Prone to Wander

-A novel-

Trudy J. Morgan-Cole

This book is a work of fiction. Any resemblance to any persons, living or dead, is purely coincidental.

Strident Books, St. John's, Newfoundland, Canada
Copyright ©2018 Trudy J. Morgan-Cole
All rights reserved
Cover and interior design: Donna Cunningham;
www.renovateyourbook.com

This is the story of how we begin to remember
This is the powerful pulsing
of love in the vein...

Paul Simon, "Under African Skies"

Oh to grace how great a debtor
Daily I'm constrained to be,
May Thy goodness, like a fetter,
Bind me closer still to Thee.

Prone to wander, Lord I feel it!
Prone to leave the God I love!
Here's my heart, oh, take and seal it,
Seal it for Thy courts above.

Robert Robinson,
"Come Thou Fount of Every Blessing"

Author's Note

JUST LIKE EVERONE ELSE, I grew up in a place and at a time that was absolutely unique, and also completely ordinary.

I was a teenager in St. John's, Newfoundland, in the 1980s. I also grew up in a Seventh-day Adventist home, attending an Adventist church and school. Some of the experiences I had growing up are common to people who lived in Newfoundland during those years. Some are common to anyone who grew up Seventh-day Adventist; many are common to people who grew up in other tight-knit religious communities. Some of the details of this world I grew up in are so specific they are familiar only to a tiny group of a few dozen people: the people who were young at the same place and time I was. It is to those people that this book is dedicated, and to whom the next paragraph is addressed.

Some of you—the old friends and schoolmates I've known for forty years—will read this book and wonder if I've written it "about you." Well, I did and I didn't. I don't base characters on real people; some writers write that way, but I can't. I can only write about fictional characters, people I've invented from the ground up. But in that process of inventing I steal freely from real life, so if you recognize a moment, or a turn of phrase, a Toronto Blue Jays baseball cap or a windy night on Signal Hill or anything else that you think you were there for: thank you, and I'm sorry. I stole our shared memories to decorate this story of fictional people in a real world.

The world of this story is mostly very real indeed: the Adventist church, school, and radio station in St. John's were real, and two out of three of them still are. Years have passed and now I am the middle-aged church lady who plays the piano in that church on (some) Sabbath mornings, when the more talented pianist is not playing. Canadian Union College (now Burman University) and Andrews University are real places, borrowed for fictional purposes, as well. There are made-up places in this story too, and churches in towns where there has never been an Adventist church, because there were places where I needed to be free to invent and not be tied to reality.

When I first began writing this novel nearly 15 years ago, I thought it might never be of interest to anyone but myself, or perhaps to those very few people who shared my roots in that place and time. But as I shared the story with a few people from very different backgrounds I found that threads in it appealed to people for a variety of reasons. It's a story for anyone who has struggled to hold onto a childhood faith in the adult world, or for anyone who has let go of that faith in an effort to find who they are. It's for anyone who has relied on the bonds of lifelong friendship as well as for anyone who has found that those ties are not enough to hold them to the person they used to be. If everything in the setting of this book is unfamiliar to you, but something that happens to one of these five characters snags at your heart, then this book is yours: I wrote it for you, too.

I apologize in advance to those people who come from the same world I do, who knew me first as an Adventist writer, who may not like this book because some of the characters swear, or sleep with the wrong people, and everything doesn't get resolved the way you hoped it would. I was trying to write a story that, though fictional, is as true as I can make it: the way the kind of people I grew up with really felt and thought and, yes, spoke, even when it has to include swear words.

This book could only be dedicated to the people who lived through it with me, and yet when I start trying to list those people, I betray the flimsiness of memory. A theme that runs through this book is how we turn our memories into stories, and none of us tells exactly the same story, so that even any list of the people who were there and lived through it with me is fragmented and incomplete. So if I were to say that this book is dedicated to Sherry and Darryl and Bob and Jim and Grace and Terry and Sarah and and and ... the rush of names threatens to overwhelm me, and I worry about who I'm leaving out, and in the end all I can say is: if you were there, you know you were there, and this book is for you.

Trudy Morgan-Cole
St. John's, 2018

ONE

Jeff

OH, GOD, IS MY FIRST last thought.

I asked about that once. In the Youth Room with the green cinderblock walls and the hard backed brown chairs. "What if your last word before you died was a curse word and you never had time to ask forgiveness? Would you be lost?"

But this isn't a curse, it's a prayer. Just like it should be. *Oh, God,* short for, *Oh God save me, send angels to lift the car up and put it in the other lane ... and if you can't manage that right now, oh, God, I'm sorry for my sins I claim the blood of Jesus please please look after my wife and kids and let us meet again in heaven, thank You for everything amen.*

No time for all that. It's compressed into that quick prayer, *Oh God.* Exactly what I would have chosen for my Last Thought, since it seems I won't be getting any Last Words.

Only, turns out that's not my last thought.

Oh my God. This time it is a swear word (*sorry*). Not because of the semi or the water on the road or the wheel twisting in my hands like a live snake, but because, *Oh my God, it's really true. Your whole life really does flash before your eyes.* A nanosecond of time slows and I see my own past projected on the windscreen.

And my next thought is, *This is what I get? I'm reliving my whole life and this is the scene I get?*

You'd think there's be some order to it, like I'd start from the beginning and see myself as a child with my parents and my brothers. Or I'd work backwards, see my wife and kids.

What I don't expect, as the semi bears down on me and I whip the wheel towards the guardrail, is Southwest Pond on a Friday night in July. I'm maybe 14, sitting on the edge of the wharf with Dave, Julie and Katie, dangling our bare feet in the water. Looking over our shoulders for a counsellor or camp director. Southwest Pond, our church campground, was a small place and it was well patrolled during Teen Camp. The four of us had sneaked out of our cabins after lights-out but we knew it was only a matter of time before we got caught.

It wasn't like we were doing anything bad. If it had been just Julie and me, we might have been kissing. We'd been going out since camp last year, making this our one-year anniversary, as Julie kept pointing out. What I really wanted was to sneak out after lights out and make out with Julie. But I was scared. Of getting caught, maybe. Or of not getting caught and not knowing what to do next. So I dragged Dave along, and Julie dragged Katie along and we made it a group thing.

I remember hearing one year that some kids at camp sneaked out at night and went skinny-dipping in the pond. Right now, dipping my toes in the water, I was thinking, *How did they not just freeze to death?* Even on a rare hot night like this Southwest Pond had the coldest water I've ever known. I knew the girls wouldn't go for skinny dipping. Julie and Katie weren't that kind of girls. Dave probably wouldn't go for it either. It would be cool to see the girls naked, but then they would have to see *us* naked.

So we sat there in the dark, talking about nothing, until we heard a noise on the path behind us. I expected some staff member on Rat Patrol with the big flashlight, booming out, "What are you kids doing down here?"

Only, there was no bright light and no booming voice. Just one person, a girl, our own age. Liz Carter by moonlight, walking softly down the path with little stones shifting under her feet. She wore flip-flops and a short skirt. I barely knew her. Her dad was going to be the principal of our church school and they'd just moved here to Newfoundland from Ontario.

"So this is where you guys went," she said to Julie and Katie. Neither of them said anything. They didn't like Liz much.

Liz stood with her toes almost hanging over the edge of the wharf, looking out at the pond. "This camp is really boring. I mean, I hate to say it but your camp sucks."

We complained all the time about how boring it was, but of course none of us liked to hear the new girl, the girl from Toronto, say that.

"There's nothing to do here. There's only one motorboat and there's no horses. At Frenda we have horseback riding. And better cabins. Your cabins suck."

We couldn't say much to this. Our cabins were made of plywood with knotholes in the walls. The mattresses were yellow foam with bites out of it, like it had been chewed by rats. That's what we used to tell the girls, that rats chewed the mattresses. The one I was sleeping on had "J.P. + T.C." picked out of it in little holes. You couldn't see a rat doing that.

"Well, if you don't like it, you don't have to be here," said Katie.

"Well that's where you're wrong, because I *do* have to be here. My folks sent me here to 'get to know people'." Liz swayed back and forth on the edge like she might fall in. If she wanted to get to know people she really was going about it badly. All week she'd kept to herself and barely talked to anyone and now she snuck out of her cabin on Friday night just to insult four people who were going to be in her class at school. "I didn't even want to come to Newfoundland at all," she added, just to make us like her more. "It's the middle of nowhere. I was supposed to go to Kingsway this year."

We all knew about Kingsway, the Adventist boarding school in Ontario. Sometimes a kid from Botwood or Marystown would go to Kingsway and come back in the summer wearing a Kingsway jacket, maroon with gray sleeves and their name sewed on the sleeve, and strut around in the jacket acting like they were too cool to live. And the real Kingsway kids, the ones from Ontario, would come down at Campmeeting to sing and do recruiting. The guys were always tall and very built and looked a lot older than they were, and the girls were all drop-dead gorgeous. If Liz was supposed to go to Kingsway this year and her parents dragged her to St. John's, Newfoundland instead, you could see why she might be in a bad mood.

"Lucky Kingsway," Dave said, not really under his breath, and we all cracked up. Liz looked out at the pond and ignored us.

"I'm going to jump in with all my clothes on," she said.

"You'll freeze to death," Katie said.

"You'll get in trouble," Julie said.

We all wanted her to do it. It was the kind of thing we would never do—almost as good as skinny-dipping—and we wanted there to be someone, one of our gang, who would actually do it. In that one second we went from thinking *Lucky Kingsway* to *Lucky us*. Because Liz was here, Liz who could insult people to their faces and say *suck* without caring and jump into the lake at night with all her clothes on. Now anything could happen.

The funny thing is, I don't remember whether she did jump or not. You'd think that's what I'd remember. You'd think if my memory was searching around for scenes from the past to light up like slides in my last minutes on earth, it would select the moment when a fourteen-year-old boy saw a tough, beautiful fourteen-year-old girl come out of the lake dripping wet with her black T-shirt clinging to her breasts. But all I see is Liz standing on the edge of the dock, and moonlight, and the four of us, my old gang, sitting with our feet in the icy water.

Look out look out look out oh god oh my god—

Remember the Feeling

2005

1979 - 1980

Julie

THE LAST TIME I FELT perfectly secure and happy in my life was ... at camp the summer I turned 14.

I'm not sure why, maybe just because later that year things got so messed up. But I'm supposed to be focusing on the good time. That's hard to do.

What I remember about that summer is, feeling like God was so close and my friends were so close and my life was going just the way it was supposed to. I don't think any 14 -year-old girl looks in a mirror and thinks "I'm pretty"—when I looked in the mirror I could always see some flaw—but I knew they thought I was pretty. Other girls ... guys too. Especially Jeff.

That summer Jeff and I had been going out for a whole year. By Teen Camp standards, we were like a couple having their silver wedding anniversary.

Things were getting more serious. Not too serious, I was hoping. Our youth leaders had started to give us little Talks about sex and saying No and stuff. Jeff had kissed me several times but he hadn't tried to go any farther. I figured he respected me and he was a good Christian boy.

I had always been a good Christian girl, raised in an Adventist home, going to church every Sabbath and all that. That summer at Campmeeting, Katie and I got baptized, wading out into the freezing cold water with the sharp rocks under our feet, catching our breath when we went under the icy surface. Afterwards, coming out of the water, I felt a holy glow, like God was living in my heart. Katie & I prayed together right before the baptism. We were so close that summer, both so on fire for the Lord.

Teen Camp was the week after Campmeeting, and the good holy feeling lasted all through camp, even while I was kissing Jeff. I believed God would always live in my heart, Katie and I would always be best friends, Jeff and I would go out together all through high school and get married and live happily ever after. And—I wouldn't have said it in words because it would sound conceited, but deep down I believed I would always be pretty, popular—the lucky one.

Well, out of that whole list, Katie is still my best friend. And I guess God still lives in my heart, but it's not the way I thought it would be. Other than that, I was wrong about pretty much everything.

That's what I wrote tonight in the meeting, when Michele asked us to write about a time in our lives when we felt peaceful and secure. Of course I didn't read it out to the group afterwards. They wouldn't understand. I have nothing in common with these women. Except.

Some of them have no shame about "sharing" their journal stuff. This one girl, Molly—nineteen, nose and lip pierced, smells of cigarettes—always volunteers to share what she's written. I can't get over her nerve. There she is, dropped out of grade 9, young enough to be my daughter (!!), never spoke up in front of a group of people in her life, and yet she has such total confidence to read out her private thoughts. Then there's me. All those years teaching kids' Sabbath School, leading out in women's Bible study groups—I freeze up at the thought of "sharing" in front of the others.

I don't think I'm going to do very well in this group.

Now I'm back at my kitchen table, this dingy depressing little kitchen, reading what I wrote. It's all true. That summer *was the high point of my life. It all comes back so vividly—the woodsy smell of the air at Southwest Pond, smoke in the cafeteria during Afterglow when the fireplace didn't work properly, the feeling of Jeff's thigh next to mine on the wooden bench as we sat in the semidarkness singing "Pass It On" or "Side by Side." Me and Katie standing just outside the cabin, lit by our flashlights, praying that God would use us to lead someone to Him. Lying awake in the cabin with the other girls, gigging about which guys were cute.*

Liz was in our cabin too—she had just moved to St. John's. I guess the next year, our Grade Nine year, was all a big competition between me and Liz. Who was going to be more popular, who was going to be Katie's best friend, who would get Jeff. All the prizes were up for grabs, and I lost it all.

Had to stop to move the laundry from the washer to the dryer and put another load on. It never ends does it? Dirty dishes in the sink, crumbs on the counter. There was a time I would have dropped dead before I'd have sat down to do anything for myself while the dishes were still dirty.

I couldn't read my journal out to the other women in the group because there's so much they'd never understand. They'd think it was weird that even though I got my first kiss the spring of Grade Eight, that was no more important, even less important, than the fact that I gave my life to Jesus that same spring. Kneeling at the front of the auditorium at the end of Week of Prayer, a small group of the other faithful around me, a larger crowd of the unsaved sitting in the back, shuffling their feet. Tears running down my cheeks as I asked Jesus to take over my life completely.

That was when Katie & I got to be best friends, and besides all the regular Grade Eight girl stuff—talking about what guys were cute and whether Stephanie had really kissed seventeen guys like she said she had—we prayed together and studied our Sabbath School lessons and talked about how God was working in our lives. Our prayers were just as important to me as the feeling I got when I sat in the dark in the church auditorium watching The Sound of Music and Jeff took my hand. God & love & friendship & growing up ... that year when I turned fourteen, it all seemed like part of the same wonderful package.

Then Grade 9 started & Liz stole my best friend. She and Katie started hanging out after school. The next day they'd be giggling over something that had happened the afternoon before. Little by little I felt Katie slipping away. It made a kind of sense, because they were both so smart and I started to feel like I would never be able to keep up with them. I used to write in a journal back then too. Liz and Katie were always writing poems and saying they were going to be writers. I remember throwing my journal in a bottom drawer and thinking, "Well, I'm not a writer like them."

Next, of course, Liz stole Jeff. She was pretty in a totally different way than I was—dark hair & dark eyes, much shorter than me. She didn't dress slutty like Stephanie Hussey, though she did wear her tops kind of tight. But really it wasn't any of that—she just had this air about her, like she knew she was special and any guy would want her. She used to play the piano and sing "You Light Up My Life" and one Friday night after youth meeting I saw Jeff leaning against the piano, looking into her eyes while she sang, like she meant it just for him.

They'd been flirting for weeks when I stopped Jeff by the water fountain after school one day and said, "We have to talk." He hadn't phoned me or anything for over a week. And he put his hands in his pockets and looked at the ground and said, "Yeah, well, I've been kinda busy." I said something like, "So, do you want to break up with me or something?" praying he'd say no, and he shook his head but said, "Yeah, I guess maybe we should. I mean, it would be better, wouldn't it?"

I wanted to scream, Not better for me! Instead I kind of tossed my head and said, "Whatever," and turned away. I walked down the hall, everything all blurry because I was bawling my eyes out.

Outside, Liz was sitting on the little concrete wall by the front door. She was the last person I wanted to see, but I had to tell somebody why I was crying. And she was supposed to be my friend—we all hung out together, this big pretense that she and Katie and I were all friends together, a Three Musketeers kind of thing. Maybe I thought that if she saw how much I cared about Jeff, she would back off and not take him. Anyway she looked up and said, "What's wrong?" and I said, "Jeff just broke up with me. I need a hug!" and went straight to her. She put her arms around me kind of awkwardly, patted me on the back, and said, "Guys are all jerks anyway," or something like that. I cried for awhile, and then I dried my eyes with a Kleenex she gave me so that when Mom came to pick me up a few minutes later, she wouldn't see that I'd been crying. I wasn't ready to tell Mom. That would make it too real.

The next day was Sabbath. Saturday night we had floor hockey at the Y gym and Liz & Jeff were together the whole evening, laughing and carrying on. In Katie's dad's car on the way back they sat next to each other in the back seat with his arm around her.

Later, Jeff's nerdy friend Dave told me that Jeff had told Liz weeks before he'd go out with her as soon as he broke up with me. That Friday afternoon when I came out of the school and cried in Liz's arms, Jeff was waiting for me to leave so he could come outside and ask her out. When I think of that moment I still feel ashamed, like it was on that day I finally saw myself for the fool I was. The fool I am.

It's nearly midnight and I've got a cramp in my hand. The dishes still aren't done & now I have to bring up the laundry and fold it. But I'm glad I wrote all that down, even if nobody ever sees it but me.

Katie

THE SLIP OF LOOSELEAF is folded tiny in Liz's palm. She sits with her chin in one hand, staring intently at Mrs. Lane while her other hand inches across the aisle toward Katie by slow, smooth increments. Just as casually, Katie lets her own hand dangle beside her desk, drifts it towards Liz's. Fingers brush for the briefest moment before Katie closes her hand over the note and then brings her fist quickly to her mouth to cough. At no time do they glance at each other.

Passing notes is serious business. It's no empty threat when Mrs. Lane she says she'll make you read the note out loud. She made Stephanie Hussey read a note she wrote to Heather about Jeff having a nice butt. Although Katie suspects Stephanie might have passed that one carelessly, wanting to be caught.

She unfolds the note on top of her *Quest* book, never looking down at it until it lies flat before her, innocent as a page of English questions. It's torn from Liz's spiral notebook: the ragged fluttering edge is ripped near the bottom. Liz's handwriting is spiky and black-inked.

The rose in my window
Blooming, dying with the dusk
Drops its petals
A challenge, a regret
a–what? Why do you ask me?
A dream of nothing.
I close my eyes.
I dream of nothing.

> *My tears fall to the windowsill*
> *A challenge, a regret.*

I wrote that last night. I've got a better one too but I'll show it to you later. Want to come to the Village with me after school?

Katie's left hand closes back into a fist. As always when she reads one of Liz's poems, there's a brief moment when she wants to take the black PaperMate pen Liz uses for writing poems and poke Liz's eyes out with it.

When Katie reads Liz's poems it's clear that she, Katie Matthews, who has gotten A's in English all her life, will never be a writer. She had better come up with another life plan, quickly. It was easy to be the smart girl, the talented writer, before Liz came along.

But Katie can't hate someone who can write like this. The prayer she has been praying all her life–to find a true friend, a real kindred spirit–has been answered at last.

On a corner piece torn from her own looseleaf, Katie writes *It's great. I love it. I can't believe the other one's better. If we go to the Village, how will I get home?*

She passes the reply across the aisle; a few minutes later the bell rings and normal communication resumes. "My dad's got a meeting here tonight," Liz says as she shoves her English books into her knapsack. "Come to our place for supper and he'll drive you home."

Outside the classroom, the hallway bustles with students opening their lockers, moving from class to class. Julie is already at the locker she and Katie share, stooping down to brush her hair in front of the small mirror stuck inside the door. When she flips back her bangs and looks up, Katie sees that her eyes are pink-rimmed. "Are you OK?" Katie asks.

Tears fill Julie's eyes, the way water bubbles to the mouth of the drinking fountain when you turn the handle, but never quite works up enough force to spurt out. "I'll talk to you later, OK?"

"OK. Umm ... hang in there."

Katie knows this is about Jeff. She also knows she should tell Liz she can't go to the Village today; she should go over to Julie's after school so they can talk. But she doesn't want another endless afternoon of why-doesn't-Jeff-love-me-anymore and I-thought-it-was-God's-plan-for-us-to-be-together. An afternoon of tears and Kleenex on Julie's bed, the Bee Gees playing softly and endlessly in the background.

In Canadian History, as Mr. Pippy drones about the Manitoba Schools Crisis, Katie studies Jeff, who sits across the aisle. So much fuss over so little, really. Katie herself had a crush on Jeff from Grade Five to Grade Eight, but she's always known he's out of her league. The thing is, Katie now realizes that while she is not in Jeff's league, Jeff is not in her league either. He's good looking and good at sports, sure, but he's a C-student and she's never had a really interesting conversation with him.

Dave Mitchell sprawls in the seat behind Jeff. Behind his tinted aviator glasses his eyes are half-shut. Katie finds herself sliding glances at Dave these days, sizing him up when he doesn't notice. She and Dave have had a few long talks lately, and he's surprised her. His grades are not that much better than Jeff's but she has a feeling that's because he really doesn't care, that he could do a lot better if he tried.

Last Sabbath in youth class Pastor Kimball was talking about how the unpardonable sin, and how if you keep rejecting the Holy Spirit then your heart will get hardened and someday you won't be able to repent. And Dave said, "But in Bible, when the Israelites were in Egypt and Pharaoh wouldn't let them go, it says *God* hardened Pharaoh's heart. So isn't it all up to God really? I mean, if God knows everything we're going to do before we even do it, if a person turns away, isn't it really God turning *them* away?"

Katie jumped in at once, defending God loudly, because she's read the same verses about Pharaoh's heart and the same thought has bothered her. Later that night she and Dave sat outside the church bathrooms talking while Pastor Kimball showed his Holy Land slides for Vespers again. They sat on the table swinging their legs and got into a big argument about predestination. Katie went home thinking about Dave, about the lost look in his eyes–behind the glasses—when he said, "Maybe some people are just God's garbage, you know? Just born to die—like they never had a chance in the first place."

The Number Seven bus leaves from the stop in front of the Salvation Army Citadel at 3:40. It's too cold to go stand and freeze out on the Citadel steps for half an hour so Liz and Katie hang out at the school, sitting on the bottom step in the downstairs hallway.

"What time is it?" Liz asks.

"Twenty after three. Should we get going?"

"Not yet." Liz glances up the stairs. Voices drift down from the first and second floors. "Who's up there? Is Jeff still here?"

Katie shrugs. "I don't know, why?"

"I told him we were going to the Village, he said he might come."

"Shoot, I forgot my Math book, and I've got to finish those questions over the weekend. I'll be back," Katie says, and races up two flights of stairs to her locker.

When she comes back down she hears sobbing in the porch. She sees Liz with her arms around Julie, who is crying. Liz's hand makes awkward patting circles on Julie's back. She keeps looking up the stairs, and moves away from Julie quickly when Katie appears.

Julie stumbles from Liz's hug to Katie's. Her pretty face collapses, a crumpled pink Kleenex. "Jeff—he told me—he said it would be better if we broke up."

"*Better* if you broke up? What a stupid thing to say," Katie soothes as Julie sobs. "Better for him, I guess he means. He's a jerk, Julie. He's not good enough for you."

A car horn honks outside. "Oh no, my mom's here," Julie says, fiercely swiping her eyes and blinking. She turns to Katie. "Look, call me tonight, OK?"

"I'll call after supper," Katie promises, as Julie runs out the door.

Liz and Katie walk down the icy sidewalk towards the bus stop saying nothing, their boots sliding on the slick black ice under the brown-sugar slush of February. It seems at the same time inevitable and almost indecent that they will discuss Julie and Jeff's breakup.

"He really is a jerk. She cares so much about him," Katie tries at last.

Liz is looking away, at cars whizzing past the intersection of Merrymeeting Road and Freshwater as they wait for the light. She shrugs. "I don't know. I mean yeah, I know she cares about him. But at some point you've got to, you know, move on." The walk signal blinks and they move on.

"Yeah, but–not like that."

"Maybe. I don't know." The bus turns the corner onto Adams Avenue right behind them; they have to run to catch it, slipping and slithering through the sludge. A fistful of snow lands inside Katie's boot. Once on the bus she takes the boot off to empty it.

"So, wanna see the other poem?" Liz dangles another piece of paper in front of her.

Katie snatches it and reads it quickly, glad to get away from the surprisingly awkward topic of Jeff and Julie.

At the Village they put their backpacks in a locker and go sit by the fountain. Liz draws a complicated heart with a scroll around it and an arrow through it on the back of her forearm with red pen. "Someday I'm going to get a real tattoo."

"Your mother will die."

"If I'm lucky. Come on, let's go to Smart Set."

They wander into Smart Set. Liz tries hats in the mirror, picks out a few for Katie to try. Then deeper into the store, to the racks of dresses and skirts. Liz pulls things off the rack almost at random, handing some to Katie and keeping some herself, then herds Katie into the fitting room. "I don't have any money," Katie protests.

"Who cares? Just try it, just to see how it looks."

They meet in the hallway between fitting rooms and stand together looking in the big mirror. Katie wears a gypsy-like skirt, almost to her ankles, with multicoloured flounces. Liz wears a slinky red dress with sequins, and a floppy black hat. Katie looks like a little girl dressing up in Mommy's clothes. Liz looks elegant, sophisticated, dangerous.

Up the escalator to Coles' bookstore, where Liz picks up books, glances at them, says loudly in a fake German accent, "Vere are de books on sex? I need sex books! Pliss, can anyvone tell me vere I might find de SEX books?" Katie laughs so hard she starts to pee in her pants and has to retreat from the store. Liz follows her, fleeing the salesman.

Their headlong flight through the mall lands them at last at the railing that looks down on the fountain below. The spray of water dances in the air just below them. Liz digs in her jeans pocket for pennies. "Make a wish," she says.

Katie drops a penny and watches it spiral down into the water below, hoping it won't hit anyone. "They say if you drop a penny off the CN Tower and it hits someone's head, it will drill a hole right through their head," Liz tells her. "The force is so great."

"I'll remember that if I'm ever up there. I'll resist the urge."

Katie gets fancy, spinning her pennies in the air before they drop down to the fountain.

Liz's hand flashes out like a snake, snatches the penny—a shiny new 1980 one—from the air, holds it closed in her fist. She pulls her hand back and opens it to show Katie the penny shining there.

Later, they will walk to Liz's house and eat supper there-vegetarian patties in mushroom gravy, potato croquettes. The phone will ring during supper and as Liz rushes for it, talking in cryptic murmurs, Katie will feel a stab of jealousy, wishing she and Liz were the kind of friends who told each other everything.

Katie will go back to her own house, where her mom reads the newspaper while her dad puts away the supper dishes, and as always after a visit to Liz's she will reflect on how completely unnatural her own house is. She will put off returning the two phone messages Julie has left for her. She will go to bed that night asking God to forgive her for not being as good a friend as she should be.

All these things she will forget. The end of the evening, and many of the events of the day that went before, will be lost in the flotsam of memory. But the moment she holds onto-the moment that shines clear in her memory twenty-five years later-is of Liz leaning over the railing, catching the brilliant coin before it falls into the spray of the fountain, holding it like a slice of time in her hand.

liz

the closet is dark and smelly as an armpit.

[possibly worst first line in history of written word?]

someone's jacket sleeve, knobbly wool, brushes my cheek as his lips touch mine. his upper lip sprouts a few wiry hairs, nothing worthy of the name "mustache." "mustache" conjures images of luxuriant black waxed handlebars twirled by the evil villain.

he is not the villain of this piece. he is a fourteen-year-old boy, hard inside skintight jordache jeans, pressing a fourteen-year-old girl against the doorjamb of a downstairs closet.

[doorjam – spelling? is this even a word?]

his tongue flicks out, tracing the circle of my lips. something flares inside like a bic lighter. i want that feeling. give me more feeling. more more more.

voices above, hammering feet.

-yoo-hoo, where are you guys? liz and jeff? are you down there all alone?? teenage giggles laced with disapproval and raw envy.

yes we are down here all alone. my hands are on his back up inside his sweatshirt feeling his skin more more more.

[what to do with quotes. i hate quotation marks but without them will i be plagued with problems of clarity]

thud-thud-giggle on the stairs. he pulls away.

-we better go up there.

-yeah okay.

walking home. hands linked, fingers twining around each other like young plants growing in the same pot. watch out. one may become a parasite.

[damn, i like this line!]

-what time is it.

-quarter after eleven.

-will your mom be mad.

i imagine her standing at the sink in our kitchen, arms braced on the counter, forming a triangle. her head is bowed. a prayer over choplets and gravy. my father rages at her back. muscles in her neck form knotty cords.

[nobody will know what choplets are — can i get away with obscure refs? as if i came from interesting foreign culture?]

-she's disrespectful at home and she's disrespectful at school don't you have any control she's as bad as her brother they're both completely out of control and you just stand there, what are you doing praying well yes you'd better pray is all i can say

all this and more waits behind the green door. jeff's mouth hard against mine then he turns to go quick before the door opens trapping me inside.

-what time do you call this.

-i call it eleven-thirty what do you call it?

[question marks — to use or not to use. i'm not being consistent — should i ?]

-i call it a disgrace, i phoned the kimballs they said you left there at ten thirty.

-we walked slow.

she sits at the kitchen table. its slick fake-wood veneer reflects the circle of yellow lamplight. her hair the same colour as the tabletop, her head bowed again.

-this is unacceptable young lady. you were out with jeff? what were you doing?

-walking home. we walked and talked that's all. oh and at the end of the street we went into the playground and he kissed me and touched my breast on top of my bra and i wanted him to do more more because I wanted to feel like i was alive.

(i didn't say all that out loud.)

[do i need this? am i trusting reader enough? too much?]

her hands rub the table in circles rubbing rubbing.

-you think you can do what you want but you're going to get a nasty shock. when you wind up pregnant on the street.

-oh my god mom.

-that kind of language is—

-what do you think i am? i just spent saturday night at a pastor's house playing a freaking scavenger hunt. like they think we're twelve. where's dad.

-don't change the subject. your father is at the school.

-it's nearly midnight on a Saturday night you're alone in the house dad is supposedly at work and you think i'm the one with the problems?

-you watch your mouth young lady—

young lady in her room alone, lights off door closed. darkness darkness. the light shines in the darkness and the darkness cannot comprehend it.

i am darkness. i cannot comprehend this light that shines for everyone i know. they walk in the light i am dark dark like the inside of my own head.

[too melodramatic?]

there may well be a god. if there is, he is nothing to do with pathetic losers and their rule book don't dance don't drink don't even get your ears pierced for crying out loud. if there's a god i want him to be bigger than giving a damn whether i have holes in my ears is that too much to ask of the almighty.

i am darkness and i do not comprehend the light.

the pills are hers for her headaches. one two three four five. chalky and bitter on my tongue. another glass of water. something rises in my throat i don't want to swallow anymore i make myself.

instead of warm darkness, cold bare light. not the light that lighteth every man but the harsh light of the bathroom flicked on while i'm sick on the floor.

[sick? puking? barfing?]

knife-white lights of the emergency room. his face her face. their eyes slide away from mine.

-she's a lucky girl she'll be all right.

-we're very sorry to bother you we just didn't know

-no no you did the right thing. do you mind if we speak to your daughter alone

-alone. without us. their eyes suspicious and shuttered.

alone with an adult who is not my parents. who says liz do you want to talk about it. about why you did this.

-not really.

-did you have an argument with your parents, with a friend?

nothing really i came home late, mom and i argued. boring teenage stuff i was just depressed i'm sorry it was a stupid thing to do.

-would you come back in mr and mrs carter. it would be good if liz could talk to someone do you have a school guidance counsellor a clergyman perhaps or should we make a referral.

my father nods he nods i'm sure we can find someone for her to talk to. he is the church school principal. his eyes tell me i will not have to not be allowed to talk to anyone.

i ride in the backseat silent home. dawn comes up over the south side hills.

[how to end this? would reader need more? will there ever be reader? is this self-indulgent drivel? why not stick to writing poems?]

Dave

I DON'T KNOW WHY the hell I'm here. It seemed like a good idea at the time.

No. I don't want to talk about that right now.

No, let's not go there. It's just—I kind of thought this might help. But so far, it's not.

Well, I could tell you a story. How about I tell you about the first time I got drunk?

It's a good story. Funny. You'll like it. It was the summer I turned 15, and I got born again, got baptized, got drunk, and played strip poker—all within 24 hours. Pretty cool, eh?

Why do I think it's cool? I don't know ... I don't think it's cool, I think it's—ironic. That's the word. I thought you'd appreciate the irony. Are you into irony?

OK, I'll tell you the story. It's a good one. And it's as good a way as any to kill an hour. Fifty minutes, whatever.

I said "born again" but we didn't use that term much. A little too charismatic. We would have said—oh, maybe "accepted the Lord" or "gave your heart to Jesus." But it was all the same thing. And that's what I did at Campmeeting the summer I was 15.

Campmeeting? It was this big church thing they used to have at the campgrounds outside town—it was a blast for teenagers, because adults went to most of the sermons and shit, and us kids were free to hang out. Some years they'd bring in a youth speaker and have special youth programs, but that year, I think all the kids went up to the main auditorium for the adult meetings, because the preacher was one of those who—what's the phrase?—appeals to young and old alike.

He was good. I can still remember him. This huge guy, like six foot six or something, big deep voice, New York accent. Used to be a street kid, in a gang, until he got saved. I guess I'd find it funny now, to hear him brag about how tough he was and how he could take anybody down. But he had us in the palm of his hand, and when he got to the part about Jesus, you could tell it was real to him. I slouched in the back row trying to look cool, but I was listening.

OK, yeah, I guess I need to back the truck up a little, explain how I came to be at Campmeeting in the first place. That means I'll have to explain about Jeff, which is kind of appropriate since I wouldn't be here if it wasn't for Jeff. He was my best friend, growing up. He lived across the street and we hung out, played street hockey and all that, as long as I can remember.

Jeff had this perfect family, like something from TV, you know? The stay at home mom, the smiling dad who played ball with his kids. They went to the Seventh-day Adventist church and the Adventist school, so Mom put me in their church school even though she didn't know Adventists from Moonies.

What? Oh, no, there was no tuition—it wasn't a private school. We had this kind of weird system in Newfoundland back in those days, all the schools were religious but they were all government funded, so it was free. So there was this small Adventist school where about one in ten kids were actually Adventist. And that's where I went.

Eventually I started going along with Jeff to Pathfinders, this kind of Scout-like program the church had, and then to youth group and stuff. By the time we were teenagers everyone at church just considered me part of the crowd. Only difference was, the others got baptized when they were 12, 13, 14. It seemed like something kids did because their families expected it.

No, my family wasn't anything—any religion, I mean. Once in school I had to fill out some form and put in what religion we were and I didn't know. I went home and asked mom and she looked at me like I had grown another head and said, "We're United!" like I was supposed to know. How would I? We didn't go, not even at Christmas or Easter.

"We're United" was a funny way to describe my family, because it was the one thing we certainly weren't.

Yeah, I know you want to hear all that, about my family and everything.

What? Because you people love that stuff. But trust me, the story about the baptism and the two-four of beer and the strip poker is a lot more interesting. I'll give you the short version on my family: folks split when I was six. Two older brothers went with Dad, me and my sister went with Mom. That was the official plan: what really happened was us kids would drift around, staying wherever, one place or the other, sometimes at Nan's for awhile. And I'm not telling you that because it's the root cause of everything that happened to me, OK? I'm telling you that so you'll know about the difference between Jeff's family and mine, and why I went to church with them.

The girls we hung out with, Katie and Julie, got real religious around Grade Eight or Nine, but nobody put any pressure on me to get saved or anything. Except maybe Katie. She used to corner me for these conversations and I could tell she was trying to work it around to my soul.

Girlfriend? Hell no. I'd never had a girlfriend at that point. All the girls had crushes on Jeff; he was the good-looking one. I was just the other guy, Jeff's buddy. Jeff used to say Katie liked me, but nah—we were more like brother and sister.

So when Katie tried to talk to me about whether I really knew Jesus, I just figured that was what she was into: Jesus. When you're fourteen it's cool to sit in the half-dark with a girl, any girl, maybe in somebody's kitchen at the tail-end of a Saturday night youth social, having these deep talks. So I didn't discourage Katie. But it was like she was talking a different language.

Yeah. I learned the language. I'm still not sure what made it click for me, but that summer, after Grade Nine, that was a weird time for me. My Dad was living in Toronto then, and he sent me a plane ticket to come see him. Up till that point I'd never thought he paid much attention to me one way or the other.

You're writing that down, aren't you? I see you. I'm telling you, you're barking up the wrong tree. My dad and me, that's not the story here. We hardly knew each other. It's just that I went to see him in Toronto that summer. Spent a month up there.

Oh, I hated it. My brother Ken lived with Dad, and they both worked construction. I basically hung around the apartment or walked the streets all day. I missed home and my friends. My brother had all these weights and shit set up in the apartment so I started working out. That's basically all I did for a month in Toronto, walk the streets or sit in the apartment lifting weights and watching TV, thinking about how nobody cared if I lived or died. Typical depressing teenage stuff, you know?

I was barely home two days and I headed up to Campmeeting with Jeff. His family stayed in a cabin; me and Jeff had a tent. All our crowd was up there, mostly without parents. Liz and her older brother were staying in their camper—their parents were up there in a cabin or something, but they let the kids sleep in the camper. Julie and Katie were in a cabin down by the cafeteria. We hung out at the waterfront all day and I got a tan on top of my brand-new chest muscles. I learned to water ski. And in the evenings we went to hear this preacher.

No, it wasn't like he was saying anything new. I'd heard it a million times before—how Jesus would have died for me if I was the only sinner in the universe—but somehow, the way he said it, he totally convinced me that God loved me. He convinced me, or I convinced myself, that I mattered to God. Even if I didn't matter that much to anyone else.

He made a call that Friday night—you know what altar calls are? Where they invite all the sinners to come to the front and get saved? They used to have them all the time at church. A few of the more religious kids would stand up and I'd stay there with my arms folded over my chest and try to look cool.

But that Friday night, the preacher from New York made the call, and I didn't even look to see what anyone else was doing. I could practically hear God—He had the same accent as the preacher—saying, *I'm right here, Dave. Wontcha give me your heart?* I went up to the front and dropped to my knees. After the meeting the preacher shook my hand and said, "Ya made the right decision tonight, kid," and I said, "I wanna get baptized tomorrow."

When I came up out of the water the next afternoon I didn't have any family on the shore to hug me and flash pictures. But Jeff had a camera, and Julie and Katie and Liz gave me big hugs and squealed because I got them all wet. Katie looked in my eyes and said, "Dave I'm so happy, I'm really really happy for you."

Substitute family? Yeah, maybe. My friends, even the church people—I guess they were always there for me. Anyhow, I went around all day on this big high. Like an adrenaline rush, I guess. After campfire that night Katie gave me another big hug and said, "This has been such a great day. I'm so happy for you." I wondered if there was anything to what Jeff always said about her liking me. But really, I think she was just being like a sister in Christ, you know?

Do you know that expression? Is this all really weird to you?

Yeah, I guess you have heard weirder. And there's weirder to come, believe me, if I stick with this. My story gets much, much stranger. Like that night, we—

What? I don't know, how the hell would I know at this point if I'm going to stick with it? You know I don't expect much from this, right? The reluctant client, is that what they call people like me?

Oh–resistant. OK. Yeah, anyway, I don't know why I'm here. I guess when a thing like this happens, you decide it's time to re-evaluate everything and—

Look, I really don't want to talk about this now. Is it OK if I just tell you about the strip poker?

So that night, Jeff and I said goodnight to Julie and Katie, and went back up towards our tent, and Liz went like she was going to her camper. Then she looked Jeff and said, "Wanna come up to the camper?"

I figured they wanted to be alone, to make out and stuff, so I said I'd go back to the tent. I was still on a spiritual high but now I felt like a loser on a spiritual high, you know? But Liz said no, her brother was up there and there might be some other people, so I should come too.

Now Liz's brother was two years older than us, and supposedly more responsible, which was a laugh, because he was a total burnout. He was home for the summer from an Adventist college on the mainland, which was why his folks, who were strict but also kind of clueless, figured he was mature enough for him and Liz to stay in the camper. That afternoon, while I was getting baptized in the frigid waters of Southwest Pond, Eugene—yeah, that was his name—drove into town and picked up Stephanie Hussey, this girl in our class who was a real tramp, and two cases of beer.

So I walked into the Carters' camper that night, thinking about how God had changed my life and I was going to maybe go away to CUC and become a minister. And there was Eugene with a beer in his hand, playing cards with Stephanie Hussey and one of the singing group girls from Kingsway College. I didn't know the Kingsway girl's name but she was pretty— they were all pretty—and that evening at the meeting she had sung the solo part in "I Believe," and here she was in a black T-shirt that said, "Good girls go to heaven—bad girls go everywhere," playing cards and drinking beer with Eugene Carter and Steph Hussey.

We sat down and joined in, and Eugene cracked open a couple more beers and Jeff and Liz took them like it was no deal at all. This was something new.

No, not for me—I'd always been around beer, there was plenty of it in our house, and I'd had a few drinks, finished off people's beer, that kind of thing. But Jeff's family and Liz's were both squeaky clean Adventist. Drinking, playing cards, going to dances—all the stuff was sinful.

Jeff paused for a minute before he handed me a beer and I knew what he was thinking—about sin, and the altar call, and me getting baptized no less than seven hours before. Setting an Example, and all that.

I took the beer and told Gene to deal me in.

I wasn't thinking about sin. I just felt happy, and anything that kept me in that mood seemed like a good thing. Drinking and playing poker were high on the list of sins I had just asked Jesus to cleanse me from, but I figured I could work that one out in the morning. It just felt good to be among friends and ... I don't know. At the time I didn't analyze it.

No, I don't really want to analyze it now. Sorry.

Somehow poker turned into strip poker. That was Liz's suggestion, and Steph was up for it too. Gene and the Kingsway girl took off for a walk, to make out, I figured at the time, although now I think yeah, maybe not. Anyway there I was playing strip poker with Jeff, his girlfriend, and Steph

Hussey who, according to school rumour, had already done it with three guys from Gonzaga.

Liz, being an Adventist teacher's kid, was a terrible card-player—no experience. She was the first to lose a hand and the first to take something off. I figured she'd go for a shoe or her watch. But she took her top off.

I got another beer, which would have been my third or fourth at that point. Next thing, Jeff takes off his shirt, then Steph—she had this black lacy bra. I already had a hard-on and I was the only one who hadn't taken anything off, because I was an excellent poker player.

We all took off shoes, shorts, watches and bandaids for awhile till we were down to underwear. Somebody walked by with a flashlight and we crouched under the table going Ssshh! Ssshh! The flashlight passed, we got up, I had another beer. Sitting there in nothing but my jockeys, holding the cards.

How did I feel? Great. Like the world was a totally fantastic place. Everything I'd felt before, about God and the Holy Spirit and all that, was nothing compared to how I felt now, sitting in this wonderful room with girls in their underwear, completely and totally plastered.

And I think what you'll find, if we keep at this, is that these are the themes of my story, the things that will keep coming up over and over again ... God, and booze of course, and occasionally girls in their underwear. These are a few of my favourite things....

Aha! See? I've got you hooked. You don't want to know about the root causes of my problems anymore, you don't want me to focus on my strengths—don't worry, I know the ropes here—you just want to know how the story ended. If I ever took off my underwear, if anyone did.

I'm gonna tell Liz that. She thinks she's the great writer, but I'm the one with the storytelling skills. I've got you hooked and even though our time's up you won't let me go till you find out who was naked at the end of the evening.

Huh? Oh yeah, still in touch with Liz—she lives here in Vancouver. And Katie calls now and then. And Jeff—well, of course, Jeff started this whole thing, didn't he? Jeff's the reason I came to see you.

What do you want to know about Jeff? All I can tell you right now is that he was *not* the first person to get naked that night. Neither were Stephanie or Liz, though Steph took off her bra. It was me. Despite my excellent poker skills, I was so completely hammered that I took off all my clothes and was lying buck-naked on the fold-down bed when Eugene finally came back and threw us all out of his camper.

Time's up. See you next time—maybe. Anyway, I gave you my story. It's the best one I've got. Hell, it's the only one I've got.

TWO

Jeff

TIRES SKID. THE WORLD BLURS past my windshield. I'm going to swerve off the side of the road over the cliff down down
    Headlights rush toward me. Coming, coming, nothing I can do to stop it. Loss of control panic and the rush of the inevitable. Reminds me of something–

Orgasm. It reminds me of an orgasm.

A crazy comparison: getting hit by a truck is like an orgasm. Maybe not so crazy if you turn it around. Coming is like getting hit by a semi ... yeah, you can see that, can't you? With the image comes another memory, lit suddenly brilliant on the screen of my frozen brain.

My First Time. Now that's the sort of thing you expect to see when your life flashes before your eyes.

A windowless basement bedroom, ugly brown wood panelling on the walls. A girl underneath me, small and dark-haired, not moving much or saying much. And I'm inside her, inside a girl for the first time in that dark room with pounding music—Queen, *We Will Rock You*—and I'm thinking, really profoundly: *This is it. We're doing it.*

It was spring, end of Grade Ten. Liz and I had been together for a year. I was crazy about her. She was different from any girl I'd ever known. Tough as nails, with her weird poetry and her black clothes and her short straight dark hair that she never tried to style pretty the way the other girls did. Later, she cut it real short and started spiking it.

She was hot. She was sexy. I loved her.

She wasn't the girl lying underneath me at the moment.

This wasn't my bedroom, where Liz and I sometimes studied after school, sneaking kisses only to be interrupted by my smiling mom with cookies and juice. It wasn't the spare back bedroom at Dave's place where we did all our exploring. It was the basement bedroom of a girl called Tina. Out in the rec room, Dave was on the couch with Tina's friend Deanne.

Dave and I had planned the evening like a military campaign. Dave's objective: get laid. Didn't matter who. My objective: get laid with a girl other than Liz, so that when Liz and I finally did it, I'd have some experience. My task: line up two slutty girls who had no connection to anyone at church or school, so Liz would never find out. Dave's task: line up enough booze and weed to make the whole process smooth.

Friday night. All our crowd was at Vespers. I hoped to get things finished in time to arrive home the same time I would have if I'd been to Vespers so my dad, who stayed home Friday nights, wouldn't guess I'd skipped out.

There on the bed with Tina under me, my mind started to wander. Not good. I thought about the music, the coats on the bed, about Dad and what he'd say if he could see me now. My dad got saved when I was about eight or nine. Before that he lived a wild life of booze and drugs and women. I remember the day he stood up in church and gave his testimony. We all stood afterwards and sang *I've wandered far away from God, now I'm coming home.* And the only thing Dad wanted was that his boys would have a good Christian upbringing and never have to wander.

He knew I was wandering. Mom and Dad saw right through Liz. They knew what was going on when I hung out at Dave's all weekend. They didn't know I was losing my virginity to a girl I barely knew in a basement on Flower Hill.

We Will Rock You ended. Now it was *We Are the Champions.* I wanted to get this over with before we got to *Get*

Down Make Love. Tina murmured and squirmed a little bit. I wondered if I was hurting her. Or could this be making her feel good? Hard to say. Her eyes were closed and her head was turned away.

I wondered how Dave was doing with Deanne. Dave was a lot more drunk and a lot more stoned than I was—par for the course. I'd wanted just enough to take the edge off. Not enough to keep me from—performing.

Tina was the pretty one. She was about as short as Liz, but skinnier, with dark brown curly hair. She wore a lot of black eyeliner. I'd only met her once or twice before but I knew she was easy and that was exactly what I was looking for. Easy. Not complicated. Dave got Deanne, who wasn't as cute. Dave was so wasted he probably didn't even know who he was with.

Tina moved again. She bit her lip and made this little noise, like a kitten. In the shadow with her hair over her face she almost looked like Liz. I closed my eyes and pretended it was Liz. *Oh no here it comes I'm coming I'm coming look out look out.* And it was over.

I lay there on top of Tina, who looked kind of shocked. She wasn't a virgin, so I figured maybe she was shocked because I didn't measure up to all the other guys she'd been with. It was dark in the room, just a little light seeping in through the crack around the door. In the dark her eyes looked like bruises in her small pointed face.

I rolled away from her and started putting on my clothes. She just lay there. Finally she said, in this tiny voice, "Did you like that?"

I leaned over and kissed her. Wanted to tell her it was great, I loved it, she was a great person. All I could think of to say was, "I'm sorry. I'm sorry."

Tina said, "No, that's OK." I left her in the bedroom and went out and found Dave and Deanne sitting on the couch watching TV. When I grabbed my jacket Dave stood up and grabbed his like it was a life jacket and the boat was sinking. We both tore out of there as fast as we could.

On the street outside I said, "So, how'd it go?"

"Oh man, it was wicked. She was hot."

"Yeah? You shoulda seen Tina. She was like ... she was wild, man." Our words echoed around the empty street as we headed up Flower Hill. An old guy carrying a dozen beer passed us. Neither of us said anything more for awhile.

I'm sorry I'm sorry please forgive me I didn't mean to God forgive me it's coming coming no stop no stop no –

Paradise by the
Dashboard Light

2005

Spring 1981

Julie

POWERLESS.

Michele says: Write about feeling powerless. I've been staring at the paper for five minutes, pen in hand, writing nothing. I'm afraid if I start I'll never stop.

It would be easy to write about Roger. But the first thing that comes to my mind is Grade Ten & Kenny Boland.

Kenny was my first boyfriend after Jeff. He lived on my street, and he was in first-year university. He didn't go to our church. I don't think he went to any church although I guess thinking back he might have been Catholic. Mom didn't have a problem with it, but a couple of people at church, like Liz's mom, gave me little "warnings" about dating someone who was so "worldly."

Kenny had a bit of money & he had a car—not a great car, but his own car. When he picked me up after school in his car I felt older, special.

He pushed a lot more, in the physical department I mean, than Jeff did. I guess because we were older, plus him not being a Christian really, it didn't matter to him so much. He French-kissed from the beginning and he was always trying to feel me up, under my bra and stuff. I kept saying No and pushing him away, but he treated that all like a big game.

One night, I think it might have been early in May, one of those rare nights in a Newfoundland spring when it's actually warm, we drove up to Signal Hill. It was a foggy night and we drove up there with the headlights glowing in the fog, crawling up the winding road because we couldn't see one thing outside the car. At the top of Signal Hill, instead of the blanket of city lights spread out below, all we saw was our own lights shining back at us in the fog. When we turned the lights off it was like we were wrapped in cotton wool. All alone in the world.

Kenny had a tape playing—Chicago I think—can't remember what song. I don't remember what he said, if he talked about what he wanted me to do, or if he just unzipped his pants. I was so innocent. I'd only learned the phrase "blow job" earlier that year. Liz had to explain it to me. I don't remember if Kenny called it that or if he said anything at all.

Here's something I do remember: he was wearing brown cords, a really narrow corduroy and kind of a sickly tan brown. I remember my face against the brown cords, staring at them. I remember his hand on my head. Pushing my head down again and again. I hated doing it, and he kept pushing.

Powerless. When it was over he asked something like, "Did you like that baby?" and of course I said yes, I loved it. At home I stared at myself in the bathroom mirror, swishing my mouth out with glasses of water and mouthwash. My face looked the same as always, though the blond hair I feathered back so carefully was all tousled and messed up. And it was like I could still feel his hand on top of my head. Pushing me down.

I didn't read out what I wrote in group tonight -- still can't imagine having the guts to do that. But when Michele asked us if anyone want to talk about it, I got up the nerve to say that I wrote about the first time I was with a guy. I found it hard to say out loud. I didn't use the slang term—I called it what it was. Oral sex. I said I still remembered that hand on top of my head, *pushing me down. Michele said that was a very powerful image & a lot of the other women nodded.*

They can't imagine how naive, how sheltered I was at fifteen. This was just such a shock to me. I remember that moment of seeing myself in the mirror. I was wearing a white blouse, I think, something ruffly. All those ruffled blouses—because of poor Princess Di. People used to say I looked like her—you know, tall & blond with a kind of clean, innocent face.

There I was looking at myself in the mirror, that horrible taste still in my mouth. Rinsing my mouth out over and over, like Pilate washing his hands of Jesus. Feeling guilty for something I hated doing—what a rip-off.

I remember thinking, I'm going to have to do this again. Over and over again. As long as I'm going out with Kenny. *Like it never even occurred to me I might have another choice, to say no.*

Why didn't that occur to me?

Michele sort of talked about that in the meeting tonight. About how girls are taught to be nice, to be—compliant, I think she said, to go along. To be agreeable. My mother was big on that. Be ladylike, be pleasant. When was I ever taught to say No? Well, yeah, we were taught in church to say no to temptation: to refuse a cigarette or a beer. Girls were supposed to say No to sex. And yet we were supposed to be nice, likable, agreeable. I never even realized till I put that on paper how tangled up those ideas were.

I stayed with Kenny Boland a few more weeks after that night. He made me do it a couple of more times. He pushed harder and tried to do more. I didn't want to lose my virginity. I didn't know how to make him stop.

So I did the only thing I knew how to do. I thought the best way to be safe from a guy I didn't want, was to find another guy.

Kenny & I had a fight. I told I had to go to the church youth rally instead of up to his cabin for May 24th weekend. Roger Petten was in with the crowd from Botwood at the rally. I knew Roger liked me. He was the only boy in a family of six girls and his little sister Samantha used to follow me around at Camp and tell me, "Roger wants to go out with you," in this singsong voice. That weekend Roger finally got up the nerve to tell me himself.

I felt safe, shivering on the cold church step with Roger's arm around me. If a guy was going to hurt me, the obvious solution was to run to a different guy. Find a nice Christian boy who wouldn't make me have sex, who would keep me safe.

Like I said, it was the only solution that ever occurred to me.

Down the hall, Mikayla and Chelsea are sleeping in the bunkbeds. Mikayla's got her arms thrown up over her face as she sleeps and Chelsea is curled into a little ball with her teddy tucked between her knees and her tummy. My little girls. My precious girls. I've raised them to be nice girls, to be pleasant, to be agreeable.

Dear God, what have I done to them?

Dave

SO, HOW'S YOUR WEEK BEEN?

Oh God, no, I'd really rather talk about your week. Or the week in sports, or the week in world politics ... let's just avoid the subject of *my* week altogether, OK?

Good story I told you last time, though, eh? The strip poker story? You want to talk about that, deconstruct it a little, we could do that.

Hmm ... what does it suggest to me? Well, it was a beginning of sorts, I guess. The beginning of my illustrious career, you might say. So many choices thrown at me in such a short time, and I grabbed for all of them. Didn't want to be left out of anything that might possibly be on the go. God, sex, booze, popularity—yep, I was going to be the guy who had it all.

I do have to say, though, that my social life did improve from that evening on. My Grade Ten year, I was a much hotter property than I'd ever been before. Now, who to credit for that? Was God blessing me, rewarding me for handing over my life to Him? Or could it have been the booze instead?

Why do I ... interesting question. Yeah, I guess in a way I do automatically assume that if I suddenly became more popular it must have been the gift of some higher power. I could give myself credit, I suppose. I grew about four or five inches all at once that summer after years of being Jeff's short friend. I kept working out. Got contacts. I guess I was better looking.

And yeah, drinking was a godsend because that smart mouth, the sense of humour that had kept me going inside my head all through "Dave Mitchell: The Geek Years," was suddenly free to come out in public. I could be a funny, funny guy with three or four beers in me. With ten or twelve, not so funny, but that comes later in the story.

Most of the credit, though, for my excellent Grade Ten year would have to go not to God or to alcohol or to my suddenly taller and more well-built self, but to my mother. That's right, Mom. All that I am or hope to be I owe to my angel mother, right? The year I was in Grade Ten, something very important happened. My mom got a job working nights, doing home care. That meant that nearly every night she was out of the house from 8 p.m. to 8 a.m. My little sister moved in with Nan. And nearly every night, people showed up at my house.

Yeah, even the church crowd, at first. Until word got around and some of the parents wised up.

Some nights a crowd of the b'ys from school would come over, and we'd party half the night. Other times there'd be just me and Jeff and Liz watching the late movie—neither of them cared what their parents said, so they were always over. After awhile Liz and Jeff would disappear back to my sister's old bedroom and it would be me alone in front of the TV. I'd work my way through a case of beer or a couple of bottles of Baby Duck, and in some ways those were the times I liked best.

Girls? Oh yeah, I went out with some girls. I lost my virginity in Grade Ten, during a double-date engineered by Jeff specifically for that purpose. Totally forgettable experience. I remember the girl's name—Tina O'Something—but I couldn't pick her out of a police line-up, I mean not even looking as she did then. I got laid a few times, but nothing serious. Nothing like Jeff and Liz, who were hot and heavy. Like I said, even though I was developing a reputation as the life of the party, in some ways I was happiest those nights in the dark living room, only the TV for light, getting drunk as quickly, cheaply and efficiently as possible.

I'm not sure when I caught on that my relationship with drinking was different from other kids. Everyone parties hard in high school, right? There were guys in my class who got drunk and stoned every Friday and Saturday night at parties. And there were kids at church, like Jeff and Liz, who had been raised to believe it was a sin to ever touch a beer bottle to their lips, but at a party they could keep up with the best of them. But for all of them, you know, even the serious party animals, it was like a – how do I put this? Like a peripheral thing. If you took it away, they might complain for awhile but their lives would basically go on.

I don't think any of them, even Russ Keating who drove his dad's car through the window of Dairy Queen once when he was loaded, I don't think any of them really looked forward to an evening alone with a couple of bottles of cheap wine. I sincerely doubt many of them had a forty-ouncer of vodka stashed in their locker at school.

Oh yeah. Well, not all the time. I wouldn't have gotten away with that. But sometimes I just needed—some backup, you know? I'd swipe the booze from my Uncle Clar's liquor cabinet, or buy it with the money I made cutting grass and shovelling snow, whatever. Hide a bottle in my locker, and buy a Coke at the store in the morning. I'd drink some Coke and then keep topping it up with vodka all day. So I could go to my locker and have a refreshing sip of Coke when things got tense.

What made it really funny was that I was living in this surreal Adventist world where drinking the Coke itself was a minor sin. Yeah, caffeine products, that was the thing there. You know, keep your body pure, abstain from all stimulants. Like the Mormons. And even though that was one of those rules nobody took too seriously, still the very fact that I always had a cola in my hand marked me out as a rebel in a small way. The fact that the can was half full of vodka was just the icing on the Coke, you might say.

You know what's great? No-one *ever* figured that out, I never got busted for it. Jeff and I used to develop pictures for the yearbook downstairs in the school darkroom, and we'd sometimes have a beer then shove the bottles up above the ceiling tiles. We'd laugh to think that someday, long after we graduated, someone would take down the ceiling and find it full of empties. But that was a shared kind of rebellion. The Coke can was my private thing.

Guilt? Oh God yes. Constant. See, I was serious about the God thing, the religion thing—it wasn't just a passing moment, a feeling that went away. I was serious about it, and I was also a serious drunk, already, at fifteen. I know the word for it today—cognitive dissonance. Sorry, two words. I've learned some big fancy words in my time. Back then, I just knew it felt like I had a nest of snakes living in my head.

Good point ... good point. Would it have made a difference, I wonder, if I'd gone to a church where drinking wasn't a sin? Where a single beer didn't condemn you for all eternity?

It would make sense to say yes. Maybe it would even be true. But the other Adventist kids I knew—Jeff, Liz, the rest of our crowd—got through that with fewer scars than I did. Jeff never took things as seriously as I did. Not drinking, not God. He could live without either of them, I guess.

And I couldn't. I'd wake up some mornings on my living room couch with empties all around me and feel like the worst piece of shit in the world. At night I'd be on my knees to God, telling Him how worthless I was and begging Him please, please accept me, forgive me, create in me a clean heart. And He would. I'd feel it, like someone touched me on the chest with an ice-pack, just for a minute, and everything was cool and clear.

It happened at church too. I was a regular at altar calls. Stumbling up to the front of the church with tears in my eyes while the pastor said, "If you've already given your heart to the Lord but you've fallen away, you know you've backslidden and you want to make it right, come to the front, just come now...." I'd come. Every time. And feel like yes, this was it, this was the start of something new. Only it never was.

Yeah, pretty sad story, isn't it? No worse than anybody else's Grade Ten year, I guess. Being fifteen sucks anyway you slice it. But you can see how all the pieces were on the board, everything in play, ready for my spectacularly screwed-up life.

Right! I knew you'd say that. Remember, I know all the jargon. Yeah, a problem-saturated narrative, that's exactly what it is. Saturated, soaked, pickled and marinated in problems.

Unique outcomes? No, I don't think I've heard that one. I guess if you want ... well, sure there were exceptions. I mean, there were times I thought I'd broken out of that cycle, actually taken a step forward. I didn't spend the whole Grade Ten year going up for altar calls and passing out drunk. I made half decent grades in Math and Science and I sucked in History and French. I bought a second-hand guitar, learned to play, took a stab at writing a few depressing teenage songs. Like I said, I dated some girls. There were hours, days, whole weeks maybe, when God and booze and the nest of snakes in my head weren't driving me crazy.

No, that's a lie. There were hours. There may have been days. There weren't whole weeks, not that I remember anyway.

OK, I remember one time—I'm not sure this counts as a unique outcome. It's just another one of those stories that seems like it might be worth telling. And it's got everything— not just God and booze but my friends and even my guitar. Oh, not much sex in this one though, sorry. You want to hear it?

Well, yeah, it is important to me, sort of. And again, it passes the time.

We had this youth rally, spring of Grade Ten. All the Adventist kids from across the island locked in the church basement for a weekend of singing and preaching and sharing. The speaker that year was a youngish guy, long hair in a ponytail which totally impressed me because I didn't think a pastor could get away with that. He made me want to get saved all over again, which was just like poking a stick into the snake den, you know. I wanted to be just like him, serve the Lord and travel around the world preaching and singing to young people with my guitar on my back.

Anyway, this guy had the idea that for the weekend rally, he wasn't going to preach—he was going to get some of us kids to do the sermons. And for some bizarre reason I was one of the ones he picked.

So Friday afternoon we gather at the church, kids from all over with their backpacks and Bibles and sleeping bags, and I panic at the thought of standing up front and preaching a friggin' sermon. But of course, I knew what would get me through.

You get *no* points for guessing that correctly.

So I went to Katie and told her I was freaking out—I didn't have to fake that part—because I'd left my notes for the sermon, which she had helped me write, up in my locker at school. She took charge of the situation and marched me up to the school with Mr. Carter's keys in hand. Carter wouldn't have trusted his own daughter, Liz, with the school keys, but he would trust Katie because she was just that kind of girl. I left her down by the door while I got the forty-ouncer from my locker, wrapped it in my sweatshirt, and stuck it in my backpack. On the way back to church I picked up a six-pack of Coke at the store.

Here's the part I remember really vividly: I can still see myself in the church bathroom, carefully pouring part of each can of Coke down the toilet and topping it up with vodka, this painstaking little ritual. I was a junior deacon in church that year, helping pass around the bread and wine during Communion—suddenly it reminded me of Communion, *This is my blood which was shed for you.*

Yeah, I had a bit of a buzz on when I went up to preach. But I didn't screw up. As I walked up on the platform I got hit between the eyes with this feeling God really *did* love me, whether I was drunk or sober. It was grace, I guess, that whole idea that the pastor used to preach about.

I never preached the sermon Katie helped me write. I started out reading it, and then I got to the bottom of the first page and I didn't turn it over. I felt so full of God's love, so sure of it, and I guess also fairly high, that suddenly I didn't have an ounce of fear in me. I looked out at the people in the pews and I ignored my carefully written sermon and started talking off the top of my head.

I had tears in my eyes by the time I said my last line—something along the lines of, "If God can save me, God can save anybody." I'd left my guitar up on the platform from song service earlier, and I went over and got it and started singing this pathetic song I wrote in the middle of the night one time.

No, I can't—well, I'm not going to sing it for you, right here. I would, but I don't have a guitar. Don't think I'm ashamed of my voice—that's one thing I'm not. But I—I can't sing it right now. I do remember the words, typical teenage songwriter shit.

Don't have much to give You
No jewels or shining gold
Just a heart that's torn and dirty
Full of dreams and full of holes ...

Not sure who I was trying to sound like at the time. I was listening to Springsteen's *The River* a lot back then so that might have been my inspiration. When I finished there was this silence, and then voices all over started saying, *Amen, Amen.* And then Pastor Ponytail—geez, why can I not remember his name?—he got up and put his hand on my shoulder and started praying.

And I felt full of the love of God, and I knew everything was going to be different. I wouldn't fail or fall again.

How do I feel about that now? Looking back? Jesus, I'd give anything to go back to that moment and make it true. But it wasn't. Of course.

Later that evening I slipped outside while all the kids were singing downstairs. I heard their voices— "Without Him, I could do nothing, Without Him, I'd surely fail ..." as I went out onto the fire escape. Stopped to grab my jacket and saw two of my remaining cans of vodka-and-Coke I'd stashed up on a shelf in case I needed them later.

I was still full of the feeling of victory and the love of God and the Holy Spirit, and I looked at the cans and said to myself, "I don't need this." And then like a brick slamming into the side of my head, I heard this other voice that said *Yes you do.* And that voice was telling the truth.

I took the cans and went out the door onto the steps. I sat there drinking and thinking to myself, *Dave, you are one sad, sorry bastard.*

When I heard someone coming and smelled cigarette smoke I knew it was another sinner coming to hide. Liz. She offered me a smoke. There I sat, drinking vodka and Coke and smoking, committing two of the worst sins we knew of in our little world. I guess if we'd taken our clothes off and screwed there on the church steps that would have topped it off. The thought did occur to me but I didn't pursue it. At that time.

I told her what I was thinking— "I am so fucked up. I am seriously fucked up beyond all repair."

You know what? She laughed. Told me it wasn't me that was screwed up, but the system—that God could still be in his heaven and we could have a few beers and a laugh. And I envied her so much then, because I could see it was true for her.

But for me? I wanted to love and serve God 100%, more than anything in the world–more than anything except another drink. Right there on the church steps, fifteen years old, ten years before my first encounter with any kind of Twelve Step program, I could see I had a problem.

Yeah, I should have been able to do something with that knowledge. Then I might not be sitting here, twenty-five years later, really and truly fucked beyond repair this time. But I put my foot on Step One and didn't go any farther.

I remember that night so well. A couple more people—good kids—came outside, and Liz and I put out our smokes. A little later I lay down in my sleeping bag surrounded by good Christian youth, and closed my eyes and wished I'd never wake up. I might have been the first time I went to sleep thinking that.

No, it sure as hell wasn't the last.

Katie

"TILL ONE DAY I MET HIM face to face, ooo-ooo-oooh, and I felt the wonder of His grace, ooo-ooo-oooh...."

Katie hates singing the ooo-ooo-ooohs. When the ragged assortment of teenage voices hits the high note on the last line— *"He's everything to meeeee!"* it sounds like cats being tortured. Jeff, next to her, stretches on tiptoe and delivers the line in a quavering falsetto.

She feels bad for laughing, because Pastor Rick is up there, lighting into his guitar with such energy and enthusiasm, his strong voice soaring over all of them, his eyes lit with the fire of God's love. Katie has spent the entire Week of Prayer in a delicious and shameful state of lust for Pastor Rick, which she has freely confessed to all her girlfriends. Sometimes when he walks down the school hallway, guitar in hand, Liz will lean over and sing in Katie's ear, *"He's everything to meeee!"*

Pastor Rick Bechtold, of Calgary, Alberta, is tall and broad-shouldered, with a handsome weather-beaten face and blond hair pulled back in a ponytail. He has preached at school every morning this week and Katie is on fire with love both for the Lord and for him.

Tonight, Week of Prayer wraps up and the youth rally weekend begins. Instead of the usual twelve or fifteen kids at Vespers there are more like forty, kids from all over the island. Katie sits next to Jeff. Liz, Julie and Dave are all up front with Pastor Rick. Liz and Julie are singing tonight, and Dave is preaching.

It's been a hectic day, a hectic week, and Katie is tired. She's worked on her own sermon and helped both Jeff and

Dave with theirs. She's phoned church members soliciting donations of food for the rally weekend. This afternoon she was the first one at church to help get things organized, and then she was sidetracked by this whole stupid crisis where Dave had left his sermon in his locker at school and she had to get the school keys and go up with him to let him in. She was glad to do it. He seemed so nervous, his need for reassurance and help so naked.

Her one-week crush on a visiting pastor is froth on the surface; what surges like the tide beneath is her love for Dave Mitchell. When Liz and Julie's song ends and Dave gets up to speak she watches how his hand quivers on his loose leaf page of sermon notes, how his eyelashes drop and rise again, how he shifts slightly from side to side as he moves his weight from one foot to the other. Inside tough, lonely, wisecracking Dave Mitchell, Katie sees the seed of a future Pastor Rick, a man who can use his words and music to charge others with God's love.

Dave gets to the end of the first page and pauses, then looks straight out at the audience. Katie can't believe he's this brave, this honest. He actually is ignoring his sermon—something she would never have the nerve to do, even though she's a much better public speaker—and talking directly to the audience. His words don't have the careful polish of the ones she helped him write: they are rough and hesitant and direct. "It's easy to fool people into thinking you're good," he says. "But it's not so easy to really *be* good. At least—I don't find it easy. And I used to think you had to be good for God to love you. But now I think that the really amazing thing about God is, that no matter how bad I am, He still loves me."

The sermon is very short–more like ten minutes than the fifteen it's supposed to be, but nobody minds, especially when

Dave picks up his guitar and finishes with a song he wrote himself.

Later in the evening, during Afterglow, some people drift outside. Katie notices when Dave leaves. She hopes he's not outside with some girl, that little blond one from Marystown, maybe.

After a few more songs Katie goes upstairs, out the front doors of the church. Julie is out on the front step with one of the boys from Botwood, but they're huddled close for warmth—it's May 24th weekend and although it hasn't snowed yet Katie wouldn't be surprised if it did. Katie waves at Julie and moves on, around the side of the church, where she finds Dave and Liz sitting on the fire escape stairs.

She sees the quickly extinguished glow of a cigarette butt on the stairs, smells smoke when she joins them. At least she knows they're not making out, like Julie and Roger, but still, the quick flare of the cigarette is enough to erect a barrier between Katie and her friends, placing her clearly on the side of the holy and uncool. She and Liz have drifted apart a bit since Liz and Jeff have been dating; Katie and Julie have discussed it and they suspect that Liz and Jeff both drink and smoke and might even be having sex. Katie hesitates a moment before she sits on the step.

"I was just telling Dave his sermon was awesome," Liz says.

"Oh, totally. It was—you know, that was a really brave thing to do."

"I know, I'd never be able to do that. I mean, just talk off the top of my head in front of people? Who knows what might come out?" Liz grins. Then, turning back to Dave, she adds, "The song was cool too. I didn't know you could write like that. You should sing your own songs more often."

"And preach more often," Katie says.

Dave picks up a can of pop that's next to him on the step and takes a long drink from it. "I highly doubt I'll be doing either of those things," he says. He looks and sounds bleak, as if the light that surrounded him an hour ago on the platform has been switched off.

"I'm going inside," says Liz, getting up. She swings herself out under the metal railing and jumps to the ground. Katie stays, unable to believe she's alone with Dave. What might happen? At least they can talk. That's worth freezing for.

She looks at his long slim fingers wrapped around his Coke can. At his face, half-hidden by his hair. Dave is growing his hair longer, down into his eyes in the front, over his collar in soft dark curls on the back. His hazel eyes are turned away from her. His lashes are dark and incredibly long for a guy's. Katie finds herself staring at his mouth, and blushes when he looks up.

"Everybody thought you did a great job," she says, wishing she could say something better.

He shrugs. "Maybe they did. But they wouldn't all be admiring my sermon so much if they'd really listened to it."

"Why, because you admitted you're not perfect, you're a sinner?"

He lays the Coke down, drops his head into his hands, runs his fingers through his hair. Katie wants to tangle her own fingers in his hair so badly she has to clasp her hands together to keep them in her lap.

"Ah, Katie, I'm such a screw-up. So totally, totally screwed up."

In the middle of his pain a note chimes in her like a bell: he spoke her name.

"Look, I don't know everything about what you're going through," she admits. She tries to guess. Dave goes to parties with Liz and Jeff—perhaps he, too, is drinking, smoking, even trying drugs? Would he do that? What else could there be? Katie realizes she doesn't know that many sins. "But look—I do know we're all screwed up," she goes on. "I mean, take me. I never get in trouble, but you know I have a terrible time with my temper, and saying things—you know, just being mean, cutting people down?" She trails off, knowing she's lost him, that he's too far inside his own problems to care about hers. "All I'm saying is, it doesn't matter what kind of sin it is. God loves us anyway."

Dave looks up, finally, from his hands, and there's a half-smile on his face. She wants to trace his lips with her fingertip, with the tip of her tongue.

"Yeah, some of us are hard tickets," he said. "God must be up there shaking His head, that's all I can figure." He takes a final sip from the pop can, stares at it for a minute, then crumples it in his hand and hurls it as far as he can. She hears a faint ping as it hits the chain-link fence.

"And now you're littering on top of all your other sins," she says, and is rewarded with a full-on look from those eyes and a genuine laugh as Dave stands up. "We better go inside before anyone thinks we're up to anything," he says.

Disappointment at going inside mingles in Katie's blood with the heady idea that someone might imagine she is up to something with Dave. Then he adds another jewel to her crown as he says, "Thanks, Katie. Thanks for listening."

She lies awake in her sleeping bag on the church floor. On one side of her, Julie snores softly. On the other side, Liz mumbles in her sleep. Katie wants to preserve every moment of this evening, frame it and keep it polished. The time on the steps with Dave—it's enough to fuel weeks' worth of fantasies in which she actually is brave enough to reach up and touch his shoulder, his face, and he completes the moment by leaning forward to kiss her.

Next morning it's her turn to stand in front of the church, making eye contact, getting encouraging smiles from her parents, her friends, random old people who have been nice to her since she was born.

Jeff preached his sermonette before hers, carefully reading the words Katie helped him write. He did fine, though he looked down at his paper too much. Katie's glad she chose to go second: people remember the last speaker best. Also, going second means she gets to choose the closing hymn. Jeff chose *Amazing Grace* for the opening hymn because it was the only one he could think of. Katie chose her favourite hymn, *Come Thou Fount.* She steps well back from the microphone and sings with her whole heart,

> *Prone to wander, Lord I feel it*
> *Prone to leave the God I love*
> *Here's my heart, oh take and seal it*
> *Seal it for Thy courts above.*

Katie does not feel prone to wander. But so many of the people she cares about *are* prone, and she wishes God could seal them all, keep them safe in Him. She learned from "The Story Behind the Hymn" on VOAR that the man who wrote that hymn wandered away from the faith himself, which makes the words even more poignant. *O to grace how great a debtor, daily I'm constrained to be.*

At the door of the church, Katie stands beside Jeff, the two of them shaking hands with people as they come out. Their friends offer hugs and congratulations. The older church members are encouraging. "Wonderful, good job, you gave a wonderful talk, the Lord is really using you," they say. Katie basks in the warm glow of admiration, even though all the praise should really go to God.

Then she hears Mrs. Martin say to Jeff, "Oh, you did a wonderful job. You should be a pastor." When Mr. Curtis goes out he says to Katie, "Wonderful, beautiful message," and to Jeff, "Good job, son. You ought to be a pastor." Three or four times, the same lines are repeated. *Katie, you did a good job. Jeff, you should be a pastor.*

The ultimate betrayal is Pastor Rick's. He gives Katie a quick hug, "Great sermon, Katie. I think it really touched people." Then for Jeff a longer, harder manly hug. "God's got His hand on you, Jeff. I expect to see you out at CUC in a few years, taking theology." As Jeff shakes his head, Pastor Rick says, "You just pray about it."

Katie walks home from the youth rally on Monday morning, the holiday Monday, as the out-of-town kids are piling onto the bus and the St. John's kids are getting picked up by their parents. Her mom sits cross-legged on the living room couch, sorting through piles of papers with a battered leather briefcase open next to her. Katie's dad is in the kitchen, making pancakes.

Katie describes her mother—to her face—as an aging hippie, and her mother doesn't seem to mind. Angela Matthews wears her hair long and straight, often in braids. She sometimes chews the end of one braid, like a nervous fourth-grader. She wears jeans frayed at the cuffs, and T-shirts bearing the logos of good causes or inflammatory slogans such as "A Woman Needs a Man Like a Fish Needs a Bicycle." She's wearing the fish/bicycle shirt this morning, as her husband makes brunch, which gives Katie a moment's pause.

"Mom, is there a reason why we don't have women pastors in our church?" Katie asks, sitting down on the couch.

Angela rolls her eyes. She works with a group trying to raise funding to open a shelter for battered women. She joined the Adventist church because she married an Adventist, and has always seemed to Katie to be a fish out of water—albeit a fish with a bicycle out of water—in church circles. She looks wrong, dresses wrong, and doesn't willingly attend either baby showers or Tupperware parties. She loves certain things about the church—like being vegetarian and not working on Sabbath—but a lot of things frustrate her.

"Basically, honey, because a bunch of uptight old white guys can't handle the idea of women having any kind of power within the organization. So they twist Scripture to their own purposes because they're afraid of treating people with the kind of radical equality Jesus did."

Katie's father has come to stand in the doorway, drying a glass as he listens with his "Now Angela" look on his face. He doesn't say, "Now, Angela," but she looks up anyway, addressing him as if he has interrupted.

"No, it's ridiculous, Ian, it is. This is a church that was *founded* by a woman, for God's sake. They put Ellen G. White into some kind of special category and make sure all the other women get locked back in the Dorcas society and the Cradle Roll Sabbath School. It's as bad as the Catholic church."

"It's not, you know." Katie's father likes to describe himself as Ian Matthews, mild-mannered clerical functionary in the Department of Education, whose astonishing superpowers remain undiscovered by those around him—or by himself. "Things are changing."

"Of course they are. I just don't understand why there's even a debate."

Katie seeks a second opinion. She knows that while her parents are smart, wonderful people, they are not the people you talk to if you want to find out the official Adventist view on things. They drink coffee and they watch the CBC news on Sabbath and they never have family worship, though her mother sometimes prays out loud at odd times, like while driving down Topsail Road. Katie wants to know what Real Adventists, people like Liz's family or the Kimballs, think about women pastors.

She chooses Liz's mother, who is the polar opposite of Angela. Liz's mom has her hair permed and always neatly styled. She owns fifty-seven pieces of Tupperware—Katie counted once, drying their dishes after a youth social—and she almost always wears skirts or dresses. If she does wear pants they're those polyester ones with elastic waists. Mother clothes. Church lady clothes.

Katie doesn't exactly admire Liz's mother, but she sees her as a kind of natural wonder, a standard to measure things by, like Cape Spear. As Cape Spear is the Most Easterly Point in North America, Liz's mom is the Most Adventist Woman in St. John's.

"Women ministers?" Liz's mom repeats. "Well you know, Katie, there are a lot of girls studying theology nowadays at our colleges. Of course they can't become pastors, God has ordained different roles for men and women, but you know, there are many ways the Lord can use women in His work. You could become a Bible worker, or teach Bible in one of our schools ... if you feel that's where the Lord is leading you. He will find a place for you."

She smiles, but cautiously, as if Katie might be a carrier for her mother's dangerous feminist ideas. "You know, Katie, every believer has a ministry. Ministry isn't just what pastors and evangelists do." She is wiping the dishes as she talks, drying the lids of her round yellow nested Tupperware. "Teaching can be a ministry. Nursing. Even being a wife and mother is a ministry." She looks past Katie, out the window.

Liz comes clattering up from the rec room. "Come on downstairs, Katie? What are you doing up here? Talking to my *mom?*" She rolls her eyes.

"Thanks, Mrs. Carter," Katie says, and follows Liz down the stairs.

liz

MY HANDS IN THE AIR my body sways. a tide of voices rises around me. no harmony, barely even melody. a chant, a tribal ritual, a liturgy of repetition.

> *[like the idea of a tribal chant. subtler way to say this?]*

we exalt thee we exalt thee we exalt thee oh god we exalt thee we exalt thee we exalt thee ooohhh god.

a woman in the pew in front of me starts. ahlalalala the babbling syllables blend into the song. she sways. another voice takes up the wordless words.

> *[haven't heard this sound in years. how best to capture speaking in tongues? could visit a pentecostal church for research purposes]*

but i am not here. i am outside the moment, an observer, a spectator. my body sways to the music of the praise band my lips obediently mouth we exalt thee. eyes fixed on the white screen at front words cast by the overhead projector.

beside me gillian drones the words we exalt thee at the front the earnest boy with the narrow leather tie says praise jesus praise jesus yes we just wanna praise you oh god bless you jesus bless you lord.

people dance around prone bodies slain in the spirit. more tongues more singing another slaying near the front. what next? bring on the snakes.

[i'm being sarcastic. is this a problem? i think not—not many pentecostals likely to read this anyway]

another sunday church-slumming again. decorous catholic crowd in dowdy polyester sunday best. old ladies with black or brown cloth hats riding their gray heads. stained glass robes candles incense the greatest show on earth.

another liturgy here, sonorous chanted words. no-one speaks in tongues or gets slain.

two orderly lines of worshippers go down the aisle to receive communion. you can't go if you're not catholic i wonder if they check id. could you get fake catholic id like you can for a bar.

if the priest looks into eyes will he know i'm not catholic? that i was taught the pope is antichrist and has 666 written on his mitre? i join the line my mind chanting silently babylon the great is fallen is fallen she has made all nations to drink of the wine of the wrath of her iniquities.

[great. now i'm offending catholics. some of whom actually do read books.]

the wine of the wrath is real wine not grape juice like ours. the bread lighter it dissolves on my tongue. i kneel obediently to receive and i feel i feel i feel nothing.

i don't want to be safe to be saved to be good but i want to feel. i read about saints and mystics about an experience that takes you out of yourself.

out of myself that's where i want to go. its getting dark and crowded in here and i want out by any means possible.

another path then. god is not the way to ecstasy. i tried drinking in grade nine and liked the feeling, the buzz, though not the hangovers. now grade ten i guess its time to try weed. my brother gene highly recommends it.

huddled around dave's kitchen table russ keating opens a bag of weed and dave shows me how to roll it. jeff tries too. we sit around the table i feel light like i'm floating my head. dave says knock knock and i say who's there laughing so hard i can't get the words out i put my head down on the table who's there who's there there's who there's who.

weed makes me silly light and giggly. but does not take me outside myself.

in a spare bedroom at dave's house jeff touches me his hands covering my breasts skimming my bare thighs. we revel in the luxury, a whole bed to ourselves. the radio plays chicago, hard to say i'm sorry.

one night, finally. the pain is short but sharper than i'd imagined. hope i'm not bleeding on dave's sheets. a frantic pushing, a film of sweat on jeff's chest and back. over in minutes.

[not really capturing this well—can't actually remember much]

he lies with his head on my bare chest his soft wings of light-brown hair feathered against my breasts.

-was that good for you he asks, a line learned from movies.

-i'm glad it was with you, i say. my first time. the best i can give him though i know he wants more.

-i'm glad too. smile.

-it was yours too? your first time? knowing that it had to be.

[do we lose track of who's talking here?]

-of course, who else would i? there's nobody but you. his eyes open and simple like a grade 2 reader.

the third or fourth time we lie on the bed he is bolder, more relaxed less nervous. queen plays on the radio, we are the champions my friend. we feel like champions, explorers, bold and daring. his fingers explore, touch there there ahhh there.

then there there oh oh yes come on baby come on. it's coming coming and yes yes yes i am i am i am.

[is there any way to write this without sounding like a complete idiot? i'm a poet. surely i can do better]

outside myself. and yet more inside my own skin than i have ever been.

[i like this though]

i didn't know. like the country song. looking for it in all the wrong places. church candles poetry music booze weed and here it was here all the time between my own legs.

jeff drives on now to his own climax and at last i know why it matters so much. this time as he lies on my chest i understand my power. who wouldn't love the person who can fit that key in the lock open that door let your fly outside yourself.

later much later i am home alone in my own dark room. my fingers follow the trail jeff has blazed. like orienteering in the woods at camp, orange ribbons tied to the trees. oh we are the pathfinders strong the servants of god are we faithful as we march along in truth and puriteee....

[guess not many people know the pathfinder song. does the irony still work?]

ah yes there there. better now with no excited boy to distract me, i find the key myself, learn my body's own language. yes and there it is there there and its coming its coming it comes.

i get up, turn on the lamp, look in the mirror, naked under my oversized t-shirt. dark hair plastered against my head. think i'll get it cut really short and spike it. i'll pierce my ears and to hell with it. twice in one night i've been where i wanted to go and i know how to get back.

the face in the mirror shines with not love not ecstasy not god. power.

i am the champion my friend.

[we get the point liz, you felt powerful! move on...]

THREE

Jeff

IMPACT.

One second of incredible pain, everywhere, chaos as the car buckles and folds around me. Then, mercifully, black.

Falling into black. Down down down. And then ...

I bob to the surface. Still dark, but peaceful. I can breathe. What's next? I've never known for sure what I believe about life after death. I know I'm supposed to sleep peacefully till Jesus comes.

Only, I'm not asleep. Not awake either. Somewhere in between.

I hear voices. Not the Voice of God, just voices. Debbie saying, "Jeff! Jeff! Would you get in here this minute!" The kids: "Daddy! Daddy!" My father: "This is not what I expected from you, Jeffrey. I'm very disappointed." Liz, sharp and clear: "I think this thing has run its course."

Has it? It's so hard to tell when a thing has run its course. I though I had years ahead of me. I thought I was half-way through my life. I didn't expect—

But that's the thing. You never do expect. We were taught in Sabbath School to look for Signs of the End—yet no matter how hard you looked, Jesus was going to come like a thief in the night. Like a semi on the highway.

I've never been good at seeing the signs.

My father was an expert on signs. He stood next to the pastor in a potluck line-up and talked about the U.S. President meeting with the Pope and how that meant the End was Near.

He knew the twenty-three hundred day prophecy better than our Bible teacher did.

He could also see signs in me. All through high school he'd seen that I was headed for trouble, and just the day before that potluck he saw the biggest sign of all. The marks for Grade Eleven publics came out and I flunked English

My father never yelled. He was always calm, always patient when he lectured me about how I was headed in the wrong direction. His lecture was still ringing in my ears that Sabbath as we gathered in the church auditorium for potluck.

Pastor Kimball called me up to the front. "It's time to pay a little tribute to our young people, some of our fine young graduates from the Academy this year, who will be going off to CUC in the fall. We're so proud to be sending our youth off to our church colleges, to prepare for a life of service to the Lord. Katie, Julie, good ... Jeff, come on up. Liz? Is Liz here?"

Liz had slipped out, sometime between church and potluck. Pastor Kimball went ahead with the rest of us, giving us each a wrapped book-shape—probably a Bible or a devotional book, I thought. I laid it down on the nearest table.

We'd all applied to CUC, the Adventist college out in Alberta, but Liz wouldn't say whether she was going or not. I assumed wherever we went, we'd go together. We could go out west to CUC, or stay home and go to public university, right here at MUN in St. John's. I knew that at CUC I could do some kind of make-up or foundation English course before I started college classes; I wasn't sure if that was possible at MUN. Liz got edgy and irritable every time I brought up college, or the future.

Pastor Kimball hugged each of us. People clapped. In the blur of faces I saw Dave sitting alone, the only Adventist kid in our class who wasn't even thinking about CUC. I wished he was. I caught his eye and he looked away, staring up at the ceiling.

After the presentation, arms reached out from all directions to hug us. Little old ladies who'd known me since I was born. "God bless you, Jeff," they said. "You go out to CUC and become a pastor. Make us proud." A couple of them pressed tens and twenties into my hand.

I picked up my plate and went into the youth room. All our crowd was in there—Dave, Katie, Lisa Kimball. Lisa's sister Debbie and Liz's brother Gene, who were already out at CUC, back for summer holidays. My own little brothers and a few younger kids were there. I sat on the piano bench with my paper plate on my knee. Classic Adventist potluck plate: a brown square of Special K roast, vegetarian patties with mushroom-soup gravy, a hot potato casserole, a cold potato salad, two kinds of jello salad—one green and one orange— with little bits of fruit floating in them. Wish I had a dollar for every time I've eaten that meal.

Liz drifted into the room and sat down by Julie and Lisa. After we finished eating people started to leave. When I saw Liz head for the door I went and grabbed her arm and pulled her back into the room.

"What's up? Where did you go?" I said.

She shrugged. "Nothing. Nowhere."

"Do you want to do anything this afternoon—go for a drive or a walk or something?"

"Not really, no. I'll probably see you tonight at Julie's."

"Look, if something's bothering you, tell me."

She looked at me, those clear brown eyes in her perfect pointed face. "It's no big deal, Jeff. I just think this thing has run its course."

It felt like exactly like being kicked in the balls. Never saw the signs. I really believed we were going off to college together and getting married someday. Partly because we were sleeping together—but also, I just couldn't imagine a life without her.

"Run its course? What the hell is that supposed to mean?" Keeping my voice down so no-one out in the auditorium would hear me say *hell*. "Are you saying you want to break up?"

She rolled her eyes. "Does everything have to be so black and white? Things are winding down, coming to a natural end. It's like if your grandfather was really old and everyone knew he was dying, you wouldn't necessarily go and stab him, would you? You'd just let him die."

I stared at her. "I don't know what you mean. Dying a natural death? Winding down? Not as far as I'm concerned. I thought everything was fine!"

She stared back, a long cool moment. Outside, a happy clatter of voices. Some little kids careening around the church basement bumped against the door of the youth room and I slammed it shut. Liz said, "Well, that's what you thought. Look, I told you, I'll see you tonight."

I stood there alone, leaning against the wall, breathing like I'd been running. They used to say, talking about premarital sex in Sabbath School, that girls used sex to get love and guys used love to get sex. Like a guy was never interested in anything more than the sex, like a guy could never be deeply in love and get hurt. Liz was my world. I was planning our future life together and she thought our relationship was dying like a sick old man.

Dave stuck his head into the room. "What's going on, man?"

"Nothing. Wanna go for a drive? Out to Topsail Beach or something?"

He shrugged. "Yeah, sure."

We left. I peeled out of the parking lot with Liz's voice still pounding in my ears.

That's the voice I hear now as waves of black roll over me, leaving me tossed up on the beach, pain returning to my numbed body. Her voice, strong and tough and confident. "I think this thing has run its course. Run its course ... run its course ..."

Up Where We Belong

2005

Summer - Fall 1982

Katie

"AND I KNOW THAT ALL OF US have the ability, all of us have the potential, to reach for the stars. That's what I want to do and I pray that each of you will make the same choice. Thank you for all that we've shared together."

Katie looks up from her creased pages of loose leaf, out over the crowded church. Her classmates sit in the first two rows, capped and gowned. Applause washes over her. She smiles and steps back from the podium.

She is class valedictorian and a semi-official high-school graduate -- nobody's really graduated yet, since public exams still have to be written and results won't be out till July. But tonight she and her classmates celebrate the end of twelve years together.

Now the hours of painstakingly folding squares of coloured toilet paper to make tissue flowers are over. The school-approved, teacher-administered, parent-attended part of grad is over, the part that the Seventh-day Adventist Academy can proudly hang its name on.

Now, the party starts.

Heather Cross has an uncle who's really rich. And possibly not that bright. He has a huge house down by Bally Haly with one of the few outdoor swimming pools in St. John's. Heather's uncle has gone out of town and agreed to let his favourite niece and her friends have the house for their grad party.

Katie's spent her whole high school career scrupulously avoiding these kind of parties. There will be drinking. There might be drugs. There may be dancing.

Her parents, like the other Adventist parents, are not thrilled about the party, though Jeff and Liz are not going to be held back by parental disapproval. In the end, Katie decides she can't miss it. Her parents grudgingly agree, with a stern warning to call them if she needs a ride and can't find a driver who hasn't been drinking.

In the church basement after the ceremony, the graduates pose for pictures. Liz and Jeff pull Katie and Dave into a picture and, belatedly, grab Julie as well, so the five of them pose together, the girls with their legs stuck out in front of their grad gowns like can-can dancers; the guys with arms draped around the girls, leaning forward. Dave's left arm is warm against Katie's shoulder.

Two hours later Katie stands behind the bar in Heather's uncle's rec room, surveying the chaos. About fifty teenagers are draped around the house. The lights are off and a strobe light flashes in time to the pounding music though nobody is actually dancing. Numerous couples are entwined in corners. The many cases of beer carried in early in the evening are stashed behind the bar. Katie is not actually bartending, but she will relax her principles enough to hand a bottle of beer across the bar to someone, which keeps her busy although she dislikes doing it.

She chose this spot because it was safe. The bar is something to lean against, to hide behind. She arrived in high spirits, elated from all the hugs and kisses and popping flashbulbs, from the ride over in the back of Gene Carter's car squashed against Dave in the backseat. When Katie came in they were playing "Up Where We Belong," one of the few current pop songs she actually likes, and she jumped up on the bar and over it, and Dave laughed. Then she leaned over and said, "What'll it be?" thinking maybe, just maybe he might say, "I'll have a kiss."

Instead he said, "Is the beer here yet?"

Katie knew then a line had been crossed. Dave and Liz and Jeff always hid the fact that they drank and smoked, though Katie was never sure whether that was out of respect or because they didn't trust her not to rat on them. But tonight, it's clear, that barrier is down. Katie is on their territory now; nobody's hiding anything.

In the rec room a bunch of people are shooting pool. Heather flits around, jumpy and excited, yelling at intervals, "Don't go upstairs! Uncle Paul'll kill me if anyone goes upstairs!"

People go upstairs. People drift by the bar and talk to Katie. Gene Carter, Liz's brother, asks Katie to pass him a beer.

"Nice to be somewhere you can relax," he says, looking at the beer with appreciation.

"Yeah? Not much of this at CUC I guess," Katie says, waving a hand to indicate not just the beer but the whole party. Gene smells like he's been smoking, not necessarily cigarettes.

"That place? Don't talk to me about that place. I'm not going back there."

"You're not?"

"Nah. If I go back to Alberta, I'll go to Edmonton. Some buddies of mine have an apartment up there. I might go to U of A, I don't know. Dad won't pay for public university."

A banshee scream from the yard is followed by a splash and a roar of approving drunken voices. "I see the throwing-people-in-the-pool portion of our program has started," Gene says, wandering towards the door.

The shouts and screams continue. it gets quiet at the bar and Katie goes out in the yard, pulling her sweatshirt over her head. It's a cold evening, with fog drifting in down here in the East End, close to the sea.

It's not an evening when anyone would willingly get in the pool, but guys are throwing girls in as the girls squeal and protest. Dave carries Stephanie Hussey, who is already dripping from a previous dunking. The floodlights shining down on the pool illuminate the scene like a dream: there are perhaps twenty kids out here but Katie sees only Dave and Steph.

Steph goes in with a splash, and Dave looks around. "Who's next? Who's next?" He lunges for Gillian Upshall, who squeals and hides behind her boyfriend.

"Oh I'll do it man, don't say I won't cause I'll do it, you better believe I would." Dave's voice, loud and manic, rises above the babble. "What's that about?" Katie says, turning to Gene Carter, who's beside her again.

Gene laughs. "Russ Keating said it was no big deal to go in the pool with your clothes on on a night like this—what'd really be a laugh would be going in with your clothes off. And then he dared Dave to do it."

"Come on Dave, I'd pay to see that!" shrills Stephanie Hussey.

The coaxing, the yelling, the drunken cajoling goes on till Dave peels off his T-shirt. He strips while the crowd around him yells, "Take it off! Take it all off!" When he gets down to his underwear somebody screams, "Put it on! Put it all back on!" Finally, still wearing his boxers, he executes a graceless dive off the side of the pool and emerges spluttering and swearing.

"OK, I did it, now who's coming in with me?" He scans the people at the edge of the pool. "Come on Katie, you're still dry!"

"No way!"

Dave chases her around the edge of the pool till he has her in a firm grip. He's cold and wet and his breath, close to her face, stinks of beer.

She struggles, but he's strong, and moments later he pushes her off the edge into the water, which is bitterly cold. She grabs at him as she falls and he falls in too, a momentary intimacy as they tangle in the water and fight their way back to the surface.

Yet once she's on the edge of the pool, shivering and soaked, Dave forgets her as quickly as he forgot Stephanie and Gillian, forgets the whole game of throwing girls into the pool and wanders back into the house. Russ Keating wrestles his girlfriend towards the edge. Katie wraps her arms around herself.

"You got anything to change into?" It's Gene.

"I do actually, but I'll look like an idiot." She came to the party wearing the pink dress she wore at the grad, now stuffed in a Sobey's bag.

"Better look like an idiot than freeze to death. Or do you want a run home?"

Katie sizes up Gene. "How much have you had to drink?"

"Like two beers in three hours. Don't worry, I'm good to drive. Do you wanna go home?"

Katie wonders if anything will happen between the poolside and the bathroom to make her change her mind, want to stay at this party. The bathroom is locked and she hears someone puking inside, so she changes in a closet and goes back through the darkened rec room, feeling bizarrely out of place in the pink dress edged with eyelet lace. She sees Dave, near the pool table, dressed again, sitting on the floor with his back to the wall cradling one of the liquor bottles from behind the bar they weren't supposed to touch. Katie stands in the doorway a minute, looking at Dave through the smoky air, wondering if he'll turn and see her. But he doesn't look up; his poolside high spirits have died down. She turns to go.

The streets are quiet at two a.m. Gene steers the Carter family car, a Chev Impala, down Prince Phillip Drive, past the university. "You going there in September?" he says, nodding at MUN.

"No ... I think I'm going to CUC."

"You're better off steering clear of that place," Gene says, then looks at her. "Maybe not. You're a different breed. You'll probably like it there."

"You mean I'm not a rebel like you."

"You don't know this, Katie, but I admire you. You're who you are because you are. That's rare. That's very rare." Something in his voice sounds almost angry as he turns on the wipers against a light spitting rain.

Katie is quiet, not knowing how to respond. "What are you going to take at U of A?" she says. "If you go there?"

"Maybe PoliSci," says Gene.

"Law school?"

"Nah, I don't know. I don't know what I want. I think I might want to get into politics. Which is weird, as I'm basically an anarchist." He turns onto Anderson Avenue, past the rundown apartment buildings.

"Yeah, that would make it hard to get ahead in politics," Katie says. "I mean, who'd vote for you? Even your own supporters wouldn't, not if they had any principles."

Gene laughs as he pulls the car up in front of Katie's house. "You don't really want to be like all the rest of us, do you?" he says, skipping back to the other conversation without missing a beat. "Drinking, screwing, and toking up. You've got more on the go than that."

Katie shrugs. "I guess." This might, she thinks, be a soul-winning opportunity. Perhaps she is supposed to share Jesus with Gene—although having grown up in the Carter house, you'd think he'd have had as much of Jesus as he needed. She's completely taken aback when Gene slides across the bench seat, slips an arm around her, and kisses her. His lips are warm and wet; his tongue probes slightly against hers but doesn't explore.

When he pulls away, Katie says, "Well, thanks."

"Thanks?"

"It's my birthday next week. I'll be seventeen. I would have gotten through the whole year being sweet sixteen, never kissed. But you saved me."

"Sweet sixteen? Really?" It's obviously never occurred to Gene that he could give a sixteen-year-old her first kiss. He smiles and shakes his head. "You're something else, Katie Matthews."

Katie takes her bag of sopping clothes and gets out of the car, running up the path to her own front door. She turns to wave. It's not what she expected from her grad night. She goes upstairs to her room considering Gene Carter. He's not exactly good looking: his hair is a little frizzy and he wears glasses. But he's smarter than most of the boys around here, and older. He's not a good Christian. But he kissed her and he was kind to her.

She lies in her bed wanting to think of Gene but sees only Dave, feels only his hands pushing her into the pool, remembers his face as sat alone on the floor of the rec room.

Gene becomes Katie's summer romance, her first sort-of boyfriend. He shows up in the afternoons at VOAR, where she's working for the summer. He kisses her in the back hallway where the records are shelved, traps her behind the transmitter and kisses her again. After work he drives her out to Topsail Beach or Middle Cove on nice days, to sit in the sun and eat Kentucky Fried Chicken. They talk and kiss. Katie enjoys Gene's mind, because he's sharp and interested in things most boys she knows aren't, like books and politics. She enjoys the kissing too, but worries that Gene will want to go too far.

He doesn't show much inclination to push. When he touches her breast, under her shirt but over her bra, Katie moves his hand away. "No?" he says, looking at her with mock-sad puppy dog eyes.

"No," she says.

"Whatever you say," Gene agrees mildly. He doesn't seem enraged by passion like guys are supposed to get after you let them French-kiss you for half an hour. Maybe, Katie thinks, he's seeing someone else too, someone who will let him do more, go all the way. He claims he slept with his last girlfriend, out in Alberta. She doesn't know whether to believe this or not. Gene doesn't act like she's always been told guys are supposed to act when you kiss them. But in spite of all the hours spent talking, she still feels she doesn't know him all that well. There are parts of Gene kept behind a locked door, and Katie, for once in her life, knows enough not to push on that door.

Locked door or not, it's nice having a guy around. Her friends are mostly coupled; Liz and Jeff still together although they're fighting a lot, Julie making long-distance phone calls and trips down to Botwood to see Roger. Dave goes around with a girl called Diane for awhile. Katie likes showing up with Gene for Saturday night pizza at someone's house or a church youth thing. At Campmeeting, he takes her hand casually as they walk around the campgrounds. She likes being labelled, seen to belong with someone.

Katie makes plans with Julie to go to CUC while Jeff and Liz bicker about where to go in September. The old gang— already Katie thinks of them that way, as her group of friends from back in high school days—gets together a few times over the summer, always with the feeling that each party, each barbecue, might be the last. Katie and Liz, Julie and Jeff and Dave all have summer birthdays, and each birthday requires a gathering tinged with premature nostalgia.

Gene takes Katie to her first movie. "Come on," he says, "I know you're not going to screw, drink or smoke dope. You've gotta let me introduce you to *some* sin. Let's go to a movie."

Katie has never been inside a movie theatre. She agrees it's time. Gene suggests *The Best Little Whorehouse in Texas,* but they go to *An Officer and a Gentleman,* which everyone has seen except them: Katie because she doesn't go to movies and Gene because he hates chick flicks. "It's not bad," he said afterwards. "I liked the part where the guy hung himself in the shower."

"You have weird taste." They are driving up to Signal Hill for the obligatory post-movie make-out session.

"Well, I'm fascinated with suicide. Not with doing it, but the idea. If you don't believe in God, it really makes sense, you know?"

Gene is an atheist. He says things like this to get Katie going, knowing she will argue. He tells her that religion is mind control, something the upper classes use to keep the lower classes in place. Katie's brain scurries to keep up with him. She's not used to intelligent atheists, atheists who grew up in church and know all the arguments and can argue back dispassionately, but arguing with Gene forces her to think about what she believes. Arguing with Gene sharpens her faith, challenges her. It never makes her want to save Gene or pray for him like she prays for Dave.

Because neither of them will ever convince the other, they segue smoothly from arguing to kissing. As Gene's tongue explores Katie's mouth, and the song "Two Out of Three Ain't Bad" comes on VOCM. Gene reaches for the button to change stations because everybody knows Katie hates that song. What kind of love song is that, she says loudly and frequently. *I want you, I need you, but there ain't no way I'm ever gonna love you?* But tonight she tells Gene, "Leave it on." From then on she thinks of it as "their song," hers and Gene's, though she doesn't tell Gene this.

Summer is ending. A couple of days later Liz tells Katie she and Jeff have broken up, that she's going to stay and go to MUN. Jeff decides to go to CUC. Gene tells Katie he's moving to Toronto with a friend. He plans to work for awhile, then apply to U of T or maybe York.

"It doesn't make any difference," Katie says. They are at McDonald's, sipping milkshakes under the glaring light at the red and white plastic table. "I mean, to us. This is just a summer thing, right? We wouldn't have been seeing each other out in Alberta."

Gene shifts in his seat and looks down at his straw, which he has chewed up as he always does. "I don't know–I guess not." He looks up. "I do like you. I mean, I like you a lot."

"I like you too," Katie says. "That's why this is easy. I mean, *like* is straightforward. It's love that screws everything up."

Gene grins. "You're refreshing, Katie. I'm not used to girls being honest like this. Most girls are so into playing games."

"No games from me," Katie says. She decides this will be her new identity, the Girl Who Doesn't Play Games. Straight up, above board, that's what she'll be from now on in every relationship. Assuming there are more relationships.

Katie spends her second-last day in St. John's with Liz. They go shopping downtown, then have lemon cream pie at the Captain's Cabin in Bowring's, looking down at the ships in the harbour. "It's weird that you're going away and I'm staying," Liz says. "You know, you love Newfoundland, you belong here. I always wanted to get away."

"Yeah, it is weird." Katie pokes at the pointy cream surface of her pie with the fork. "Are you ever going to tell me what happened with you and Jeff?"

A pause. Liz looks out the window, blurred with rain, and then back at Katie. She leans forward as if she's about to share a confidence, then sits back and eats another forkful of pie. "I don't know. We just outgrew each other. It wasn't undying love. It was—like you and Gene, kind of." Liz has heard the whole story on Gene and Katie and heartily approves. "You made the right choice. I mean, my brother's cool but he's not the guy you'd want to settle down with, long term."

"And neither is Jeff?"

"For somebody else. Maybe it's me who's not the settling down type. Me and Gene both—maybe it's something hereditary."

Katie wants to spend her last day with Dave. When she calls that night, he says sure, come over, they'll hang out together.

It doesn't work out. Katie's last-minute stuff -- packing, shopping -- takes longer than she expects, and when she calls Dave's place there's no answer. Late afternoon she finds herself walking around the neighbourhood to places Dave might be— Russ Keating's house, Brewer's store, even down as far as Bannerman Park because he sometimes walks that way coming back from work. About suppertime she finally gets to his apartment and climbs the million steps and finds Dave home, asleep on the couch.

He gets up, washes his face and changes his shirt, says they should go out for supper. They walk down to Leo's on Freshwater Road. Katie could get the car and they could drive somewhere, but it's a nice warm night and she wants to keep walking around her old neighbourhood, the tangle of streets she grew up in, past her house, past Vokey's store and Coady's and the school, past Chalker's and Henry's and the smell of fish and chips in the air, down to Leo's.

Dave apologizes for not answering the phone earlier. "I was home, but I was -- asleep. Big party down to Russ's place last night." He smiles but looks at his chips, sprinkling vinegar on them, and Katie feels the hugeness of the space between them.

"Sometimes I don't know what's gotten into you," she says, not sure whether she should sound cross or sad.

"Hell of a lot of vodka, Katie, that's all that's gotten into me."

"I hate to see you doing this to yourself."

"You make it sound like such a big deal. I'm not *doing anything* to myself, just having a few laughs. I'm sorry, I don't believe in—all the church stuff. Everything we used to believe in."

"Not even God?"

He shrugs. "Maybe, maybe not."

It's a long way from her intellectual sparring with Gene. Katie doesn't want to argue with Dave, doesn't want to convince him of God's existence. What she wants is something else, something she knows is impossible.

They walk very slowly down Pennywell Road, up Adams Avenue past Booth and Mary Brown's, past their old elementary school and the gas station, down to Katie's house.

"OK, well, I guess I'll see you at Christmas," Dave says. He reaches forward to give her a hug.

And Katie, the Girl Who Doesn't Play Games, decides this is the moment to lay all her cards on the table yet again, just to make sure he won't completely forget her. She puts her hand on the back of his head and moves her mouth to Dave's, to the lips she has dreamed for years of kissing, which are just as full and soft as she's always known they would be. Dave is shocked and for a moment doesn't kiss her back, but then he responds. Katie links her arms around his neck because she knows that lifts her breasts a bit and he'll feel them pressed against his chest, such as they are. She darts her tongue into his mouth and again after a moment's quick surprise he responds too, a real passionate kiss that touches Katie in places none of Gene's kisses ever did.

When Katie pulls away she looks in Dave's eyes again, and he says, "Wow. Well. Wow."

"See you in December," she says, and forces herself not to look back as she goes up the steps of her house.

liz

I WALK DOWN AISLES LINED with cough medicine, aspirin, toothpaste, shampoo, nylons. find a row of boxes with discreet pink script. stand a minute staring. pick up a box by the corner with two fingers.

two hunched women in lumpy cardigans turn into the aisle. i slip the box back on the shelf.

-...yes my dear and tis some hard to find them, the right kind i mean, they stopped carrying the ones i liked. in the orange box.

-the doctor scholls, sure they still got those i saw them over in the other aisle i think.

they brush past pushing a rattling cart.

-oh yes the doctor scholls yes but it's the size my dear i can't seem to find the size i want.

[how good is my ear for a st. john's accent? it's been years since i heard it regularly...]

they reach the end of the aisle at last and turn again, a final querulous note hangs in the air --
-...and me corns me corns are killing me...

i pick up the box with the pregnancy test and try to hold it so no-one who might pass, no church member, no friend of my parents might see what i'm holding.

at the checkout heart pounding in the hollow of my throat. when jeff buys condoms is there this furtive shame, this sneaking and peeking around corners. or is it a badge of pride. virile young man buys extra-large condoms at shoppers drug mart, film at eleven.

not that it matters as it seems the damn things may not have worked anyway.

two weeks late. i wake every morning and realize another day has come and my period hasn't.

i think of a seed growing inside me, a hideous sci-fi movie creature that will burst out of my body, devour my late teens, my twenties, my life.

[like this image...not sure if it's actually good or i just like it]

at home the square box burns in my pocket. where to do it. not at home where she may interrupt see guess find the box in the garbage no not at home.

-can i take the car

-are you going out again

[still haven't figured out what to do with question marks or punctuation in general for

that matter. must i bow to conventions of prose?
on the other hand do i imagine i am ee
cummings?]

-just out to the radio station to see katie

-katie's so smart getting a job there it will look so good on her resume i don't know why you wouldn't apply it's not like we can pay your way for the rest of your life you know

[am i capturing her voice here? a deeper worry
than just getting the accents of the women in
drugstore. i want it to be true, not a mockery
despite my teenage anger my anger still today.

i should be in therapy not writing book.

unless writing book is therapy.]

-fine can I take the car

-oh take the car.

at the radio station religious music drones out of the big reel-to-reel tapes turning lazily on the machine. katie goes on air every fifteen minutes gives time and says what song we just heard the easiest summer job in the world.

i sit on the desk out in the office tuck my feet up under me make small talk while my mind races the test the test the test. finally katie has to go on air i say i have to go to the bathroom.

break it open read the instructions this is grade eleven chem lab all over again. vials to pour things to mix and above all my pee the vital ingredient. and time. what the hell am i going to do with this test-tube vial for an hour?

the radio station washroom is the smallest in the world. the sink hangs at a crazy angle like a shirt button about to fall off, blocks the doorway. i squeeze past it to crouch over the toilet and try to direct my pee into the tiny glass. no bigger than a shot glass or a communion cup.

[it's worth writing all this for a chance to immortalize that bathroom. you'd sit on the toilet and yr chin wd be in the sink]

then open, add, stir. my fingers tremble. katie outside. are you ok in there? did you get flushed down?

-i'm ok not feeling very well i think i might have a bit of a stomach bug.

not entirely a lie as nausea rushes in. morning sickness, i think. that's the first thing. then i'll get fat and everyone will see me and know. jeff will be a hero and offer to marry me. that's what he wants anyway marriage house K-car two-point-four kids. i for one would rather drive out to middle cove beach and walk slowly into the sea. though the waters close over my head yea i am with me.

[was i right? is that what he wanted? if so he got it, up to a point anyway]

wait wait wait. how long can i stay in the bathroom. i go out, close the door, sit on the floor leaning against the door.

katie comes out in the hallway to shelve records. how're you feeling?

-pretty awful.

katie chatters. she's getting her stuff packed for cuc blah blah blah. i try to picture an adventist college out on the godforsaken prairie, nothing around for 500 miles but jesus freaks in suits and princess di ruffled blouses i will die out there and my bones will be bleached in the sun and the vultures will circle.

[obviously i mean the guys are in suits and the girls in ruffed blouses though this was the 80s and i can remember some pretty frightening wedding tuxes]

-i'd like to go to mun i tell katie. i love the mun campus the library all gleaming and glass the courtyard outside with the broad steps where students sit and study and smoke in the sunshine the underground tunnels unwinding like catacombs full of stoners sitting on the floor blasting their radios.

my whole world i see now for seventeen years has been home church and church school three points in a triangle so neat and self contained you could drop a plastic bubble over it and seal it off so nothing from outside could ever get in. turn it upside down and shake it to make it snow.

[love this image. should use it in a poem. maybe should stick to writing poems. pare this whole thing down to a haiku. there's a writing exercise for you]

katie goes back on-air. a song plays with happy bland anonymous christian voices singing about happiness all the time wonderful peace of mind when you've found the lord.

-that's why i don't want to go to cuc. it's going to be full of people exactly like that. is gene picking you up today?

katie is dating my brother gene a fact which seems amazing. i think of them both as asexual beings, like plants.

[odds are good if this is ever published both gene and katie will read it. wont they be thrilled to be likened to plants. tho obviously i have more info now on both of them than i did then. but trying to put myself in that teen headspace]

i'm sure they're not doing it though. no little glass jars of pee for clever katie to worry about.

finally finally back in the bathroom i stare into the tube. what the hell is the ring supposed to look like. i don't see a ring or do i? why don't they give you a picture of what it would look like. i hold it at eye level, tilt it, shake it. now i think there was a ring and i've disturbed it by shaking.

i pour the whole mess down the toilet sweep all the paraphernalia into the drugstore bag cram it back in my jacket pocket and flush.

three more days and still no period. jeff is at me to make up my mind about cuc, are we going, what are we doing? we we we all the way home.

sabbath morning i wake feeling sick again. run to the bathroom but can't puke. they are doing a thing in church today giving some little gift to the kids who are leaving for college. i will stand up there and take my gift and smile. no-one will see the scarlet "A" on my sabbath dress.

in the middle of sabbath school i feel it something damp and cold between my legs. i go to the washroom and there it is praise jesus the blood the precious blood. there's wonderful power in the blood.

i put in a tampon and walk not back into the youth room but up the stairs out the doors of the church down aldershot street. i feel like aunt marjorie. aunt marjorie had cancer they were going to operate then she went in to see the doctor and he said marjorie your cancer's gone i can find no trace. well her prayers were answered she told us god had given her life back to her and she wasn't going to waste another minute she had always wanted to try scuba diving so she did.

i know just how she felt.

walking around the dingy streets of rabbittown, the centre of st. john's, kicking at crushed pop cans and chip bags under an august morning sun, i make resolutions for my new life. at home that afternoon i write them in cherry red lipstick on my bedroom mirror.

1- i will go to mun in sept.
2- i will move out of my parents' house
3- i will break up with jeff
4- i will go on the pill
5- i will not live another minute inside a plastic bubble.

[actually wrote these in my journal but i wish i had written on the mirror with lipstick. would've been a bitch to clean off though]

Julie

JOURNAL PROMPT #5: WRITE about the idea of being in "a new place" and what that means for you.

I've always loved moving into a new place. I love walking into an empty house, walls bare, floors waiting for you to walk on them. Mom & Jeannette & I moved a lot when I was a kid, after my dad died. Roger and I moved a lot after we were married, too—pastor's families always do. I'm used to unpacking my boxes, taking an empty space and making it home.

I cleaned the apartment today—scrubbed and swept and dusted. I bought fabric to make curtains for the kitchen window—meant to sew them tonight after the kids were in bed, but I ran out of steam. I had to leave my beautiful sewing machine behind and I can't face hand-sewing them. I'll go over to Mom's and use her machine tomorrow. I'm here at the table, curtain fabric all around me, writing about making a place into a home instead of actually doing it.

That "new place" feeling—I never had it with this apartment. The day we moved in, after three weeks in Mom's one-bedroom apartment, I was too numb to even care. The place was already furnished, ugly stuff I would never have chosen. The girls started bouncing on the couch & I didn't even care enough to stop them. Maybe that's why this has never felt like home to me: it's filled with someone else's bad taste. I've left so much behind.

Every time Roger got called to a new church, I spent hours painting, making curtains, putting up wallpaper, sewing new throw cushions. Half the time it didn't need to be done: the manse had been painted after the last pastor moved out; my old curtains would have fit the new windows just fine. I loved doing it. Now I look back and see myself with my paint roller in hand, frantically trying to cover up the past, put new wrapping on a sad old package. Each new house would be the place where I'd finally get it right, I thought.

Instead, this dingy 2-bedroom apartment in a low-rent building is the place where I have to get it right.

I'm lonely. When I moved before, I was never the adult in charge. I did the painting and papering, the sewing and decorating, but there was someone else–first my mom, then my husband–to handle the rent, the insurance. There was always a grown-up. I was a little girl with a new dollhouse, rearranging the chairs and tables, making up a story.

The only other time I moved without a "grownup" to take care of me, was when Katie & I went away to CUC my first year. We caught a lift to K-Mart in Red Deer, and I bought two cheap matching bedspreads, off-white with sky-blue ruffles, a pair of tie-back curtains to match, a couple of new posters & a lamp. Katie bought an extra bookshelf.

I loved that room. I loved college, loved that everyone there knew me as Roger Petten's girlfriend. People liked Roger. His teachers in the theology department had him picked out as having a great career ahead of him. He had worked so hard to lose his Newfoundland accent, and when he preached, especially, he sounded so smooth, all the edges polished away, like a real pastor.

Roger was into everything—choir, clubs, the whole bit—had a ton of friends, and lots of girls liked him. But he only had eyes for me. I felt so secure, having this wonderful boyfriend, this stable relationship. That was how I'd always wanted to feel. Safe in the arms of Roger.

I'd stand outside Lakeview Hall in the mornings, my backpack of books beside me on the pavement, waiting while girls poured out of the lobby. I loved to look around on those clear, crisp fall mornings early that school year, before the Alberta winter cold set in. Until I got out there I didn't realize how much I was used to the landscape of St. John's, a city nestled in a narrow harbour valley, houses sloping up the sides of the hills around. Alberta felt so open—the sky was so big and the land stretched so far in all directions. Lakeview Hall was a little lower than the rest of campus, so Roger would come down over a little hill to get me in the mornings so we could walk to breakfast together. If I looked the other direction while I was waiting for him, I could see miles of fields and trees rolling on forever, out to the horizon. That view, more than anything, made me feel like I was in a new place, a different place. A place that was scary, unprotected, but where anything was possible.

Then Roger would come down the path to meet me and I'd watch him from a distance. He wasn't real tall, but he had a very solid, blocky, muscular figure. He wore his light blond hair short, with a mustache that made him look much older, and when he saw me standing outside his face would just light up and he'd take me in his arms and give me a gentle little kiss. Then I'd turn my back on those open fields, on all that possibility, and walk up to the cafe with Roger's arm around me, feeling sheltered, cared for, safe.

Dear Lord, I'm sitting here at the table surrounded by blue-and-white floral curtain fabric, reading that last sentence over and over. So often when I write my journal entries turn into prayers. Please be here with me, God, in this new place that doesn't feel hopeful or joyful.

I'm wasting time. Maybe if I put this away now I can at least get the curtains measured and cut before bed.

Dave

OK, FIRST UP... THANKS for rescheduling. I'm sorry about last Wednesday. I thought I was going to be here and then ... then I wasn't. I wasn't going to come back at all. I'm sorry about that.

Uh, nothing really, just changed my mind. Well, it was a hell of a week. A lot of stuff happened. I met Liz. I mean I didn't just run into her; she called last week and said we should get together. That's not unusual. But she was acting weird—said she had something important to tell me and then said she couldn't tell me yet, had to wait till "the time was right." Unsettling. And I saw my son too. That's always unsettling.

He's, um, sixteen. And a hell of a lot too much like me at sixteen for my comfort. Everytime I see him I think, this is going to be OK, I'm going to be patient, I'm going to listen to him, accept him for who he is. And I just end up wanting to shake him.

Yeah, so those were two of the big things. And another thing— a guy I know called me. These guys I know, guys who have a band. They wanted me to play a gig with them. I haven't played or sung in—well, awhile. And it's been years since I tried to do it—well, on my own.

I'm just realizing how many things there are like that. Things I've never done sober. Don't think I've ever slept with a woman when I was stone-cold sober. Playing the guitar. Just talking to people, having these tough conversations ... without having a drink first, several drinks, to get through it. I don't think I've got what it takes.

Being born again, they say in church. Now I know what it feels like. Babies come into the world butt-naked, not knowing the language, smaller and weaker than everyone else. So that's ... yeah. That's where I was, this week. And that's why I skipped Wednesday, why I almost gave up on this whole thing.

Yeah ... no, that's the big question, isn't it? No, I didn't. I cancelled my meeting with you, I didn't get out of bed actually, stayed in my room all day with the shades drawn, thought about doing some very stupid and self-destructive things. But I didn't drink. Yet. I think we both know it's only a matter of time. I'm not kidding myself anymore.

See, Wednesday, I started the game again, telling myself there's really nothing wrong with me, I don't need you, I don't need AA, I don't need help. Denial. Not just a river in Egypt, right? You may laugh, but denial's gotten me through some tough times.

OK, right, you're not laughing. What do I mean? OK, one time—this was years ago—I was talking to Katie. On the phone. I told her some shit that was going on with me, kind of justified it, and then I said, "I know, you're going to tell me that's just a defense mechanism." And she said, "Hey, don't knock defense mechanisms. You know where we'd be without them? Defenseless."

So, yeah. Denial. Denial saved my life. Remember I was telling you about me in high school—that feeling that I had a bunch of snakes loose in my head? Because I was so strung out, see, drinking and trying to be good and feeling guilty and hating myself, I finally got to the point, I'm not sure when this was, but a point where I thought I might kill myself.

But I didn't do that. I coped. I handled it. I just adjusted my strategy, reframed the problem. That's good, right? By the time I was in my last year of high school, my Grade Eleven year, I'd stopped kicking myself around and feeling guilty. I told myself I wasn't an alcoholic or anything like it, it was impossible to be an alcoholic at sixteen. I was just a guy who liked to drink and party, a guy like any other guy.

Well, of course, right, I had to drop the other side of the equation too: God. I decided that this whole nonsense about God caring for me, having a plan for my life, wanting to lead me–that was all bullshit. Liz used to say if there was a God He had to be concerned about bigger things than whether she got her ears pierced or not. I decided if there was a God He wasn't too worried about me getting wasted now and then.

How did it work? Denial? Worked like a charm. By the end of Grade Eleven—that was the last year of high school in Newfoundland in those days—I was living with my brother Tony and one of his buddies in an apartment on Liverpool Avenue, near our school and church. Great place—this big old two-storey house that someone had built a third-floor extension onto. The third floor was our apartment: two bedrooms, a kitchen, bathroom and a tiny living room. I slept on the couch and didn't pay any rent, just had to buy some food or beer now and then.

The one drawback to this place was that the steps up to the apartment were on the outside of the house, this incredible open staircase that went up to the third floor, forty-six steps. Now this was bad enough in summer, climbing up all those steps, especially if I was coming home drunk and always in danger of slipping. But imagine—

Right! Imagine a Newfoundland winter ... months and months of slush and ice and snow, a buildup of black ice on those steps, the icy wind cutting you in half while you climbed up. We moved in in the spring and didn't really realize till January what we'd got ourselves into. I'll never forget those steps.

So ... right. What was I telling you? Oh yeah, I finished high school. Don't remember much about my grad—passed out at the grad party and missed they part where they rode up to Signal Hill to watch the sunrise. Wrote my public exams and surprised myself by scraping through with passing grades, so I figured I might go to MUN. Got my license and drove around in my brother's old Dodge Dart that looked like shit but could do a hundred and fifty on the highway. Worked at a drugstore down on Rawlin's Cross. Sat on the top of all those steps on summer nights playing my guitar. Denial worked great for me. It was an excellent summer.

My old gang of friends was all splitting up—moving on, I guess. We hung out together a little that summer, but we were drifting apart. I spent more time with these guys I knew who were starting a band. Thought it was the beginning of my great musical career.

I had a Martin D-1 guitar that summer, a beautiful guitar I bought with the money my grandfather sent me for grad. That was the guitar that—

I'm getting confused. There's so much I want to tell you, I'm going off in all different directions. The guitar. My old friends. Denial. I promise you, this all ties together.

I guess when I was up playing with these guys a few nights ago, you know, it brought me back. The band I was in that summer, after Grade Eleven—well, we sucked, of course, but we had a hell of a time. Even got a few gigs. I knew I wasn't going to seriously be a rock star, but it was close enough for me at seventeen.

So yeah, I went to university, lived in this apartment with my brother and this other guy, played in a band, partied. At first it was all rolling along fine but of course eventually it had to come down to a choice between partying or studying if I was going to get through exams, and I'm sure you can guess which one won out.

Yeah, the deal at MUN was that if you failed all your classes, or most of them, you'd get this letter saying you couldn't come back the next semester, you had to stay out and re-apply or something. I got that letter one day over the Christmas break, this horrible stormy sleety day when I woke up with a killer hangover. My grades were in the mail and somehow I was hoping I had scraped a pass, so it was brutal to see my failure there typed out on paper.

All these other people, my friends, guys in the band, somehow managed to pass, most of them, and they converged on the apartment that night—Liz was there too, I think, the only one of my old gang who stayed home and went to MUN. Of course she had straight A's or something like that. Anyway, it was this big party, everyone celebrating and me drowning my sorrows, and sometime after midnight I went out on the steps, completely shitfaced, sitting up on the rail in this snowstorm playing my guitar. I remember Liz and these other girls laughing, telling me to come inside, stop being an idiot, and then I jumped off the rail and—yeah. Wow. Straight to the bottom, me and the guitar.

I don't remember the ambulance or anything, but I remember being in the emergency room, my ankle hurting like crazy—it turned out to be broken—and all I could ask anyone was where's my guitar, was it OK?

Of course it was totaled. Destroyed. And so was I, in a way— the ankle was the least of it. Kicked out of school, lost my job, trashed my beautiful guitar.

Yeah. You'd think it woulda been some kind of—wake-up call, or something. But I keep sleeping through those.

But you see, don't you, why playing with a band this week, playing sober, might be a tough thing for me? I know I can't do this stuff if I'm not drinking. Of course, the stuff I do when I am drinking, that's not so nice either, so I'm kind of between a rock and a hard place.

Time's up, eh? How was it for me today? Actually, talking about this has clarified things a lot.

There's no good way for this to end. I've been down all these roads before—detox, rehab, AA, therapy, all this shit. I'm forty years old, and my body's shutting down on me and in all honesty I'll be relieved when it does.

Yeah ... I'm sorry. You know, I pretty much had myself reconciled to this. After all the shit with the hospital back in the summer—well, I had no intention of giving it another try, not at my age, not after all that's happened.

Why did I come? In the first place? Because of Jeff. Because it should have been me, I knew that. It was my number that was up. And then there was this cosmic bureaucratic screw-up, and

I'm still alive. And I thought I would give it one more try. Have one more shot at the thing I've never mastered.

What? Oh, just—being alive. I was going to give life one more chance..

FOUR

Jeff

THE PAIN IS INCREDIBLE.

Where am I? Not in the car anymore. Lying down somewhere. My chest my back my legs. Pain shoots through everything. Black turns to blinding white. Can't see can't hear. But I can feel.

Run its course this thing has run its course oh God I'm sorry where are they were are they where are they?

My wife and kids. Mom and Dad. People ... there are people I need to see.

Weight crushes my chest, collapses my ribcage, makes every breath a fight. Force myself to suck in air. There are people I need to see.

In ... out ... in ... out. Every breath a knife through my lungs. I try to hang on to the present but the past floods up again with each painful breath.

The same feeling—air sliced in and out of my lungs, each breath like my life depended on it. My legs pumped, my heart raced, as I cut across the ice. My stick reached for the puck, lifted it from Gary's stick, turned it around up the ice as I passed to Nathan. Then the offense was driving towards the other team's net and I waited, not moving but poised and alert, waiting for the puck to come back to my end and my own body to move in response.

Saturday night hockey at CUC was the high point of my college life. I crouched on the ice watching the puck, sprang to action again as soon as I saw it move down the ice towards me.

I watched every player, every move. Calculated where the puck would be next, what moves I'd need to make to keep it clear of our net.

When the game was over I skated over to my one-woman cheering section. I pulled off my helmet—I had classic hockey hair at this point, short in the front and long in the back—and Wendy kissed my sweaty forehead. "You were awesome out there!"

What a woman. Positive affirmation in a fuzzy pink sweater. I couldn't get over my luck. Wendy was short and a little on the hefty side, but in the good curvy way, nice big boobs and butt. She had brown curly hair and a great smile with dimples. We'd started dating that September, beginning of our sophomore year.

What a change from Liz. Liz and Wendy were like the photograph and the negative. Where Liz was dark and cynical, Wendy was bubbly and sincere. They both loved to laugh, but at completely different things. Liz dressed mostly in black. Wendy's wardrobe was a rainbow of neons and pastels. Liz loved to criticize people and make fun of them. Wendy wrote little notes of encouragement on heart-shaped pink paper and dropped them on people's desks.

Liz was hot for sex like she was never going to get it again. Wendy giggled and pushed me away, both her little hands on my chest, whenever I tried to do more than kiss her.

Was I frustrated? Hell yes. There was so much to Wendy, and I was dying to get my hands all over her. But CUC dorms were strictly patrolled. While guys had smuggled girls into Maple Hall, it required total co-operation on the part of the girl and a considerable risk. Public displays of affection were banned and there weren't many places you could display it privately. It was forty below for six months of the year, so romantic meetings under the trees were not exactly ideal.

Couples could find the place and time if they really wanted it. But if one of them really *didn't* want it—if one of them was totally convinced that she was saving herself for her wedding night because it would just be so much more special—then the whole system was in place to back her up. There wasn't much a guy could do except beg.

Coming out of the rink my damp hair froze in the December air. The knife-sharp cold of an Alberta winter was so different from the long damp soggy Newfoundland winter that stretched on forever. I've heard people from the East Coast say it doesn't feel as cold out west because it's a dry cold. Well, it was dry all right, I'll give it that. They gave stats on the forecast telling you how many minutes it would take for exposed skin to freeze.

After the game, Wendy was waiting outside with Debbie Kimball and Debbie's boyfriend Chuck in Chuck's car. I wanted my own car out at CUC. "Next year I am definitely driving out here," I told Wendy as we headed down the dark road in Chuck's backseat.

I could hear the pout in her voice. "Next year I won't be here. You should come to Union with me."

Wendy and Debbie were both transferring to Union, the Adventist college in Nebraska, to finish their nursing programs. The only tension between me and Wendy—other than sex—was whether I should go with her. I wasn't thrilled about it. I liked CUC, and Union would be a lot more expensive.

I kissed her, mostly to shut her up. When we came up for a breath I said, "I'll be finished at the end of next year." I was in the business program, doing a three-year diploma. "Then maybe I could move down near Union and get a job."

"Oh, that'd be *great*," she sighed, all breathy and smiley. "Then we wouldn't have to wait till I graduated—we could get married right away."

Whoa. *Married.* Did I hear that right? I kissed her again. This bought me time to think. She snuggled closer to me, her boobs pressing against my chest. *Married people have sex every night,* I thought.

From the front seat, Debbie screamed.

Chuck yelled, "Look out!" The car moved sideways, like it was weightless, floating. Wendy clung to me.

The car spun. Headlights raced toward us. My heart felt like it was going to burst from my chest. *No no not yet not yet!! I can't die yet! I haven't done anything!!* Everything Wendy and I had just talked about—career, marriage, the future—flashed through my head. My life was unrolling in front of me, long and straight like one of those endless Alberta roads. Nothing unexpected was going to stop me before I had a chance to live.

The car skidded. We were thrown against my door, Wendy on top of me. Screech of brakes from the highway—the other car, I guess. It sped past. We were on the shoulder, shaking but alive.

"Black ice," Chuck said after a minute. "Hit a patch of black ice. Didn't see a thing."

We sat there in silence for a minute. I think it was Debbie who said, "I prayed. Did anyone pray?"

I didn't pray. All I thought about was my life, how I wanted to live it. The stuff I wanted to do.

Whether I prayed or not, God spared me that night on the highway outside Lacombe. He didn't spare me this time. Maybe I ran out of chances.

Now I'm in the dark, fighting for breath harder than I ever did on the ice, a wind colder than Alberta winter slicing into my lungs, robbing me of breath. Something I didn't expect came around a corner. But this time, I'm not thinking *There's stuff I need to do.* All I'm thinking is *there are people. People I need to see....*

Total Eclipse of the Heart

2005

1983 - 1984

liz

THE SMALL ROOM IS institutional-ugly with sagging torn leftover furniture. the air is a haze thick with smoke of all kinds, the tables littered with ashtrays beer bottles coffee cups pizza boxes pencils and paper paper paper. the muse office where a group of dedicated, manic, often stoned university students gather weekly to churn out the campus paper.

i scrawl articles on yellow legal pad then tap them out on the typewriter. i do layout, staying awake until four a.m. in a daze of creativity, booze, weed and hormones to paste up lovingly detailed pages of news and opinions.

the editor is a fourth-year english major named mark malone. he wears his long black hair dissheveled over a worn t-shirt and skintight black jeans. he chain-smokes and bitches at people and has a violent, almost psychotic temper when people miss deadlines or the printers screw up. he is believed to be brilliant although he spends 20 hours a day at the muse office the other four at the breezeway and has never been seen to open a book of any kind.

[apt character sketch...yes i think this sums him up]

he is my lover. not boyfriend. jeff was my boyfriend. mark is my lover. we never had a first date. we worked late put the paper to bed then to bed ourselves on the stained and sagging office couch.

my friends are artsy, angry, theatrical. we laugh at everyone who is not lucky enough to be us. mark and my new friends know nothing of my family my old friends my old church but if they did they would laugh and that laughter liberates me.

i am majoring in english writing papers on macbeth and john donne getting drunk on words as often as wine writing writing my own words too my poetry finally set free from teenage angst. i imitate donne, eliot, cummings, dickinson, trying to find my own true voice.

[dickinson. at least i have one female poet in there. probably accurate to my reading at the time though]

late one night in a high november gale i sit at my window and try to write about the night. but the poem is about me. i go back over the scrawling sprawling lines and pull out words. i cross myself out of the poem and try to make space only for the night the trees the moon. the poem grows shorter and shorter. it is twelve lines, eight lines, five.

[note: writing about writing harder than writing about sex]

i add words carefully like salt to soup. not too much, don't throw them in with a free hand or i'll lose the flavour. two hours later the finished poem is ten lines long.

i have to show it to someone to anyone to mark.

when i find him at the office he is hunched over his typewriter. i say i wrote a poem and he nods and turns back to his editorial.

-i wanted you to see it. i wanted .... your opinion. to know if you think it's any good.

this is not true but makes him look up as i knew it would. then as he reaches for the paper and begins to read suddenly it is true. i do need to know if he thinks its good.

he raises one eyebrow. he can actually do this. pushes hair impatiently out of his eyes. yes yes it's very good very tight great image nice very nice.

-i thought i might send it in somewhere, tickleace or somewhere you know try to get it published.

-oh. he has handed it back but now reaches for it again. do you want any suggestions for editing.

no. yes yes of course please i say out loud.

[this is clear isn't it? again i'm seeing how and why quotation marks became so popular]

he edits lightly, a word here, an arrow, a question mark there. i fold my lightly battered poem in the back pocket of my jeans.

[lightly battered -- good!]

141

later, much later, i look at the poem again. the deadline for the provincial arts and letters competition is in february. i type the poem out with mark's edits. then i type it without them. i lay both sheets on my bed.

the day of the deadline i slip the copy without mark's changes in the envelope. seal it quickly. put on a stamp and drop it in the mail.

weeks later i dance into the office waving the letter over my head. i won i won my poem got an honourable mention. my friends scrabble for the paper oh my god liz how exciting.

several student poets a few of them friends of mine organize a reading two weeks later i am asked to read my honorable poem. the reading is at the ship inn and our friend larry is playing with his band afterwards.

i agonize over what to wear trying shirts dresses hats on in the mirror. mark tells me to calm down or he'll go without me.

walking through downtown streets towards the ship mark says i entered too you know.

-what you what?

-the arts and letters i entered too. i entered a poem and a short story.

-oh mark. i'm sorry. but why tell me now i wonder.

[do i need more dialogue here or is it clear what he's doing?]

our crowd spills onto two tables at the ship. everyone claps and cheers when i read. friends crowd around liz that was great fantastic.

another round of drinks. tasha raises a pint. a toast a toast to liz and her literary success.

-no shush no its not that big a deal

tasha quite drunk stands up and when others raise their glasses she stands on her chair. to my friend liz carter the poet....

-someone shut her up she's making a bloody fool of herself. mark's voice sharp as a papercut. don't go overboard for god's sake it was only an honourable mention.

i look at him in the dark smoky air he's drunk but not that drunk. i haven't really looked at him before. and he has never looked at me.

i go home that night alone and the next day in the sober light of day i tell mark its over. i have a speech all prepared when he asks why, i will tell him my writing is the most important thing in my life and i need someone who will nurture me not pour acid on my softly budding leaves. or words to that effect.

but he doesn't ask.

two days pass before i climb the stairs to the muse office. the door is closed. i hear voices and laughter. someone comes out its tasha my friend one of my best friends. she does not hold the door ajar for me but lets it shut behind her.

-mark's in there she warns as she goes down the tsc steps.

after a minute i turn and leave.

i think about the doors of my parents house of my old friends houses of my church and now the door of the muse office. i believe i am on a journey to become myself. all around i hear the sound of doors closing.

[melodramatic?]

alone in my rented room i pick up the phone.

-dave its liz do you want to go downtown with me and get completely shitfaced.

-you even need to ask.

-meet me at the sundance in half an hour. i'll be the one wearing black and crying in my beer.

-i'll be the one carrying a rose between my teeth.

old friend old door never completely shut. the light seeping beneath that door is enough to take me a few steps farther on.

Katie

ALPHA, BETA, GAMMA..."

Katie's concentrating so hard she almost walks into a tree.

"Daydreaming?" says a voice behind her.

"You could say that. I was practicing the alphabet. The Greek one—I'm pretty good with the other one."

"Yeah, I've been known to get pi and phi mixed up." Charlie Gurnkowski chuckles. He's the kind of person who actually chuckles and it sounds just like what you'd think of when you hear the word "chuckle." He's about five inches shorter than Katie, a little overweight, and has a bad home perm. He's also flattering himself; Katie knows Charlie is capable of getting not only his pi and phi but also his delta and epsilon mixed up. He's barely keeping his head above water in Greek I.

She understands that Charlie is not trying to flirt with her. Nor is he a friendly classmate starting a casual conversation. Today in Old Testament they discussed Deborah, prophetess and judge, and Katie said it was interesting how there was no record of anyone in Judges questioning Deborah's right to lead Israel. Nobody responded, but Katie knows this is why Charlie's falling into step with her on the way back from class. Charlie Gurnkowski has an Agenda.

It's a sunny day in early December, and although the Alberta air is colder than Katie would have believed possible outside of a commercial freezer, the brilliant blue sky and the ice sparkling on the bare trees puts her in a good mood. She doesn't want to be on anyone's agenda. She scrambles to think of a neutral topic to raise with Charlie, to steer him away from the subjects of Judges, theology, and women in the ministry.

"Going to the Oilers game Saturday night?"

It's the most innocuous thing she can think of, since nearly everyone on campus *is* going, but Charlie recoils as if she's slapped him. Katie realizes he thinks she's asking him for a date. The pitfalls of college life never cease to amaze her. She makes a good save, continuing to talk with barely a pause for breath.

"Julie's trying to talk me into going but honestly, I'm looking forward to the dorm being quiet with all the hockey fans gone. I mean, I can get some studying done, finally." She sees her friend Monica sitting at a table with one empty seat and waves vigorously. "Oh, there's Monica and the gang, gotta go. Good luck with that Greek, eh?"

Numerous lies in that sentence, Katie thinks as she sets her tray down across from Monica. First, it's not "Monica and the gang." Katie doesn't have a gang. She has, on a tiny campus of just two hundred students, about a hundred and eighty to whom she can smile and say hi, about forty with whom she can sit down and have a ten-minute conversation, and about five she would call friends.

Another lie: she's not going to study Saturday night. She'll spend the night reading a novel and writing home. She pretends to study a lot more than she does, because she's known as a straight-A student. People would be suspicious if they knew how little she studies. They'd suspect she was very, very smart.

It's her second year at CUC and Katie is tired. Last year, when she was taking general first-year courses, wasn't so bad. But this year, now that she's declared a Religion major and, worse yet, put herself on the pre-professional track, people who once ignored her now seek her out. They want to know why a girl is studying for the ministry. She's had perfectly sane cafeteria lunches turned into polemic Bible studies as some fourth-year theology student whips out his gigantic King James, slaps it on the table and says, "Let the women *keep silent*," stabbing 1 Corinthians with a stubby finger.

After lunch, Katie works her shift at the library, which is shorter on Fridays because the early winter sunset brings an early Sabbath. The light has changed by the time she walks back to the dorm: the shadows of buildings and trees lie long across the path, the sun slanting between them.

Miraculously, Sabbath has come to her dorm room too. Katie feels it as soon as the door swings open. The chaos of books, papers and clothes that cascaded over her own desk this morning has been cleared away: books and papers in a pile on the end of the desk, clothes tossed in the laundry. Both beds are made, the carpet has been vaccuumed, and the soft perky voices of the Heritage Singers drift up from the silver tape player on the dresser.

"Julie, you shouldn't have."

"No, but I did." Julie is lying on her bottom bunk. "Anyway, I think we'll get the good note this week."

The dean of women does a room check each Friday afternoon. One of two notes appears on the door after this check: the good note is on a small square of pink paper with a frilled edge; the bad note is mauve. Both include a quote from *The Adventist Home*, about how wonderful it is when a home is ready for Sabbath. The pink note goes on: "How lovely it was to see such a pleasant room!" and commends the occupants on tidying their living space appropriately before sunset. The mauve note says: "College students lead such busy lives. Yet if we take those few minutes to prepare our homes and lives for Sabbath, we can create an environment in which Jesus and the angels will feel comfortable. I hope that next week your room will be ready for Sabbath, just as your heart is." The mauve note is phrased so gently that it took a few weeks for Katie to realize it was a reprimand.

Friday evening descends. Vespers is a slide show, scenes of the Rocky Mountains merging in and out of each other in that multi-image effect all the A-V guys think is so cool. Against a background of the Maranatha Strings and verses from the Psalms, images of snow-capped peaks, mountain goats, and the Northern Lights flood the screen. At the end, a girls' trio sings "Day is Dying in the West" in close harmony, their voices braiding into a golden rope that marks off a space in time.

For a day of rest, Sabbaths are actually pretty busy for Katie, since she teaches a Sabbath School class of earliteens at the College Park church and is also a deaconess. She closes the day by giving the worship talk in the girls' dorm chapel. Mindful of the upcoming Oilers game, she painstakingly constructs her 10-minute talk around a hockey analogy. She's not sure it works. Is God playing offense or defense?

She doesn't mind a quiet Saturday night. There's that lingering sense of guilt: she ought to be doing something fun, ought to have a date. But the pool of people she's really comfortable with here is so small, and her days are so full, that it seems like a waste of a good Saturday night to sit in a cold stadium with a bunch of people she only vaguely cares about, watching toy-sized men far below chase a miniscule black dot around the ice. Instead she curls up for an hour with *My Name is Asher Lev,* which she's reading for fifth or sixth time, and then gets some looseleaf from her binder and sits on the bed with the binder propped on her knees, writing a letter to her parents and one to Liz.

She's asleep that night before Julie returns, and wakes in the morning to hear how great the game was and how much fun everyone had. They go to the cafe for cheese blintzes, the best thing about Sunday mornings. Katie walks from the cafe to the library, where she's scheduled to work, and runs into Dr. Worthington, her favourite prof, on the steps.

"I heard you gave an impressive talk at Vespers last night," he says. "Something about keeping your eye on the goal?"

Katie looks at her feet. "Uh, something like that, thanks."

Dr. Worthington half-turns as if to go down the steps, then turns back to her. "I hope you don't get too discouraged, Katie. I know there's a lot of—well, you have to put up with a lot, sometimes, from the other—from the fellows in the class."

Katie waits, not knowing how to jump in and save this conversation.

"Things are changing in the church, Katie," he says finally. "There are several young women studying at our seminary, now, doing their M.Div. You're probably the best theology student I've seen in awhile—it'd be a shame if...."

"I'm doing OK, really. Thanks for, um, all the kind words."

"Yes. Well. Be of good courage," he says, and goes down the steps.

Out the library window, later that afternoon, Katie sees a group of young men under a cluster of maple trees. A photographer kneels in front of them, capturing the group as the back row links arms over each other's shoulders, the front row each on one knee with chins cupped in their hands. They are mostly back-on to Katie and all wearing CUC jackets, but as they shuffle around and move into place she can identify them all. There's Roger, in the back row; there's Charlie, in the front row between Kevin West and Derek Schaeffer. They are her classmates along with the third- and fourth-year theology students. The young men studying for the ministry. She watches as they pose for several shots and finally wander off in twos and threes, punching each others' arms, making jokes. Male bonding.

Katie tries to keep silent. It doesn't work. At supper she asks Roger, "Who was posing outside the library today?"

Roger's eyes slid away: to his plate of veggie spaghetti, to Julie, across the cafe. "Oh, just some of the guys, you know, the theology guys. Future pastors, you know."

"All my class was there. And yours. And the seniors." She waits. Roger doesn't look back at her. Julie nibbles her garlic bread. "Nobody mentioned it to me."

Roger clears his throat and wipes his mustache with a paper serviette. "Uh, no, well, it wasn't for anyone. Just the, you know, the pre-ministry people, the—I mean, there were people taking religious studies who weren't there. The ones, you know, people who are going to be Bible teachers and stuff. This was just for the—like I said, for the future pastors."

"Not including me," Katie says.

Roger crumples the napkin, throws it on the table. "Katie, let's not go into this again. If you'd rather listen to your own opinion than to God's Word, I'll leave that to you." He stands up, picking up his tray though he's not finished, kicks his chair back, and stalks away. A few people at nearby tables turn to look.

Julie and Katie are left alone at the table with half-eaten plates of spaghetti. Julie looks at Roger's retreating back, then at Katie who is blinking hard and fast. She will cut off her own hand with the butter knife before she cries, here, surrounded by everyone.

Julie says, "I'm sorry," in a little half-voice.

Katie twirls spaghetti on her fork, watching out the cafe windows as the sunset blazes down over the open fields.

"It's just awkward for him," Julie says, looking down at her plate. "You being my best friend and all. I mean, I understand why it's important to you, sort of, but I don't like seeing him upset."

"What about seeing me upset?"

"I'm sorry about that too, of course I am. But I mean, it's your choice. You don't have to do this to yourself."

"Do what to myself?"

"Beat your head against a brick wall. Try to get in somewhere where you're never going to get."

Katie puts down her fork, looks straight at Julie. "Jules, a couple of generations ago women couldn't be doctors or lawyers. Is that what you would have said to those first women who went to med school or law school—stop beating your head against a brick wall?"

Julie, too, has finished her meal now. She stares at her empty plate. "That's different. God never said women can't be doctors or lawyers."

"Oh, and He said they couldn't be pastors?"

"It's right there in the Bible."

"Are you sure that's what it says? Or do you only know what Roger's told you? I've studied this, Julie. If I think God is calling me, of course I want to make sure it's according to His will!"

She's not hoping to convert or convince Julie. The best Katie hopes for is detente, for Julie to say she respects Katie's opinion. Instead she gets silence.

"I can't believe you said that. I can't believe that's what you think of me," Julie says finally. "You make it sound like I'm Roger's puppet."

Something mean rises in Katie, something that wants to hurt. "Well, *do* you ever have a thought of your own? Or does Roger pull the strings and you dance?"

Julie makes a tiny noise, sucked-in air and a sniffly nose. "It doesn't take a man or a Greek dictionary to tell me what the Bible says. You pray for Liz and Dave, but you know what? I pray for you, because I can see what you're headed for. And that's not Roger's opinion, that's my own!"

"Well it's a miracle then, it must be the only opinion of your own you've had since you started going out with him!" Katie picks up her tray and leaves.

Much later that night, Julie will return to their dorm room. She will make the first step toward reconciliation with a hug. Their friendship will heal itself, the scar tissue bumpy and white for awhile. But they will continue to room together till April, the end of the school year, the end of Katie's second and last year at CUC.

When Katie goes home she takes with her, along with her books and clothes, a CUC yearbook -- the *Borealis* -- with pictures of herself and her classmates. Her back page is not filled with loving tributes from friends as Julie's is, but she has a respectable number of notes and good wishes. *Thanks for helping me with Greek! Good luck in the future!* writes Charlie Gurnkowski. *I'm sorry you're going. I'll miss the prayer groups in your room,* writes Monica Nolan.

Katie takes the yearbook out often that summer at home, turning the pages, reading the signatures, looking at the pictures. The photo captioned Canada's Future Pastors shows them all smiling, squinting into the winter sun, looking hearty and ready to take on the world. On the same page are pictures of the religion faculty, including Dr. Worthington with his thinning dark hair and silver-rimmed glasses.

Over the years, Katie will turn back occasionally to that yearbook page, looking at the faces, trying to keep track of what has happened to the Future Pastors, the glorious highs and shameful lows of their careers. After several years it's hard to know, because she's lost touch with so many people. A few are easy: Roger, of course, never leaves her range of vision.

Charlie Gurnkowski becomes a conference president, out west somewhere. Dr. Worthington becomes notorious after he leaves the church and writes his infamous book. Katie Matthews (not pictured), puts the yearbook on a high shelf and moves on.

Dave

HI.

You're surprised, aren't you? You didn't expect to see me today.

No, it's OK, you can admit it. I saw that little flicker of surprise. I don't think there's anything wrong with admitting that you give up on people sometimes. Sure, you believe in the potential of every human being and all that, but you've been working with us human beings for a long time and you know that you win some and you lose some. Remember, I've been around the track a few times. The counsellors in rehab, they always had an opinion about who was going to make it and who wasn't. Nobody would say it, of course, but ...

I had this same conversation with Katie, last time I was home. She's in your line of work. I tried to get her to admit that there are kids on her caseload that won't ever get their lives together. Not that you still don't give them your best effort, but ... I don't know why shrinks and social workers and addictions counsellors aren't allowed to admit defeat sometimes.

Yeah, but doctors do it. The cancer doctor, the heart doctor, they know there are some people who won't pull through. My mom was like that, at the end, with cancer. They have this little talk to you, they say, "I'm sorry, but there's nothing more we can do for you medically. No further treatment. Go home and spend your last weeks with your family in peace."

I like that. I admire that. Why shouldn't you be able to say, "Mr. Mitchell, there's nothing more we can do for you. We've all tried our best but you're a hopeless drunk. We'd appreciate if you'd take this fifth of vodka and go home so you can start drinking yourself to death as peacefully as possible."

You think that's what I'm doing? Setting myself up for failure so I won't get my hopes up? Trust me, I haven't been getting it up much—I mean hope, of course—in quite some time.

And yet, here I am. Back again. Was this a good week? No. Am I still cruising along, six weeks into my latest bout of sobriety? No. Did I drink this week? Yes.

Yeah, last Friday, right after I left here. Wasn't in the greatest mood. Hit the liquor store on the way home and loaded up on the cheapest vodka I could find, and then went home and drank till I passed out.

When I woke up Saturday, sick as a dog, of course the only thing I wanted was another drink, but I'd finished all the vodka so I had to leave the house again. At which point a funny thing happened.

No, not odd–funny. Genuinely funny. I went to church.

Yes, on a Saturday morning. I used to be a Seventh-day Adventist, remember—don't you people read over your notes? I had to pass their church on the way to the liquor store. Never been in there in all the years I've lived here, but it was just after eleven o'clock, there were cars parked outside, music coming from inside–I went in and sat down in the back. Left before the service was over.

It's funny, you know, but when I used to go to church, that was some kind of—what do you call it?—a test, a litmus test, for how friendly, how welcoming, a church was. Bring in some unshaven bum off the street, wearing jeans and a stained T-shirt, reeking of booze, and what'll happen? Will people edge away from him in the pews, or will they rush up to embrace him, invite him to stay for the potluck? Well, this church fell somewhere in the middle. Nobody edged away, a couple of people smiled. But to be fair, I didn't want to meet anybody, certainly didn't want a potluck dinner. I just wanted to sit for awhile.

No, don't worry, I'm not here with another conversion story. I didn't fall to my knees at the altar and get saved or anything like that. I told you, I don't have the energy for another rebirth.

But even though there was no altar call and I didn't pray or sing or whatever, something must have worked. Maybe it was just sitting still. Anyway, I slipped out during the closing hymn and walked back home and called Rick—that's my sponsor—and he took me to a meeting that afternoon. And another one on Sunday, and another one on Monday and Tuesday. And here I am today.

So that's what you call a unique outcome, is it? Well, good. I'm glad you got one. About time, eh? I don't know, though, I really have been giving you the problem-soaked narrative. I mean, like I said before, it's not like being a drunk has been my whole life. I had a career, I've been in love, got married. I had kids ... I had a life, of sorts. I've managed a few unique outcomes in my time.

I guess one of the better times would be—oh, take my second year of university, for example. I did go back, yeah, because after I got kicked out I had a lot of time to think, and drink, and decide that I really didn't want to work on carryout at

Sobeys—that was the job I got after my ankle healed up—for the rest of my life.

So there I am, second time round, taking first-year courses again, and there's this girl in my English class, Renee Lawson. Renee, Renee, Renee. She looked like her name sounded … elegant, sophisticated, a cut above everyone else in English 1010. I used to sit in class and stare across the room at her. She had this long red hair, worn really straight at a time when most of the girls had frizzy perms, and that was typical of her—she had her own style and she didn't care what anyone thought. Before I got to know her I used to call her the Ice Princess.

I hardly ever spoke up in that class, because English wasn't my thing at all. At the time I was taking a computer course, one of the first ones they offered there—BASIC programming. Poking around the computer lab, trying to learn what I could about the mainframe system—I had a friend who had a Commodore 64 and I had messed around inside that a fair bit, I found computers interesting. But Shakespeare? Hamlet? Give me a break.

So one day in English class, the prof is on a roll, explaining all this stuff about tragedy and throwing in these Greek words, catharsis and a whole bunch of other Greek shit, talking a mile a minute about Hamlet and his tragic flaw and how we could use this and that in our papers, and finally she turned back to the class and said, "Does anyone have any questions?" It was totally quiet there for a minute, like we were all shell-shocked from the barrage of information, and I raised my hand and said, "Do you know if there are any openings in the meat-cutting course at Trades College?"

Oh yeah. I was still using the smart-ass charm. It worked, too. Later that day I was at my locker down in the tunnels and Renee passed by, and for the first time she stopped and spoke to me. She said, "That was funny today, about the meat-cutting course." She didn't actually laugh or anything, just said, "That was funny" like she was awarding me points for my performance.

That broke the ice with the Ice Princess, so to speak, and eventually I got up the nerve to ask her out to the Breezeway after class, where I really concentrated hard on having a few drinks and stopping before I got shitfaced. I didn't need to worry, though, because it turned out the Ice Princess could drink most guys at the Breezeway under the table when she got going. I almost had to admire her just for her capacity, you know?

She wasn't like me at all—about drinking, I mean—but she turned into a different person when she had a few. Suddenly she was this hot sexy girl who loved to laugh and tell dirty jokes, who once got up and table-danced at a party at Trevor Canning's house.

And then there was sex. Ahhh yes ... sex with Renee. I'd like to think of Renee as my first lay because honestly, nothing before that really counted. She was my first experience of a real woman, I guess, and I loved the way that Ice Princess composure would crack when she got turned on.

One night we came out of the Breezeway and Renee had to go to the library and get some books for an assignment. We were up in the stairwell leaning against the glass walls and kissing, when suddenly Renee said, "Know what I've always wanted to do, ever since I came to MUN? Do it in the stacks." Her whole face lit up like someone had flicked a switch, and I got extremely turned on and said, "You want to?"

Of course we did! You think I'd make this shit up? One of the proudest moments of my university career. Up against the back wall -- she just hiked up her skirt and we did it and then collapsed giggling.

It didn't last, of course. In the end, I found out that the girl who could drink guys under the table and screw in the library bookstacks was just a mask she was wearing. After all this time I'd spent trying to get past the Ice Princess and find the "real" Renee, it finally hit me that the Ice Princess *was* the real Renee.

Near the end of Winter Semester, a couple of weeks before exams, she dumped me. Stopped calling, stopped answering my calls. Finally in the middle of the square in a torrential March downpour, she leaned forward and gave me a kiss told me we'd had fun, she didn't want some long-drawn out break-up scene. She was going out with another guy, an Engineering student. I was thinking about doing Engineering but I didn't have the marks to get in. That Renee, she knew a loser when she saw one.

Sad story, hey? Boy meets girl, girl breaks boy's heart. Pretty typical first love I guess. And I'm sure you don't need me to paint you a picture of how I reacted to having a broken heart. Let's just say that when Winter semester was over I got another one of those notes from the University saying that I wasn't welcome to re-apply till the following winter, and I could see it was going to take me awhile to get a degree at this pace. After two years I'd accumulated five credits, so I forgot that whole planning-my-future thing and went back to basically planning my next drink, which was manageable.

So ... that's not really a unique outcome, is it? I don't know, I had a semi-adult relationship, I picked up five university credits—and a few weeks later, I actually quit drinking.

Oh yeah, that was when all the old gang came home for the summer break. Julie, the girl Jeff used to go out with before Liz, another one of the crowd from school and church—she got married that summer and we were all involved in the wedding somehow. Hell of a wedding—no bar, no dance, and I have to say the bride and groom didn't look like the two happiest people on earth, but we all got through it.

I drove up to Campmeeting on the Sabbath, end of July, just to see everybody and hang out for awhile. All the old gang was there and everyone was making a big fuss over Julie and Roger, the newlyweds, while Liz and Katie hung around in the background making sarcastic remarks. Katie had her CUC yearbook up there and everyone was passing it around looking at it, pictures of Jeff playing hockey, of Katie up front speaking at some church thing. That Saturday night while the meeting was going on I sat with Katie out on a picnic table while the sun went down behind the trees. I leafed through that yearbook looking at pictures of this place that looked so clean and well-scrubbed and so far away from St. John's.

I asked her if she liked it and she said it was a good place, just not for her. She was transferring to some other Adventist college. Out of the blue I said I was thinking of going to CUC with Jeff and she said she thought I'd be happy out there. I said I hoped so, but I'd have to clean up my act a lot.

I asked her to pray for me—I meant in a sort of general way, but she said, "Right now?" and I said OK. She prayed for me there on the picnic table, prayed God would come into my heart and give me the power to live the way He wanted me to live.

I guess it sounds very cliché to you, even to me in a way, but it was—yeah, it made an impact on me at that point. I wasn't sitting in the meeting and I didn't go up front for any altar call, but out there on the picnic table with Katie I decided I was going to make a new start, pack up and head west, for CUC.

I wonder was that the night Katie kissed me? I don't think so. But it was one of those nights, one time we had some deep serious talk and out of the blue she kissed me like—God, I don't know what. This from a girl who was never anything more than a friend, right? I never have understood women, and at forty years old things don't look good for me ever getting them figured out, you know?

Sorry. Getting off topic. But I did it, you know, I quit drinking, saved a few bucks from my job, and at the end of August Jeff and I piled everything into his crappy old car and we took off driving west across Canada, into the sunset, into my new life.

So, is that a unique outcome? Does that count? Because, you know, in the end it turned out the same as all the other stories. That's what gets me down, you know? Every time something works out, every time it looks like a happy ending, I've got a pretty good idea how it's going to end.

Sorry, we're over time. Isn't it your job to keep track of stuff like that? You're supposed to boot me out.

No, it's OK, really. I've got to go. And I'll—I'll see you next week.

Julie

THE ENGAGEMENT WATCH

Back in the 80s, Adventist girls didn't wear engagement rings, because that would be wearing jewellery. Nowadays I see girls in church with diamond rings, but that would have been unthinkable for me in 1984, even more so since my future husband was going to be a pastor. But there was always a back-up. The Engagement Watch.

Maybe that seems silly now. But then I believed wearing jewellery was vain and worldly. A watch was useful, functional, and at the same time pretty and elegant.

Ever since I got out to CUC Roger had been bringing up how nice it would be when we could get married, have a little place of our own. I didn't want to wait till after graduation, either. I dreamed about married life, being with Roger all the time, having a little place of my own to make nice & cozy— and after we graduated, a baby. I was ready for the next step.

So he came to visit me one evening in the girls' dorm lounge & said he had something very important to talk about. I sat down next to him on the couch, the one turned to face out the window so we'd have a little privacy from the other girls hanging around in the lobby. It was January of my sophomore year—we were just back from Christmas break.

Anyway, Roger started in with this whole little speech. It's only now, looking back, that I realize that speech was all about him—his plans, how he was doing in his classes, how his profs all thought he would be a really great pastor. How he was graduating in a year and they looked more favourably at candidates for the ministry if they were married. When I play it back in my head it was actually more like a job interview than a proposal.

Then he took my hand and kind of abruptly went down on one knee, fished the little watch box out of his pocket and said, "Julie, will you make me the happiest man on earth by agreeing to be my partner in life and ministry?" I knew he'd memorized it, probably even practiced it alone in his room.

The watch was gold, with a small white face and gold numbers and a very delicate gold chain. I still have it, in a box with some other keepsake stuff. I remember how I showed it around the dorm that night and all the girls squealed and hugged me. They were happy for me because my real life was beginning.

I did some free writing in group tonight. I've been feeling this need to go back to the past, to examine things, as if I were going back through a piece of knitting to see where I dropped a stitch. I used to knit a lot—and sew, crochet, quilt, cross-stitch & do plastic canvas. I had our place filled up with afghans and ruffled cushion covers and quilts and cross-stitched wall hangings.

Anyway, I thought it might do me some good to remember how Roger & I started out. If I'd read this piece out to the group I'm sure they would have howled about the watch thing. But I was proud of my watch and what it represented. We planned a Christmas wedding the following year—I loved the idea of wearing a velvet-trimmed ivory gown with my bridesmaids dressed in dark green velvet, poinsettias all over the church.

Katie agreed to the green velvet dress & the poinsettias, even though I knew she wasn't crazy about the groom. She and Debbie Kimball and my sister Jeannette were going to be my bridesmaids. I started buying the bridal magazines and getting patterns for dresses.

Things changed between Roger and me after I started wearing the watch. He got even more possessive. That was one of the reasons Katie never liked him, but I remember telling her that I liked manly guys, not wimps, and if he got jealous I knew he valued me.

Roger got manly several times that year, at me and at guys I was friendly with. Even got into a fight with Jeff—Jeff and I sometimes ate together in the cafe and stuff, and of course it was no good telling Roger that I had no feelings for Jeff anymore. He blew up at me one night in the dorm lobby, right in front of a bunch of people, and stormed out, and later I heard that he and Jeff had an actual fight over it in the guys' dorm. I actually felt proud, like it was a big accomplishment to have my man fight for me.

He changed in another way too. Before we got engaged we'd french-kiss passionately for half an hour if we got the chance, but Roger wouldn't push any further than that, not even to touch my breasts or anything. Just clinging to each other, kissing and moaning and then pulling apart saying, "We really should stop this." We both had such a strong feeling about doing what was right, waiting till marriage—especially where he was going to be a pastor.

One night about a month after we got engaged he asked me if I wanted to come to Nick and Teresa's trailer on a Saturday night to watch a video. Chariots of Fire, *I think it was. He said he had a surprise for me. Videos were a really new thing then— hard to imagine now! What did people ever do on Saturday nights? Nick and Teresa were married students, and they were the only people we knew who had a VCR. But the surprise, the thing Roger hadn't told me, was that Nick and Teresa were away for the weekend. Roger was house-sitting.*

I never saw the end of Chariots of Fire. *We started out cuddling on the couch, moved to making out, and soon Roger was pulling off my blouse. I asked if he was sure it was OK, and he said yes, yes it was all right because we were engaged now. So I just closed my eyes and tried to enjoy it.*

There was a lot more pain than I expected, and I was worried about getting blood on Nick and Teresa's couch, and the whole thing just seemed so sudden, and almost violent. No, I don't mean Roger was rough with me. I should be clear about that, make sure I'm remembering things correctly. It was just— the whole thing of sex itself. It felt like something animals should be doing. Not romantic, not like the movies where they lie in bed, gaze into each other's eyes, and then it all fades to black. I probably hadn't been watching the right kind of movies to prepare me for this.

After that, Roger wanted to do it every chance we got— though there weren't many, CUC being the kind of school it was. In March I missed my period. At first I didn't tell anyone, then I told Katie, and she made all the arrangements for me to get to a clinic in Red Deer and have a pregnancy test.

Roger exploded. He was furious. He yelled at me, said I was going to ruin his career, called me names I didn't even know. His pastor-voice would slip when he got mad and you could hear that he was just a boy from Botwood, that accent he worked so hard to hide.

Katie and I quickly regrouped with the wedding plans. Green velvet dresses were out the window and so was a custom-made gown for me. Debbie said it was so exciting that we were getting married in the spring but she couldn't make it back to Newfoundland on such short notice. We told everyone that Roger and I had just decided to move the wedding up a few months, and everyone smiled and nodded like it was sweet that we were so much in love we just couldn't wait.

I'm sure Roger was right, no-one was fooled. But as the end of the semester drew closer Roger had a talk with Dr. Devlin, who was kind of his mentor, and Dr. D. told him that while it was a sin to sleep together before you were married, doing it while we were engaged was a sin people could overlook. As long as we got married before I started to show. In other words, he didn't think it would hurt Roger's chances of getting a job the following year.

I did worse in my exams that April than I'd ever done, what with wedding plans and worry and morning sickness, but I passed everything and flew home with three weeks to go before the wedding date.

Mom & Jeannette were great, & all the church ladies at home. They had a big shower for me and I got all this great wedding stuff, although it was weird because in a way I was expecting baby stuff too, which of course I didn't get. But the women, my family and friends and the church women, they were just like a river that carried me along right up to the wedding.

I still have this box of wedding stuff back home and I used to take it out and look through it every time we moved. There's a church bulletin from the wedding, listing the wedding party. I didn't have that much family compared to Roger's crew from Botwood, but my friends turned out in full force. Debbie couldn't make it with the revised wedding date but I had Jeannette & Katie standing for me, Jeff & Dave were ushers and I even asked Liz to sing. Not one of those people liked Roger or really approved of me marrying him. In a weird way the fact that they disapproved of Roger, even though it made me sad, kind of made me feel like—I don't know, like these were the people I could be sure of. The ones I knew were on my team.

What else is in that box? Some photos, me and Roger posed in front of a pool and under a tree in Bowring Park. A little bag of rice for throwing, and our unity candle.

There's nothing in the box to show how three days before the wedding, I started to bleed and bleed like I was having the worst period in the history of womanhood. Nothing to show how I sat on the toilet in Mom's bathroom, terrified with tears rolling down my cheeks. How Jeannette drove me to emergency and confirmed what we all knew. I'd lost the baby. Nothing to show how I cried all night and how Katie came over and sat with me, holding my hand, not saying anything.

There's no memento in here for the day I told Roger about the baby, the day before our wedding. There's no photo in here of the look on his face, the rage, the—I can't find a word for it. He slapped his fist into his palm over and over and I knew it was me he wanted to hit. He called me a slut, a whore -- oh God, it hurts to write those words down. I'd ruined his life, I'd tricked him into this shotgun marriage, and now there wasn't even going to be anything to show for it. He made me feel like our baby was something I'd carelessly laid down in a store and forgotten, or a china plate I'd broken while drying dishes.

I cried all that night before the wedding. My biggest fear— he'd cancel the wedding. But everything rolled on just as planned. I walked down the church aisle on my mom's arm, Mrs. Tilley at the organ playing Pachelbel's Canon. Roger was waiting for me, his face like a mask I couldn't read at all. Like nobody was home behind his eyes.

Remember how we prayed that night, Lord? Did You hear Roger's prayer, in our hotel room, after he held me in his arms and said he was sorry. He asked Your blessing on our new life together. You didn't give us that blessing, did You? Or maybe You did and we're the ones who screwed it up.

Roger never mentioned that baby again.

FIVE

Jeff

I'M IN FREEFALL. SOMETHING has happened, something huge. But I'm nowhere, suspended in midair. I don't feel angry, or hurt, or alone. I'm don't feel anything. I just think: What's next?

Another random picture fills the screen. Burger King: Calgary. Two months after CUC graduation. I wore gray pants and blazer and a blue oxford shirt with a white collar and narrow navy blue tie. Dress shoes and a leather briefcase. It was mid-June and 30 degrees. I was starving and coated with sweat.

Exhausted after a morning of beating the streets with my resume in hand, I stumbled in to Burger King and started reaming change out of my pockets. A few nights before I'd sold all the cassette tapes I owned to my roommate's buddy Trevor for forty bucks. I'd used the money to buy Pop-Tarts and ramen noodles and make a bunch more copies of my resume. I had $3.69 left, enough for a burger, Coke and small fries—barely. When they gave me the cup for my Coke, I filled it with about 90% ice.

I was living in a two-bedroom apartment in a twelve-storey building with some guys I didn't really know. One of them was a cousin of my girlfriend -- correction, my *ex*-girlfriend -- Wendy, and since Wendy and I had had such a happy, positive breakup, no hard feelings, she had asked her cousin if it was OK for me to crash on their couch for a few weeks till I found a job and a place of my own. Craig—the cousin—said sure.

I was on Plan B for my life and starting to realize that I didn't have a Plan C.

Plan A had involved graduating, moving to Nebraska, and getting a job there while Wendy finished her nursing degree. I had started the process of getting a U.S. work visa when Wendy told me over the phone that it would be better if we started seeing other people.

I wanted to say, "It would?" or "Better for *who* exactly?" Instead I sat there like an idiot with the phone in my hand, my jaw hanging.

Two o'clock that morning, lying awake, I caught on. When she said we should see other people, what she meant was that she was seeing other people. Other person. *Another* person.

I called back to confirm this.

Wendy was as sweet and understanding as could be. Yes, she was in fact already dating a pre-med student named Bill. The conversation got a lot less pleasant after that, with me standing on my bed yelling into the phone. The guys in the room next door banged on the wall and yelled at me to shut up. Little Miss Sunshine said she wanted us to always be friends. She didn't want a nasty break-up. I did everything I could to make it nasty but it was like getting into a fight with one of those molded jell-o salads my mom used to make. No matter how hard you hit, the jello's never going to hit back. You're just going to come out all sweet and sticky.

That was in early March. Only a week before my best friend and roommate had been kicked out of school for his annoying little habit of stashing bottles of cheap vodka in our closet. With Dave gone and no hopes of reuniting with Wendy, I was ready to leave CUC. My parents came up for grad and helped me pack everything up. Then they flew home and left me in Alberta to pursue Plan B: Get a job and enjoy the single life.

I put stale fries in my mouth one after another. I stared out the window at the street full of busy people with stuff to do. It was 1985. The unemployment rate in Canada was at an all-time low. Calgary, Alberta, in the midst of an oil boom, was probably the easiest place in the world to find a job. I saw "Now Hiring" signs everywhere I went. There was even one here in Burger King. There was no job shortage. Just no job for me.

There was even one here in Burger King.

Plan C was driven by hunger and desperation and a deep-in-the-gut fear that told me I might never get a real job, that my college education was a waste. I guess I was going through a kind of post-grad depression. And I really, really, really wanted another Whopper. Preferably a double Whopper.

July. Burger King. Every college graduate's worst nightmare: flipping burgers for a living. On my time off, I looked for a real job. I wasn't getting doors slammed in my face, but I was getting: "Well, we're not hiring for anyone in this particular area right now, but in a few months...." or, "We'll keep your resume on file...."

August. Still at Burger King. Eleven o'clock on a hot Friday night. I was cleaning the grills. I hated Whoppers, hated fries, hated the uniform, hated my life. I was afraid I might spend the rest of my life sleeping on the couch of my ex-girlfriend's cousin, smiling and saying, "Would you like nuts on your sundae?"

I left work and took the bus back to Craig's place. Craig and his roommate and a few friends were sprawled around watching a video. I was tired and just wanted to sleep. But they were sitting on the couch where I normally slept, so I went into the kitchen to find something to eat. Anything that didn't have a BK logo on it.

I was putting some ramen noodles on to boil when Craig came in to get a drink out of the fridge. "Uh, Jeff," he grunted.

He was kind of a grunty guy, big and burly and not really talkative.

"Hey, Craig," I said, breaking up my noodles and poking them down into the bubbling water.

"Uh, I've been meaning to ask you, you know, when you think you'll find a place to live?"

Up till that moment I'd thought I had a place to live. We both knew what he meant, though

"Because, you know, classes start in a few weeks and once we're in school, me and Keith, y'know, we pretty much use the living room to study in."

"I'll see what I can do."

"Thanks, man."

"Whatever."

He went back out to watch *Return of the Jedi.* I turned off the burner and drained the noodles. I ate them straight out of the pot, mixing the little powdered flavour packet in. I stood at the counter, trying to figure out what to do next.

Plan C wasn't looking good. I was running through life plans so fast I figured I'd soon be down to *Plan 9 from Outer Space.* Before things got that bad, I was ready to try Plan D. The three-digit figure in my bank account was good for one thing other than a portion of a month's rent. It was enough to buy a one-way, student standby ticket from Calgary to St. John's.

On Monday I called Dave, who was living in Red Deer with a girlfriend who was driving him nuts, and asked if he wanted to come home with me.

End of August. Me and Dave on a plane flying east. Suspended in midair—which pretty much summed up how I was feeling. I'd spent four months in Calgary and I wasn't one step further ahead than I'd been that day I sat in the Burger King. Still didn't know what was going to happen next.

That's what I feel now. I think I'm lying somewhere, maybe on the ground, maybe on a stretcher. Things are very noisy but I can't see anyone or hear any voices I recognize. And I can't feel anything, anything at all. Like I'm cut off from my body. Something has happened, something huge. And yet here I am in freefall, waiting. Waiting for what happens next....

Glory Days

2005

1985

Julie

LAUNDRY

I went to the laundromat last night. The girls came with me—Mikayla begged me to let them stay home and she'd watch Chelsea. I'm not ready for that yet—Mikayla's only eleven. At first it was kind of fun: the girls helped load the machines & sat on top of the washer & laughed about how it jiggled them around. But the wait for the dryer took too long and they got whiny & difficult. Finally I drove them home and let Mikayla "babysit" for twenty minutes while I drove back up to Merrymeeting Road and unloaded the dry clothes back into the car. Normally I prefer folding them in the laundromat as soon as they come out.

Going to the laundromat takes me back to the early years of my marriage. I folded mine and Roger's clothes in so many little small-town laundromats before we finally got our own washer and dryer. How thrilled I was the first time I could put on a load of clothes in my own house and then go upstairs and get dinner started, instead of being stuck in the laundromat reading tattered People *magazines.*

I'd like to believe that someday I'll own a washer and dryer again, that I won't spend the rest of my life lugging my clothes back and forth the laundromat. I guess there are people who never do get that far in life, or people like me who get that far and then slip back downhill.

As you can see I wasn't really in an inspired mood to write anything deep and meaningful in group tonight. That's probably why I finally felt brave enough to read out a little bit of what I'd written. I figured they'd laugh because my laundry meditation was so stupid. But it seemed to really hit home with a lot of the girls. Not just about what a pain it is to go to the laundromat—that part about getting ahead in life and then slipping back downhill. A lot of them feel like that. A lot of us.

Isn't life supposed to be about moving forward? You're a kid and you live in your parents' house. Then you move out on your own and have a little independence -- in my case that would be my two years in the dorm at CUC. And then you get married and you live in a tiny apartment or in our case a trailer. Roger & I shared the same trailer that Nick & Teresa used to live in, after they graduated. Neither of us ever mentioned the fact that we'd had sex there for the first time.

I think we were happy in that little trailer. The unhappiness I felt right after the wedding, after I lost that baby, got folded up and tucked away somewhere small inside me. Roger wanted a fresh start, so I tried to forget the past and concentrate on being a good wife. I threw myself into cleaning and decorating that trailer and learning to cook tasty vegetarian meals and of course doing the laundry. I used to go up to the girls' dorm with our laundry, hauling pillowcases full of it across campus.

We were both so busy that year. Roger was graduating in the spring so he was busy, not just with classes but also travelling around preaching in different small churches— ministerial students had to do that. We both worked part-time to pay our tuition. In my spare time after school and work I had the housework to do, but like I said I really didn't mind that because I took such pleasure in making a home for us. And I enjoyed the little bits of time, usually on Sabbath, that Roger was able to spend at home just relaxed. He could be very sweet and kind to me. He used to come home and put his arms around me & kiss me & say how nice it was to come home to such a cozy little house—much more peaceful than the boys' dorm.

I missed dorm life more than Roger did, because of course I'd been in the girls' dorm where what I remembered was late-night talks in each others' rooms & sharing homemade cookies in the lounge. I guess the things Roger remembered from dorm life were more like guys playing hockey with pop cans in the hallways while he was trying to study, fistfights breaking out, stuff like that. Even though I liked married life, I missed having the other girls around all the time. Sometimes at night I'd be in the trailer when Roger was out, and I'd sit alone with my books at the little table and stare out the window & wonder if this was what my whole life was going to be like.

Kind of like I do now.

One Sabbath I convinced Roger to invite some friends over for Sabbath dinner. Roger lit right up at the idea and had several suggestions of people we could invite, his theology friends and their girlfriends. He said we would need to practice the gift of hospitality for when he was a pastor. I knew what he meant. In church at home growing up it was always Pastor and Mrs. Kimball who had a big crowd over to Sabbath dinner

I wanted to invite Jeff & Dave—Roger wasn't too thrilled about that. He still had this old jealousy thing going on about Jeff, and as for Dave, Roger said he was a loser & nothing but trouble.

I insisted. I didn't often do that, but this time I dug in my heels. Roger said if we wanted people from back home we could invite his classmate Ed and Ed's girlfriend Brenda, and wouldn't it be nicer if it was just couples? I agreed to Ed and Brenda but I said also Dave and Jeff. I guess what I really wanted was some kind of connection to my old life, my own life.

Instead of trying to explain that to Roger, I pointed out that they were single guys far from home and they probably never got a home-cooked meal & it was our duty to share our hospitality with them. Finally he gave in.

Our first try at hospitality went pretty well, six of us squeezed around the tiny table in the trailer eating veggie lasagna. Roger was even decent to Dave and Jeff at first, until he decided the Sabbath afternoon conversation should take a more spiritual tone, and they wouldn't stop cracking jokes and discussing hockey.

Finally Jeff said they had rented the video of The Day After, so we got onto talking about nuclear war and the end of the world. Roger got very solemn and said something typically pastor-like, about how the signs were all pointing to the end and the old world didn't have much time left before the Lord returned. Ed, who had been face and eyes into the hockey conversation, remembered he was a ministerial student too and chimed in with "Wars and rumours of wars" or something like that.

I remember how Dave got this wicked little grin and said something about the last plagues, and how we must be having the plague of unending cold, and Jeff jumped in talking about the plague of the block heater.

Dave said something like "And the fourth angel poured out a vial of ten-foot snowdrifts, and behold, it all landed upon Lacombe, Alberta." He said it in this loud, resonating preacher voice, Generic Adventist Pastor with just a hint of a round-the-bay accent behind it—well I mean, he was obviously making fun of Roger.

After they were gone I moved around the tiny kitchen tidying up, my voice chattering away in the silence of the trailer, saying how nice that was, how much fun it was. I heard Roger get up and walk over to the sink as I paused by the window, looking at our guests' footprints in the snow outside.

I heard the crash as Roger slammed the glass down in the sink -- the tinkle of broken glass. I wanted to ask if he'd hurt his hand, but I also wanted to pretend nothing unusual had happened. I just stood there watching the footprints in the snow, wishing Jeff or Dave had turned back to wave goodbye before they disappeared out of sight.

Dave

SO WHAT KIND OF STORY from my lurid past do you want to hear today?

Oh, come on, admit it. You're enjoying the stories. My past is much more interesting than my present.

No, no, that's a good thing. A boring week is a good week.

This week? Nothing to tell. Really. Other than going to AA meetings and trying to take up running—which I suck at, no surprise there—I haven't had any drama to report. Played my guitar a few times, fixed a friend's computer problem. If you want to know the truth I feel raw, like I'm learning everything from scratch. How do you get through a day? What do people fill their time with? How do you talk, what kind of a meal do you cook for yourself? I mean, it's not like I've never done these things, it's just ... well, it feels different now.

Yeah, I know I've had to do this before. Every time I quit drinking. You'd think I'd be able to learn something from all that experience. Thing is, it usually didn't last real long, and there was often a lot of other stuff going on—school, marriage, kids, work—to occupy my time. Now here I am, much older and in much worse shape, learning to walk on my own.

OK, good question. What *can* I learn from those other times? Well, take the time I told you about last week, when I decided I was going out to CUC and live the squeaky-clean life of the

Christian college student. That actually went OK for awhile. Best part was the drive out west. Jeff's old Horizon used to break down every hundred miles or so. Whenever it was running we'd drive through the night, taking turns sleeping, to make up time. And in between we'd end up spending hours in garages in little one-horse towns off the Trans Canada. By the time we rolled into Lacombe nearly two weeks later we were exhausted, filthy, broke, and the car was pretty much a write-off.

Best road trip of my life. The weather was fantastic and the stuff we saw along the way—well, I was this kid who'd grown up in St. John's, Newfoundland, you know? Apart from my one trip to Toronto I'd never been anywhere, and it was all just so beautiful, so big, and I felt like we were off on an adventure.

I brought my guitar along—a cheap secondhand one I got after my Martin got destroyed—and I remember one night when we were both too tired to drive we scraped up the cash to pull into a public campsite, and I lay out on the hood of the car looking up at all these pine trees and the stars in the sky above me, playing the guitar, for about an hour. I can't remember ever feeling like that before. Like just being there, in that moment, was enough. I didn't have to worry about what came before or after.

Yeah, Jesus and me were going steady again. Things were good. At first, anyway. While I was playing by the rules.

I remember one time on the road, we were stalled in this little town in—Manitoba, I think it was—the kind of place where there was nothing to do and nowhere to go. We were wandering the streets, waiting for the muffler to get put back on the car or something, and we passed a bar and Jeff suggested we go in for a beer. And I felt this kind of panic. I was far from being able to tell myself or anyone else that I had a real problem, but I knew it wouldn't be a good idea for me to go into that bar. So I said, "No man, I don't think so." We went to a corner store and bought a Coke instead, and for the rest of that trip Jeff never suggested having a drink.

Yeah, nice while it lasted. When we got out to campus, reality struck pretty quickly. I knew living in the dorm at CUC wasn't going to be like MUN. I'd quit drinking and also, by the way, quit smoking which wasn't easy either, just so I could avoid trouble out there. But there were so many other rules—having to show up to dorm worship and chapel, being in by curfew.

Yeah—in college. Can you believe it? But that's what these little Christian colleges were like—maybe still are, for all I know. It all seemed so surreal, I mean coming from MUN where people were practically screwing in the tunnels—up until the tunnels caught fire anyway, after that they had to keep them clear but people found other places to do it.

No, not everyone at CUC played by the rules—not by a long shot. There were different crowds out there, a crowd that was good and religious and all, a hard crowd that was always getting into trouble, and you could more or less pick and choose where you wanted to belong. I knew by the end of the first week which guys in the dorm were drinkers, who'd have beer or maybe even liquor hidden away in their rooms. For someone like me it wasn't hard to spot that and keep that information kind of on file. But I stayed away from it. A unique outcome, one of those things you like.

I'd say the good times lasted well into the New Year, but I started getting stressed out in the second semester—you know, I don't think I've ever gotten through a second semester anywhere? What kind of a track record is that?

I was getting tired of putting in all this effort, and it was so friggin cold all the time, and I didn't have a girlfriend and I didn't have that feeling anymore, that feeling of strength and energy and whatever, like God was carrying me through. I was just tired.

So one day when Jeff and me and a couple of other guys took a drive into Red Deer to catch a movie, one of the guys suggested we drop into a bar afterwards. I figured, what the hell? I hadn't had a drink in six months. That was long enough to prove that I didn't have a problem, that I could control it, that I could quit anytime. I figured it wouldn't hurt to relax with a couple of drinks before we went back to campus.

Yeah, I can spot the flaw in that reasoning now. Couldn't then. All I could see was the bar in front of me, the other guys around me ordering beers, and I had a Black Russian—one of my favourite drinks ever. I just remember lifting the glass, smelling it before I tasted it, and knowing how damn good it was going to feel. God, it was better than sex.

Things unravelled fairly quickly after that. I kept it quiet for awhile, managed to keep up the double life, although I got a few warnings from the profs that my grades were slipping. Slipping? Hell, they were going downhill like skiers on a double black diamond, but I really didn't care anymore.

Oh, definitely, there were consequences. I got caught a couple of times-once hiding a forty-ouncer in my room, once coming out of a bar in Lacombe, another time—yeah I guess it was a couple of times. The dean—can't remember his name—used to haul me into his office for these little lectures and give me warnings. He gave me second and third chances, but I didn't give a damn. Finally I made my last visit to the office. Damn, it's bothering me, his name. Can't remember it for the world but I'll never forget his face. He sat there behind his desk, leaning back in his chair like he was trying to get as far away from me as possible even though the desk was already between us. He had a short, bristly buzz cut going gray, and his eyes behind his glasses were like steel. He was extremely pissed and making no effort to hide it.

He read me the riot act, about how many chances I'd been given and all the people who had tried to help me out and the good people back home who'd sent money to help with my tuition, and blah blah blah. I got the bottom line, which was that I was expelled effective immediately.

I scraped up what little cash I had and bought the old Horizon off Jeff for $400, although I didn't have the whole $400 to pay him at the time. Jeff felt bad about me getting kicked out, although looking back I guess he should have been pissed at me because the booze was in his room too, and he got hauled over the coals for it as well. I made sure they knew it was me and not Jeff who kept it there, I didn't want any trouble for him.

No, didn't really have a plan. I had this vague idea that I'd hop in and drive back across Canada again, all the way home, although realistically I knew the car wouldn't make it past Red Deer. The day after my talk with the dean I was standing out in the parking lot, packing the trunk, getting ready to say goodbye to that place forever. The assistant dean— now his name I do remember, because it was a stupid sounding name, Wayne Wiley, and I always felt sorry for him having to go through life with that name—anyway, Wayne Wiley came out and said goodbye to me. He was a young guy, much younger than the head dean, probably only a few years older than me. He'd always been pretty decent to me. That day he came out looking unhappy, and he leaned on the hood of Jeff's old car and told me he was sorry I was leaving.

I kind of shrugged and said, "Guess you shouldna kicked me out then," but he surprised me. He said he wasn't supposed to tell me this, but he'd voted against expelling me. I didn't see why—the rules were pretty clear and I made no secret of the fact that I'd broken them.

Wiley said, "Well, I just thought you had—" and I figured for sure he was going to say "potential," because, you know, I've heard that the odd time or two. But instead he said he thought I had some problems, some shit I needed to work out. He didn't say shit—stuff. I knew what he was getting at. I slammed the trunk down and told him he had it all wrong—I didn't have a problem, I could keep the rules if I wanted to, I just didn't give a fuck. I did say fuck.

He pissed me off. Ruined the satisfied, you-can-all-go-to-hell feeling I had driving away from campus that day. I was finished with CUC, with the church, with God, with being good. I wanted to make a clean break, and then this well-meaning asshole had to go spoil it by acting like he actually looked at me and saw a human being.

Afterwards? Oh, I stayed for a couple of weeks with some guys from the college who lived in Lacombe. One night at a bar I met this girl named Tammy. She had no connection with the school or with Adventists; she was a tough, hard-drinking, slutty-looking little girl with the kind of hair that's usually called dirty blond, only in her case it actually looked dirty. We got plastered together one night and I woke up in her bed in the morning, and the next day I kind of moved my stuff into her place. I thought it would last a couple of weeks, because she wasn't my type at all—no brains, not much in the way of looks, bad temper and not even really good for a laugh.

Geez, what a way to talk, eh, about my ex-wife, the mother of my children?

Oh yeah. That's a long story, how I got from Point A to Point B with Tammy. And for once, you know, I'm not that interested in telling you this particular long story. You're right: maybe we should be focusing on the here and now. Like right now, after I leave here, I have to get something for my supper and figure out how to spend the rest of the evening. Got any suggestions?

liz

I'M TRAPPED CAGED IN THIS tiny place the bars closing in around me and outside is danger danger i hear the shouts the gunfire they're coming closer rhythmic blasts almost ringing and zing zing zing—

i'm awake. heart still racing from an incomprehensible dream i roll over and hit the snooze button. the ringing continues. finally i realize grab the phone. the glowing read numbers read 2:15 a.m.

-gene? what the—

-did i wake you up

-no gene i'm routinely awake at 2:15 in the morning.

-oh sorry is it that late there.

this might be barely forgivable if it were the first time or if gene lived on the other side of the international date line. he lives in ottawa, one and a half hours behind st. john's and does this every single time he calls.

-gene you asshole i have an exam in the morning.

-how can you have an exam classes haven't started yet.

-well screw you i'm in an accelerated program. by this time i'm semi-awake and laughing and so is gene my brother the person walking around out there with the dna that matches mine there's nobody quite like him. many better some worse but nobody quite like gene.

-so have you seen the folks.

-i'm sorry did you call to talk about something in the real world or about ancient history.

-no no i'm serious I called them last week remember I told you I was going to

-oh yeah the coming out party, how did that go.

-as well as you would expect. Or worse. But did you even know they were leaving.

> *[he said she said. would a little attribution kill me? even i get confused rereading this. is it clear gene is the one who knows about the move and i don't?]*

-they're what?

-dad's got a call they're moving to the states. apparently god does answer your prayers.

there was a time when i wanted my parents in another country preferably on another continent. now they just seem irrelevant. they might as well be in the states for all i've seen of them this last year or so.

i ride the route seven bus through safe suburban west end streets. alien territory now. i am a downtown girl my turf defined by walking distances and taxis. i study at mun sleep in rabbittown party on george street. everything west of pennywell road might as well have dropped off the map.

i get off at my old stop walk past the tidy two bed bungalows one after another white pink green yellow their smug complacency makes me want to hurl.

[ha! smug? who's smug here! remember i was 19. do i mention that anywhere?]

i stand in front of the house with a for sale/sold sign in the yard. walk past a few paces then turn and walk back. a curtain moves. somewhere in there she's watching.

up the concrete path the steps to the green door with three windows shaped like teardrops.

ding. dong.

she opens the door slowly. she wears brown polyester pants with a short-sleeved blouse featuring large green and orange flowers accented with the same brown as in the pants. her hair is recently permed, glossy and unmoving.

what she sees: a nineteen-year-old girl wearing ripped black jeans and a white t-shirt under a second-hand men's grey sport coat with the sex pistols logo hand-sewn onto the back of it. long straight black hair under a black fedora and lots of silver jewellery.

we are creatures from different galaxies i can't imagine what we will say i doubt the universal translator will even work in this atmosphere jim.

[star trek allusions shd be a relief after obscure adventist church allusions]

-liz. come in.

i perch on the edge of the couch like a guest.

-it's been awhile. we've missed you.

-gene told me you guys were moving. were you planning to ever tell me.

-well we had a hard time getting hold of you. i finally tracked down your number and called several times but you were never there.

-oh. well i'm not home that much.

silence. clock ticks fridge hums my mother's fingers rub at a spot near her knee.

-so where are you moving to.

-kansas city your dad has an offer to be principal there.

-good that's good.

-and what about you what's happening in your life. Our eyes do not meet.

-university starts next week. oh i wrote a poem that won a prize.

-that's wonderful you always had such a talent with writing. sigh. i always hoped you would use it in the lord's work.

-mom. please.

tears in her eyes in her voice. well i'm sorry liz i don't know what you want me to say. i only ever had one task to do in this life only one thing that mattered to me raising my two children for the lord my only purpose in life and i've failed at it.

-well jesus mom did it ever strike you maybe you should have had some other purpose?

-is it too much to ask you not take the lord's name in vain in this house.

shit. i should have watched my mouth for once. i just said something important to her and all she hears is jesus.

-i think back to you and gene two little children in cradle roll sabbath school singing jesus loves me and it just breaks my heart to think of both of you now not in the church. and this latest thing with gene... did he tell you...

-of course he did mom. i've known gene's gay for like… i don't know. two years. he didn't want to tell you because he knew you'd react like this.

-i just wonder what we did wrong. your father and i. to have both of you turn against the lord like this

i stand up. i only came to say goodbye. i don't need this mom.

she stands up too, follows me to the door.

-look do you have a piece of paper. i pause in the porch on my way out. she hands me a little piece of notepaper from beside the phone. philippians 4:13 is printed on the bottom amid a border of sunflowers. i take it and scrawl my mailing address on it and give it to her.

-drop me a line when you get there. good luck and—tell dad i said good-bye.

[stayed up till 1:00 writing this last night and couldn't sleep till dawn. must remember that just because reading this tears the lining out of my stomach does not necessarily mean it's good. must workshop this]

Katie

MARIA! I JUST MET A GIRL named Maria! Lalala lalala Mariiiiii-yaaaaa!!"

Katie dissolves in giggles as Nola dances along the sidewalk that leads from Burman Hall to the cafeteria. They've just left the Saturday night movie, *West Side Story*—Saturday night movies at Andrews are often classic musicals, which Katie and Nola leave dancing and singing badly.

A knot of people on the walk in front of them turns around at the sound of Nola's decidedly unmusical soprano. "You guys going to the Snack Shop?" says their friend Vicky.

"We were thinking about Chez Marie's."

"Oh, let's go to Chez Marie's—I love that place!"

The sky deepens to dark blue over the tops of the trees that line the campus. As they pass Meier Hall, Vicky says, "I'm going in and see if Andy wants to come."

"Have you got any money?" Katie asks Nola.

"I've got ten dollars. I'll treat you."

"OK. I'll treat you next time."

Their group grows as they cross campus. Vicky's boyfriend Andy joins them with his roommate Jake. At Lamson Hall they collect Katie's roommate Eileen and her friend Alice, who need a break from studying for an anatomy exam. As they cut across campus towards the highway, singing tunes from *West Side Story*, they meet Darryn coming back from the library and convince him to join them.

Chez Marie's is a tiny ice-cream shop across the highway from the Andrews University campus, and the only off-campus restaurant within walking distance. This is an important consideration, since only a few of Katie's friends have cars and those who do often don't have gas to put in them.

At the end of the road that marks the border of campus they wait for a break in traffic. Cars in this area often carry bumper stickers that read "I Drive U.S. 31/33: Pray For Me." Berrien Springs is a one-traffic-light town, but because of the highway, it can hardly be described as slow-moving.

As usual, Chez Marie is deserted when they get there. Katie often wonders how the place stays in business. She and her friends are there a couple of Saturday nights a month, but they rarely see any other customers. The restaurant does not offer the intimate French-bistro decor the name promises: it is a fluorescent-lit room with shiny formica tables, dominated by a huge ice cream bar where you can look down through the plexiglass top and choose one of thirty-six flavours. Some things are encouragingly French: the ice cream crepes are excellent, and the owners are two massive and imposing French women for whom English is not only a second language but a very distant second. Never having learned the women's names, Katie's crowd refers to them as Shay and Marie.

Flooding into the restaurant, they push two tables together and drag chairs from around the room to accommodate their group of eight. Marie comes out waving her ice-cream scoop in the air. "Ah! Allo! 'Ow are you all?! What you 'ave?"

Placing orders takes the better part of half an hour, and it's already after ten. By the time the crepes and sundaes arrive, Vicky and Jake are deep into a discussion about the relationship between *West Side Story* and *Romeo and Juliet*. Andy is analyzing the upcoming anatomy exam with Eileen and Alice while Darryn tells them to shut up, please shut up, he gets enough of this rooming with a pre-med major and he doesn't need to come out on a Saturday night to hear about people's innards, please. Nola is telling Katie a funny story that's not really funny about something Insensitive Ted said in their Pastoral Counselling class. Everyone is talking at once, cutting into and out of each other's conversations, using flamboyant hand gestures, sometimes shouting.

Katie shuts off her attention from Nola's anecdote for a moment—she's heard enough Insensitive Ted stories—and looks at her friends. They're not all close friends, of course: she doesn't know Alice that well, and she only knows Jake as Andy's roommate. But they are, as a group, people she can call friends. For the first time in her life Katie is a place where there's an abundant supply of people who think like she does, care about the things she cares about, enjoy talking about the subjects that interest her.

Ever so often, since reading *Our Town* earlier this year, Katie has gotten into the habit of stopping time, pausing to look around her and realize how happy she is, how lucky she is to be here, with these friends. She doesn't want to wake up dead some morning and realize that she never appreciated life while she had it. She will be the rare person, the saint or poet, who pays attention.

Now she surveys her assorted friends: red and yellow, black and white, all precious in her sight. Nola, short and chunky, has the kind of medium-brown skin and wiry black hair that invites awkward questions like, "So, um, what *are* you—I mean, um, where are you from?" To which Nola, whose mother is Filipino and whose father is African-American, correctly replies, "I'm a theology major, and I'm from Chicago."

Katie likes the theology department at Andrews better than the one at CUC, in spite of Insensitive Ted. She's not the only woman: she and Nola are both in the junior class, and in the senior class, graduating this year, is Beatrice Grant, a fifty-seven year old retired teacher. Katie and Nola call her Auntie Bea, at her request.

By quarter to twelve the talk has worn down and everyone has scraped up the last chocolate syrup from their plates. Byzantine negotiations regarding the payment of the bill have begun: "Well you treated me last time so I can pay for you this time, only I don't have any money on me but Andy owes me for buying him a burger at the Snack Shop yesterday, so Andy, if you have a ten ... does anyone have change for a twenty?" In the middle of the discussion Shay—or is it Marie?—comes out, vast and imposing in a floral-print apron, waving a bill as incomprehensible as a doctor's prescription pad. "Oo pay?" she bellows with some concern. "Oo pay?!"

The bill is paid: they drift out into the night. "What time is it?" Katie asks. "Five to twelve," one of the guys replies. "Have you girls got late passes?" Everyone is supposed to have a pass if they're going to be out after eleven on a weeknight, midnight on a Saturday night, except those over 21 who can come and go as they please. Only Eileen and Jake have attained that status, but Andy and Darryn aren't worried because the guys' dorms don't really track or care about late passes. Katie and the other girls pick up the pace, hurrying past the rows of married-student townhouses and across the dark lawn of Pioneer Memorial Church.

Despite the threat of the getting marked late, Katie lingers outside the door for a moment to say goodnight to Darryn. "I'll sign you in," Eileen promises as she, Alice and Nola go inside.

Darryn is another member of the extended friend-group. He and Katie have been hanging out a lot since Christmas, but you couldn't call it dating: he doesn't refer to her as his girlfriend and they've never kissed. They wind up almost accidentally going to things together; they sit on benches under the trees and have long talks about the meaning of life and stuff. Katie knows there's a girl back home, an old high school girlfriend, but Darryn's not big on spelling things out.

"Hard to believe the semester's over in only three weeks," says Darryn.

"Yeah, I know. I really have to get cracking on studying for exams," Katie says. "Greek is going to be a killer, I know."

Darryn is majoring in History, a junior like herself. He's thinking about law school, maybe, but he believes God has called him to be a missionary and he agonizes of how to fulfill that call and still study law. Darryn agonizes a lot, mostly over God's Will.

"But soon you'll be back on your tropical island," Darryn says. Katie has taken full advantage of the fact that no-one at Andrews knows anything about Newfoundland. She told several people that she lived on an isolated northern island off the south coast of Greenland, that her father made a living trapping inland seals for their pelts and that she had gone back and forth to high school by dogsled. She told an equal but unrelated number of people that her home was a small tropical island called New Finland, colonized by Finnish settlers who had shed their clothes and adapted to life in the tropics but who still subsisted mainly on the boiled salt cod of their ancestral homeland.

The luxury of re-inventing herself, far from home and people who knew her there, is irresistible. She's cut her hair boyishly short, and is only sorry she didn't start out at Andrews by introducing herself as Kate. She's always wanted the more grown-up version of her name and this year would have been an ideal time to launch herself under a new label.

They stand by the round globe light on the lamppost in front of Lamson Hall. Darryn reaches up to brush a strand of hair out of Katie's eyes. The gesture, more intimate than usual, makes Katie brave enough to say, "I'll miss you over the summer."

Darryn sighs. "I'll miss you too. We've had a lot of fun this year." He doesn't let go of that tiny piece of her short hair, twirling it between his fingers. "It's so hard to know sometimes, Katie, what's the right thing to do. Isn't it? I mean, I pray so much about finding God's will, letting Him lead in my life ... sometimes I wish He'd just spell it out for me."

Katie would like to climb the wall of Meier Hall some night and spray-paint: "MARRY KATIE MATTHEWS" backwards on Darryn's window, so he'd see it as a message from God. Katie's own view of God's will is still developing, like photographic film immersed in fluid, waiting under the red light till the picture becomes clear. She does not think, however, that God has a divine roadmap somewhere with every step of her life, every decision she's supposed to make, marked down on it.

She flies home in the third week of June and goes back to her usual summer job at VOAR. Home seems quiet after leaving her circle of friends at Andrews. Most of her St. John's friends are away, except for Liz who is spending her summer playing Celia in *As You Like It*. "I'd rather be Rosalind," she confesses, "but I'm working my way up. Last time I was an extra. Hours and hours of showing up at rehearsals for five minutes on stage whispering 'Peas and carrots!' to the other extras and looking shocked at the goings-on of the actual characters." Katie had a small part in an English department play this year: swapping stories of theatre life bridges some of the gap between the worlds she and Liz now inhabit.

Two pieces of news mar Katie's summer. One comes from New Orleans, where the Seventh-day Adventist church in its General Conference session has not voted to ordain women to the ministry, instead referring the matter for "further study." It's judged to be potentially too disruptive to the worldwide church to introduce such an innovation at this time. Katie's mom is furious and stays home from church for three weeks. On the fourth Sabbath she shows up wearing jeans and her fish/bicycle T-shirt.

The second piece of news comes in late July, when Katie gets a large cream-coloured envelope in the mail. It's an invitation, in curly embossed script, to the wedding of Darryn Paul Kaye and Lisa Michelle Krantz, in their hometown of Paduka, Minnesota, on the weekend of September 6, 1985. A soft-focus oval photo of Darryn with Lisa adorns the invitation. Katie sends back a firm "will be unable to attend" on the RSVP card, and slips it in with a "Best Wishes on Your Wedding Day" card and an American $20 bill.

After getting Darryn's wedding invitation, Katie spends several evenings driving around in her mom's car, listening to her heartbreak tape. It includes songs guaranteed to wrench a tear from her even when she's in a good mood. *How Am I Supposed To Live Without You? I Can't Fight This Feeling Anymore. Against All Odds.* She leaves the tape in the car's cassette player and lets it play over and over, end to end.

"It's like a kick in the gut," she tells Liz one evening over dinner at Sidestreet. "It feels exactly like that. Not that I've ever *been* kicked in the gut. But it couldn't be worse."

"I know," says Liz, who has told Katie all about her awful boyfriend from last year, the one who put her down and wouldn't give her any credit for being a good writer. "I wonder why that is—I mean, is that the origin of the phrase 'broken heart'? You can feel it in your chest, but it's really more the abdominal area. Why didn't people start saying, 'My stomach is broken?'"

"And why should you feel it as a physical pain at all? Is it some kind of thing about hormones or adrenaline or something? I don't see why emotional pain should hit you in the middle of your stomach. I can still feel it now, although it's shrinking."

"And eventually it shrivels down to the size of a walnut, but it never quite goes away," Liz pointed out. "I wonder how many of those you can carry around inside you? Don't you think we'll accumulate a lot of them, over the course of a lifetime?"

Both girls are quiet at this thought, winding fettucine alfredo onto their forks.

"Oh, did you hear?" Katie says, hoping Liz will take it as a non-sequitur. "Jeff and Dave are coming home."

"They're what? I thought they were both staying out west."

"No, Jeff's mom told me at church he's coming home this weekend, and Dave is coming with him. I don't know if it's just a visit or if they're home for good."

"We should all get together before you go back," Liz says. "Go out for dinner or something."

The next Sabbath Jeff and Dave are both in church. So, to Katie's surprise, are Julie and Roger. She hasn't seen Julie since her wedding, and their hugs are hasty and, on Julie's part, teary-eyed.

"I wish we had time to visit! We're only home for a couple of weeks while Roger's helping his brother build a house out in Botwood. I really wanted to stay at mom's for my birthday, but Roger wants to drive back tonight after sunset."

"Couldn't you stay in for a few days?" Katie suggests.

Julie looks uncertain. "I guess I could—I don't know. I'd have to take the bus out...."

"I could drive you on Monday, if you want to stay in for the weekend. My mom won't mind lending me her car. It'd be fun—a girls' road trip. Come on, tell Roger you're going to stay in for a couple of days."

Julie hesitates, her eyes meeting Katie's for a second then shifting away. "I'll ask Roger," she says finally.

On Sunday night Katie and Julie are the first to arrive at Mr. Jim's Pizza. Liz comes next, all in black with her punk-girl look, apologizing loudly for being late. Katie works hard to keep a three-way conversation going until Jeff and Dave arrive.

"Oh-ho, Miami Vice!" Liz cries when Jeff walks in, and Katie echoes, "We're so honoured, Mr. Johnson!" Jeff tells them to shut up, but he is indeed wearing a melon-coloured T-shirt and aqua-blue blazer over rolled-up khaki pants, and deck shoes with no socks. He's also sporting a fashionable sheen of stubble.

Dave, on the other hand, has gone for the simple classic look -- white T-shirt and blue jeans. His hair is still long and tonight he's wearing it loose instead of tied back. Katie fights the urge to tangle two handfuls of it in her hands and pull him towards her and kiss him like she did that one time, years ago. Has he forgotten?

They settle in and catch up on news. There are awkward pauses. In the gloom of Mr. Jim's Katie remembers the brilliance of Chez Marie's and her colourful, witty college friends. Her old friends, by comparison, are black-and-white photos captured on a yearbook page. But the book's binding is cracked and it falls open, always, to this page, these faces.

They talk about school, about jobs, about break-ups and broken hearts.

"Not everyone's love life sucks," Liz says. "Look at Julie. Happily married. I knew you'd be the first one of us to get married, Jules."

Julie is quiet. "So, are you going to spill the beans on married life? Tell us all about it?" Katie probes.

"Oh, I've seen them," Jeff says. "Her and Roger walking around campus, all lovey-dovey. It's enough to make you sick."

"It's different, that's all," Julie says finally. "Just very different from being single or even dating. And one of the differences is, your life is more private. You don't really talk about your marriage with other people. It's like your own private world."

There's silence then, for a moment. The pizza is finished; they look around at each other, not sure what to do next. Then Liz speaks up, in a flamboyantly bad English accent—she and Katie have watched a lot of Monty Python videos this summer. "I've got an idea. Let's us—let's *all* of us—drive up to Signal Hill!"

"Oh, do lets!" "Ra-*ther!*" "Let's *all* of us—" They all plunge with enthusiasm into the loud, campy accents, repeating the plan over and over before they actually leave into the restaurant and pile into Katie's mother's car to drive up there. The heartbreak tape is still in the cassette—*Summer of 69*—as they drive the winding road up to Cabot Tower.

The night is clear and the southwest wind is fit to blow your head off. They get out in the parking lot, still giddy with the Python accents and something else, egged on by the night wind. Dave is the first to climb on the roof the car; he pulls Katie up and the others follow. They and sit looking at the city lights and sing Happy Birthday to Julie, and then Happy Birthday to each of the rest of them since they all have had birthdays this year.

"Twenty," Jeff says, above the wind. "Not teenagers anymore."

"We should make a sacred vow," Liz says. "No matter where our lives take us or what we do, to meet every year on somebody's birthday, here on Signal Hill."

Katie loves the idea, but Julie says, "We couldn't do it every year."

"OK, maybe every five years. We could meet back here when we're twenty-five," Liz amends, shouting a little to be heard over the wind. "And then again when we're thirty!"

Twenty-five, thirty seem impossibly far away. They all agree.

"And until then, we'll swear an oath," Katie suggests. "We'll promise that whatever happens, we'll remain forever young."

There's general agreement, except for Julie who says, "We might not always want to be young. I mean, you have to grow up sometime."

"What would your oath be, then?" Jeff asks her.

"To be forever—strong," Julie says after a pause.

"We could each put in one thing," Katie says. "One adjective."

They shift on the roof of the car so they're in a circle, facing each other rather than the city lights. "We vow, then," Liz says, "by the sacred tower of Cabot, to meet here again in five years, and to remain forever young, strong ... um, free ... and—Jeff?"

"Positive," says Jeff.

"Dave?"

He thinks a minute. "Outrageous," he says finally.

"That's it then." Katie grabs his hand, and Julie's on the other side of her; they all take hands. The wind rises, threatening to blow them off the roof, and they all shout to be heard, joining in on the chorus of adjectives. "We vow to remain forever young, strong, free, positive, and outrageous!"

The wind carries their words over the parking lot, beyond the rocks and the lighthouse, out over the dark and churning sea.

SIX

Jeff

YOU'RE HERE. YOU'RE HERE. Everything's going to be OK now isn't it? Something went wrong, something went terribly wrong. But now you're here. I can see your face. Everything's going to be OK.

Her face bends over me, her hair like a curtain. I think there is a curtain around me. I'm not sure where I am. But she's here. I can see her eyes.

Funny, I have no memory of the first time I saw her. I have that sharp memory of the first time I saw Liz. That was the dividing line for me between being a kid and growing up. You'd think I'd have a similar memory of the first time I saw the girl I was going to marry. She arrived from away, like Liz did. But when the Kimballs moved to St. John's, I was only ten or eleven. I didn't register anything beyond the fact that they had two girls, no boys. Bor-ing.

Later, I thought her little sister was cute. Lisa. Pretty little Lisa, always flirting with boys a couple of years older. Boys like me. We almost went out one time, before Liz came.

Debbie was a year older, a year ahead of me in school. We didn't hang out together until CUC, when I dated her friend Wendy. Debbie and I had that common background, growing up in St. John's. But that was it.

Then one Sabbath I went to church in Vancouver and there she was. This beautiful blond babe with amazing blue eyes, standing in the church lobby next to Aunt Shirl.

Aunt Shirl wasn't my aunt. She was Mom's friend. Every couple of months she'd call and invite me to Sabbath dinner. The promise of a home-cooked meal was enough to make me haul my ass out of bed Sabbath morning. Aunt Shirl could report to Mom that I was in church. Everybody's happy.

Shirl said, "There's someone here you should meet." The blond turned, like slow motion, her white dress swirling. Great legs. I did a double take. It was Debbie Kimball. I gave her a big hug. For a minute I was back home, fourteen again, remembering Pathfinders, Sabbath School and Saturday night socials.

Aunt Shirl and her husband invited Debbie home for lunch too. I was glad Dave had been too hungover to come to church with me. I had Debbie all to myself. She leaned across Shirl's dining room table and told me she had just moved to Vancouver. We talked about old times, traded news of people we both knew. I forked up Special K roast and scalloped potatoes with a silly grin on my face.

When Debbie said she had to get home, I offered her a ride. It was miles out of my way. I was low on gas. I didn't care. I enjoyed driving with Debbie beside me. She looked great, her hair pulled up in some kind of thing on the back of her head, a big shawl-scarf kind of thing thrown around her shoulders. I remember glancing at her ears and noticing that she had them pierced but wasn't wearing earrings today, not to church. That said a lot to me about what kind of girl she was and how well we'd fit together.

She told me nursing stories, about her patients and various disasters she'd had on the unit, funny stories that made me laugh as we drove along. Finally she said, "So, what are you doing these days?"

The topic of my job hadn't come up at lunch. Probably because I kept steering the conversation away from it. I don't know why. It's not like I was still working at Burger King. I just didn't feel that selling carpets—which was basically what I was doing, even though my title was "manager"—was up there with being a nurse.

But I told her the truth. I said, "Well, I'm managing a store. A carpet store. Not just carpet but all kinds of flooring, really. But mainly carpet."

"Manager? That's great. You must have a lot of responsibility," she said. And suddenly I felt, like, *Wow, I have a lot of responsibility! I'm the* manager! One sentence from her made all the difference.

I talked about work as we drove along, racking my brains for witty carpet stories. On another level of my mind I was planning how to get her phone number. Unfortunately it seems my mind doesn't have that many levels. I completely forgot about the level that was supposed to watch where we were going.

I looked around. We were in a completely unfamiliar part of the city.

"Do you know how to get to your place from here? I'm a little lost," I confessed.

She looked around like she also had just realized we were in unfamiliar territory. That was good. It meant she'd been paying attention to me and not to the street signs. On the other hand, it meant that she wasn't going to be much help getting back.

I realized I wasn't looking so smooth. I meet a pretty girl, drive her home, and get her stranded out in the wilds of North Vancouver.

I thought we were getting somewhere until we passed a Petro-Can and realized we'd passed the exact same station five minutes earlier. As we turned west again the sun hit my eyes and I realized it was near sunset.

Then Debbie started to sing. She started singing, *Day is Dying in the West*, the old standard Adventist hymn for Sabbath sunset. I looked over at her. She grinned at me, and I started to laugh. Then I joined in. I pulled the car over to the curb and stopped, and we sang to the end of the verse. Then I turned to her and said, "I guess it wouldn't *kill* me to go back to the gas station and ask for directions."

I went to start the car again, to head back to the gas station, and realized we were out of gas. Totally. I could usually get it to turn over when it was on empty but the tank must have been bone-dry. Debbie got more and more giggly. Finally she said, "Let's get out and walk. I think there's a gas station somewhere near here."

We got out and started walking down the sidewalk, a block or so to the Petro-Can. At one point she stumbled. I took her arm. She looked down and said, "Darn," and took off her shoe. She'd broken her heel. I waited for her to freak out, like a lot of girls would do, but she just looked up at me and smiled this wonderful glowing smile and took off the other one. I took her arm and we walked across the gas station parking lot, Debbie in her stocking feet, both of us in our church clothes.

I was planning to do everything right and not mess things up. I was going to get her number and call in a few days and invite her to a movie. Then another couple of dates. I wasn't going to rush into things. But suddenly I stopped under the big red maple leaf of the gas station sign and took her in my arms and kissed her. It must have been the right thing to do, because she kissed me back.

I was twenty-two. My life was far from perfect. I was a long way from home. I worked in a job I didn't like much. I lived with my best friend who was somehow turning into a stranger. He was shortly going to move out and I was going to be stuck with an apartment I couldn't afford and forced to downsize my lifestyle. But standing in front of a gas station kissing this girl I'd known all my life who laughed at disasters, suddenly I knew everything would be OK.

I'm here. Jeff, can you hear me? I'm here. Everything's going to be OK.

I can hear you. I hear you. I'm still in here. Everything's OK.

You May Be Right, I May Be Crazy

2005

1987

Julie

I JUST WENT SHOPPING. I bought myself some new clothes.

Flipping back through the pages of this journal I see myself complaining about the apartment, the laundry, being poor, etc etc etc. Poor poor me. Today I've decided it's time to write about something good.

I got my HST rebate & bought some new clothes for the girls, stuff they can wear to school, then got myself a pair of jeans & a pale pink sweater. It's very soft wool and needs to be handwashed—not at all practical. It wasn't from Wal-Mart either—I got it at Fairweather. It has tiny white rosettes sewn in a pattern on the front. I tried on the jeans & sweater tonight for Mom & the girls and they all said I looked great.

I used to enjoy dressing up and looking pretty. I never let myself go or looked sloppy—I just stopped enjoying it. And I remember exactly when and why I stopped.

We were in Nova Scotia, Roger's first job as a pastor. He was pastoring three churches in the area, all tiny, and we lived in a basement apartment underneath a church member's home.

I was sorry we'd left CUC before I'd had a chance to finish my education degree, but I liked church work and Roger & I were a good team. I felt closer to him than I had when we were married students. Everyone liked us and said what a sweet young couple we were.

Of course there were always those few people who'd never be content. We got some complaints: the old pastor was better at visiting the seniors, his sermons were shorter, Roger was trying to bring in too many new programs the church couldn't afford. He was usually upset when he got home from a church board meeting. But in spite of all that I felt like we were in a good place.

Our second year there, Roger planned an evangelistic crusade. We didn't have the budget to bring in a speaker but Roger was going to do the speaking himself. We sent out thousands & thousands of invitations and put ads in the paper and on the radio. We rented a hall and set up chairs for a hundred and fifty.

There were twenty-five loyal church members & about fifteen visitors there that first night. I've learned since then that in evangelistic crusades, the first night is usually the best. People come out of curiosity, then attendance starts to drop.

Our attendance for that crusade levelled off at about five visitors. A good Adventist crusade goes on for five weeks, with meetings three or four nights a week, time to cover all the doctrines. Roger had the whole set-up, the slides of the beasts of Revelation and the image of Daniel 2. Every night he beat himself out giving these wonderful sermons, a full hour long, for the sake of five people. I could tell he was getting discouraged by the poor turnout, so I just threw myself into giving him all the support and encouragement I could. I told him those five people meant as much to the Lord as two hundred, and if he could bring even one of them into the church, he'd be doing the Lord's work.

Three of them were sort of drifters who seemed a bit dazed and confused and not sure what they'd wandered into—one of the men may have been a mental patient. But there was one couple, probably in their thirties, nice, well-dressed, educated people—just the kind of people we wanted to bring into the church. I really went out of my way to be friendly to those folks. I got very close to the wife, Elaine, even though she was about fifteen years older than me, and by midway through the series of meetings she and I would get together to go for walks along the harbour.

The tricky point of any Adventist evangelistic series comes a couple of weeks before the end, when the preacher presents the Sabbath message and people realize they've been worshipping on the wrong day all these years. That's a tough stumbling block for some people to get over, even with all the Bible texts that make it clear as can be. Not everyone's ready to hear it. But with this crusade, we really didn't have a lot of people left to lose. I prayed extra-hard that week.

Roger introduced the Sabbath message on Friday night; the next night he was supposed to preach the second part and make a call for commitment. Sabbath afternoon I went for a walk along the harbour with Elaine and we had a great talk about the things she was learning at our meetings. I felt good because God was using me to share the truth. I ended up having supper with her and Jack and driving to the meeting with them, getting there just in time to play the piano for song service at the beginning.

Roger preached the second half of the message, the really hard-hitting half that called on people to make a decision about the true Sabbath. He made a call at the end and we were supposed to all be there with heads bowed & eyes closed. I was playing the piano—"Softly and Tenderly, Jesus is calling...." — & I glanced around a bit. All the church folks were standing of course, and the three other visitors, but Elaine & Jack were still sitting down.

After the meeting Jack & Elaine stayed to talk to Roger for a long time. Jack did most of the talking and their voices got loud at times—I could tell Roger was working hard to keep his temper under control. I stayed in the background, helping the deacons pick up the songbooks and generally clear up the hall. I was out in the lobby putting Bibles in boxes when Jack came striding out of the hall with Elaine kind of scurrying at his heels. She threw me one sad look before she left, almost like an apology.

Suddenly one of the church ladies came over to me. She was one of those little old ladies every church has three or four of: cranky, self-righteous—no, sorry, I'm being petty. She meant well. They always do.

I stood there in the lobby feeling sad about Jack & Elaine and worried about Roger, and this tiny woman with the tightly permed gray hair lit into me, criticizing me for showing up in jeans instead of a dress. I was wearing the clothes I'd worn to go for a walk with Elaine, my good jeans and a nice red sweater I'd bought the day before. She criticized me for the little bit of lipstick and eyeliner I wore. She quoted 1 Peter at me, about how godly women should adorn themselves with modest apparel, not with gold or pearls or costly array.

Roger was out in the lobby too, listening, and I kept waiting for him to say something, to defend me. Instead, when we got in the car he started criticizing me too. I didn't act or dress like a conservative church would expect their pastor's wife to, I wasn't supportive enough, I spent too much money on clothes for myself.

We baptized two people from that crusade. The mentally ill man and one of the women. Months later I saw Elaine in a store and she smiled at me politely, as if she were trying to place me.

Tonight, while I was trying on these jeans and this sweater I was carrying on this little monologue inside my head -- rehearsing all the reasons why I could afford it and why it was OK to buy it, promising myself I wouldn't buy anything else for a long time. It wasn't till I got home and tried the stuff on for my mother and daughters that I realized there was no-one I needed to say this to.

I really can't describe how that felt. Years ago, I think in school or church, they showed the movie Pilgrim's Progress I loved that moment when Pilgrim kneels down at the cross and the burden he's been carrying falls off and rolls down the hill. We used to sing in Sabbath School: Roll, roll, your burdens away. Tonight I stood in front of the mirror in my jeans and pink sweater and felt that burden just rolling, rolling away.

Dave

SORRY I'M LATE. I SHOULD have called ... we'll probably need to change the time if that's possible. See, I'm working now, and it's a bit of a rush to get the bus here after work....

Or what? No! No Jesus no. You're not serious.

No, I definitely do not feel ready to stop. Sure it's only these last few weeks that I've started to feel ... well, like I was even ready to be here. Like this might be getting me somewhere, finally. I mean, I know things are tight and this is a non-profit and you've got a waiting list and all but ... you can give me a few more weeks can't you?

OK, OK. Sorry I panicked. I guess when you asked ... well, what I heard was that maybe *you* were finished with me. Ready to push me out of the nest or whatever. And I can tell you, I could go to a meeting every night, have my sponsor on speed-dial, whatever, but I am not in *any* way ready to start flying on my own yet. Got that? Seriously, when the time comes ... I'll tell you, OK?

I'm not bad eh? From resistant client to completely counsellor-dependent in, what, less than two months? You gotta like that.

So, yeah. Now that we've bypassed that little obstacle ... yeah. Working. Back to pulling down semi-regular hours at an actual job. It's been ... yeah it's been awhile.

I don't know—uh, four, five years? After I was in rehab, I had a job for awhile. When I lost that, I worked on my own for a bit. Just being, you know, the guy you call when things break down. You have to have a lot of energy, you have to hustle, to sell yourself in that kind of business, and obviously in the last couple of years hustling wasn't my strong point. I'd say it's been—yeah, at least three, four years since I worked at all.

Before that? Oh, my resume doesn't look bad if you can ignore the last few years. The guy who offered me this job, he knows me and I didn't have to tell him any lies. It's only part-time and I know the reason he called me was partly to try to help me out. Help me get back on my feet, as they say. But it's going to work. I'm going to make it work.

I didn't go looking for it. I'd been thinking about it, because I'm getting a little sick of the place I've been living, which is basically a bedsitter. I'm actually getting to the point of feeling like I might deserve to live in more than one room, you know? I'd like a small apartment—nothing fancy, but a place with my own bathroom. Maybe a stove instead of a hot plate. I didn't really have myself worked up for the whole job-application, handing out resumes, going to interviews song and dance. Then out of the blue this guy I used to work with when I was with the government calls me up. He's got his own company now, it's to the point where they need a part time systems administrator, and he wants to know will I come in and interview.

Lucky? Oh yeah. Well I've always been lucky.

OK, I know that sounds crazy, given the stories I've been telling you, but we're talking careers here now, and I have been lucky in that way. Things have dropped into my lap a time or two, I've been in the right place at the right time. I'm pretty good at what I do and I guess if I'd been the least bit ambitious or had any real drive, I might have done real well for myself.

No, never finished university. CUC was my last shot. By that time I'd flunked out of two different schools, and you know, I can take a hint. I drifted around Lacombe for a couple of months, got a part-time job, lived with Tammy. Went home to Newfoundland for awhile, but there was nothing on the go there. After a few months Jeff and I both packed up and headed out west.

A guy from our high school class was out in Vancouver making decent money in construction and we stayed with him. Both of us got jobs, and the money wasn't bad. I bought myself a used computer and took an evening class in microcomputer systems. When that class was over, I found a job working in the customer service department of a computer store.

Yeah—you old enough to remember the late 80s? If you bought a computer from the store and it broke down, you'd bring it in and the tech guys would actually fix it. Ancient history, I know.

Yeah, that was another of the good times, I guess. Good job, half decent apartment. I found some guys who were starting a band and got into playing with them. I was the nerdy tech support guy Monday to Friday, then on Friday nights and Saturday nights our band played in bars and I got to be cool rock star guy.

Oh, and girls—well of course there were girls. Easy to pick up girls when we played in bars. One night we were playing at a place that was slightly less of a dive than the places we usually played, and when the set was over I was starting to pack up my guitar and stuff and this girl comes over and says, "Hey, Dave."

I looked up and it took a second to register. This was Tammy—I'd had no contact with her since I left Alberta. She was out in BC visiting a friend, and we hung out that night and she gave me her number. She was looking pretty good—had her hair all sprayed up into this big-hair look -- late 80s, remember?—and she was wearing white pants and a shirt that was silver and sort of—I don't know, kind of sparkly? After that she used to call me from time to time, tell me I should come and see her if I was ever back in Alberta, although at that point that was nowhere in my plans.

So ... yeah. How'd we get started talking about Tammy? I told you I didn't really want to talk about her.

Oh right ... work. I was telling you about work, how I got started in computers. And how well things seemed to be working out when I was twenty-two–decent job, playing in the band, steady girlfriend, nice apartment with my best bud–as far as I was concerned, I had it made.

What? Oh yeah ... you never get too far off topic, do you? OK, given the context here, it's a fair question. How much *was* I drinking at this point? Uh, well, you won't get any bonus points for guessing "quite a bit," now, will you? But this was another one of those times when I had things under control, you know? I didn't want to screw up work or the band. When the show was over, it was party time.

Anyway, it was my drinking, I guess, that finally got me back together with Tammy. Jeff, of all people, starting giving me a hard time about it. I mean, you've got to picture it—me and Jeff, friends as long as I can remember. I could count on Jeff never to judge or criticize.

But suddenly, and this was after nearly two years of living together, he catches on that something's not quite right. I have to laugh, honestly, at my church friends. Not that Jeff was going to church at that time, but you know, he shared that background. And like all the Adventists I knew, he only knew two ways to look at booze. Either you were a good Adventist, going to church, and it was wrong to touch it at all. Or else you were bad, and you'd left all that behind, and there was nothing wrong with it. It was very black and white for him. It amazes me now that he lived with me for nearly two years before ever seeing what was right before his eyes.

Anyway, one morning he came out of his room and saw me on the couch, TV still on, empty bottle of incredibly cheap vodka tipped over on the floor next to me, and he shook his head and made some comment—"You're pathetic, man"—something like that.

He got into the habit then, dropping these little comments, and I'd brush it off. He'd say I needed to get my shit together, and I'd say he needed to go to hell.

It all blew up one night when I was home alone, hauled off in front of the TV watching, I don't know, *Dynasty* or some crap. Jeff comes in through the door, home from a date, and makes some smart-assed comment like, "Whaddya know, there's Mitchell, not passed out yet."

I told him to shut the hell up, but he wouldn't. Started going on at me, and soon enough we were yelling at each other and I told him he sounded just like his old man. Well, he went wild then. Took a swing at me. My reaction time wasn't the greatest and when Jeff hit me I went down like the proverbial ton of bricks. I went after him and we were all over the apartment, me getting the worst of it by far, until I tripped over the arm of the couch and fell on top of the bottle, broke it and cut my hand open. Jeff had to drive me to the hospital, and I got four stitches.

We had a good laugh and I guess the whole thing might have blown over except as we were driving home, early in the morning by that time, he said, "I'm sorry about the fight. And I'm sorry about your hand. But you gotta know I meant what I said, before. I think you're headed for trouble."

Yeah, typical reaction. I just blocked it out. Looked out the window at the streets and houses rolling by and thought, *I don't need this.* Later that day I called Tammy and said, "Hey babe, what if I came out to Red Deer, could I stay at your place for awhile?" And of course she was thrilled to say yes. And I quit my job, quit the band, left Jeff high and dry without a roommate—just got the hell out of there and headed east, moving in with Tammy.

For weeks after that night I carried those stitches around in my hand, and for whatever reason they didn't heal up properly. I was always at them, picking at them, kind of absent-minded when I was at work or whatever. They got sore, and a bit infected, and I ended up having to go back to the doctor a couple of times. I cursed at Jeff every time I had trouble with that hand, because I figured it was all his fault. I've still got the scar, a white line that cuts right across my palm—see? Never did heal up entirely.

I figured I'd stay with Tammy a few weeks and then I'd shake her off and find something else, someone else. Go back to Vancouver or back home or something. Instead of a few weeks it turned out to be seven years and a lot of water under the bridge. A lot of water and a hell of a lot of booze. But that's another story.

Now look what you did. I come in here in a good mood, all happy about my job and everything, and you get me started on Tammy and my marriage and the whole shitty past. Now I'm so depressed I'm going to be hard-pressed to find my way home. You sure they're paying you for this?

Nah, don't mind me. I'm only giving you a hard time. I mean, this is the stuff, right? Some of it hurts even to touch or think about. Like the stitches, you know? Stuff never heals right and then it keeps giving you trouble down the road. I'm trying for a metaphor here, something profound, give me a break. I'm giving this my best shot—you know that, don't you?

You see I'm not finished yet, right? You know I'm not ready to go.

Katie

"I DON'T *DISAGREE* WITH the program in principle, I just think we need to be wise stewards of the Lord's resources. We might want to give five hundred dollars but are we sure of how—"

"—I really don't see the problem. We're more than ready to fork over money for roof repairs or paving the parking lot. But when it comes to the heart of this church, our young people—"

"Where's the money going to come from? I've got the budget in front of me and I'd like to know which account this five hundred dollars is supposed to come out of!"

"Katie? Do you have any suggestions on that?"

Katie knows nothing about the church budget and has no suggestions. Church board meeting has been going on for two hours. Katie has been tuning much of it out, including the endless wrangling over whether the church auditorium is big enough for the seniors' dinner—last year some of the older folks had difficulty navigating around the tables. They have finally reached item 10 on the agenda, which is Katie's request for funding for a series of youth coffeehouses.

This request has sparked forty minutes of debate. Concerns voiced: Where will the money come from? Will this be effective as an outreach to neighbourhood youth as well as our own? Do we in fact want neighbourhood youth in contact with our own? Will the music played at this event be appropriate? What type of music *is* appropriate and who gets to define that? What can we call it rather than a coffeehouse, since we don't promote the drinking of caffeinated beverages?

Concerns unvoiced, but hanging in the air: can this twenty-two year old girl who has infiltrated their church under the title of Taskforce Youth Worker be trusted? Should her innovative ideas be tenderly nurtured or nipped in the bud? How will the church in High Valley, British Columbia, mold and shape Katie Matthew's desire to serve the Lord in ministry?

She gets two hundred dollars for the Un-Coffeehouse, as the board would like it to be called unless Katie and the young people can come up with something better. Two hundred dollars won't be enough to rent a location outside the church, which Katie would really like to do—partly because it will be easier to get community youth to come if they don't have to come to the small, out of the way Adventist church, but mostly because she knows she'll have more trouble about the music if it's on church property.

Karl wants his band to play at the coffeehouse, and Katie wants him to, even though she personally finds the music of Karl's band about as enjoyable as listening to a cat being run through the dryer. It would be good for Karl. Karl is the grandson of a church member, recently released from a juvenile detention centre and anxious to turn his life around. Getting Karl involved in church and youth group is Katie's biggest personal success since arriving in High Valley in September.

Katie needs a few success stories. After her first year in seminary she decided that a year working taskforce, actually volunteering in the ministry, would be a great foundation for her future career. The church in High Valley had advertised for a student volunteer to assist the pastor, work with the youth, and do outreach in the community.

Doing outreach in the community turns out to mean going door to door distributing literature and attempting to generate "interests," a job Katie hates so much she actually throws up in the mornings before going out to do it. Pastor Boone tells her in his hearty bass voice, "I always tell the young men training for the ministry, learn to do door to door work. If you can get into people's homes, that's where you can really do the Lord's work."

Assisting the pastor means that Katie alternates preaching duties with him, switching back and forth between the High Valley church and an even smaller church thirty miles away. Katie enjoys preaching as much as ever, but the congregation's response can be disconcerting—some members like to criticize, and others agree heartily with things she isn't sure she said.

Working with the youth is the best part of Katie's job description. There are just seven of them, ranging in age from thirteen to nineteen. Several other families in the church have teenagers, but about half of these are away at boarding academy while the other half simply don't attend. Katie's goal is to seek out the latter half and find a way to make the church youth program so appealing and exciting that they won't be able to resist coming.

She teaches youth Sabbath School and plans a weekly Sabbath evening vespers followed by a social at someone's home. The Saturday night get-togethers started out with four regulars. Gradually, and entirely through Katie's tireless efforts, the group has grown. Last Saturday night, in the Boones' downstairs rec room, Katie organized games, popcorn and a video for twelve. She wishes someone, anyone, would come up to her and tell her how wonderful this is.

Instead, she gets pulled aside for a little talk with Mrs. Callahan, who has noticed Karl Philips's interest in her daughter Nina and wonders if anything can be done about this. Yes of course the church is a hospital for sinners, dear, but we also have to think about the well-being of our young saints, don't we?

Katie scores a coup when she arranges to use the gym of the public elementary school as the site for the Un-Coffeehouse. On Sabbath afternoon, as soon as the early winter sun sets, she borrows the car to pick up Karl and his friends and their band equipment and brings them to the gym to set up.

She makes several other trips: to the church to borrow sound equipment; to Tim Horton's for donuts; to the supermarket for pop and paper cups. Her youth group members trickle in between seven and seven-thirty, while the band is doing a sound check. Bobby Szabo puts his hands over his ears. "I don't know if I can stay in the room if they're going to be playing all night," he says.

Katie's not sure she can either, but she hates smug conservative Bobby Szabo so she says, "Broaden your tastes a little, Bobby. Open your mind."

"Have you ever heard of being so open-minded that your brains leaked out?" Bobby says.

Bobby, homeschooled at sixteen, lives to challenge Katie. He's already given her a couple of Bible studies on women's role in the church, and, in preparation for the Un-Coffeehouse, loaned her a book about how rock and roll is the devil's music.

The Un-Coffeehouse is a success. Maybe there really isn't that much to do in High Valley on a Saturday night in January. All the church kids and semi-church kids show up with friends and dates in tow. At the height of the evening, as Katie passes out donuts and root beer, she counts twenty-seven teenagers sitting around the tables. Bobby Szabo stays until ten o'clock, never sitting at a table but hovering in a doorway, hands in pockets, watching. Karl's band plays loudly and forcefully all night, except for a break between sets when they are replaced by taped music. Katie's head is pounding by eleven o'clock, when she closes up.

Pastor Boone arrives with his truck to bring the sound equipment back to the church. Karl's friends leave with their guitars and drums in someone's van. Karl stays behind, along with the Callahan girls, to help Katie mop the floor and stack the tables and chairs.

This was great," Nina Callahan says. "We should do this, like, every Saturday night."

Her sister Georgina is doing little dance moves to the music still playing on Katie's ghetto blaster, using the mop as her partner. "That's right! What's more important than having a place for us and our friends to hang out?"

"You said it," Karl agrees, walking past with a stack of chairs. "Jesus said we needed to bring the gospel to the least of these, you know? And who's the least if not the young people, you know?"

Katie knows, and is thrilled by these kids whose earnestness so reminds her of herself just a couple of years ago. She gives all three a ride home. After dropping the girls off Katie drives Karl to his grandmother's place, which is across town, literally on the wrong side of the tracks, in the same block of government-subsidized row houses where she once handed out Bible-study enrollment cards.

Karl is elated by the success of the evening and keeps talking after Katie has pulled up in front of the house. Katie listens as he talks about how he'd like to start a band playing just Christian music. She gets home about one o'clock to a quiet house and locks the door behind her.

In the morning she comes down for breakfast and finds Pastor Boone sitting alone at the kitchen table with a cup of Postum.

"What time did you get home last night, Katie?"

"Um, I'm not sure. It was after midnight."

"Well, it was already past eleven when I left the school with the sound equipment. I was just wondering what took up all that time."

Dimly, through a Sunday morning sleep-fog, Katie realizes she's in some kind of trouble. "We had to clean up the gym and then I dropped Nina and Georgina and Karl off," she says.

"I've already had a call from Mrs. Callahan. She's very upset about how late her girls got home. It was past midnight, and I quite understand her concern. But according to the time I heard you come in last night, it was well past one when you got in. I'm sure it didn't take you that long to drive Karl downtown and get back."

"I—uh, we talked. Karl sat in the car and talked to me for a little while afterwards." Katie wonders would it be OK to sit down at the table or should she stay standing, like a kid in the principal's office.

"Katie, I've told you before that I'm concerned about that young man and his influence on the other young people. I'm concerned, too, about your relationship with him. I don't think it's appropriate, and it certainly doesn't look good."

Temper flares in Katie, quickly choked and corralled. She plays with a spoon lying on the tablecloth, turning it over and over in her fingers. "I'm trying to *help* Karl, and all anyone else seems to want to do is condemn him." Tears are starting and she fights hard to keep them back. Pastor Boone sees, though, and shakes his head.

"Now, there's no need to get emotional about this. Seeing those teardrops makes me even more sure that you're in over your head here, Katie."

Katie wants to explain that she is actually very mature, and not at all naive or emotional, but it's hard to convince someone of that when you're crying.

There are complaints about the Un-Coffeehouse. The music was inappropriate. "Even some of our own young people didn't feel comfortable with that noise they were playing," Bobby Szabo's father tells Pastor Boone. Nobody comes directly to Katie with their complaints: they go to the pastor, who tells Katie she may plan another Un-Coffeehouse in February, but there will be some restrictions. Karl can't play; the musical choices will have to be approved by Pastor Boone, and there will have to be adults on-site to supervise. "You mean *other* adults," Katie says evenly when the edict is handed down.

"Other adults?" Pastor Boone repeats. "Well, the board members I spoke to thought yes, one or two adults should be present—"

"Other adults," Katie says again. "In addition to me."

She goes on meeting with the youth group, planning another Un-Coffeehouse, listening to Karl. One Sabbath he doesn't show up to church, and Nina Callahan, teary-eyed, tells Katie that Karl hasn't been answering her calls. On Monday night she calls to tell Katie that Karl wasn't in school, and can Katie please find out what's wrong.

The next afternoon Katie walks across town to Karl's house, but finds nobody home. She doesn't want to raise the topic of Karl with Pastor Boone after the talking-to he gave her, but later that night Pastor Boone sits her down for another chat. His face is solemn but it's obvious he's enjoying this, holding this knowledge she doesn't share. "This has been quite a busy few days, Katie. Your young friend Karl Philips was picked up after school Thursday afternoon, by the police. His grandmother called me on Thursday night. She was quite distraught. He was arrested for selling drugs on school property."

Katie feels her heart fall—she knows the feeling well—but says nothing.

"Apparently it's been going on for quite some time. Some of the other young people spoke to me about it. He's been known to have drugs on him at school and at church functions as well. It was only a matter of time." The pastor has been looking out the window but now turns to look at Katie. "I'm sorry. I know you were fond of the young man, you had a lot of faith in him. Misplaced faith, as it turns out."

"I don't understand—why wasn't I told about this? I'm supposed to be the youth worker, I knew Karl better than anyone...."

"Well, perhaps that was the reason why. We didn't feel you had the necessary—distance, from the situation." He puts a hand on her shoulder, much as she did for Karl in the youth room. "I'm sorry you had to experience this, but I think in the long run it will be good for you."

Alone in her room later, Katie tries to think who to call or write to, who might understand. Nola, perhaps. But Nola is in seminary, where Pastoral Counselling and Youth Work are classes, things you can study for and write papers on. Like Katie, she excels at these things. But she might not understand how messy they can be in real life.

What Katie really wants is to jump in the Boones' second car and start driving east, through the mountains, across the prairies, east and east to the ocean, the real ocean. Home. She wants to be home again, though arriving on the lam in the pastor's stolen car might not be the best way to get there.

Katie takes out loose leaf and begins something she hasn't tried in a long time. She starts to write a story, shaping her hurt into words that might make some sense of it. She writes about Karl, not from the perspective of the youth pastor who tried to help him or the teenage girl who loved him and wanted to heal him, but in Karl's own voice, trying to understand how he could turn away from and then back to the life he'd known before.

She fills eight pages of loose leaf on both sides, buoyed by a sense of accomplishment entirely unconnected to any work she might do in the High Valley church. She might even edit it a bit, try to get it published.

It's two a.m. in B.C., nine-thirty in St. John's. She talked to her parents last night and if she calls again tonight they might think something is wrong. Katie dials Liz's number instead.

Loud music plays in the background, but Liz is ready to talk. "I'm just running lines for a play, but I'm by myself," she says. "Some people are supposed to come over later." Liz lives a wonderful bohemian life in a downtown house with half a dozen other people, acting and writing and working as a waitress to pay her modest share of the rent. She's full of news: the theatre group she's working with has workshopped a play she wrote and may produce it in the fall; she won another award for a poem; one of her short stories is going to be in a literary magazine.

Katie tells the story of Karl, thinking how different her life and Liz's are now, how irrelevant her dreams and goals must seem to Liz who never goes to church and has no use for God or religion. *She thinks I'm wasting my life,* Katie thinks.

"Is this really what you want?" Liz asks.

"Is what? To be a pastor?"

"I don't really know about being a pastor," Liz says, "but I'm listening to your voice while you're talking and I'm hearing about the church board and the whiny members and you just sound really tired and discouraged. And the only time there's any life in your voice is when you talked about Karl, about trying to help him. Are you sure the church board and all the rest of the job is really what you want—or is it just Karl?"

"I just want *Karl*? Liz, the boy is seventeen, give me some credit, I'm not a freakin' pervert."

"I don't mean *that*. I don't mean, you *want* Karl, as in him, personally. I mean—you know, the Karls of this world. You've always wanted to help people. Do you still think the pastor thing is, you know, the best way to make that happen? I mean, I'm only asking."

When Katie hangs up she reads her story over again and then slowly tears it up. She thinks about Liz, whose plays are produced, whose stories are published, whose life is moving forward. Katie lies awake, unable to sleep, unable to imagine facing Pastor Boone over the breakfast table. Unable to imagine what comes next.

liz

OUR HOME'S BEEN NOTHING BUT A *playpen. i've been your doll-wife here just as i was papa's doll-child at home....*

[italicize? as if anyone might confuse ibsen's words with mine....]

-no liz no you sound like you're about to give torvald a smack upside the head.

-well i'd like that very much.

-yes liz we know that but the point is what does nora want.

-i'd say she probably wants to smack him upside the head too.

-stop projecting your own feelings on the character. be nora, liz. be nora.

tara the director sits backwards on a straightbacked wooden chair, smoking, scribbling notes in a spiral bound exercise book. lewis is being torvald, wearing jeans and a bauhaus t-shirt incongruous with the square-trimmed beard he has grown for the play. he is impeccably the nineteenth century gentleman hurt betrayed in his own home by his own wife. a plane crashing into the roof of the lspu hall would not make lewis break character.

-let's give it another try.

fifteen minutes later tara calls for a break. we all go outside and smoke. chris bums a smoke and a light off me.

i watch the door for lewis. he won't come out till he's shed torvald like a snakeskin. it takes him longer than it takes the rest of us.

he comes out and sits by me. lights his pipe. the latest affectation since being cast as torvald. any little thing, he says, to help him enter the character.

> *[am i being fair to lewis? on the one hand who gives a shit? on the other hand fr. a literary point of view i owe it to the work not to make him a caricature. unfortunately if i write him true to life he is a caricature]*

-sorry if i screwed up that scene a bit. i would not apologize to tara, would fight for my vision of the character. but in the face of lewis' impeccable torvaldity i know my surface-level reading of nora does not measure up.

> *[torvaldity. torvalditude. i should coin words more often. it's fun!]*

-well i feel you're kind of still finding your way into the character.

-yes that's it that's it exactly. i read her as a twentieth century feminist. i can't get inside her head. a woman who takes it for granted that it's all right for a man to own her, to play with her like a doll. it's like thinking in a foreign language.

next to us tara is talking with chris about the set. the furniture will not do. it is not period.

-i hate period pieces tara says.

-yet you choose ibsen.

-it's a great story. if it were up to me i'd direct it on a black stage with prop boxes.

-well let's do it.

debate ensues. what would they do about costumes then? the elaborate period costumes on the blank stage. would that work.

-you're all friggin insane says marilyn. this thing opens in a week we are not suddenly going to start stripping the stage and putting the actors in one-piece white jumpsuits. it's a friggin period piece live with it.

i relish nora's costume the full skirt the corset-tight waist the feathered hat i put on as i sweep out the door. a guilty pleasure i indulge with secret delight.

we sit and smoke and look down at traffic passing on duckworth street. tara says come on guys let's get back to work and chris says yeah lets get out early i fully intend to go home and get pissed tonight.

-everyone hear that? party at chris' place.

rehearsal finishes at eleven. we reel exhausted to chris' apartment but lewis insists on leaving early.

i lie in bed next to lewis listening to his slow sonorous snore.

[justifiable alliteration? not sure]

a solid blocky man well built for playing torvald the beard looks at home on his sleeping face. he is nearly thirty almost eight years my senior. not a boy but a man.

our bed is a futon on the floor. beside it books are stacked in milk-crate bookcases. empty wine bottles and unframed posters decorate the room. a streetlight shines through the bare window.

unable to sleep i run nora's lines in my head. a woman from another place another time another world. a woman whose husband calls her his doll-wife and yet she feels no need to give him a smack across the face.

i see this woman not in her period home with the nineteenth century settee but standing in a 1980s kitchen her brown hair lit by the glow of the swag lamp, her arms braced a triangle on either side of the sink. her head bowed. are you praying yes you'd better pray. i only ever had one purpose in my life and i failed at it.

[i have recreated this moment and yet i do remember thinking of my mother while onstage playing nora. did i always see the connection or was there a moment like this when i made the link?]

why have i not seen her face in nora's before? it's a trick of the light i see now she was there all along the first time i read the part. A woman locked by faith hope love into a set of choices so narrow they are defined in the light cast by the swag lamp.

can i enter her dark and narrow world enough to bring her voice to life, to give nora her sad passion. afraid afraid afraid. there are hallways we do not want to go down. and let the women keep silence.

the corset laces pull and tighten. i catch my breath. project project to the back row breathe from the diaphragm. fabric rustles over my head around me i am a prisoner in petticoats.

[again with the alliteration]

lewis passes in costume. he is not yet torvald but almost.

i step out on stage and give myself to nora and she gives herself to the audience. i am a nineteenth century norwegian woman who has never heard of gloria steinem or read ms magazine. i am a submissive christian wife who only wants to be a helpmeet to her husband. nora's anger my mother's anger my anger is pushed deep inside.

before all else you're a wife and mother.

i don't believe in that anymore. i believe that before all else i'm a human being no less than you—or at least i ought to try to become one.

-liz that was fantastic you were on fire out there. better than i've ever seen you. tara kisses my cheek she is alight elated.

we get a review. the production is praised tara's direction the lavish period set a whole paragraph on lewis' masterful torvald. one sentence: newcomer liz carter plays a passable nora but lacks the maturity to make the character's anguish believable.

[no imaginative recreation here. i remember every word of my one sentence]

lewis clips the review his good review and pins it to the wall. in our room. in my room.

SEVEN

Jeff

VOICES YELL AROUND ME. *Multiple system trauma! I've got a rhythm but no pulse! Oh shit—hemothorax!*

Debbie's face is beside me. She's holding my hand. Then she lets go. She's moving away—no, I am. They're taking me away from her. I want her next to me. But she stands there smiling at me. Her eyes are locked to mine. As long as I can see her eyes, it's OK.

"Do you, Jeffrey Stephen, take this woman, Debra Elaine, to be your lawfully wedded wife, to have and to hold from this day forward?"

Yes, yes I do. For better, for worse, for richer, for poorer. I looked at Debbie, her face glowing beneath her veil. I couldn't imagine what "for worse" might be like. Poorer I could imagine, sickness I could imagine. But with this woman next to me for the rest of my life, I couldn't really believe that there'd ever be any "worse." It would all be for better and better.

Sappy. I know. But if you can't feel sappy on your wedding day, when can you? And the amazing thing is I feel the same way today. It's the worst day of my life. Maybe the last day of my life. But when Debbie smiles, I'm OK.

We'd been going out for two years and getting married felt right. I hated the wedding fuss as much as most guys do—the tux, the decisions over flowers and invitations and food. But I was happy to put up with it all, just to marry Debbie.

It worked out that a lot of our old friends from home were able to be there—Debbie's sister Lisa, of course, and Dave, and also Liz and Katie, since they were living in Ontario at the time. We got married in Oshawa where Debbie's parents lived. So my wedding was kind of a reunion for the old gang, though since it was my wedding, I didn't get to hang out much.

My parents and my brothers came up a week before the wedding. We did a bunch of family stuff together with the Kimballs, but I tried to avoid situations where I was alone with Dad. I wanted to get through the wedding without any little father-son talks.

No such luck. Right before the wedding, while I waited in the anteroom off the sanctuary, Dad stepped into the room. He came over the adjusted the flower in my buttonhole.

"Are you nervous?" he asked.

"Not really."

Wrong answer. "Marriage is a serious responsibility," he said. "Not something to take lightly."

"I'm not taking it lightly."

"Debbie's a lovely girl—good Christian family. Your mother and I like her a lot. This is a good time to ... well, think about your priorities. Work hard, support your wife, put God first—make us proud of you."

Make us proud of you. Would have killed you, Dad, to say *I'm proud of you?* Just this once.

A noise made us both turn. Dave was in the doorway, my brothers Ed and Larry just behind him. "It's showtime," Dave said.

Dad opened his mouth to say something else, then closed it. He patted my arm and turned to go. Dave came up and straightened my bow-tie. "You look like a dork," he said.

"Thanks, man. I'll do the same for you when your time comes." He was my best man. We weren't that close anymore, really. Our lives were heading in different directions. Dave was drifting around—he'd lived out in Vancouver with me for awhile, then back in Alberta, then Ontario, still living that party-animal life. He seemed stuck in a stage I'd already left. But when I had to choose a best man, I didn't think twice. He was more my brother than Ed and Larry were.

Now he grinned at me. "Might be sooner than you think," he said, and gave me a little push towards the door.

I walked out onto the platform, into the church filled with people, and all I could hear were my dad's words: *Make us proud of you.* What if I couldn't? What if I couldn't make Debbie happy, couldn't succeed at marriage or a career or anything?

Then the music changed, the doors opened, and I saw her on Pastor Kimball's arm. I don't remember a damn thing about her dress or her veil or the flowers. All I remember is that her eyes met mine and my heartbeat slowed to something like normal. The organ music swelled, drowned Dad's voice in my head. Debbie smiled at me.

The ceremony went off without a hitch. We took pictures on the Kingsway campus and went to the Kingsway cafeteria for the reception. There was no dance, of course, just the dinner and speeches. Debbie and I circulated around to the different tables to visit with our guests.

Katie and Liz were at the table with my parents and Debbie's folks—the crowd from home. Katie talked a mile a minute and kept everyone laughing. Liz was quieter than usual. She looked pale, and not that pretty. Strange to remember I once believed I'd marry her.

Dave and Lisa both came over, and we all got talking about old times. "Don't forget," Katie said, "We've still got a vow to keep. We're supposed to all get together next summer, on somebody's twenty-fifth birthday."

"A vow?" Debbie said.

I didn't know what Katie was talking about, but Liz said, "Oh, not all of us. It was just me and Katie, Dave and Jeff–and Julie too, wasn't Julie there?"

"Yeah. All the people with the summer birthdays," Dave remembered. "Weren't we supposed to meet on Signal Hill every five years?"

"We swore an oath," Katie said.

"This is coming back to me," I said. "We made a bunch of promises."

Liz and Katie looked at each other and said, almost in unison, "To be forever young, strong, free, positive, and ... what was the other one?"

We all fumbled around for a second trying to remember. "Outrageous," Katie said finally.

I ticked them off on my fingers and grinned at Debbie. "Well, I'm five for five so far."

"You just got married, you're hardly free anymore," Dave said.

"But you're young and strong," Debbie added.

"And definitely positive," I said, smiling back at her.

Liz leaned forward, holding up her glass of fake wine. "What about outrageous? You got that covered?"

"He will in a few hours," Dave said, and everybody cracked up. I shot my parents a worried glance but even Dad wore a tolerant smile.

Making Love out of Nothing at all

2005

1989

Katie

SEPTEMBER SUN LEAKS THROUGH a hazy yellow-grey sky onto the tiny balcony where Katie lies reading a textbook. Falling asleep over a textbook, to be more accurate. It's hot enough that she considers going down to the pool, one of the major perks of this apartment building.

The screen door opens and Dave comes out on the balcony, leans against the rail. "This is great," he says. "I mean, it's very relaxing, being here."

"Relaxing for you, maybe," says Katie, who has an exam the next day.

"Yeah, maybe a little too relaxing," Dave laughs. "Obviously if I stick around here I'll have to get a job. Can't laze around sleeping late forever. It's a nice change though."

"From life in Alberta?" She hasn't asked, but she knows he had a job and a girlfriend out there. Something must have gone wrong.

"Life in Alberta, life with Tammy. We just—you know, things weren't working out." He shrugs, shifts position to stand leaning over the rail, looking away from her.

A few weeks ago, when Katie had just arrived in London, Ontario, and was looking for a roommate, Dave appeared without warning in the lobby. He said he'd driven eighteen hours straight from Red Deer—"just went to Calgary, hung a left and kept going"—and needed a place to crash.

Dave offers to pay half the rent for as long as he stays there. When friends from church ask who she's living with she says an old friend from home is crashing at her place for a couple of weeks, because otherwise it might seem like they're living together. Katie herself struggles to take it in stride, to feel that it's no big deal that suddenly, after all these years living on the other side of the country, Dave Mitchell is using the same shower she is, eating breakfast at the same kitchen table.

Not that Dave actually eats breakfast. He quickly gets into a routine of staying up late and sleeping in past the time Katie leaves for classes in the morning. Mostly they see each other at suppertime. Katie occasionally cooks a meal, or they go to the Taco Bell conveniently located at the other end of the parking lot below Katie's building.

He hasn't said much about why he's here, why he left Alberta. "You wanna talk about it?" she says now, since this is the closest he's come to the topic.

He turns to grin. "No fair trying to be my counselor."

"Oh well, it was worth a shot."

"I bet you're good at it, though."

Katie lays down the book and joins him at the rail, leaning and looking out. "I think I might be. I hope I am. Social work seems like a better fit than going into the ministry, anyway."

"Yeah. What with you not having the balls for it and everything."

"Shut *up*." But it's true, in both senses, that in the end she didn't have the balls to be a pastor. Katie Matthews, who is no quitter, is a seminary dropout. She's not sure if this is God's Will. It seems less and less likely that God has a roadmap, although she does feel that she and God are on a weird road trip together. He sits behind the wheel but keeps asking her which exits they should take. Not unlike how her mother and father drive on family vacations.

Dave checks his watch. "I'm going to head out for awhile," he says.

"OK." Katie used to say, "Who with?" or "Where are you going?" but she quickly figured out those were questions she wasn't supposed to ask.

Dave doesn't move for awhile; they both stand there watching the yellow seep out of the sky; the grey darken to purple. When he finally goes inside Katie says, without turning around, "Take care."

"See you tomorrow," he says.

Katie invites Liz, recently split from her boyfriend, down from Toronto for Thanksgiving weekend. "We should do something real traditional, like cook a turkey, put on a big Thanksgiving dinner."

"And for whom exactly would this be traditional?" Liz asks. "My family always had that veggie sliced turkey stuff, rolled up around dressing and baked in a pan with gravy. With toothpicks stuck in to hold the veggie slices together."

"Yeah, I think we did that one year. My mom was very excited about Tofurkey when it came along, as I recall. Anyway, I'm not vegetarian at the moment, are you?"

"I think we need to push the envelope on this," Dave says. "Can you make cranberry jelly with real cranberries?"

"You mean, can I personally do it, or is it theoretically possible?" Katie asks.

"I guess that answers that question."

Katie's delighted that Dave is so into the Thanksgiving project. He's been moody since he arrived. Sometimes he talks like he's going to find a job and stay in London; she wonders whether that means staying with her. Would it work as a permanent arrangement? Other times he talks about going on home to St. John's, or back out west. "The truth is I haven't got a friggin clue what I want to do with my life," he says one night as they sit in front of the TV. *Family Ties* is blaring away although neither of them is really watching it.

She looks up from her book. "Maybe this is what you're here for—like a space in time, to figure things out. Maybe this is, you know, where God wants you to be right now."

Dave rolls his eyes. "Well if God's got anything up His sleeve, I wish He'd let me know." He reaches forward to change the channel on the TV. "Why haven't you got a remote? This is such crap, is there anything else on?"

"Turn it off, please. I hate all the Keatons, each one in a special and unique way. You're not even watching it."

"I know, but I like to have some noise in the background. I don't like it quiet."

"Then put on some music."

Dave flicks off the TV and goes over to the stereo. Their tape collections have merged over the past few weeks, though Dave likes to mock Katie's pop-music tastes. Looking at his back while he rummages through the tapes, she thinks of a number of songs she'd like to hear now. *With or Without You.* Cyndi Lauper's *Change of Heart. Misguided Angel,* by the Cowboy Junkies. These are the songs on her internal soundtrack, now that Dave is in the apartment.

He picks up The Smiths. "Not that!" Kate warns him.

"Are you ever going to let me play The Smiths?"

"Sure, when I'm out of the apartment."

"Frankly, Mr. Shankly, I'm disappointed to hear you say there. OK, let's go for the compromise position."

"Surprise, surprise," says Katie. They've been playing the same tape over and over for the past few weeks, one of the few they both agree on.

Dave picks up his guitar and starts picking out a tune, playing along with Paul Simon. Music floods the room, making it warm and full. "I love this album, but I don't get most of the lyrics," she says after a few minutes.

"You analyze them too much. Just enjoy."

"But seriously—Graceland? I mean, I get that it's about pilgrimage, and I guess Graceland is sort of the modern pilgrimage, the whole Elvis-is-God thing, but still ... I don't really understand it."

Dave shakes his head and looks down at his fingers as they fly over the strings. "That's funny. I mean, you have a degree in theology and everything."

"And this is relevant because...?"

Now he laughs, singing along for a line or two. "Katie, it's not Graceland just because of Elvis. It's Graceland because ... you know ... *grace?* And maybe there's a reason to believe, we all will be received in Graceland."

"Oh. Oh yeah." The pieces fall into place and the song with its catchy tune and bouncing bass line is suddenly like an Escher drawing that, seen in a different light, reveals an entirely new picture. "Oh my gosh. That's great. I love it."

"I like it too, even if I don't believe it."

"Don't you?"

Dave looks down at his fingers. Paul Simon sings again that we'll all be received in Graceland. "Not so much, not really," Dave says. The moment is there, open and filled with music, and if the Holy Spirit was going to give her any words this would be a good time. Katie says nothing, and when the song ends Dave puts down the guitar. "Think I'll go out for awhile," he says.

Liz arrives on Friday afternoon. She brings a grocery bag of assorted items that may or may not fit with the traditional Thanksgiving feast: goat cheese, pomegranates, rye bread. A bottle of wine—"You don't mind, do you Katie?" she says. "Just for the dinner."

Katie figures she'd better start learning to be a little more open-minded and says it's OK. She inspects Liz's other offerings. "The bread's not going to keep till Monday," she says. "And really, why should it? We've got two days to get through before Thanksgiving, I'm sure we'll be eating other meals. We can break open the goat cheese and pomegranates anytime."

"Yeah, I'm just in the mood for goat cheese on rye," Liz says. "On the other hand, didn't I pass a Taco Bell on the way in here here?"

They eat take-out burritos and pomegranates on the living room floor. Liz, who's working at a coffee shop in downtown Toronto, says she had an awful time getting the whole weekend off. "I was *this* close to telling them to take the job and shove it," she says. "Which would have been kind of a disaster since I'm having a hard enough time making rent as it is."

"How's your book coming?" Katie asks, knowing that Liz has been working on a collection of poems.

"We will not speak of my book," Liz says, in tones suitable for a funeral. "So, how are things with you, Dave? Did you break up with, what's her name, Tina?"

"Tammy," says Dave. "We will not speak of Tammy."

"Speaking of breaking up—" Katie begins.

"We will not speak of Lewis."

Liz looks more fragile than Katie can remember seeing her before. She's dressed mostly in black with lots of jangly silver jewellery, and her hair is very short. Her face looks pale and thinner than Katie remembers it.

"Lots of fun areas for conversation this weekend," Katie says.

Liz licks grease from her fingers. "So, are you guys going to the Wedding of the Year?"

Dave sits up. "Hell yes. I'm *in* the wedding of the year, which totally blew me away."

"Why? You and Jeff practically came out of the womb together."

"Yeah well. We don't keep in touch that much since I left Vancouver. It was decent of him to ask."

Within the last few weeks they have all received invitations to the wedding of Jeffrey Evans and Debra Kimball, to be held at College Park Church in Oshawa on the 28th of October. "Who has a wedding at the end of October?" Katie wonders. "What are they going to have, a Hallowe'en theme?"

"I've never understood this thing about weddings having themes," Liz says. "I mean, you're getting married, isn't that enough of a theme? Although if I ever get married, I'm going to have a death theme. I think that will be unique."

"It's because of Debbie's family," Dave says, responding to Katie's comment rather than to Liz's. "Apparently trying to co-ordinate their schedules is like landing the planes at Pearson airport. This was the only time they could get everyone together."

They sit around till about nine-thirty talking and finally Liz says, "Does the film festival start tonight?"

The weekend has officially been dubbed the Old St. John's Gang Thanksgiving Turkey Dinner and Film Festival, because everybody's rented a video they think the others should watch. Katie's pick is *The Sure Thing*, because it's funny and John Cusack is sexy. Liz has picked *Chitty Chitty Bang-Bang*, because it's a childhood classic she never got to see, despite having learned all the songs from the record. Also, she says Dick van Dyke in his prime is sexy in a way John Cusack will never be.

Dave says they need something darker to balance the chick flick and the kiddie flick. His choice is *A Clockwork Orange*, but not because anyone in it is sexy.

Three videos for three nights should work out, but Katie doesn't want to watch one on Friday night. "I'm going to go to bed early," she says. "I don't care if you guys watch *A Clockwork Orange* tonight." Having read the book, she's pretty sure the movie's not going to put her in a Sabbath mood.

"Is it OK to smoke out on the balcony?" Liz asks before Katie turns in.

"Dave does."

In her room Katie lies in bed and tries to read Madeleine L'Engle. She pictures Liz and Dave, sitting up late, watching the movie, smoking on the balcony and having some deep conversation. At eleven-thirty, still awake, she puts down the book and puts on her bathrobe. The hall and living room are dark and silent. She goes into the kitchen and looks out onto the balcony. Dave and Liz are both out there; Liz's cigarette is a tiny orange glow in the darkness. Dave sits on the chaise lounge and Liz sits in front of him, leaning back against his chest, his arms loosely tucked around her sides. Katie stands for a minute watching, then turns to go back to bed.

The next morning, Katie pushes that memory away, tries not to dwell on the thought of Liz and Dave together. It's a good weekend. They all stay up late Saturday night talking, sleep late in the morning, eat junk food, watch *The Sure Thing*. On Sunday evening they take a break from watching *Chitty Chitty Bang Bang* to gather round and solemnly observe the turkey, which has been sitting in a sinkful of warm water all day. Liz prods it with a fingertip. "Do we know what it feels like when it's thawed?" she asks.

"Like *flesh*. Soft warm living *flesh*," says Dave.

"I can't believe we're going to eat this tomorrow," Katie says.

Liz has decided the entire turkey procedure should be captured on video. "It'll be like an art film," Liz says. "We can enter it in some short film festival and get rich." She begins on Sunday morning with an extreme close-up of the bird's carcass and shots of Dave and Katie trying to figure out which end is the neck. "Because the cookbook says to put the stuffing in the neck. What happens if you accidentally shove it up the bird's arse?" Katie wonders.

"It won't work. The bird will become constipated and refuse to cook," says Dave.

"This has to be the neck. It's narrow and tapered like ... well, like a neck."

"But it's right between the legs. What does *that* suggest to you?"

Liz is laughing so hard she has trouble holding the camera straight.

Katie makes an arbitrary choice of orifice into which to insert the stuffing. Soon the bird is in the oven and there's cranberry jelly—from scratch—simmering in a pot on the back of the stove while Liz, having handed the camera to Dave, peels potatoes.

By five o'clock they are ready to eat, though first there's an extended video mix of Dave carving the turkey while lip-synching to Weird Al's "Like a Surgeon." It doesn't taste bad; a little dry, but there's gravy. The cranberry jelly is inedible, but the potatoes, carrots and turnip are OK.

Katie leans on her elbows happily and surveys her dining room table as Dave pours wine for Liz and himself and ginger ale for Katie. "See, this is what being single in the modern world is all about," she says. "You don't have to be part of a nuclear family. We create our own families, families of choice, to share the love and warmth of special occasions." She raises her glass.

"And she's the one who's *not* drinking," Dave says.

The very act of explaining how wonderful it is to be single in the modern world plunges Katie into self-doubt. "Jeff's getting married, Julie's having a baby," she says. "Is there something wrong with the three of us? Are we late bloomers, or what?"

Into the pause the follows her words Dave says, "Well, I'm having a baby."

Liz sips her drink. "Call the *National Enquirer* on that one."

"Well no, not me personally. But there's a child, there's going to be a child, that I'm going to be the father of."

"You're what?"

"Tammy. My ex-girlfriend. She's having a baby."

"What? When?" Liz and Katie both lean forward. Katie can't believe Dave has been here nearly a month and hasn't mentioned this little detail.

"I guess it's due in—I don't know for sure, in the winter sometime. January or February, maybe?"

"You knew this before you left?"

Dave looks down at his plate. "That was kind of why I left, I guess. The whole idea—fatherhood, parenthood, freaked me out. I mean, me and Tammy weren't even that serious. And then out of the blue—you know." He looks up and shrugs.

Katie struggles not to say something judgemental, something that will sound churchy and disapproving, but Liz's jaw drops. She stares at Dave. "Your girlfriend told you she was having your baby, and you skipped town? Let me get this straight—you left the woman who was going to have your baby, left her to deal with it by herself."

"Yes. Yes, I did that." Dave looks back at her evenly.

"OK. I just wanted to be sure I heard that correctly." Liz stands up and starts to clear the table, clattering forks and knives against the plates.

They've barely finished dessert when Liz jumps up and starts throwing things into her overnight bag. "I've got to work tomorrow morning, so I need to catch the early train."

Katie drives her to the station: Dave is gone when she returns. Katie looks over the mess of dirty dishes in the kitchen, cuts another slice of cheesecake, and puts *The Sure Thing* back in the VCR.

It's past midnight when Dave comes back in. He stands in the doorway a minute, lit only by the blue light from the TV screen. Katie looks up at him. "Want some more cheesecake?" she says.

"Not at all." Dave sits down heavily next to her on the sofa and leans back, closing his eyes. After a minute he says, "Liz was a little freaked out about the baby thing, eh?"

"I was surprised too. I mean, you never mentioned it."

"Didn't wanna think about it." Dave's words are running together and Katie realizes he's drunk. She doesn't usually see him like this. They have lived in the same four rooms for a month but have kept their lives compartmentalized. Why should she be surprised to learn he's deserted the mother of his child?

"Liz was really mad, wasn't she? Like she was ... disgusted. With me."

"Women look at things differently, I guess," Katie says.

"But not you. You're not—I mean, you don't judge me. You're a good friend, Katie. A good friend when I need a friend."

Katie doesn't know what to say. "I've tried to be...."

"You have been. You're a beautiful woman, Katie." Dave takes her face in his hands, one hand cupping either cheek, and brings it towards his face. There's no mistaking the overpowering smell of alcohol on his breath, which would normally revolt Katie, but right now it just adds to the strangeness of the moment, carrying her on a wave of desire so strong it's almost like nausea. Dave's lips are on hers, for the second time in her life, his mouth as warm and alive as the last time, as in all her dreams.

They kiss until Katie finds herself slipping back on the couch, lying back, Dave leaning forward to lie on top of her. She can feel his heart beating as fast as hers is, against each other's chests. One of his hands traces a line down her neck into the neckline of her blouse, fumbles with a button, slips inside her shirt, inside her bra. Cups her breast for a moment, then moves lower, curving over her belly. Her pulse races in her throat.

Katie is twenty-four, and a virgin. A complete virgin: she's never even had a really close call. She's been planning to save it for marriage but these days she sometimes thinks that marriage is a remote prospect. If Katie never meets the right person, will she be a lifelong virgin, buried in a coffin marked "Returned Unopened," as scandalous great-aunt Martha used to quip about her spinster sister? If Katie's going to lose her virginity, if she has to lose it someday, who else would she want to lose it to but to the person she's been in love with since she was fourteen?

Dave moans her name: *Oh, Katie,* into her hair as his body fits itself to her shape and his hand continues to explore, back up inside her shirt, pushing aside her bra. She slips her own hands under his T-shirt, running them up his smooth warm back, and hears him moan again.

In a swift motion Dave sits up and pulls his shirt over his head. Which is OK, but the next thing he does is unzip his jeans, and that's a mistake.

Because it gives Katie a moment to think, to see clearly: *I'm going to have sex with Dave.* And every neuron in her body is saying *Yes! Yes! Yes!* because she's wanted this so badly, for so long. Until she looks in his flushed and tired face, and her brain, ignoring her body, tells her *No, no, no.* Her heart is undecided, pulled in both directions.

She reaches up to touch his cheek as he moves to kiss her again. "No," she says. Her heart pounds; she wants to erase the words even as she speaks them.

"What? What the hell...?"

Katie wriggles out from under Dave, fastens a token button on her shirt. "I'm sorry," she says. He sits beside her on the couch, rubbing his face, looking not so much upset as dazed. "*I'm* sorry," he said. "I kinda got the message that you wanted ...*"

"I did. I do. But it's not right."

"Oh God. What is it, sin again?"

Katie shakes her head. It's not sin, really, or even the wanton destruction of their friendship. It's nearly having what she wants, and then realizing she doesn't want it like this. Dave—drunk, with the girlfriend, the baby, even whatever he's got going on with Liz—she wants Dave without all that baggage. And she sees, now, that Dave without baggage is something she's never going to get.

She wants to touch his face again, his bare chest. Her palms are hungry for the feel of his skin. But she stands up. "I'm going to bed," she says. "I've got class in the morning."

The next night when she comes home from a late class she finds Dave lying on the couch, watching TV. He's made a start at the dishes; Katie pitches in to finish them, and after awhile Dave comes to join her, picking up a cloth to dry.

"Look, about last night—I'm sorry. I was drunk. And, you know, an idiot."

"It's—OK. It doesn't matter."

She washes and he dries in silence punctuated only by the clinking of cups and silverware. "I won't be around to make an idiot of myself much longer, anyway," Dave says. "I'm going back to Alberta."

"You are?"

"Yeah. I called Tammy today. We talked for a long time. I'm going back to give it another try."

"That's—that's probably the right thing to do."

"Yeah. I mean, I'll stick around till Jeff's wedding, then I'm going to drive back out west."

Katie just nods. She keeps rinsing dishes and putting them in the drain rack, though Dave has stopped drying. He stands there wiping a single long-stemmed glass over and over.

"I'm going to try and do this right," he says finally. "Get married. You know, give the kid a good start and all. Tammy, she—she's made a lot of changes. She quit drinking, she's going to AA, says it really helps." He talks faster and wipes slower. "I never thought I'd have any time for that, self-help groups, all that crap, but I should probably—I think I'm going to give it a try. Since she is." He looks up, finally, at Katie.

"Is that what you think you need?"

"I think so, maybe, yeah."

"Then that's what you should do." She smiles at him, willing warmth into her smile. "And you know—you're always in my prayers. They have a pretty good track record."

"Yeah. They do. Maybe there's a reason to believe."

"We all will be received, in Graceland," Katie finishes, like a liturgy. "And, Dave?"

"Yeah?" His eyes catch hers and they're so full of hope and fear she can hardly look in them.

"That glass is probably about dry by now."

Dave

SO, I SAW BRETT AGAIN TODAY.

Brett, my son. Remember? OK, we'll let that slide. I've probably only mentioned him once or twice. It's weird, isn't it? You know the names of all the people I went to high school with, know all these intimate details about them, yet I've hardly talked about my son and daughter.

Yeah, I know why that is.

I've told you a lot about things I've done, and I'm not particularly proud of them, but I can't say there are that many things I really feel ashamed about. Shame. Not a word we use that much, is it? Except in, like, therapy and shit. But yeah. This is the one thing I'm ashamed of, that I wasn't a good father.

I remember my own dad when I was fourteen, sending me a ticket to fly up to see him in Toronto. Did I tell you that story? This guy who walked out on my mom when I was six, suddenly trying to make everything right with a plane ticket and a three-week visit. I felt nothing for him, nothing. I looked at him and saw this stranger. And now I look at my son and I see the same thing.

I think that's the saddest fucking thing in the world. And yeah, I'm ashamed of it.

My dad? Died ten years ago—just before my mom, in fact. No, he—he was in a car accident. It was quick. We never—I mean, after that time I went to Toronto, I probably only ever saw him two or three more times. He wasn't a part of my life. After Tammy and I split up, well I hoped things would be different with me and my kids. I'd be a different kind of absent dad. But I didn't do any better. I haven't seen Sara—my daughter—in ages. It's Brett who makes the effort sometimes, calls me up when he's going to be in the city, says we should get together.

Oh, I just take him out, you know, to some pizza place or fast-food place. This time we went to a movie afterwards. A movie is good. You don't have to talk much.

He's a good-looking kid, sixteen, tall as I am already, and I know Tammy has a hard time with him. Her husband Bob, he's an all-right guy I guess, but Brett doesn't have much respect for him and they have a rough time at home. You know, the whole "You're not my real dad, you can't tell me what to do," routine.

As for his real dad ... no, he doesn't have much respect for me, either. He sits across the table from me while we're eating and I can see it in his eyes, that he sees this washed-up old drunk, a guy who looks ten years older than he is and takes the bus to meet him because he can't drive anymore. He knows what he's seeing.

I think the problem was, we got off on the wrong foot from the start. Having a kid, starting a family—those were the farthest things from my mind. Tammy and I had been living together, oh, nearly two years by that time, and somehow I was still thinking of this as a temporary arrangement, a short-term fling. Things were still going pretty well for me—I liked the work I was doing, I was playing with the band from time to time, we had enough money to live in a half-decent apartment and have a good supply of booze on hand. My needs were simple. Somewhere down the road, I figured, there was another woman—someone prettier and sexier and smarter than Tammy—but until she came along, Tammy would do.

Then one evening Tammy drops the news in my lap like a gift-wrapped brick. "I'm pregnant," she tells me. "What are we going to do about that?" Great way to put it, eh?

Problem-solving wasn't my number one skill, so after the crying went on for awhile I left Tammy there and went out to a bar and got shitfaced. I met this girl there and went home with her, which was a first for me. I wasn't in love with Tammy or anything but I hadn't bothered to cheat on her before. However, the night she told me she was carrying my child, that seemed like an appropriate time to start sleeping around.

You can see why this whole story is not one I'm particularly proud of.

Yeah, that's how I coped for the next few weeks—maybe it was months. Tammy refused to even consider the idea of an abortion. She was determined she was going to have this baby. Finally one night she caught me with another girl and made a scene in the bar. I went home and packed a couple of suitcases and my guitar and just hit the road.

Funny, isn't it, how often we see me doing that? There's another recurring theme in my story ... Dave runs away to start a new life. Except it's never a new life, it's the same old life some other place. And like some kind of spawning salmon, I just started doing the only thing I knew to do: driving east.

When I got to Ontario, I stopped. Katie and Liz were both living in Ontario at the time, and I got to Katie first, since she was in London. She needed a roommate and she let me crash there as long as I could split the rent. I didn't see it as a permanent place to stay—but then I'd never seen living with Tammy as permanent either, and look where that got me.

Oh no, don't get me wrong. I wasn't "living with" Katie the same way I was living with Tammy. Roommates only. Katie and I were always just friends and on top of that, of course, she was as pure as the driven snow. But she was a good sport and good for a laugh and I always felt—I don't know, kind of safe around her. That faith that I had as a teenager, when I was convinced God actually cared about me and had a plan for my life—well, Katie was the one person I knew who still believed that as an adult. It was kind of fascinating to watch her, just to be around somebody whose life wasn't a total disaster.

She was nosy though, and a real nag, God love her, so I had to kind of revert to adolescence while I stayed with her. You know, going out of the apartment to drink, stashing a bottle of vodka in the closet in my room. But given the living situation I'd just left, crashing at Katie's place was like a vacation.

One weekend while I was there, Liz came down from Toronto. I'd never been as close to Liz as I was to Katie, but that weekend, I don't know, something really clicked between us. I guess I finally gave up thinking of Liz as Jeff's ex-girlfriend and really saw her for herself. And what I saw was someone who was—like me. Not that she had the exact same set of problems I did. But that something in her was hurt or bent or twisted the same way something in me was. Those nights at Katie's place, Katie would go to bed early and Liz and I would sit up and talk, go out on the balcony for a smoke and maybe have a discreet few drinks, and I just felt for the first time that I was with someone who really understood me, you know?

Yeah, OK, she was really hot too. Tiny and dark and very trendy-looking in the way she dressed, sort of artsy, lots of black—that kind of look. As different from Tammy as a girl could be.

So this weekend—it was a long weekend, I think Thanksgiving, and we made a big production of cooking a turkey—I really thought something was going to happen between me and Liz. And then it all fell apart, because like an idiot I told the girls about Tammy and the baby.

I would've expected Katie to be one who disapproved, with her morals and all. But Liz acted like I'd left Tammy and her baby living under a bridge gnawing on crusts of bread or something. Suddenly, it was like she had no time for me.

Fine, I thought. It was a long shot anyway, me and Liz. But she made me feel guilty, and I phoned Tammy to see how things were going.

Tammy surprised me. She told me she'd quit drinking and she was going to AA, and that if I was ever thinking of coming back she'd expect me to do the same.

I said, "You'll be waiting a long time, honey." I mean, who did she think she was? I'd left her, and I hadn't ever said anything about wanting to come back, and now here she was laying down conditions. Wasn't something out of whack there?

No, I didn't go back right then. I hung around in London, waiting for Jeff's wedding which was going to be up in Oshawa. I didn't even know if Jeff and I were still friends after I left Vancouver, but then he called me up to say he was getting married and asked me to stand for him. I was like, "You sure?" and he said, "Gotta have someone from the old gang, b'y."

Anyway, my last couple of weeks in Ontario were kind of a blur. I was calling Tammy, and drinking a lot, and one night— I can't even remember when this was, if it was the weekend of Jeff's wedding or sometime before that—I was so drunk, and so desperate, that I even came on to Katie.

Oh, she set me straight on that, no doubt about it, and I apologized, but I felt embarrassed about it for a long time afterwards. Like I said, she was a really good friend to me when I needed it. In some ways my friendships have turned out to be the most durable things I had.

No, I don't know why that is.

Anyhow, I stood for the wedding, and then I got in my car and headed west again. Back to Tammy and the baby she was having. Back to the prospect of getting sober and going to AA meetings for the rest of my life. I wasn't thrilled about any of this, but I decided it was the right thing to do and I was going to do my duty. Be a man, you know? Driving west again, hoping for another fresh start, another clean slate ... even praying a bit, I guess, because old habits die hard and I still hoped God was going to be there to get me through it.

So when I look at my son now, at this teenage boy who looks so much like me, this kid I hardly know—that all comes back. The way I acted when I found out he was coming into this world. The way I went back to his mother like a man going to face a firing squad. The way I tried, tried the best I could. The way, in the end, I failed.

Tammy? Oh hell yes. Tammy, she'd be one of your success stories. Brett is sixteen, like I said, which means Tammy has been sober sixteen years. Sober, remarried, decent job, did the best she could with my two kids, mostly on her own.

I haven't had a good word to say about that woman in years. She's a forty-year old who tries to dress and do herself up like she's twenty-one, and she's got a mouth and an attitude on her like she'd as soon smack you as look at you, and she is, as I said before, not the sharpest knife in the drawer. But she's done for sixteen years what I never managed to do. I never loved her and I don't even like her much, but by God I've got to admire her.

Or maybe it's just that I envy her. I'd give fucking anything to have those sixteen years back.

liz

I EAT GRAPEFRUIT AT A COUNTER littered with toast crumbs juice-glass circles newspapers cigarette ashes. behind me lewis hums through his morning routine.

he is busy full of energy full of purpose. he has the lead in a play at the bathurst street theatre. his life has a shape, it is definite, with boundaries.

my life is an amoeba. it moves shapeless towards nothing, pseudopodia appearing and then being reabsorbed into the amorphous body of my existence.

>*[the amoeba image was a good idea but it's gotten away from me. grown out of control like that ivy i once had.*
>
>*now i'm using metaphors to analyze my metaphors. i. need. help]*

i have found nothing in the theatre in toronto and after months of looking i remind lewis i never meant to be an actress. what i was supposed to be was a writer.

-so write, he says.

writing means i sleep late. writing means i read a lot, and pace our small living space. i sit at the messy counter with an open exercise book in front of me tapping my pen on the paper, running it up the spiral binding. flip back and read old poems. get bogged down revising an old poem because it is brilliant and i will submit it for publication. read it over and realize it's crap.

writing means i go out and walk the streets, go for coffee, apply for a job at the coffee shop.

i miss my period. i write a poem about fear and babies and death. i say nothing to lewis.

days unroll into weeks. i cross out whole pages in my notebook and write nothing new.

finally the drugstore, the kit, the pee.

[do we need a second description of a pregnancy pee-test? gut feeling says no]

so different now from doing it at 17. no more hiding from parents who disapprove of my sex life. now i hide from a partner who disapproves of my carelessness.

-how could you let this happen liz i think you may have done this deliberately are you trying to sabotage my career.

later he returns repentant. i shouldn't have been so harsh i know this is as much a shock for you as for me. we can take care of this. i'll support you one hundred percent.

-no matter what i choose to do.

-well but well i assumed of course i assumed that you would ...

-of course. but if i decide to keep it, you're still there, one hundred percent.

-liz you have to understand. the idea of family, of parenthood, has no appeal for me. i don't want a child. you don't either if you're being honest.

this month he is playing rosencrantz. he and guildenstern are dead. but i look at him and see torvald helmer, square-cut beard and topcoat with tails. he knows what i want. he will support me one hundred percent as long as i want what he wants me to want.

what do i want. i walk the streets. i cannot see myself raising a child. i cannot see myself giving up a child never knowing what happened to it. i cannot see myself taking a life.

i cannot see myself.

i stop in front of store windows but the girl in the long skirt and gypsy earrings is no-one i recognize.

lewis hovers. time is slipping by liz have you made an appointment have you made a decision do you know do you know what you're going to do.

-if i decide to keep it. what will you do.

-what are you, pro-life all of a sudden? fundamentalist upbringing coming back to bite you on the ass?

[should i take time here to explain adventists not actually as into pro-life scene as most evangelicals? or just allow reader to share lewis' assumptions?]

i sit on the end of the bed watching him undress. springy red hairs cover his chest. a stranger. a man who will leave me if i give birth to his child.

i tell him i'm leaving. i'll look for another place.

-no need. i have some friends who are looking for a housemate. you keep this place.

generous very generous. the act of an honourable man. with lewis gone (where? friends? what friends?) the bedsit closes in like the walls of the trash compactor in *Star Wars*.

[hokey image with the trash compactor but can't think of a better one. surely this is virtually universal for people of my generation anyway]

thanksgiving weekend i take the train to spend the weekend with old friends. katie's apartment is that bright airy space i have needed. i wish i could sleep on her couch forever never need to take a breath or make a choice just curl up safe as a child in the backseat of daddy's car. safe in the arms of jesus safe on his gentle breast.

it's not jesus' arms around me but dave's. dave, old friend, fellow teenage rebel. dave of the long slim guitar fingers and deep haunted eyes. we share a lounge chair on katie's balcony shivering as the evening grows cool. dave's lips brush my hair gentle as leaves drifting to the ground.

katie was crazy for dave all through school and long after. now i watch her watching him, watching us. i want need his touch but she is my oldest friend. i am not that much of a bitch.

i lose myself in laughter and old friendship and hokey videos. i drown in an image of myself in katie's apartment raising my child along with dave who will love me and love my baby. katie will care for us like a benevolent maiden aunt. sheltered and coccooned in such love i will finish my book and birth it as i birth my child into a world of love security acceptance.

[this part makes me laugh. any chance reader might react the same way? i can only hope]

we pull drumsticks from the overcooked turkey. drown it in lumpy gravy and laugh.

dave tells us he left his girlfriend in alberta because she was having his baby and he couldn't handle that whole family scene, man.

the room grows cold a chill spreads over the table congealing the gravy. why did i think this was a safe place. there is no safe place. i look at dave there is nothing in his lovely dark haunted eyes that wasn't in lewis' eyes.

i ride the train back to toronto in darkness. out the windows the urban sprawl the city that never ends slips past me but i see nothing because it is light inside and dark outside. all i see is my face. my own face.

on the sidewalk outside the clinic a woman pushes a pamphlet into my hands. i let it drop but another woman presses closer with a plastic object a misshapen white doll. this is what the baby looks like at twelve weeks see the little fingers see the little toes.

my hands and legs shake but i walk past year blocking out their cries my own cries i walk up the steps. in the glass front door i see the reflection of a young woman alone. i raise my eyes to hers and we nod in recognition.

[am i flogging the reflection image to death here? perhaps delete reference to train window. just need to show that i can see myself again.]

Julie

THE FIRST TIME

I WAS SEVEN MONTHS PREGNANT, walking home across campus on a clear fall evening. My feet kicked through piles of fallen leaves from the red maples that lined the walkways. The undersides of the leaves as they fell were pink and it was like walking on a lovely soft carpet.

I climbed the step to our apartment and let myself in. It was late—I'd just gotten off work. I took two classes & worked half-time as a secretary in the English department. I was tired & my blood pressure was high.

I sat down on the sagging couch and put my feet up on the coffee table, thinking what to have for supper. As usual there wasn't much in the fridge—sometimes ramen noodles were as good as it got. There was a can of Saucettes in the cupboard—I could fry them up and maybe put on some Minute Rice and steam the broccoli that was left in the fridge. OK. I closed my eyes.

I heard Roger at the door & felt my muscles tense, that flutter in my stomach that had nothing to do with the baby kicking. Somewhere over the four years we'd been married I had started to feel nervous every time my husband entered the room, trying to figure out what mood he was in and how I could keep him happy.

He was hardly ever happy that second year at seminary. Classes were hard, money was tight, and my surprise pregnancy had thrown off our plans.

"What's for supper?" First words out of his mouth.

I told him what I had planned and he told me to hurry, he had a meeting at seven.

At supper I mentioned that I'd had a letter from Katie. The old gang was all going to Jeff & Debbie's wedding that weekend—I said something about how nice it would be if we could go.

Roger didn't want to hear about that. He hated any mention of my old friends, and he started talking about how I was always making eyes at other men—that's what he called it—and how I wouldn't be able stay away from Jeff, even if it was Jeff's wedding. He was yelling, calling me a little tramp, and then he crossed the floor and hauled me to my feet & pushed me back against the kitchen counter, right up in my face, yelling. I kept shaking my head, until finally I made the mistake of saying something like please, please get a grip, you don't know what you're saying, you're crazy.

He lost it then, I guess, and hit me across the mouth with the back of his hand. Then he grabbed my hair and pulled my head back, slapped me again across the face, and then punched me right in the stomach. I doubled over with the pain and all I could think of was the baby, the baby, please let the baby be all right.

Roger came back really late that night and sat down on the bed where I was lying awake. He touched my face very gently, I think maybe to see if there was any swelling, anything anyone could see. He told me how sorry he was, how stressed-out he was, how nothing like that would ever happen again.

I took his hand and tried to think what I could say. I think I told him that it was—not OK, because even I knew that was a stupid thing to say, but that I understood how hard things were for him and I would try harder to be a supportive wife. He asked if he could pray with me, ask God to forgive him and pray that we would both do better.

I wrote that last night, getting ready to bring it to group tonight. And I read it out loud in front of everyone. I've never told that story to another living person, and tonight I told it to nine women who are as different from me and each other as nine human beings could be. And every one of them nodded, & had tears in their eyes, & every one of them hugged me afterwards. It's sappy to say it, but yeah. They hugged me like we were sisters.

EIGHT

Jeff

A moment of clarity. Everything white and in perfect focus. No familiar faces. Everyone is masked. A machine beeps.

I want Debbie. I want Mom. I want my boys. No ... not the boys. Not here. Too scary. I'll see them when it's over. I'll hold them in my arms and *I swear God I'll never take another moment for granted, life is precious I'll value every day I have with my wife and kids, my family and friends I will never let another minute slip through my fingers just keep me alive just give me a little more time ...*

" ... a little more time ... Yeah, we'll get it to you by Friday. We just need another day or so ... it's not us, it's the trucking company ... yeah, sorry about the delay."

The hospital room, the masked faces, the machines disappear. I'm in my office at Rocky Mountain Furniture and Appliances. I hated that place. The scarred old wooden desk, the wood-panelled walls. A calendar from ABC Trucking showed June 1992. Debbie was always after me to hang my Business degree up on the office wall. I never did. That would have made the place even more depressing.

A sign on the office door said, "Jeff Evans, Manager." I was the manager of this hellhole. It was the Burger King of the managerial world. I'd been here for three years.

One of the salemen came in with a bunch of purchase orders. A customer showed up to complain that the couch she'd ordered was delivered with the wrong colour cushions. The clock hands crawled towards six p.m.

I pulled open the bottom desk drawer. I had something hidden there that I only resorted to when the job was so dull I couldn't make it through the day.

It wasn't a bottle of whisky or a bunch of pills. It wasn't a screenplay I was secretly writing in hopes of getting famous. It wasn't even a pile of skin magazines.

It was a brochure for a course in real estate sales. Yeah, I had wild fantasies at that point. Fantasies about having a job I didn't hate. I imagined going to bed Sunday night and not wanting to shoot myself because Monday was coming.

The phone rang again while I was turning the pages of the brochure. I pictured myself showing some rich people around a huge mansion on a sunny afternoon. I'd be my own boss and set my own hours. If I was good at it, I could get rich. I'd make as much money as Debbie, anyway. Right now I was making about half as much.

Debbie said she didn't care, but I hated being the failure while she moved up through the ranks, getting promotions, making more money. Oh, and saving lives while she was at it.

At least this was Friday. I'd be home by six-thirty. The hours were regular, that was the good thing about being manager. If I worked in real estate I'd be doing evenings and weekends. I'd be back to working Sabbaths. Debbie worked Sabbaths, but that was OK in everyone's eyes because she was a nurse. Saving lives gets you an exemption from the Sabbath commandment.

I sank down into a brown velour Lazy-Boy, just for a second. I wasn't supposed to sit on the furniture. The door pinged and I shot out of the Lazy-Boy like a BB from a gun.

Good call. The man walking through the door had a leather jacket and a very large mustache. He swaggered in and looked around like he owned the place. His name was Ned Chernipeski, and he owned the place.

He owned about seven or eight businesses. He and his wife drove matching BMWs and had a vacation home in San Diego. I wanted to be Ned Chernipeski. I wanted everything he had. I wanted to learn the secrets of success.

I was about to learn the most important one.

"Jeff, hey, how's it going?" Ned's voice was pointed at me but his eyes were all over the store, taking in the stock, the way we had it displayed, and most of all the empty aisles where the customers weren't.

"A little slow today, Ned, tell you the truth." Never any point putting the best face on things with Ned. He hated optimists. You always had to come clean with him.

"Yeah, it's kinda quiet." He finished scanning the floor, met my eyes, and nodded at my office.

I knew what was coming. Lately every time Ned called or dropped in, he was worried about the sales figures. The store had had a bad year. I was doing my best to keep things in the black but it had been a long time since I'd seen Ned happy.

He pulled out the extra chair in my office and turned it around to sit on it backwards while he talked about how bad sales were. He'd made me lay one of the store employees off a month ago, but that wasn't enough to help. Finally he got to his point.

"I've had an offer on the building and I'm going to sell. It's just not viable." He stood up and put his hands in his pockets. "It's not your fault, Jeff. I mean, I don't blame you. It's a combination of things."

"Yeah. It's, uh—yeah. Just a bit of a shock. When—how much longer do we have?"

"End of the month. We'll have the going-out-of-business sale, of course. Unload some of this shit." He looked out at the showroom floor filled with three-piece living room suites and six-piece dining room tables. His other businesses were restaurants and bars, mostly. "I hate furniture," he added.

"Me too," I admitted.

Ned frowned. I don't think he expected me to say that.

"Big going out of business sale," I repeated. "I'll get right on that, Monday morning."

After he left I sat in my ugly little office. Suddenly it felt like a safe place. Everything there was predictable. I knew what was going to happen when I came in every day. Except for the day the boss came in and told me he was selling my job out from under me.

I put my head down on the desk. I couldn't picture going home and telling my beautiful, successful wife I'd been fired. I couldn't picture explaining this to my parents next time they called. I had no idea what to do next.

All I wanted to was to be successful, to get ahead. *Why isn't that ever enough, God?* I prayed, alone in the manager's office. *I'm doing my best. Why isn't that enough for you?*

Now darkness closes in and I wonder: *Did I do enough? Try hard enough?* I want to go back to my life, to my wife and kids, to my family and friends. If I can't do that, let me go on so I'll know everything, know the truth, once and for all.

Just don't leave me hanging here in limbo.

Time after Time

2005

1992

Dave

HEY, HOW'S IT GOING?

Not bad, not bad. Just got off work, got something coming up tonight I'm looking forward to— another gig with the guys in the band. Feels good to be playing again. I know I'm a little rusty, but they don't seem to mind.

So, let's see, where were we? Right, I was telling you about when Brett was born, how I quit drinking and moved back with Tammy. We got married in a civil ceremony, very quiet, no fuss— Jeff came out and stood for me like I'd done for him a couple of months before, and I settled into trying to be a good husband and father. Started going to AA, even though I have to say I thought a lot of what went on there was bullshit. I kept at it, though, because I knew this time I had to—

What? What do you mean you don't want to hear about this? What the hell are we here for if not to talk about my life?

My life *now*? Look, sweetheart, I give you an update on that every week. You know what I'm doing; I told you five minutes ago. I'm sorry, but there just ain't that much more to tell.

Isn't this what you people are supposed to do? Dig into the past, figure out the root causes of my problems, find out why I'm so fucked up? No, I'm not interested in your bloody here and now focus. Here and now is pretty straightforward, honey. I'm trying to dry out, I'm hating every minute of it, but I'm doing it. End of story. I go to a fucking AA meeting every other day if not every fucking day. The only reason I'm seeing you on top of all that is because I want to make it *work* this time, I actually find that I want to go on living, which I won't do if I start drinking again. So I have to figure out why I've always screwed up in the past and how I can avoid doing it again. That's what you're here for, that's your function on earth, to help me figure this shit out, so don't tell me you're not interested in hearing my stories!

No I don't want to bloody calm down!

Oh, God. Jesus, I'm sorry about that. Look, I shouldn't have— I'm sorry I lost it, sorry I yelled at you. I can be an asshole. I've been told.

No, let's just forget it. I lost my temper, I shouted, I'm sorry. Can we just move past it? I don't want to pick it apart, analyze why I got angry or what it says.

Pretty damn persistent aren't you? OK ... OK, look, I'll try. But I just want to say that I'd rather be telling you a story.

I think ... I guess I got mad because I'm giving you the best I've got, and you're telling me it's not good enough. All I have is my past, all I have are these stories. And I'm convinced that somehow if I tell them to you, if we take them apart and put them back together, there's some magic key I'm going to find, something that's going to make me go, "Aha! That's why I've always screwed up! That's why I can't stay sober." And when I have that key, then like magic it'll fit into the lock and everything will change. Things will get easier.

Right now they're very hard.

Yeah. Fair enough ... I guess it is easier to talk about an AA meeting I went to fifteen years ago than the one went to yesterday. OK, maybe you have a point. Half a point.

But I've still gotta argue that the past is relevant. I mean, isn't that the way it works in the movies? A guy goes to see a shrink because his life is all screwed up and for three or four sessions they bullshit about stuff and finally the guy breaks down and tells the shrink the story of the time his father strangled the kitten with his bare hands in front of the kid's eyes ... and that's it. The guy breaks down and starts to cry, and he understands this is why his life has always been screwed up, and then he's better. He can go forth and conquer. He's got the key.

No—to the best of my knowledge I've never watched anyone strangle a kitten. It was an example, I pulled it out of thin air. I'm just trying to make a point here, that there's always supposed to be some—some *thing*, what d'you call it? Some trauma, in your past, that explains why your life's been the way it is. I tell you stories because I'm hoping one day we'll hit the one that will make me break down snotting and bawling and suddenly everything will be clear.

What? Yes of course I bloody use sarcasm as a defense mechanism, do you think you're supposed to get points for observing that? Geez, I've been doing that since I was twelve.

OK ... so I'll try and make a connection here. I've been thinking about AA, about the time Brett was born and I started going to meetings, because I was at a couple of meetings this week, and I think I'm sort of hung up on a couple of the steps, on the fourth and fifth steps. I've been thinking about this ever since I saw Brett last week.

It just seems like too much, you know? The idea of a fearless moral inventory, much less making amends for the damage I've caused. Sometimes the damage has just gone too far, you know? What kind of amends could I ever make to my son, my daughter, my ex-wife? At this point?

Back then, it seemed simpler. I didn't mind AA too much. I mean, it pissed me off sometimes— then and now—but I guess it was a good fit for me because it was so much like church.

Some of the people at the meetings I go to, around here, they have a big problem with the concept of the Higher Power, because they threw out the whole idea of God a long time ago. So they have to do a lot of fancy footwork to come up with a Higher Power they can live with. For some people it's the Universe or the Great Spirit or the Goddess—that goddess shit reminds me of Liz, that's stuff she gets on with. Or if they're total atheists, maybe their Higher Power is their True Self, or the spirit of support and love that they find in the group ... whatever. I mean, I'm not knockin' it. Whatever the hell works for you, whatever gets you through the night, that's a good thing, I guess.

But for me, there was never any scrambling around trying to find a Higher Power. My Higher Power was the same God I gave my heart to when I was fifteen. I felt such guilt because I let Him down, and such anger because He let me down. I've struggled with God over the years, like Jacob wrestling with the angel, but there's never been any question about Him being there.

So AA made sense to me. God was there, and you had to rely on Him just like they told you in church. Leaning on the everlasting arms. And you had to be sorry for your sins and try hard to do right. And that was me those couple of years after Brett was born—trying hard to do right. To make amends.

No, that's the thing, I didn't really make amends. I did try to be a half-decent dad to Brett. He was a cute little thing, especially when he was a toddler. I'd do the stereotypical stuff, ride around with him up on my shoulders, fly him through the air like an airplane, shit like that. It seems pathetic to me now, to think that was what I thought being a father was all about.

Tammy? We still weren't getting along. Maybe even less than we ever had before. Now that we weren't drinking anymore, we had absolutely nothing in common. Tammy wasn't particularly interesting before, but she was downright moronic when she was sober.

I'm sorry, yes, I am doing it again. I'm obsessing about the past. Is there a connection in there to what I'm feeling now? Hell yes. I don't need you to make the links for me. Of course I'm scared— I've always been scared that if I stopped drinking no-one would find me interesting or witty or whatever. The problem with that, of course, is that once you get to a certain point with drinking, like say the point where you're passed out on somebody else's bathroom floor with your face in a pool of your own vomit—then you're not so much witty or interesting anyway. So it's kind of a lose-lose situation.

You what? Well, thanks. That's ... good to know. And you know, you've only ever seen me sober, so if you think I'm funny and smart, then, who knows, there's hope yet.

It's just—God, it's just so frightening, you know. That thing about having replacement addictions, I don't think I'm doing that this time. There really isn't anything else that absorbing in my life. Just life itself. That's what makes it all so frightening.

What's frightening, specifically? Well, you take women as an example. Remember I told you once I'd never had sex when I was sober? I realized after I told you that it wasn't the literal truth. I was sober for nearly two years after I first got married, so obviously I've done it. A few times.

Yeah, literally, just a few. It was never what you'd call a great marriage, and once we both quit drinking and Brett came along—I mean, the times we did have sex, I sort of—I don't know. Distanced myself. Like I was never really there. I don't know how to be—intimate, I guess you'd call it.

But we stumbled along, and the only thing in my life I was at all happy about was my music, the band I was playing with, and they were about to go on tour. It might have been our big break. Then Tammy hit me with the news. Apparently one of those few times we managed to sleep together had hit the jackpot, and she was pregnant again. She didn't want me to go on tour; she wanted me to stick around with her and Brett and the baby.

The other guys in the band were all single, no family concerns tying them down, and did I ever envy them. But in the end, I stayed. They replaced me and went without me. I guess the real shitty fairy-tale ending would be if they'd hit it big and become some enormously popular band that you'd instantly recognize the name of. That didn't happen—but they had a pretty good run, all the same.

How'd I feel? Pissed. I stayed. I did the responsible thing. But I cut myself a deal. Since I'd given up this dream, this thing I wanted so much, I would reward myself. I'd allow myself to start drinking again—but only moderately. A couple of drinks after work in the evening.

So yeah. I'm mired in the past, I'd rather tell you stories than take a cold hard look at myself as I am today and try to make some progress with that. But isn't there something I can learn from this story? From all the stories.

OK, I'll take a shot at it. The first time I quit drinking, back in university, I guess I did it for God. And when He didn't come through and make everything easy for me, I started again. The second time, I did it for Tammy, for my kids, my family. And when that didn't turn out to be all rewarding and good, I drank again. So now I ask myself: what am I doing this before? I've been sober since the fifteenth of August—what is this, the first of November?—with one brief lapse, as I'm sure you'll recall. What's driving me this time?

The easiest answer is that I'm doing it because of my health—like I told you, after what happened to Jeff, I realized maybe I wanted to go on living, and it's been made pretty damn clear to me that if I keep drinking I won't be doing that. But let's say, now, tomorrow I were to go to the doctor and get diagnosed with some shit—cancer or something. Would I say, OK, that's it, I'm dying anyway so I may as well have a drink? Jesus, I hope not. But it just goes to show, doesn't it? That no reason I have for quitting will ever be good enough. If I want a loophole, a way out, I can always find one.

No, I don't, not right now. Like I said, my life is weird now, scary and boring at the same time, but it's a hell of a lot better than what I had before. It's just the fear of the future that's getting me, I guess.

Right, right, one day at a time. I should get a bumper sticker.

Here's what really scares me, though. Maybe here's why I keep going over the past, why I'm afraid to stop talking about it. I'm absolutely shitbaked that someday I'm going to run through all my stories, I'll have uncovered everything, and there'll be no magic moment. I won't break down in. I'll have the whole story out there, my whole sordid past, and I'll be just as fucked-up as I've always been. I'm scared to discover that it really is just one day at a time, and it never gets any better or easier. I'm scared of finding out there really is no magic key.

liz

COFFEE SHOP SMOKY WITH cigarettes cappucino lust and ambition. in one corner a mike stand and podium.

[mike? mic? i always see it spelled mic but in my head i say mick when i see that. i will spell it mike. it's my book]

the well-known novelist has finished reading a chapter from his work in progress. a lesser known, emerging writer is paired with the well-known novelist for this reading. well-known writer is there to ensure people will actually come out.

they have come. they crowd around the tables eyes hungry for a glimpse of the novelist ears open for his witticisms. now finished he sits down at a table full of his friends.

and now folks let's welcome an award winning poet whose poetry has appeared in grain tickleace dandelion quarry all the way from the far east coast to the far west with a short stop in toronto on the way but we can forgive her for that can't we heh heh heh here's emerging artist liz carter.

[i like "grain tickleace dandelion quarry." like mythical horny four-headed beast of revelation, only four-headed beast of Canadian 1990s lit mags]

i emerge.

my hands shake my lips are dry. this is not my first poetry reading i have read at home in st. john's and often in toronto but this is my first time baring myself before the vancouver arts community. a little fresh meat folks.

five poems. my five best or at least those most agonized over most tortured. the lines sound amateur and drop on the audience with all the resonance of dinner plates shattering. people stop whispering and talk out loud abandoning all pretense of politeness. the well known novelist guffaws out loud at a comment from one of his confreres.

[guffaw? confreres? can i really use these words? why would i?]

anger flares ignites my voice gives a poem about loss and abandonment an energy it did not originally possess. the novelist looks up with mild interest. fifth poem finished i stumble away from the podium blind deaf dumb. i have come too far west i have passed the point of no return i need to go home wherever home is.

the novelist turns as i pass his table. hey lisa it's lisa isn't it?

-liz.

-liz right liz. great reading loved that last poem you've got great energy there.

-thanks. another step almost past but i can't keep it shut. of course i needed a certain amount of energy to be heard over the rude assholes laughing at the table in front.

[can't remember what I actually said but wish it had been as witty as this]

walk away. don't look back. nice exit liz. the evening is redeemed. how i love to proclaim it.

he stops by my table before leaving. i sit with andrea and her partner teresa my first lesbian friends. my only vancouver friends so far. andrea is a writer teresa an actress both know the famous novelist enough to say hello.

-andrea, teresa, hi. lisa, you're a bit of a bitch but i've gotta say you were right. i was an asshole. if someone had done that to me at my first reading i would have been scarred for life and i wouldn't have told them off either.

-liz. it's liz. and it wasn't my first reading. i read at harbourfront in toronto perhaps you've heard of it.

-shit you are one tough cookie aren't you?

-that's the way this cookie crumbles. i can't decide if this line is witty or disastrous but it's out of my mouth before i can analyze it.

-since i seem to have difficulty remembering your name is it all right if i call you cookie.

-it is not at all all right.

-liz then.

-yes.

three weeks later after two chance meetings three let's go for drinks two meet me for coffees one dinner and a play the well-known novelist sits astride me naked on the futon in my room. he is in his early forties well built still slim red hair good in bed. self-absorbed irritable and happily married but you can't have it all in one tidy package.

[readers -- should such exist -- probably finding parade of my lovers indistinguishable. artsy self-absorbed pricks. if accused of lacking originality i can only plead that art imitates life]

i make friends. his friends. writing friends artist friends separate from the circle of friends he shares with his wife his high school sweetheart a tax attorney. two children both in junior high. people tell me he will never leave his wife.

-will you ever leave your wife?

i whisper it in his ear after lovemaking. we are outdoors on the beach at midsummer a hot july night a secluded sleeping bag. we have been together six months. he is revising his novel i am writing poems with feverish energy a pile of paper growing beside my newly acquired computer.

waves rush onto the surf i taste salt sweat on his face as i lick the words into his ear. he pretends not to hear.

we lie side by side in the dark. let me tell you a story he says.

it's a story as familiar as a good date movie. boy meets girl in law school. they fall in love and marry. boy quits promising law career to write great canadian novel. friends and family scoff and shake their heads but girl stands by her man and goes to work the hard daily grind while he churns out page after page and eventually after years of struggle stress and self-doubt his novel is published to huge acclaim.

-and you tell me this story to inform me that you stay with your wife out of gratitude.

-no. for gratitude i send someone a large bouquet of flowers. perhaps a bottle of wine. what i'm trying to tell you is that a marriage is something other than love other than romance. it's about being connected in a much more profound way. i'm passionately in love with you liz. i want to have sex with you all the time. because i'm hot for you, does my sister stop being my sister? does my brother stop being my brother?

> *[incredible as it may seem this line of reasoning quoted almost directly from the man himself.]*

-uh no.

-exactly. and my wife does not stop being my wife.

-i'm sorry i'm missing something here.

-i need you. i couldn't live without you. but it doesn't change the fact that i am related to margery in a very deep way as much as if by blood.

-and margery understands all this does she?

-margery allows me a certain amount of space she understands what is necessary for the creative process.

> *[should i name him? make it a roman a clef so everyone will guess which canadian novelist i slept with?]*

passion sex anger hurt fuel my pen and i write write write into the early morning hours and rise after a brief sleep to pour coffee for commuters. i am in love i am betrayed i am angry i am in esctasy i am coming alive.

Katie

KATIE RUNS DOWN THE STEPS, pulling her jacket on. Her breath makes soft white puffs in the night air as she hurries toward her subway station.

It's nine o'clock. Katie allegedly works nine to five. There never seem to be enough hours in the day: she spent most of today in her office with a suicidal sixteen-year-old sex worker. After finally leaving the girl temporarily safe at the shelter Katie sat down to face the pile of paperwork she'd neglected all day. At seven-thirty she finished writing the proposal she needs ready for tomorrow's meeting, took a little time to tidy off her desk, and figured she could be home by nine-thirty.

Katie isn't crazy about walking alone in downtown Toronto after dark and is anxious to get back to the relative safety of her apartment in Scarborough. She walks with her eyes fixed straight in front of her, trying not to make eye contact with any passersby.

Then, just before she goes down the steps to the subway station, she sees a boy sitting on the concrete step of a store. A familiar boy: it's Scott, who sometimes stays at the shelter.

"Hey, Scott," she calls. He looks up, trying to focus on her. He's high, of course. Katie goes over and sits down next to him. He's wearing a short-sleeved T-shirt and faded jeans although it's a couple of degrees below zero tonight.

"Hey, Katie." He looks up at her, his eyes dark in his white face under spikes of dark hair.

"You got anything warmer than that to put on?"

Scott shakes his head.

"Where you staying tonight?"

"Don't know." He looks at her. "Can I go to the shelter?"

"Shelter's full tonight."

"Shit." Scott kicks at a Coke can on the sidewalk.

"You gotta go somewhere, Scott. You'll freeze to death out here."

"Can I come to your place?"

Katie laughs. "No, Scott, you cannot come to my place. But maybe I can help you find a place. Got any friends you can stay with? What about your cousin?"

"Kicked out," Scott says. He leans back against the wall of the building, closing his eyes. "I could hold up a store and get in the lock-up for the night."

"Yeah ... let's try to find a better option. Come on, you want a coffee or something? Have you had anything to eat?" She ends up taking the boy to a sandwich shop, buying them each a sub and coffee, walking with him through the dark and crowded streets. Oddly, she feels less nervous this way, walking a teenage drug addict like a German Shepherd. And Scott is not bad company; funnier when he's not high, but still amusing when he is. He comes from Cape Breton: somewhere in the Highlands there's a mother crying her eyes out over her troubled youngest son lost in the big city. Oh where is my wandering boy tonight. At twenty-seven Katie is far too young to be feeling maternal about a seventeen-year-old—isn't she?

She gets Scott into a shelter for adult men: they don't really want him, but the director owes Katie a few favours. "Hey, thanks Katie," Scott says.

"No problem, Scott. It's my job."

She gets on the subway at King and begins the long ride north. At College the hockey fans flood the car, leaving the game at Maple Leaf Gardens. Katie gets off with a small crowd at Shepherd and finds her car in the parking lot.

As she unlocks the door to her apartment and steps inside she remembers Scott's comment—"Can I come home with you?" and her own laughing refusal. There was a time when she probably would have been just naive enough to invite a homeless teenage junkie into her house. She may not now be the queen of boundary setting, but she's learned a few things.

Her kids—as she sometimes calls her teenage clients — prey on Katie's mind as she lies in bed. Cheryl. Felicity. Scott. Scott most of all, perhaps because he's the most recent. But there's no denying it; while she works well with young women, Katie's real interest is screwed up teenage boys—always has been. Only, these days it's a professional interest rather than a personal one.

She guesses that on some level every disturbed young boy she's ever worked with is some kind of substitute for Dave Mitchell. Is she trying to save them the way she always tried to save him? The real life Dave is, by his own account, doing fine now: living in Alberta with his wife and child and another baby on the way, working, playing in a band, getting on with his life. he thinks briefly of her old friends, all out west, all farther from home than she is. Will they ever meet again on Signal Hill to keep the old vow?

God, please be with Scott tonight, she prays before sleeping. *Please be with Cheryl. Keep them safe—long enough for them to get better, long enough for someone to help them. Help me to help them. Help me know if I'm doing the right thing.* The differences she's able to make in her clients' lives seem minuscule. She's dreamed of boys like Scott, dreamed of rescuing them from the street, helping them kick their addictions and finish school and find meaning in life. Instead, she's given Scott coffee and a sandwich and helped him find a room on a cold night. Tomorrow he'll get up and leave the shelter and go down Yonge Street and panhandle enough cash to buy crack and get high again. Katie loves the hands-on practicality of her work, but there's a certain hamster-wheel futility about it at times.

By four o'clock on Friday— the one day she never works late—she's more than ready for a Sabbath rest. She's also ready for the company of someone other than troubled teens and the sometimes troubling adults who work with them. After work she showers, changes into a skirt and sweater, and goes to Vespers.

At Vespers her friend Brenda, a nurse at the Branson, asks, "Have you seen the new guy?"

"Who? Where?" Katie says, her head going into an exaggerated swivel, nostrils flaring. Brenda giggles and pushes her back into her seat. "He just started coming to church. Came in during the crusade."

"Oh." Katie sits back. She hasn't been involved in the evangelistic crusade her church has just finished, since several things about public evangelism make her a little queasy, and she's automatically suspicious of any guy who would have joined the church during a crusade. This is, after all, a person who must have been attracted by promotional advertising showing luridly coloured Beasts of Revelation, someone perhaps a bit needy and unbalanced, potentially fanatical.

"Is he cute?" she asks, as an afterthought.

Brenda shrugs. "Not my type. A little too skinny and white for me. But he's from down east, like you."

"How old?"

"Not sure. Thirty-ish?"

"Divorced or never married?"

"Hmm. Don't know."

"What does he do?"

"Something manual. Carpenter? Something like that."

"Oh." The new guy, all in all, doesn't sound like much of a catch, though the bit about him being from "down east" might make him worth checking out. *Who am I kidding?* Katie thinks. She'll check him out. They all will. She and Brenda are two of about five mid-twenties single women in their large Adventist church. They vary in racial background, career path, interests, personality. They are united in their disgust at the lack of single Adventist males in the city and the smug conceit of the few they do meet. The sheer weight of demographics means these guys can afford to be cocky.

Word of a new man on the scene—someone who's recently joined the church or moved to the city, even a recent divorcee—spreads quickly through the network. Once, Brenda and Katie drove all the way to Oshawa on Sabbath morning with their friend Shari just because Shari said there was a new guy at College Park church who was kind of cute.

"Ooh, he's there, there he is," Brenda says, digging Katie in the ribs.

"Be quiet," Katie hisses. A musical group sings softly at the front of the church. "I'm here to welcome the Sabbath and meditate on the love of God, not check out guys .... Where's he sitting?"

"Two rows back, on the right."

When they stand for the opening song Katie turns carefully back to drape her coat over the seat behind her and spots the unfamiliar face. Not a stud by any means, but not bad either. A little skinny and white, as Brenda says, but Katie doesn't mind either of those things.

As they thread their way over to him after the service Katie says, "Brenda, this poor guy. He's got to know we're circling him like vultures. Anyway, he's probably got a girlfriend."

"He had one, but she broke up with him when he joined the church," Brenda whispers. "Mrs. Eliot told me."

"Oh good, so he's on the rebound too. This gets better and better."

Face to face with Sam Patey, Katie needs to hear no more than his warm pleasant "Hi, nice to meetcha," to realize the truth.

"You're a Newfoundlander," she says. "Where from?"

"Mount Pearl. But my mother's people are from Trinity Bay."

"I grew up in St. John's."

"Really? What school did you go to?"

"The Seventh-day Adventist school."

"Oh right, sure, of course. I went to Mount Pearl Senior High."

"Did you ever know Craig Hussey? His sister Stephanie went to our school."

"Hussey, Hussey ... I knew a bunch of Husseys. Did he play hockey?"

"I think so, yeah." Brenda steps quietly back into the shadows, mission accomplished as Katie and Sam fall into the time-honoured Newfoundland pastime of tracking, sorting out mutual acquaintances and common ground. The next day after church, he sits with her at potluck.

"Not bad," she tells Brenda later on the phone. "He asked me to dinner and a movie."

"A movie's good," Brenda says. "You know he's not *too* conservative."

"He seems nice," Katie says. "But I could never marry him. Think about it -- Katie Patey? That's never going to happen."

Sam's story unfolds over the first few evenings they spend together, simply and without angst. He grew up going to the Salvation Army, drifted away from it as a teenager, always had an interest in the Bible. Came across the flyer for the Adventist meetings, went to them, studied his Bible, decided this made sense. He works as a contractor, working for another guy now but eventually hopes to go into business for himself. Makes decent money, enough to live on—his needs are simple, he says.

He's twenty-nine but looks a little older, his sandy hair thinning on top. He has a boyish enthusiasm for model planes and Monty Python; he comes to Katie's apartment and cooks lasagna. "Sounds too good to be true," Liz says, when Katie phones to tell her about Sam.

"Yeah, I'm pretty sure he's actually a serial killer with a closetful of dead ex-girlfriends."

"Been over to his place? Anything smell funny?"

"Yeah, I've been there—classic bachelor chic. It's not a dump, it just doesn't look comfortable. Oh, and he has a collection of pylons."

"Pylons?"

"You know, the orange traffic cones? He collects them from all over, places he's visited. They're in the living room."

"Sounds harmless enough. Unless of course each one marks the spot where he murdered someone."

"Yeah, there is that. But you know, Liz? I keep waiting for him to open up, to reveal his dark side. And I'm starting to suspect that maybe he hasn't got a dark side."

"And this is a problem because...? Are you saying he's boring?"

"No, he's not boring. He's got a good sense of humour, he's smart, he's fun to be around. But I keep waiting for a glimpse of his tormented soul, his inner anguish. What if he hasn't got any?"

"Would that be so bad?"

One Sunday morning in spring Katie wakes up early despite putting in an evening shift at the shelter the night before. There was a fight at the shelter last night and they'd ended up calling the police. Katie got home late and slept badly.

Sam is picking her up for a day's visit to Niagara-on-the-Lake. Eating her usual bowl of Raisin Bran she realizes her stomach is queasy and puts it down to lack of sleep. By the time Sam arrives there's no doubt she feels nauseated. Well, at least there's no worry that she might be pregnant, seeing as how the question of sleeping together hasn't even arisen yet. Still, Katie doesn't like the prospect of having a day trip ruined by her weak stomach.

"We don't have to go. I'd be OK with staying home, going another day," Sam says.

"No, I've got stuff going on every weekend for the next month. We're never going to get a day as good as today, and the weather's perfect. I'll be fine. I'm sure I'll be fine."

Sam rummages around in her kitchen cupboards. "Have you got any plastic bags?"

"Under the sink. Why?"

"We may need them."

They arrive in Niagara-on-the-Lake late in the morning as the sun is bursting forth in its full brilliance from the sky, and as they walk hand in hand down the main street Katie is glad she came.

After three months of dating, Katie's and Sam's relationship is at an impasse. Sam would like it to be more serious: he says he loves her. Katie likes him but tells him she needs time. Somewhere, she thinks, there will be a moment. He'll share some dark secret with her, and she'll know that he needs her. A song will play, a bird will sing, small pieces of paper will flutter down from the sky with "Marry Sam Patey" written on them in divine calligraphy.

"Oooh, let's go in there," Katie says, pointing at a shop that sells hand-knit sweaters. "I want to try a—oh my...."

"You OK?" Sam says quickly.

"Yes, I'm—no, no I'm not—quick, where's the plastic bag?"

With commendable efficiency Sam hands her the bag and Katie runs a few feet away as she begins to retch. She turns her back to the sidewalk, hoping people won't stop and gaze at the young woman throwing up into a Loblaw's bag. She heaves and heaves, bringing up the all-too-recognizable Raisin Bran, and barely notices cool hands touching her hot sweaty face.

Sam stands behind her, holding her hair back in a makeshift ponytail. He lets go as Katie stops throwing up. She wipes her face with a Kleenex and leans back against the wall of the nearest building. How hideously unromantic. "Must be—some kind of stomach bug or something," she apologizes. "Sorry."

"Could be," Sam says, ignoring the apology. "One of the guys I work with had one of those twenty-four hour stomach things last week. Here, give me that." He reaches for the Loblaw's bag. Katie's eyes widen. "What for?"

Sam grins. "Going to throw it in the garbage, what else? I'll be right back."

Katie watches him as he walks down the pretty tree-lined sidewalk, this unremarkable young man in jeans and a polo shirt, a bald spot starting to show on the back of his head. This man, on a fine spring day, walking down the road carrying a bag of vomit—of *her* vomit. Nothing remotely like this has ever happened to her on a date before.

In a flash Katie, still shaky and a bit sick, can see years into the future: she sees hospital birthing rooms and dirty diapers and sick kids and dead pets. She sees someone who can deal with all that, someone who will be there for her. Who will be there.

"Let's find a place where you can sit down for awhile," says Sam, back from the garbage can.

"That sounds good," Katie says.

Julie

JUST GOT OFF THE PHONE FROM *talking to Kyle—poor kid. He's trying to make up his mind where to spend Christmas: with me or with Roger. No fifteen-year-old should have to make that choice.*

I'm trying not to push him one way or another. This must be awful for him—it must seem like I planned to leave Roger as soon as Kyle's back was turned. Of course, it wasn't that way at all. But it was easier, once Kyle went to Kingsway.

Kyle's always been close to his dad. I can't say Roger was a bad father. Is it wrong to shatter his son's image of Wonderful Daddy? But I miss Kyle so much—and besides, I don't want him spending any more of his time with Roger, looking up to Roger, learning to be like Roger.

When Kyle got off the phone I was shaking. I needed to talk to someone. But who? I hate to burden Mom—she's so frail these days. I should be supporting her, not unloading on her. Katie—my tower of strength—wasn't home when I called.

Then I thought of the girls in my group. I know should say the women, not girls, but so many of them seem like girls to me, so young to have been through so much. We are so different—but I realized last meeting when I read that piece about the first time Roger hit me—we're closer than I ever thought possible. I wanted to be sitting around the table in that shabby little room with Michele and the girls, telling them about this phone call from my teenaged son, about how painful it is to tear a family apart and try to stitch something new together from the scraps.

I've never been into all that feminist stuff like Katie and Liz are. Sisterhood and all that. But I do believe that women should encourage and support and pray for one another.

In every church Roger pastored after we left the seminary, I always started a women's Bible study group. Usually we'd meet once a week, study a Bible passage together & then pray for each other's needs.

Roger had kind of mixed feelings about the groups. He had to approve, because it was exactly the kind of thing a pastor's wife should be doing, but he was uncomfortable with it. Scared, I think now. He used to lecture me about how it was important to keep our discussions to Scripture, not to indulge in "pop psychology" or a "gossip session."

He used to remind me that his reputation was important and that he had to avoid the appearance of evil. I guess that meant that I shouldn't confess to anyone that sometimes I was so discouraged & lonely that I'd cry for no reason at all. And I should avoid mentioning that my husband, the handsome & dynamic young pastor, was beating me up on a fairly regular basis.

It was the same old story every time—always a big outburst, and then the apologies & tears & prayers afterwards. I felt sorry for Roger in a way—he tried so hard to do everything right and make a good impression, and yet he had this thing inside him he couldn't control that tripped him up & dragged him in the dirt. I used to pray God would set him free, help him change.

I prayed for him, but I hated praying with him—those prayers after he apologized. Once I told him I didn't want to pray with him. I thought he'd hit me again, he was so mad, but instead he took me by the shoulder and actually forced me down to the floor, and kept his hand there, pressing me down, kneeling beside him while he prayed for God to help both of us work harder at our marriage.

God got me through those years, I know that. I felt like I was two Julies, the outside happy pastor's wife, and the inside one only God could see. I prayed so much & I would read my Bible & there'd always be some verse that would give me strength. And yet every time Roger would force me to kneel down and pray with him I'd have that feeling again, like God must really be on Roger's side. In my head I started to split God into two, Roger's God and my God.

There was one time I came close to breaking, letting the inside life spill into the outside life. It was in one of the women's Bible study meetings—in Saskatoon, I think—a really close & supportive group. One of the women was going through a terrible divorce where her husband left her for another woman—another had breast cancer. It was so wonderful, the way we all rallied around those women, supported them, prayed with and for them, helped with babysitting, housecleaning, meals.

One night the lady who had breast cancer had just finished her last round of chemo and we had a little party for her, with a cake and candles, and we all held hands and sang "We are One in the Spirit." After that we broke up into twos and threes to pray. I was with the lady who had cancer and the lady whose husband had left her. They were both really strong Christian women, they had such faith, and they were so loving & kind. And as we started sharing our prayer requests, I suddenly wanted to be on the receiving end of some of that love and caring. I was only going to say that I needed prayer for my marriage, that things weren't always easy, just ask them to pray for me.

One of the women said how grateful she was for all the support the church had given her, and then she reached out and took my hand. "And Julie, your husband, well the Pastor has just been like an angel. He doesn't just preach the Word, he lives it." She dabbed tears away from her eyes as she spoke.

I reached out and pulled her into a hug and she held on tight, and I was thinking how close I'd come to destroying everything: her faith and trust in her pastor, the good work that Roger was doing in that church. I promised myself I'd never make that mistake again.

And I never did.

NINE

Jeff

I'VE ALWAYS BEEN CURIOUS about near-death experiences.

It's just like in the *Reader's Digest* articles. A long hall and a white light. Or maybe I'm awake again and this is a hospital corridor? But it's so quiet. And I'm not lying down. I'm upright, moving forward.

If I get back, I'll talk to the pastor about this.

Near-death experiences are hard for Adventists to get their heads around. Most Christians love them because they're evidence that there's "something more" after death. But we were always taught that death was just like sleep. The dead know not anything until Jesus comes to wake them on resurrection morning.

I was never real religious as a kid, but like most boys I was fascinated by gross stuff. I sat in church hearing a sermon about the resurrection and wondered what it would be like to wake up in a box under the ground. How would the coffin open? Would it explode outwards? Would you have to tunnel up through the ground? What if your body was partly rotted, would that be fixed before you were resurrected? I was probably about eleven at the time and eleven-year-old boys can keep going for quite a while on this kind of thing. I brought it up later, over potluck lunch, hoping to gross out Julie and Katie.

The thing is, if you're just going to sleep, why the tunnel and the white light? One time in youth Sabbath School Dave tried to trip up Pastor Kimball with that one. What did

323

Kimball say? That there was no real proof of near-death experiences. They could be hallucinations. Or Satan could be deceiving people.

Still, at this point it seems like a good idea to keep an open mind.

There's an open space ahead. I guess there should be figures in white robes, if the stories are true. Instead I see, in that bright lit space, a man in blue jeans and a work shirt. A heavyset, balding man, completely human and familiar. Wait, he's not dead. Am I? This is confusing.

"Jeff! Jeff, what are you doing?"

"I don't know, Dad."

He sits down on a kitchen chair—there's a chair—and gives me a long hard stare. "Well, that about sums it up, doesn't it?"

I stand in front of him like I stood so many times when I was a teenager and he'd talk to me, always in that quiet voice. Disappointment behind every word. Why was I out so late? Was I with Liz? What were we doing? Was that beer on my breath? Cigarette smoke on my jacket? The bottom line was usually that I was grounded for two weeks, which I always skipped out on. I built up a time debt to the point that if he'd ever called it in, I'd have been grounded till my second year of college.

After I moved away, he'd grill me every time I came home. Was I going to church regularly? Was I studying hard, working hard?

This room I'm standing in no longer looks like an open space at the end of a long white tunnel. It takes on the shape of my parents' kitchen. Dad used to sit here at the table, reading the paper, waiting for me when I came in late. I see yellow linoleum between my feet. That's what I usually looked at.

He wasn't a harsh man. Never angry without a reason. Just—serious. He had high expectations and I didn't meet them.

I thought it would change as I got older. Married, working—I thought I had things going well. But I was still a disappointment to him.

Debbie and I came to St. John's one summer, a few years after we got married. We planned to spend a couple of weeks going around the island, seeing the sights. We stayed with Mom and Dad while we were in town.

Katie and Sam got married that summer, and the night before the wedding we went over to their new place with a crowd of people. It was great to be back with old friends again—Sam already felt like an old friend although I'd only met him the day before.

Debbie and I got home late that night. When I went inside I saw my dad was still up, sitting in the kitchen reading Saturday's *Telegram*. He got it delivered every Saturday and never opened it till after sunset. He looked up when we came in and said, "Have a nice evening?"

I said yeah. I felt sixteen again.

He said, "Want a cup of tea or anything?" Debbie said no, went off to bed. I put the kettle on.

He folded the paper, laid it down on the table. "You gave us a lot of worries when you were growing up, Jeff."

I shrugged. What could I say? "I was a bit stunned I guess. Sorry about all that."

"I never wanted to see you make the same mistakes I made." He looked down at his tea. "Well, it's water under the bridge now. You're married to a nice girl, doing well in your job."

"Yeah, it's—things are going good."

"Real estate's a tough business, I hear," he said after a minute. "Good money to be made, but hard work. You doing OK?"

"We're doing all right."

"Hard job to be in and take Sabbaths off, they tell me. How'd you manage?"

Ah, there it was. The catch. "Well Dad, you know, I'd like to have Sabbaths off too but like you say it really isn't practical in real estate. Saturdays, that's when people go out to look at homes, you know. Debbie has to work Sabbath shifts too—we get to church whenever we can."

"Debbie's job is different. It's essential. You could have your Sabbaths off if you really made it a priority. There's an Adventist realtor up in Oshawa—your mother knows her, a lady realtor—she does real well. And never works a Sabbath."

"It'd be nice to get to that point someday, Dad." My hands were shaking, jiggling the teacup. What was I scared of? He no longer had the power to ground me or take away the car keys. Why did I have to remind myself I was an adult?

"You get to the point when you have enough trust in God to do what's right. It's nothing more than what the hymn says, b'y. Trust and obey. For there's no other way."

I stared down into the dark-red centre of the teacup. It was bag tea, not steeped, but I think I would have had a shot at reading the tea leaves if there were any. I wanted to see into the future, to know when the day would come when he'd shake my hand and say, "Congratulations, b'y. You've done it. You grew up and made me proud. You're good enough."

Now I stand in front of him and he looks at me. Am I finally going to hear those words? Slowly he shakes his head.

As I stare at him, excuses and explanations on the tip of my tongue, his face changes. It's not the face of my father I've known all my life but a much older man, wrinkled, his jowls sagging, his thin wisps of hair almost white, his eyes watery and bloodshot. My father as he really looks now, though in my mind he's forever forty-five and vigorous. The world tilts and I'm not standing looking down at him but lying looking up at him. His face looms over me, large, larger than the sky. His loose old lips tremble. What's he saying? Just my name. "Jeff."

In the background a babble of voices without meaning rises from the stillness. "We're losing him! Check the levels! Stat!"

"Jeff ... Jeff ... *Jeffrey!*"

Diamonds on the Soles
Of her Shoes

2005

1995

liz

WALKING ALONG THE SEAWALL in stanley park hand in hand with my famous married lover. he stops, kisses the back of my neck.

-come to the island with me this weekend.

he has a place on galliano island. a place just ours where his wife does not go. she must know. we have been together over two years.

> *[amazingly it seems from what people have told me since that she didn't know. still find this hard to believe]*

-i'd love to but i really can't i've got a reading.

-blow it off. i need you up there. you're going to newfoundland for two whole weeks what will i do without you?

-i'm not blowing off my reading i need all the promotion i can get. poetry collections don't sell like novels you know.

-that's why we need to go to galliano. to celebrate your book.

-can we drive up after my reading?

-i guess. we won't have saturday up there then. he pouts. poor baby. i have already given in now he will have to give a little too. the art of compromise.

later in my apartment the phone rings.

-liz it's me mom.

-mom.

when did we last talk was it christmas was it my birthday last year they have retired in kelowna but i have only once made the trip to see them.

-one hand holds the phone the other plays with my earring. so how are you how are things.

-i'm not calling to chat liz. it's your father he had a heart attack.

my father my father is dead the patriarch who strode through my childhood parting the waters with his staff is dead. i pull on the earring so hard it pops out of my ear and the pain makes me say oh shit.

[should i have her react to the swear word? i don't know if she would have at that point]

-they said it was fairly severe it happened at about lunchtime they're keeping him in intensive care. i've already called gene and he's flying out do you want to come.

i stare at my earring in my hand not understanding. intensive care. keeping him.

oh. he's not dead. not a fatal heart attack, the other kind.

-liz hello hello are you there are you still there.

-yes yes sorry mom i'll be down in the morning first thing.

i should go tonight. i should drive through the dark night to be at my mother's side at my father's bedside. he may die before dawn i should be there.

i don't have a car i'll need to take the bus. unless.

i can't call my lover's home phone i use a friend to relay messages. tell him to call me tonight if he can i really really need to talk.

[how convoluted life was before cellphones]

half an hour later i sit in the dark room. the phone rings.

-what is it baby did you change your mind about galliano? wanna go up right away?

-my mom just called my dad's in hospital in kelowna with a heart attack. they think he'll pull through but they want me to come down. i told her i'd catch a bus in the morning.

-guess that shoots the weekend on galliano then. how long do you think you'll be down there.

i don't even ask him to drive me. there's always a good excuse. what would margery think. margery won't mind if we screw on galliano island all weekend but if he drives me to kelowna to see my possibly dying father that will somehow shatter our carefully constructed glass house.

i arrive busshevelled and weary in the late morning. gene meets me at the station.

[another word i've coined as far as i know. should email websters so they can be sure to include the lizwords in the next edition]

gene has not visited my parents since he came out to them ten years ago and dad made it clear he wasn't welcome. mom keeps in touch with him by letters and phone calls. yet here he is now.

-how is he.

-hooked up to machines that make a sucking sound reminiscent of darth vader. they say it's too early to tell.

at the hospital my large father is engulfed made small by tubes wires a mask over his face. despite the breathing sound the effect is the opposite of darth vader he becomes less threatening more human.

though if he opens his eyes and says i am your father liz i'll be out of here pretty damn quick i can tell you.

[ok i'm pretty sure this is my second star wars reference. probably one too many. find and delete the other as vader image is central to this scene]

i sit beside her on a hardbacked plastic chair. how are you doing mom.

-not very well honey.

she gropes for my hand and holds it. i am a small child again skipping down the sidewalk hand in hers mommy mommy see my pretty dress mommy mommy.

she doesn't even know i wrote a book. i never told either of them. they thought helen steiner rice was a great poet they would loathe my poems they would feel shame. or so i tell myself.

[problem: surely no-one who might read this would know who helen steiner rice is. is name self-explanatory? surely everyone knows poet with three names is a hack?]

-how long can you stay? gene has to go back wednesday.

lucky gene who lives in ottawa with his university job and his boyfriend bob and their two golden retrievers. He says boyfriend not partner because partner is confusing with bob being a lawyer and all. they've been together four years and would be married if it was legal probably. gene looks professorial wearing a sloppy knit sweater his balding head emphasizing the high forehead his nerd glasses finally having shaped face and body to meet their stern demands.

-i'm supposed to leave on the 7th for katie's wedding.

-katie's getting married. gene smiles the fond sepia smile he always reserves for mentions of katie. first marriage?

-yeah her first. too bad you missed out there, apart from the gay thing and all.

-apart from that little thing, yeah.

-oh if you could stay a little longer liz, mom says. i don't know how long he'll be in how i'm going to care for him when he gets home it's all so overwhelming.

i want to tell her to lay all her burdens at the feet of jesus. it's worked so well all her life why would he fail her now? look back in the sand mom there's only one set of footprints. isn't he carrying you?

i am thirty years old and not as cruel as i once was. i make my calls. cancel a reading a workshop an interview. call my lover who says he'll miss me. call katie who says sure it's ok if you come at the last minute or if you can't come at all of course tell your mom she and your dad are in our prayers.

i'll tell them. prayers can pass through me like a conduit.

i drive my mother's car through unfamiliar streets. she can barely give directions. she has been at the hospital thirty hours.

-i shouldn't have left the hospital liz what if something happens to him while i'm gone.

-you're no good to him or yourself if you collapse. gene is there.

-gene is no good to him you're no good to him i'm all he has. we had such hopes for you both he was so proud of you and then these last years we kept asking ourselves where did we go wrong.

-maybe you didn't go wrong.

neat suburban streets unroll beneath the car. families pour out of minivans into tidy three-bed bungs irish setters galloping after them. everything about this life makes me shudder.

and yet. and yet. a small girl maybe four or five stands on the clipped front lawn of a house wearing underwear and an umbrella dancing singing. harried suburban mother runs out the door i expect to see a slap a reprimand but in the moment before the car turns the corner i see the woman dancing on the lawn beside her daughter.

mommy mommy see my pretty dress. see me dance. i'm going to be a belly dancer when i grow up. i think i may have meant ballet dancer.

no sweetheart jesus doesn't want his children to be belly dancers.

and yet in memory i see a moment when she unties her apron and dances beside me. a trick of memory perhaps.

-i don't know what you mean. raising you children to serve the lord meant everything to him to me.

[is the switch from memory to dialogue too difficult to follow here?]

-i just published a book. my own book, words i wrote. it won an award, a major award. gene is associate professor on track for tenure at thirty-two. these things may mean nothing to you beside the fact that we don't go to church and we drink wine and swear but you have to see you didn't do so badly.

-you're right those things mean nothing to me.

-how about this then. he's sick possibly dying and we're here. we're not perfect but we're both here.

more streets unroll beneath the wheels. one two three stoplights before she says yes. yes that does mean something.

home to this house i have visited once. she lies down and tries to rest finally i pass the room see her in an uneasy sleep. in the living room i thumb through old photo albums 3 x 5 matte photos with rounded edges frozen scenes of childhood vacations and birthday parties. happy christian family in front of our happy christian house flattened under cellophane sheets like one-celled organisms caught under the coverslip.

[i like the coverslip image]

an early photo two of them his arm around her young young gene a toddler in arms she smiling broadly beneath her big beehive hairdo one hand laid gently on her rounded belly. me.

last year i was a week or two late. after two scares i know the routine go to the drugstore pick up the test a little cardboard packet with no more emotional weight than a pack of kleenex. slap it on the counter take it home.

negative. the next night i whisper into the dark. what if i had a child. your child. he does not answer because he is in his house sleeping with his wife to whom he is related as if by blood.

a little girl on the lawn dancing in her underwear. a little girl in white dress and shiny black shoes clutching a white child's bible see mommy i was good in sabbath school i got a sticker. a wild dark little girl, gypsylike with long dresses and floating scarves, a little girl with a strong celtic name morag branwen fiona dancing dancing by my side down a city street in a park at a jazz festival she is dancing beside me reaching out for my hand. dance with me mommy.

-liz liz. she stands in the doorway her clothes rumpled from sleep her hair untidy face flushed. what time is it did gene call.

-nobody called let's get something to eat and i'll take you back.

-no. nothing to eat. i need to be back there. i can't leave him alone.

she reaches for my hand.

[too blindingly obvious or just the right note to end on? also is this the place to end it? do i need to write about what happened to him or is this story really about my mother and me and my unborn daughter?]

Katie

FRUIT TRAYS! FRUIT TRAYS comin' through!"

Sam sidles into the house holding fruit trays aloft, pushing through a crowd of people children. "Look out! Flying fruit!" he shouts, and Mikayla, the flower girl, looks up and giggles, her face brilliant as a buttercup in the grass. Katie, just coming downstairs after changing from her jeans into a wrap-around skirt, stops for a moment and watches Sam with the kids. *Yes*, she thinks, as if there was any doubt. *Yes.*

So far, she has had no doubt, no pre-wedding jitters. She and Sam have been together three years and they're back in St. John's, where they belong. They've bought a downtown row house that Sam is fixing up. It's going to be a showcase when it's finished—a live-in advertisement for Sam's business. It's a long way from that yet. But it's finished enough to move into, finished enough that on this warm August evening they can fill it with family and friends for their combination rehearsal dinner and housewarming party.

"Sam! Have you got the fruit trays?" Katie's mom is in the dining room, arranging food. "Carol! Bring in some more paper cups!" When Katie drifts into the kitchen her mother glances up at her. The mother of the bride wears a knee-length tie-dyed caftan, her graying hair caught up in a loose bun from which damp wisps escape to stick to her face.

Katie pushes through the kitchen, where a clutch of eccentrically dressed older women—her mother's friends -- are nibbling their way through a cheese ball while badmouthing the premier and urging one another to run for the NDP. "My gosh doesn't she look lovely Katie, come here and let me have a look at you," says Carol Davis, grabbing Katie around the waist. This particular group of women—fifty-something divorcees, lifelong single women, lesbians, one ex-nun—are refreshing. They like Sam, but they bring a healthy skepticism to weddings. Unlike the church ladies of their generation, they don't act as if getting married is the single most important accomplishment of Katie's life.

Katie's friends from work are mostly out on the back deck. She detaches her co-worker Shelagh from the group and leads her down the steps. "Time to get acquainted with other bridesmaids," she says. "This is Julie, my best friend from high school, and Nola, my best friend from university. Liz, my other best friend from high school, should be landing in about, oh, two hours."

Nola works as a hospital chaplain in California: she and Katie haven't seen each other since Katie left the seminary. Shelagh and Nola quickly discover a mutual interest in grief counselling and start comparing notes. Julie calls "Kyle!" to her son in a warning tone, and then Roger strides past, heading for the fence where his son is clinging. "Standing there whimpering his name isn't going to do much," he tosses over his shoulder at Julie as he passes.

"Oh, there are some vaguely connected relatives up there—two old ladies who might be either my aunts or Sam's, I'm not sure—that I have to go speak to," Katie says, excusing herself. But before she reaches the mysterious old ladies she is stopped by her father, presiding at the barbecue, who hands her a burger.

"I can't eat this Dad, somebody's put ketchup on it," Katie says. "Not to sound ungrateful. You're terrific to do all this."

"Here, I'll swap, I haven't put anything on mine yet," says Debbie, handing Katie a plate. Jeff leans against the rail and Debbie perches next to him, his arm around her. The setting sun illuminates their hair and makes them glow, appropriately, Katie thinks, because they really are the golden couple, both blond and beautiful. Katie takes Debbie's unsullied burger and Jeff says, "Who's going to pick up Liz and Dave?"

"Half a dozen people have offered, but I'd really like to go myself," Katie says.

"Can I come?" Jeff says. "You want to go, Deb?"

"No, that's OK, there's some people here I'd like to catch up with. Anyway you might not have enough space for both of them and their luggage," Debbie says.

Katie squeezes Sam's hand as she passes him. "I'm going to the airport to get Liz and Dave," she says. "Jeff's coming with me."

"Help! My bride's running away with another man!" Sam shouts.

"Ah, she's got more sense than that," Jeff says.

At Torbay airport they stand behind the rope that cordons off the Arrivals door. Children whine and parents soothe them. People wait with empty baggage carts for their loved ones. "I hope they had the sense to only bring carry-on," Katie says. "I don't want to wait for their luggage. At least the flight's on time." She feels a little trembling in her stomach; meeting old friends after a long time apart is more nerve-wracking than getting married, it seems.

A flight attendant opens the doors and the first arrivals trickle out, looking vague and disoriented until they spot their own particular cheering section in the crowd. Katie, having flown in to larger, more anonymous airports, loves the "Torbay welcome" and enjoys watching other passengers reunite with their loved ones. Tonight, though, all her attention is focused on scanning for Liz and Dave. "I might not recognize them," she says. "You'll have to tell me."

Liz , Dave, Jeff and Debbie all live in Vancouver now. Only Liz would make the long trip home just for Katie's wedding; it's sheer luck that Jeff and Dave have other reasons for coming home that make it possible for them to be here at the right time. "I don't see all that much of Liz anymore," Jeff says. "Dave sees her more than I do, I think. Oh, there he is now."

Katie looks up at the tall dark-haired man who hasn't yet made eye contact. A stranger, at first glance. Then he sees them and smiles in recognition. She looks for Liz beside him, but he's alone.

Then Dave is hugging her, her face pressed into the zipper of his brown leather jacket. "Did Liz call yet?"

"What? Isn't she with you?"

"No—no, she called me this morning. Her dad's taken a sudden turn for the worse. They're not sure he's gonna pull through."

"Oh, how terrible." Katie thinks about Mr. Carter—hardly a beloved figure but a towering one from her adolescence— possibly dying. She thinks of Liz and Mrs. Carter, who have never been close, facing this together. She thinks of how to adjust the wedding party to account for only three bridesmaids instead of four.

Katie walks between them as they head for her car in the parking lot. Though she still thinks of them as teenaged boys, they are both men, thirty years old. Dave has gained weight and his face, darkened with long-past-five-o'clock shadow, looks older. Jeff still has a great body but his hairline is in retreat: he's started to comb it forward, which is the beginning of the end as far as Katie's concerned. On a straightforward scale of male hotness they're probably both better-looking than Sam but neither of them looks as pleasing, as *right*, to Katie.

Seeing Dave was some kind of a test for her, she realizes. Not that he's about to storm the wedding, stand up and say "I object!" when the minister asks for any reason why she and Sam should not be lawfully joined. But she had to see him, to be sure that if for some reason he did object, she wouldn't follow him out of the church.

Back at the house, the crowd has thinned a little, though there are still upwards of twenty people hanging around in the living room, the dining room, the kitchen, and out on the back deck. Julie puts shoes on a reluctant Kyle and a drowsy Mikayla. Dave leans close to Katie, watching Julie tuck Mikayla's feet into pink jelly sandals. "Wanna know what Liz said when she got Julie's Christmas card with their picture on it?" he whispers.

"What's that?"

"If this image of Christian family life were any sweeter I'd be in a diabetic coma right now."

"Yeah, that sounds like Liz," Katie says, missing Liz more than she expected.

The phone rings about half an hour after they get back from the airport. Katie takes the call up in the bedroom. "Hey. Sorry if I've screwed up your wedding," says Liz.

"How's your dad?"

Silence on the other end of the line. "He didn't make it."

"He what?"

"He had another heart attack this morning. Massive. Funeral's on Monday. I'm supposed to be a bridesmaid on Sunday, instead I'm burying my father on Monday. If they weren't on opposite ends of the continent I could probably hit both."

"Liz, are you OK?"

"Reasonably. I've got some pills into my mom, over her protests, which seems to be helping. Gene is a tower of strength. Hard to believe, but true—apparently he really comes through in a crisis."

"I can believe that. Listen, I wish I could be there with you."

"I wish I could be there with *you*. Even an Adventist wedding would be more fun than an Adventist funeral. Listen, I can't talk long, but I'll give you a ring on Sunday morning, OK?"

Downstairs, Katie looks for her mother to tell her the news, but instead gets swept up into an argument in the kitchen over the government's scheme to dismantle denominational education, with Katie's church friends fervently on one side and her work friends as ardently arguing the opposite position.

By ten-thirty almost everyone has gone. Nola, who's staying in the guest bedroom, goes to bed early, pleading jet lag. Katie sits on the back step drinking lemonade, the night still warm enough for bare arms and legs. In the kitchen, her mother and assorted church ladies, treading lightly on the edges of the Sabbath, finish cleaning up. The back windows throw rectangles of golden light onto the deck. Katie's father looks out through the back door. "We're off now," he says. "Anyone need a ride?"

"We're going to walk," Debbie says. "It's such a nice night." She and Jeff are sitting on the grass. Sam sits a few steps below Katie, leaning his head against her knee. Dave stands against the rail, jingling keys or change in his pocket. "Ummm ..." he says. "No, it's OK. You go on. I'll stay a little longer."

They have all been talking, but after Katie's parents leave silence falls over the yard. After a while Jeff says, "We could drive out to Cape Spear, for old times' sake."

"Or up to Signal Hill," suggests Katie. But no-one makes a move to leave. "We could go tomorrow afternoon," Sam says.

"Yeah. Maybe we can see if Julie and Roger want to go. Too bad Liz isn't here—we could do the vow thing," says Jeff.

"That's right! Who's got the nearest birthday—isn't it yours, Jeff?"

"It's obviously going to take more than a birthday or even a wedding to get all five of us up to Signal Hill."

"Maybe a funeral," Dave suggests.

"You're in a cheerful mood," says Debbie. She looks up at the house rising above them. "You guys are so lucky to have this house. Do you know what you'd pay for a place like this in Edmonton or Calgary?"

"About two hundred and fifty thousand—but I could get it for you for two twenty-five," Jeff puts in quickly, and they all laugh. "What'd you really pay?"

"You'll kill us," Sam says. "Seventy-five."

"Holy shit," Dave says.

"The joys of living in a depressed economy," says Katie. "The house is a steal at seventy-five thousand, and we've probably only put about fifteen thousand into it so far, with another thirty or forty thousand to go before we turn it into our dream home. Then, if we wanted to sell it, we'd probably clear—oh, eighty."

"Eighty-five if we're lucky," Sam says.

"Is that what you want to do—fix it up and flip it?" Jeff asks.

"Heck no. This is our home. We're building for generations here," says Sam.

Debbie nods. "A home to raise your kids and grow old in."

"And die in," says Dave.

"Another cheerful comment," Jeff says. "That reminds me—what's the news from Liz?"

Katie stares at Jeff, appalled to realize she hasn't told anyone. In the bustle of her own pre-wedding party she has actually forgotten the news of her best friend's father's death. She feels as self-obsessed as a Hollywood starlet.

When she tells them, everyone but Sam shares in a brief burst of reminiscing about Mr. Carter. "Remember the time he took us to the bird sanctuary and blew up at us on the way back...? He was wicked on the ice, remember his slapshot Dave ...? Remember the assembly where he bawled us out about graffiti in the bathrooms...?"

"Oh, I remember that one," Debbie says. "He held up two fingers, first and second—" she demonstrates, "and said, 'There are two groups of people here. Those who did it, and I don't expect them to confess—and he folded down the index finger—and those who *know* who did it, and I hope they will come forward."

"All the while shaking the middle finger at us, not even knowin' he was doin' it," Jeff says, and they almost roll on the grass laughing, Sam joining in as everyone waves the middle finger in honour of the late Mr. Carter.

"This is shocking," Katie says, a weak protest.

"Ah, he'd want us to remember the good times," Jeff says.

"No he wouldn't," Dave says. "But Liz would."

Another moment's silence falls, and Debbie turns to Sam. "You promised you were going to show me the molding over the fireplace."

"Getting ideas for your dream home?"

"Maybe." Debbie and Jeff follow Sam into the house, leaving Katie alone with Dave.

"How was Liz doing when she called?" Dave asks, sitting next to Katie on the step.

"OK. A bit shaken up, you know." Katie glances up. "You and Liz see a lot of each other these days?"

Dave shakes his head, shrugs. "Yeah, a bit, I guess. But not, you know, like that. Just to hang out. Like you and me would, I guess, if I lived here. Only not so much, now you're getting married."

"Why not? You said it wasn't like that."

"No, not like *that*, I mean, but—things change when you get married."

"Maybe you're a little cynical about marriage."

"At the moment. Yeah." Dave's divorce has just become final.

Jeff comes out of the house alone and joins them on the step. Through the open door they can hear Sam and Debbie talking about Sam's grand plan to expose the brickwork around the fireplace and the beams in the ceiling. "What's up?" Jeff says.

"Dave's saying bad things about marriage."

"Marriage? Don't listen to him. Greatest institution on earth."

"If you like being in an institution," Dave says. "You'll do OK though," he adds to Katie. "Sam's all right."

"He better be," Jeff says. "If he doesn't treat you right, you call me and Dave, we'll fly home and beat the crap out of him."

"Damn straight we will," Dave says. "You got no brothers."

"Somebody's gotta do it," Jeff agrees.

Sam and Debbie come out onto the deck. Katie tilts her head back to look at Sam. "These guys are just telling me they're going to beat you up if you don't treat me right."

Sam looks from Dave to Jeff, a slow measured look though not an unpleasant one. "Yeah. I got the message," he says.

Debbie stretches. "We'd better go, Jeff. See you guys at church in the morning."

"You need a ride somewhere, Dave?" Sam says.

"Yeah, if you don't mind. My mom lives up on Shea Heights."

"No problem."

Goodbyes, and they're all gone. Katie stands on the front step watching Sam drive down Gower Street with Dave. A nice thing for him to do, though he probably had reasons of his own. She goes back into the house and shuts the door, walks through the rooms of her house. The living room with the small fireplace under its elaborate mantel. The dining room and kitchen where they will someday knock down the wall to make a big eat-in kitchen. Up the stairs to the bedroom, picking up stray paper cups from steps and windowsills as she goes. The master bedroom with the big four-poster and the handmade quilt, an early wedding gift from Katie's grandmother. The bed where, on Sunday night, she and Sam will lie down for the first time as husband and wife. The bed where they will conceive their babies, where she will nurse their children and—she hopes Dave's right—the bed she will someday die in.

For now, though, the bridal bed.

Dave

HI. ME AGAIN.

Yeah well, I'm glad to see you too. I thought maybe after last time you might have made an excuse to be conveniently unavailable for further sessions with me.

Well it's nice of you to say that. Very professional. I guess you people are trained in how to react when somebody freaks out and starts cursing at you, eh?

Yeah I bet you have seen worse. Hell, I've *been* worse.

So yeah, I'm going to make an effort to keep my eyes on the here-and-now today. No more straying over the back roads of the past. I'm going to talk about my life today and....

OK, well, that's refreshing to hear. So you don't completely mind digging up the past a little? Yeah, I kind of see what you mean. Not just the past for its own sake. But there's something there I need to look for. Maybe it's not a magic key or whatever shit I was talking about last week, but there's stuff I still want to understand, to make sense out of.

But for now we'll stick to the present. Good week. Honestly. Not as tough as ... well, as the weeks have been. I'm working, I'm going to meetings ... it hasn't quite been 90 in 90, but damn close. Messing around a bit with the guitar, trying to write a song actually. Haven't done that in awhile. Oh, and I met Liz for coffee.

Good, it was good. We've gotten together a few times, several times, since we got back from St. John's in August. Kind of gotten back into the old habit of meeting every few weeks to catch up. Of course, in the old days we generally used to meet at a bar for a few drinks. Now we hit coffee shops.

Remember I told you ages ago that I met up with Liz and she said she had something to tell me, something important, but she wouldn't tell me what it was? So naturally I've been bugging her about it every time we get together. But she still won't say. Says she's waiting for the opportune moment.

I haven't told you as much about Liz as about Katie or Jeff, except for that one weekend at Katie's place when I thought something might happen between Liz and me. It never did, but I've probably ended up being closer to her than any of the old gang. Of course, that's partly geography. We've both lived in Vancouver for the last ten-plus years, so naturally we're going to keep in touch more than we do with people who live on the other side of the country.

But yeah ... there's more to it than that. We're fundamentally the same in some way.

No hell no, I don't mean—no, she's not like me. She's not an addict, she's not a loser, she's a smart, successful woman. She's got, like, two or three books published, she speaks and reads and teaches at conferences and stuff. If writing poems made you a real celebrity like playing hockey does, everyone in Canada would know Liz's name.

She gets me, though, I guess that's it. She takes me as I am. People have always tried to change me, make me shape up. I don't blame them.

In all the years I've known Liz she's never tried to do that to me. I mean, she knew I was making a mess of my life and I'm sure had I asked her, "Liz, do you think I should quit drinking" she would have said yes. But I didn't ask—obviously—and she just accepted me on my own terms. And for a person like me, once in awhile it's very restful to have someone do that.

Well yeah, of course. That's a luxury you can afford if you're an old friend who sees me once every few weeks or months for an evening. She never had to live with me, or work with me, or put up with my shit. It's not fair to compare her to, say, Tammy. Tammy didn't take me as I was, but I can't blame her for that. She had to live with me and try to raise two kids with me. She put up with enough.

I told you I started drinking again about the time Tammy got pregnant with Sara. For the next couple of years we lived under a flag of truce, you might say. Tammy was still sober, still doing AA, trying her best to raise the kids with some shred of a normal life. I worked hard all day and came home and sat in front of the TV and got drunk every night. I had almost zero interaction with the kids—I'd put up the effort to be Dad for maybe half an hour, an hour after I got home, but if they came in and saw me in the recliner with a drink in my hand, they learned pretty fast to leave Daddy alone. Hell of way to grow up, isn't it?

But I believed I was still doing OK. Great how we manage to kid ourselves isn't it? Pulling down a steady paycheque made it possible to delude myself. I mean, if you can hold down a job without getting fired, you can't be a drunk, right? Drunks can't hold a job, everyone knows that.

Right—functioning alcoholic. You people have a word for everything. That was me. I functioned. I supported my family and I showed up every night. Whenever Tammy tried to talk any kind of sense into me, I just gave her back those two facts, like they were some kind of entry card that would let me in anywhere. "You wanna be a single parent, fine," I'd tell her. "I can put my child support cheque in the mail just as easy as bring it home to you. You want them to have a dad coming home every night, this is the dad you get."

What a friggin' bastard, eh? I mean, that's in retrospect. At the time I thought I was pretty smart for laying down the law to her like that.

It took a while for things to get out of control. A couple of years, anyway. I think Sara was about two when I started giving Tammy shit about going to meetings. She was going to AA and to Al-Anon too by this time, out two nights a week, and that meant I was home responsible for the kids. Babysitting, I used to call it. She'd get the kids bathed and in bed before she went out and my babysitting consisted of doing my usual vodka-and-TV routine, only with the kids asleep upstairs.

Yeah, maybe I was punishing her for going to meetings. I know I used to make fun of her for it, tell her she was an emotional cripple who couldn't survive without some kind of a crutch to keep her going. Did I mention she was also going to church at this point? Some kind of charismatic Pentecostal thing. One more thing for me to bug her about.

Anyway, after awhile what I used to do on the nights she had meetings was, I'd stop by a bar on my way home from work. I'd come in half cut just before she was due to go out and take up my usual position in front of the TV. A few times she got home to find one of the kids upstairs bawling their eyes out, maybe having pissed the bed or something, or just waking up from a nightmare, and I'd be down in the recliner passed out. Oblivious.

Finally she laid down the law. Quit drinking, go back to AA, or she was kicking me out of the house.

How'd I take it? I just laughed at her. Told her it was my house, bought with my money, and if anyone was leaving it was her. She said if she left she was taking the kids, and I said fine, go.

No, I never really expected her to do it. But the last laugh was on me. She had a pretty good lawyer too, and in the end the easiest thing to do was to sell the house, split the profits, and leave town. That's how I ended up back out in Vancouver.

Sure, of course I thought of going back home. I'm a Newfoundlander, we always think of it. We just don't ever actually do it. You sit up here on the mainland thinking, "Better to be back in Newfoundland on one meal a day than up here living off the fat of the land," but in the end you stay, because life's easier here.

I only went back home once for a visit. Not long after Tammy and I split and I moved out here, I went back to see my mom. She'd just got diagnosed with cancer and I knew she wanted me home. Liz was going home that summer, and Jeff and Debbie too. Katie was getting married, Liz was in the wedding, and Liz convinced me to go home and visit my mother, go to the wedding, get in touch with my roots or whatever.

Why'd I need to be talked into it? Well, it was a rough time for me. I know what you're thinking–they were all rough times. But that particular summer—what would that be, summer of

95 maybe? The year I turned 30. You turn 30 and you're supposed to be able to look at your life and see some progress.

I looked at my friends' lives and they all seemed to be moving somewhere. Liz had a book published. Jeff and Debbie were this perfect couple, both moving up in their careers, living the good life. Katie was getting married to a nice guy, she was living back home, she loved her job.

You think it wasn't hard to put myself up against that crowd, let everyone back home see how I stacked up? Dave Mitchell, nerdy computer tech guy, failed musician, divorced deadbeat dad, drinks maybe a little more than he should. That's how I would have seen myself that summer. I didn't want to hang around and watch all my old friends being happy and successful.

But I went, by myself as it turned out. Liz's dad took a heart attack and died just as she was about to come down, so she stayed and I went to the wedding.

Yeah, it was as bad as I expected. It was like going back to your childhood home and finding new people living there. Back in St. John's, visiting the old church, hanging out with the old gang ... all the while knowing I didn't fit in and I never would again.

I'm sorry. I really can't explain it any better than that.

My mom was going through all these tests, and it turned out to be bone cancer, very fast-moving, very nasty. Unlike Liz with her dad, I didn't stick around to see that through. I left while Mom was in hospital, and she died six weeks later.

My sister was still living home. She coped with everything. Maybe it's always the women who get stuck with the real bad shit, the births and deaths, the messy stuff. On the other hand, there could be guys who are there for that stuff too. I've just never been one of them.

What, now? Has that changed? Well, nobody around me seems to be in imminent danger of giving birth or dying so it's a little hard to tell. I'd like to think I could be a bit more—a bit more *there* for the people I care about, now. But until somebody puts me to the test, I won't know for sure.

What really scares me is that I might never find out. I mean, I don't see myself getting involved with anyone anytime soon. I know it's not even supposed to be a good idea, when you're in recovery. But let's say I get through these next few months, this year ... where will I be then? Sober, straightened out ... and alone? I haven't been great at being around for the people I care about. My kids, a few old friends ... that's about all the ties I've got left. Forming new ones is damn hard.

Oh, something good I forgot to tell you—I moved. Out of the bedsit and into an actual apartment. It's nothing fancy. I won't be holding dinner parties anytime soon. But it's clean and it doesn't smell of piss, and that's about as high as my standard for accommodations is right now.

I moved my stuff in by myself. Later I thought about Liz and figured if I'd called her, she might have come over and help me unpack my one or two boxes. Sometimes I don't think about things like that till it's too late. I'm very used to being alone.

I walk into that apartment and the emptiness just scares me, you know? I've lived alone ever since I left Tammy. But when I was drinking, I never felt like I was there alone. Hell, half the time I never even felt like I was *there*, period. Now I'm wandering from room to room in this bare unfurnished apartment, seeing how small and pathetic my little pile of stuff is, and wondering if that's how I'll always be—alone.

Julie

SATURDAY NIGHT- I'M SITTING AT *the kitchen table in my bathrobe. Another Saturday night and I ain't got nobody. I don't mind. It's been a good day.*

I sang in church this morning. Mrs. Elliott called Tuesday and asked if I could do special music. I was scared. I wasn't sure I could still get up in front of church and sing. But Lord, I asked for strength and You came through. Again.

Through it All *is an old favourite of mine. The first lines— my voice almost broke then and there—"I've had many tears and sorrows, I've had questions for tomorrow, there've been times I didn't know right from wrong." God, I do believe you've been with me through it all. But did my trials come "to only make me strong"? I'm not sure. I don't like the idea that you're up in heaven pushing a button and saying, "Julie Cuff needs to be a little stronger—let's give her an abusive husband and see how she handles that!"*

It was scary to stand up front again, especially here in our old church, the church I grew up in. Mom was there, and Katie, and so many other people who've known me all my life. What do they think of me? My old life was so easy to approve of. Now I know there must be people who disapprove, who talk behind my back—who blame me. But when I stood up in front there this morning and looked at the faces in front of me, I couldn't guess which smiles hid condemnation. I got a lot of Amens.

The girls & I went to Sam & Katie's for lunch, then we all drove out to Cape Spear. It was a cold day but brilliantly sunny—the girls all had fun clambering around on the rocks & exploring the tunnels.

I haven't been to Cape Spear for years. I have so many memories from childhood and my teenage years of coming out here, going for walks on Sabbath afternoons. I looked down, like I always do, to the waves crashing on the rocks below. It's not hard to believe some people have ventured to climb down there and been swept off to their deaths. I wouldn't set a foot off the path, myself. I've always been cautious.

But what I remembered this afternoon was the time I didn't go to Cape Spear, the day before Katie's wedding. She got a crowd together to drive out there on Sabbath afternoon. All the old gang— Katie and Sam, Jeff and Debbie, Dave, some of Katie's family and friends from away. I told her Roger & I & the kids would be there, no problem.

Roger flat-out refused to go. Bad enough he had to go to the rehearsal dinner and the wedding itself with my old friends, that stuck-up townie crowd he'd never liked. I offered to take the kids and let him stay at my mom's place and get some rest, but then he turned mean. Talking, like he so often did, about me throwing myself at men, about me and Jeff. "I s'pose you can't throw yourself at Jeff, not in broad daylight with his wife there, although I'm sure he'd do it quick enough if her back was turned. Maybe you'll have a shot at Dave? He might have you, he'll probably be too drunk to know the difference."

I was so angry I was shaking. We were in Mom's spare bedroom—Mom and the kids were only out in the living room and could have come in any minute. But Roger didn't raise his voice. He was an expert at saying terrible things in a low, calm voice if anyone else was nearby.

I told him not to talk about my friends that way, and he kept on in that soft terrible voice, telling me what bad people they all were, how Katie and Sam were sleeping together before they were married, the filthy stuff Liz wrote in her books, the way Jeff and Debbie only cared about looking good and making money. *"Lovers of pleasure rather than lovers of God,"* he called them.

It wasn't what he said that made me so angry. Half of it was true anyway. It was the pleasure he took in it—the sheer joy of hatred that showed through in his eyes and his voice. It made him so happy to list off people's sins.

He had me crying by the time he'd finished badmouthing all my friends and telling me how worthless I was. Then he told me that instead of going out with them, I was going to stay home and be a good wife. He smiled at me as he locked the door, just as if we were so madly in love we couldn't get through Sabbath afternoon without sneaking off for a quickie. Afternoon delight.

He pushed me down on the flowered bedspread, pulling my skirt and nylons down to my knees. "Come on baby, that's right, give it up to me." At times like this he liked to talk dirty. Not just dirty but mean dirty. "Give me what you'd like to give Jeff or Dave or the rest of the fellows. Hell, you'd probably even put out for Sam if you could get hold of him before the wedding, wouldn't you? You'd like that wouldn't you?" On and on as he grabbed my breast and crushed it in his strong hand, pushed himself between my legs, covered my mouth with his so I couldn't cry out. He put his hands on either side of my face and squeezed till I thought he would crush my jaw.

Oh, God. Writing about this is harder than writing about when he hit me. My hands are shaking. When I was young I was taught to save sex for marriage, not because it was bad or dirty—I was never taught that, even though some people who grew up in church say that was what they were told—but because it was this special and precious thing that would bond a husband and wife together in union like Christ and the church, a bond that could never be broken. What will I tell my children about sex when the time comes? How can I tell them it's a beautiful and wonderful gift?

I didn't mean to go down this road. Too raw, too painful. I stood next to Katie at Cape Spear today, remembering all this, wishing I could say something. Stood there and stared off into the distance—next stop, Shannon, Ireland—until Chelsea and Mikayla came running down the walkway, Sam behind them with Charlotte on his shoulders.

It was a good day. I don't know why I had to stir up all those awful memories, but they're there and they won't always lie quiet like I'd like them to. They're the trials that came to make me strong.

Only, Lord, I'm not sure I'm strong enough.

TEN

Jeff

I WAKE TO PAIN. MY SPINE is on fire. Needles shoot into my head. Even my eyeballs burn.

If being alive feels like this, maybe dying won't be so bad.

But if I'm feeling pain, that's a good thing, right? I'm still here. Still able to feel something.

Voices shout my name. "Stay with me Jeff! Come on!" I want to say, *I'm with you. I'm here.* But I can't say anything. It hurts so much.

Women always say that a man can never have any idea what the pain of giving birth is like. But I figure dying's got to be worse. Only no guy ever makes it back to tell his wife: *I've been there. You're right ... the pain is unbelievable.*

I didn't think Debbie would be the type to make a big deal about the pain. She could handle anything. Plus, she was an obstetrics nurse. She helped bring babies into the world every day. She even considered studying to be a midwife. She was big into natural birth, no drugs, she knew all the breathing exercises, the different positions. She used to say, "Sure, it's painful. But it's a healthy pain. It's the kind of pain you have from doing hard physical labour. That's how you need to think of it: pain with a purpose."

"I don't have to think of it *any* way," I told her. "You're the one who has to do the workout."

"You'll be my coach, my partner," she said. "We're totally in this together."

But I knew that wasn't true. No matter how much I wanted to be part of the team, there was no way this was a real team effort. This was Debbie's show. She would be feeling all the pain, doing all the work, pushing this live human being out of her *body*, for crying out loud—and the best I'd be able to do was squeeze her hand and tell her when to breathe. My best-case scenario would be if I didn't pass out in the birthing room.

I had so many doubts about fatherhood. We'd been married eight years by the time Debbie got pregnant with Brandon. At first we both wanted to enjoy being married, get ahead in our careers, have enough money to put a downpayment on a house. After the five-year mark, Debbie started making noises like maybe it was time to go off the Pill and start "trying."

I used the same old excuses: we weren't making enough money, we were living in an apartment, there was still plenty of time. Finally one night we were lying in bed after sex, and she leaned on my chest and said, "That was great. But you know what would have made it even better?"

Like most guys, I wasn't crazy about hearing things could be better. But I tried to keep an open mind. I figured she'd read some article in a women's magazine about something new to try in bed. I said, "No, what?"

"If we'd just made a baby," she said.

"Sure … someday." What I always said.

"I'm thirty-three. Time's passing. I'd like to have kids before I'm … well, I used to think thirty-five. Two kids before thirty-five. I'm willing to adjust that. But I don't want to wait till I'm forty."

I lay there amazed that she had things planned out like this. She kept talking. "The problem here isn't my biological clock, Jeff. It's something in your head. You're stalling and I don't know why. I need you to *talk* to me." She was big on that whole communication, share-your-feelings thing. All the girls I'd ever dated were.

"OK. Well." My mind raced, trying to think what I could come up with to tell her. Something I hadn't said a million times before, that would sound convincing. Suddenly I had an idea. Maybe I could tell her the truth.

"I think what it is ... I know a baby would be cool. And I know you'd be a great mom. It's ... this is really all about me."

"You're worried about ... being a father?"

"I'm worried about being a *good* father."

"Why?"

"I don't know. It's just ... it scares the crap out of me me."

Having a baby was a big thing. A huge thing. Bigger than even a job or marriage, because you could always back out of those things. One a baby was in the picture, that was a whole human being you could screw up. It was too scary. Too big a risk.

"Jeff, why do you think I want to have a baby with you?"

"Um ... because I'm your husband and you're basically an old-fashioned girl?"

She smiled. She was next to me again, lying beside me smiling, doodling on my chest with her fingertip. "I picked you, Jeffrey Evans, as the father of my children. I picked you because you are kind, and sweet, and smart, and hard-working, and caring, and funny, and ... did I say kind?"

"You didn't say good-looking. Weren't you thinking about my gorgeous genes?"

"Yeah yeah yeah. But good-looking guys are a dime a dozen. Kind ones ... not so much."

"You really think that? That I'm kind?"

"It's your outstanding quality."

Nobody had ever told me that before. Kind. When a guy thinks about what he wants to be, he doesn't usually think, *I want to be kind*. But on the lips of a beautiful woman, it sounded pretty good.

"Is *kind* enough, though? Enough to raise a kid? I mean, I always thought you had to be ... you know, *wise* and stuff."

Debbie laughed and kissed me. "If we're waiting around for you to be wise, bud, you really *will* hear my biological clock ticking."

Ten months later I stood in a birthing room in the hospital, watching this same beautiful woman going through a kind of agony I couldn't even imagine. Her face was streaked with sweat. Her hair was plastered to her face. She'd actually broken blood vessels in her cheeks. She had been in labour for thirty-seven hours. Without drugs. Now she was pushing. She'd been pushing for a long time. The doctors were getting worried.

They baby was in distress. Debbie gripped my hand so hard I thought the bones might break.

"Mrs. Evans, we're sorry but the baby's heartbeat is unstable. We're going to have to do an emergency section."

All I could think was, *Thank God. It'll be over.* I looked in Debbie's eyes and saw a quick flicker of disappointment. I understood something about my wife then, something I didn't have time to examine. Suddenly everything moved in a blur and our birthing room turned into an operating room.

And then he was in my arms, this red squalling thing. Blue eyes so bright they startled me peering out of this tomato face. My son.

Later I lay on the bed with Debbie in her hospital room watching Brandon nurse. It was the most amazing thing I'd ever seen. "You felt bad about having to have the section, didn't you?" I said.

"Just for a minute, this momentary thing. Like you'd feel if ... if you'd trained for the Olympics, and run the race, and you came in second by a zillionth of a second. I mean you'd be on the podium getting the silver medal, but still ... silver."

"Not quite perfect."

"Yeah. But, you know, then I said to myself, Don't be stupid. Healthy baby, that's all that matters here."

I leaned over and kissed her, then kissed Brandon. His eyes were shut tight, totally content. I looked back at Debbie. Such a perfect girl, always needing to prove she was perfect. Didn't take a genius to figure out how the two of us had ended up together, did it?

The picture lingers in my mind—Brandon at Debbie's breast—for a second, and then it's gone, torn to shreds by the white-hot knives of pain, pain, pain. *Make it stop make it stop I don't care let me go I'll do anything just make it stop....*

In the Living Years

2005

1997 - 1998

liz

OK WATCH FOR THE STEPS NOW   take it easy...good. don't worry, i'm right here.

-what's your problem i go up and down these steps every—

-oops. that's ok now. does your ankle hurt? do you want to go back?

-i want you to take me home.

-this is your home.

-it's not. i remember my home. it was a white house with a green door. i had flowers planted outside.

she's thinking of the house in st. john's. out of all the places we lived that's the one she remembers as home.

> *[not true. she described the house in kansas city. but st. john's is so central to this story the detail fits better]*

her hand light as a flower petal on my arm.

-we need to go back now. i have to go home soon.

-you just got here.

it's four o'clock i've been here since nine this morning. i block off whole saturdays to come see her an absurd kind of penance for not living in another place time existence where i might take her under my own roof spare her this indignity.

it's a good home owned by church people small personal lots of stimulation. gene is footing most of the bill. along with her savings, dad's insurance. my poems and their critical acclaim would not pay for many cheerful nurses' aides.

after he died she cried slept late asked for prayer but slowly slowly began to emerge. thy will be done. we'll understand it all by and by. she prepared herself for genteel widowhood, god as her live-in companion.

then she began forgetting things. keys dates phone numbers. i'd laugh on the phone. it's a senior moment mom. we would both laugh. so long since we had shared any kind of laughter. look at me mommy, i'm a princess and i have a pet tiger he's tame.

then she forgot dad was dead. she talked to him. i called gene.

-i remind her he's dead and she keeps on talking to him. does that sound serious?

-that's frightening liz.

-you really think she's losing touch with reality.

-i don't recall her ever being in touch with reality but she's forgotten that the dead know not anything. once she starts losing key adventist doctrines you know it's time to call in medical help.

easy for him to laugh safe in ottawa. a son is a son till he marries a wife but a daughter's a daughter all the days of her life. well gene didn't marry a wife and to be fair his corporate lawyer boyfriend is helping him pay the bills for this place. but still. he is there and i am here. i am a daughter all the days of my life.

the expected unexpected diagnosis. early stage alzheimer's. do we want to try the experimental drugs some people see some improvement for some time. she tries. we see no improvement.

when she starts a small fire with a forgotten piece of toast gene says it's time to get her out of there.

She wanders the halls of the personal care home looking lost no matter how many times gene and i show her to her room.

-we can't stay here we can't live here. using the royal we she has adopted.

-of course you can mom see here's your room your bedspread pictures of the family see your favourite plaque on the wall see your bible here beside the bed.

but no no no. she balls her hands into tiny fists.

[not sure i like "balls" as a verb. it's had such a sucessful life as a noun like an actor who's been

*typecast i can never really accept it in another
role]*

today i am missing a wedding to be here. though i would have missed it anyway because i was not invited. the famous novelist my lover of four years who would not leave his wife left both his wife and me eight months ago for a girl of twenty three.

today they are getting married in the house on galliano island. they have not only written their own vows but published them in a limited edition chapbook to be given as gifts to the wedding guests.

*[ok...all hopes of anonymity lost with the utterly
true chapbook detail.]*

i would like to tell my mother this but cannot shape it into language she will understand. she rages about the lunch we have just finished.

-i do not understand why the vegetables have to be so overcooked. it's not healthy and it's unpalatable. i called the manager and i told him your kitchen staff are torturing the brussels sprouts.

From the fog of alzheimer's my gentle mother has emerged an angry activist. sixty-six years of smiling acquiescence have dropped away she complains she whines she bitches.

sometime to my delight she even swears mildly. i tell her it's time to take her pills she says i don't give a damn about the damn pills. we smile like schoolgirls caught smoking.

i went once to a support group for family and friends of alzheimer's patients. weeping they told how their father mother husband wife had turned into a different person angry hostile. he's like a stranger i don't know him anymore they said through tears.

for the first time i know my mother. layers of costume and stage makeup have been stripped away to reveal her at last.

we cross the footbridge that leads to the front door. the grounds are lovely everyone says with a sigh. i remember my dream of walking through parks and streets with a tiny laughing little girl at my side. i remember walking by my mother's side laughing dancing through puddles tiptoeing look at me mommy look at me. yes look at you my silly princess.

> *[is this clear? the substitute daughter? there are so many layers here i'm not sure i'm unpacking them all well. also hate the word unpacking and have no idea why i just used it]*

i test this strange new intimacy. i'm glad i came to see you today mom. a man i used to be in love with is marrying someone else today.

she looks at me her small face crumpled in shock. oh liz oh my darling baby girl. are you angry?

-angry well yes maybe a little.

her small pink mouth never touched by lipstick makes an o. well if that happened to me sweetheart i'd be really pissed off.

waves of laughter almost knock me off my feet. i sink into the adirondack chair by the door she slowly lowers herself into the matching chair. smiling too enjoying my laughter though she doesn't get the joke. what's so funny dear?

-oh mom i just never expected you to say that. it's just so funny. jesus christ.

the little round o again in shock this time. not the disapproval i remember so well but a surprised hurt.

-oh honey you mustn't speak that way about jesus. he's my best friend you know.

peel away the costume peel away the stage makeup this is what you find here at the core. as real as essential as the anger the swearing the laughter. don't talk that way about jesus honey he's my best friend.

Katie

DAWN SPILLS YELLOW LIGHT OVER the quilt and pillows. Katie stirs and shifts, half-waking, then burrowing deeper under the covers.

Sam moves, not really awake but drawn by the movement of her body. His arm hooks around her and his fingers slip under her nightshirt, feeling their way up the warmth of her belly, to cup her breasts. He still breathes slowly and evenly as if asleep but his fingers are bringing her nipples to life.

Katie yawns, stretches, turns around and in a single fluid motion takes the basal thermometer from its case on the headboard.

She has vague memories of a time when her husband's sleepy morning caresses made her think of passion rather than of ovulation. Now she takes her temperature, trying to be surreptitious so as not to alert him and break the mood. She studies the thermometer. Yes! Today may well be The Day. She shifts to fit her body against Sam's. His eyelids flutter, revealing pale-blue eyes.

"Is it OK?" he asks.

"It's OK," she says, and they kiss.

The monthly cycle of hope and frustration has been going on for over a year. At first it was, "Let's start trying and see what happens." Then it was official: "We're trying for a baby." After six months, Katie began reading up on the art and science of conception. She bought the thermometer. She developed a level of familiarity with her own cervical mucus that she'd never expected to have. The truth was, she had never imagined saying—or thinking—the words *cervical mucus*. But that was the price she had to pay, it seemed, for wanting a baby.

Katie's sure it's her problem. Sam's sure it's his. They've danced around the idea of getting tested, but in the end they always say "One more month." According to the charts, the temps, the mucus, the phases of the moon, the alignment of the chicken entrails, this sunny October morning will be their best chance this month. And if it doesn't happen, she'll definitely call the doctor and make an appointment.

Katie expects her period around the end of the month, but Hallowe'en comes and goes and the only blood she sees appears on the ghoulish masks of children at her door. She waits another day to tell Sam.

On the first of November she sits in her office with Tanya Foley. Tanya is fifteen and pregnant. Her mother wants her to have the baby and let her, Tanya's mother, raise it. Tanya doesn't know what she wants.

"Like Missus up at Planned Parenthood, she said I could still get an abortion, right?" the girl says, cracking her gum. "But my mom says that's a sin and I'll burn in hell. But I'm not even sure I believes in hell. What do you think I should do?"

It's an excellent opportunity to practice non-directive counselling, as Katie neither knows nor cares what Tanya should do. *Get your tubes tied, you brainless little twit, and leave baby-making to the people who are actually capable of caring for a child.* She doesn't say this. She leans forward in the attentive listening posture and says, "Tanya, let's brainstorm a little. Can you think about the different choices you have, and what might happen to you if you made each of those choices?"

"Well I can only make *one* of them," Tanya says, rolling her eyes.

Throughout the interview Katie tries to ignore the thin twist of pain in her gut, the cold dampness between her legs.

When Tanya leaves, Katie goes to the bathroom and, heart pounding, pulls down her pants to reveal the dark blotch of blood against the white cotton. Hot tears spring to her eyes and roll down her cheeks. Her fists pound her thighs.

She goes to see Diane, her supervisor. "I'm having kind of a rough time," she says. "I wouldn't mention it only I think it's affecting my work. I'm having a hard time dealing with pregnant teenagers all of a sudden. Sam and I are trying for—" Katie's voice breaks. She's horrified. She doesn't cry at work. "For a baby," she says, swallowing. "I'm having some— problems. I think it's affecting my ability to be ... empathetic. I don't know what to do about this."

"You had Tanya today?" Diane says. Katie nods.

"Why don't you talk to Anne, see if you can swap Tanya for one of her clients. Tanya's worked with Anne before, I think she'd be OK with that."

"Thanks. Sorry to be such a wimp."

At suppertime she tells Sam, sees the disappointment in his face. "Oh well," he says, smiling. "Guess we'll just have to keep on having sex."

"Bummer."

They eat spaghetti in silence for awhile. "Do you think we should—"

"Talk to the doctor?" Sam finishes. "Sure, if that's what you want."

"Maybe it's time. You know, to get some tests and stuff."

"OK."

"It's a pain in the neck. You have to give a sperm sample, all that stuff. There's a lot of poking and prodding."

Sam just nods. "I think I can rise to the occasion."

Katie gives his joke the half-smile it deserves. "I've been reading up on this, Sam. It's really a long process." She's checked books out of the library, titles like *Taking Control of*

Your Fertility. They finally have a new computer powerful enough to surf the web, and Katie's bookmarked websites, learned that TTC is the acronym for Trying To Conceive. She's become an expert in this alien field in a few short months. "It kind of takes over your life. And it's expensive too. It's not all covered by MCP."

Sam gives her a careful look over his forkful of meatball. "How important is this to you, Katie? How badly do you want a baby?"

"Badly. I want one a lot. Don't you?"

"I do, but I guess I just always thought it would just—happen, you know? I never thought about how much trouble I was willing to go to, to get one."

"I know."

"The thing is—the poking and prodding? It's going to be mostly you they poke and prod at, probably. If I have to give up a few of my guys in a sample jar, that's not going to kill me. But your body's the one that makes the babies, and I think you should get the final say in this. When to start. How far to go. When to stop."

"We'll stop when we have a baby," Katie says, her voice trembling. She looks out the new bay window they've put in the dining room with its view of the long narrow backyard. The maple tree gives up its last golden leaves to the frosty ground below. Sam raises his glass of ginger ale.

"To our baby, then," he says.

There are tests. There is poking; there is prodding. Katie tries a few cycles on Clomid, which worries her mother. "Fertility drugs," says Angela. "Isn't that what these poor women take and they end up having quadruplets and quintuplets? It doesn't seem a like the kind of natural process you want to be messing with."

"In the good old days I would have been called a barren woman," Katie points out. "Sam would have the right to put me aside and take another wife. So let's try to make a truce with modern technology, shall we?"

Clomid starts in the New Year, appropriately for a venture of hope and optimism. Christmas cards and phone calls have been filled with news of pregnancy and babies. Julie is having her third. Jeff and Debbie have a little boy. Katie's college friend Nola is suddenly married and pregnant after years of being contentedly single. "Next Christmas there'll be more," Katie says to Sam. "And every year, the pictures. The baby pictures."

One evening in April Katie stands at the sink doing dishes when Sam comes up behind her, slips his arms around her and begins kissing the back of her neck. The back of the neck has always been Katie's biggest turn-on.

Now she stiffens. "What are you doing?"

Sam draws back; says nothing. She can feel his hurt.

"I'm sorry, but this is not the best time in my cycle and I just wanted you to know before things got too far, OK? Tomorrow, the day after, will be fine."

"Excuse me," Sam says, and heads for the basement steps.

"Sam, wait. I didn't mean—you can go on kissing me—."

"No, that's fine, thanks," says Sam, closing the door behind him.

Katie wants to follow him down there but besides being the cornerstone of his business, the basement workshop is also Sam's retreat, his private sanctum. Generally, she's welcome there, but at times like this she treads carefully.

When the dishes are finished, Katie goes on-line and posts a few weepy messages on one of the TTC forums she haunts. Then she opens a WordPerfect file. She has not written a piece of fiction for many years, but she starts a story now. She writes in the voice of a pregnant woman -- not a thirty-five-year-old woman desperately trying to conceive a much-wanted baby, but a fifteen-year-old who would like to have an abortion except that she may then go to a Hell she doesn't believe in. Katie rediscovers the sheer joy of losing herself in words, creating a fictional reality that, as long as the computer is turned on, seems as durable and important as her real world.

She writes for an hour, then goes to the basement, tapping lightly on the downstairs door. Sam stands at the workbench with his back to her, carefully sanding a piece of elaborate hand-made molding.

"Can I come in?"

Sam shrugs. Katie hesitates, then steps forward. They have been married nearly three years. She is starting to learn the rules of this marriage, the next step after the rules of engagement. Or rather, she and Sam are constructing those rules, one day at a time, learning when to be silent and when to speak up. Now Katie follows her instincts and goes into the workshop, curling up on the wingback chair in the corner, her chair. For awhile she says nothing, just watches his hands moving over the wood.

"Sometimes I think it would be more satisfying, doing what you do—instead of what I do," Katie says at last. "Working with things instead of people."

"Well, it's certainly easier," Sam says. "More straightforward. Wood doesn't have a mind of its own. And once I fix something, it stays fixed. The hardwood floors we refinished last week wouldn't suddenly go out and cover themselves with wall-to-wall carpet once my back is turned."

Katie smiles, thinking of Tanya Foley, now eight months pregnant, who has moved back in with the boyfriend who cheated on her. "Wish I could say the same for my clients." A pause. "I'm sorry. I was being stupid."

"No, you're the one who knows when it's safe to do stuff. If you say it's the wrong day, it's the wrong day," Sam says, not looking up.

"That doesn't mean you can't touch me or kiss me. And besides—sex shouldn't be like something you do in the lab. I hate the way this baby-making business changes everything."

Sam lays down the sandpaper and comes over to squat in front of her chair. "It's wearing you out. Are you ready to—I mean, do you ever think about quitting?"

"Quitting?" It's the last thing on her mind. They're still at the beginning of a very long and tiresome road. "I still really, really want a baby, Sam. But you know after the next few months on Clomid, if nothing happens, they're going to go back and ask whether we want to try in vitro."

"Then it really *will* be something we do in the lab," Sam says.

Katie wipes her eyes with the back of her hand and Sam hands her some industrial-strength brown paper towel. It's already April. Too late now, even if things worked out this month, for a baby picture in the Christmas card. Next year? Maybe. She nods. "Whatever it takes. Even if we have to clone you."

"Nah, can't do that."

"How come?"

"Sure, everyone will want one."

Julie

FILL IN THE BLANKS

I left because: I was afraid of what might happen to my kids.

I went back because: I was afraid of what might happen to Roger without me.

I left because:

I went back because:

I left because:

I went back because:

I left because:

I went back because:

I left because:

I went back because:

I left because:

I went back because:

I left because: I realized God loved me as much as I loved my kids and He would never want to see me hurt.

I won't go back because:

As you can see from the above, I left a lot of blanks in the fill-in-the-blanks exercise at group tonight. Michele started off by telling us that most women in abusive marriages leave an average of SEVEN times and go back to the guy before they make the decision to leave for good. I would never have guessed that.

I didn't have as much to write about as some of the others. Up till this time, I only ever left Roger once, when I was pregnant with Chelsea. Mikayla was five & Kyle was seven.

We were in Ontario, Roger's biggest church yet. It was a large church with a lot of problems, and he was run ragged trying to keep everything going, keep the peace and all. It was kind of like his big break—he knew people in the conference, at the union, were watching him to see how he handled this "challenging" church—it was important for his career.

I taught part-time that year in the church school, on top of looking after the house & kids, and helping with church work. With how tired & stressed we were all the time, well, I guess tempers were even shorter than usual at our house. One night Roger pushed me over the stairs. He usually hurt me in ways that wouldn't show or leave any bruises, but when I fell over the stairs I twisted my ankle and ended up having to go to emergency. The next day I was on crutches telling people I'd tripped over one of the kids' toys on the stairs. Roger told Mikayla it was her Barbie and she cried, thinking it was all her fault.

I was about three months pregnant—of course my ankle was the least of my worries. But I didn't have any bleeding, so I figured things were all right.

But it scared me. I lay awake at night to the sound of Roger's snoring, thinking about how my baby might have been hurt or I knew I'd always blame him. And what about Kyle and Mikayla? He'd never touched them except to spank, and he didn't spank excessively hard or anything. I wondered, was it only a matter of time?

That Sabbath in church he preached about Jesus blessing the children. "Suffer the little children to come unto me, and forbid them not." I sat there passing out crayons and colouring books to the kids to keep them quiet while their father stood in the pulpit and told people in his wonderful, gentle voice how much Jesus loved the little children.

I was shaking inside. I had to get the kids away from him. But where would I go?

I had a cousin in Toronto. She wasn't a really close cousin and it was a couple of hours on the train but I decided to go. I didn't even call first. That afternoon Roger had to go to the hospital and visit some sick church members so I packed one bag for me and the kids and called a taxi to get us to the train station.

I called Laura, my cousin, from the train station. I just asked if it was OK for me and the kids to come on a spur-of-the-moment visit.

I didn't leave a note or anything for Roger. I didn't know what to say. When I got to Laura's that evening I called him. He was frantic. I told him that I thought it would be better if I spent a little time away so we could both cool down and think things over. I hung up the phone while he was still yelling, "You can't leave me Julie! You can't do this to me!"

It was a rough couple of weeks. The kids were confused—why were we taking this unexpected vacation? Laura was really supportive: I didn't tell her about the abuse but just that things were difficult with me and Roger. One day I looked up the number for a women's shelter. I even dialed, but I hung up when someone answered.

Two weeks after I went to Toronto, Roger came to bring me home. He cried and told me how much he loved me and needed me. He said if I left and took the kids he'd lose his job and his self-respect and his whole world would fall apart. He said I was the only thing keeping him sane and if I left he would not only leave the ministry but leave the church and probably fall apart completely. He begged me to come back and promised he'd never do it again.

I had so many things I'd planned to demand from him. I was going to insist that he go get counselling. But once he was actually in front of me, holding my hands and weeping, I couldn't do it. All I saw was this guy I fell in love with when I was 15, the cocky little bayman in the Kingsway jacket trying so hard to be a big man on campus, so desperate to get ahead & win approval. I didn't see how either of us could make it without each other. Laying down the law just wasn't possible.

I gathered up the children and got in the car with him, praying all the way that God would finally change Roger and make him into the man I wanted him to be.

It never happened, did it Lord? You never answered that prayer. Now I know it's pointless to ask You to change other people. You can change me, but You can't change Roger unless he wants to change.

I called him tonight. I haven't talked to him since the week after I came in here to St. John's. He used to call every night and finally I told him I wouldn't take any more calls. For over three months I haven't spoken to him at all.

He wants me and the kids to come home for Christmas. Mikayla and Chelsea are always asking me why we don't live with Daddy anymore, is Daddy ever coming in here. Being together as a family for Christmas would be ideal from the kids' point of view.

I told him I didn't know, that I would have to think it over. I know the right thing to do is to stay here. Or is it? Was it really right to walk away from my marriage? I tell myself I miss being married, not Roger himself. But is that true? There's so much good in him. I loved him for so long. He tells me he's changed. Maybe this time he really has.

If I never go back, how will I know?

Dave

REMEMBER I MENTIONED A FEW weeks ago that my life these days was kind of boring? Boring in a good way—no unexplained accidents or injuries, no crises—but honestly, a little on the dull side?

Yeah well I think I've got that problem solved.

Well, it's been quite a week. Lot happening. And strangely, much of it's been good stuff. Or at least potentially good. One thing is ... well, I got a piece of news this week that was very ... interesting.

No, I'm still kind of thrown by it. I'm not ready to talk about it yet. I need to just ... sit with it for awhile, I guess. Not something I was expecting or prepared for at all. Something that has the potential to grab me by the scruff of the neck and fling me forward into the future a little more forcefully than I wanted to go. But let's talk about that later.

Other stuff I can tell you about. Let's see ... OK, a good one would be that I had a doctor's appointment this week. I hate going, but I've been trying to do things right, check in regularly. This time she had the results on the last batch of tests she ran.

And you know what? It wasn't all that bad. I mean, nobody's going to confuse me with a healthy forty-year old man who's been taking care of himself. But the human body's pretty amazing, isn't it? The level of punishment it can take and the way it'll bounce back.

The long and short of it is that all the unpleasant shit with my liver isn't getting any worse and probably won't as long as I stay sober, eat right, all that stuff. If I take care of myself I can probably keep using this liver for awhile, which is good because I'm pretty attached to it.

Yeah, I left the clinic feeling pretty damn good, better than I've felt in awhile. I said screw the bus and walked home, just to feel ... I don't know. Alive, I guess. Glad to be walking on the earth a little longer. And you know what? Feeling like that, good and healthy and alive—it scared me shitless.

Why? Because it suddenly hit me that if I can really stay sober this time, if I can find a way to move forward from here ... then forty isn't all that old. I mean, yeah, it's halfway to being dead, and you still don't know what's coming around the next corner, but ... I could live a long time yet. These last few years I've gotten used to the idea that I didn't have much time left. I'd never really banked on having to live out the second half of my life, you know?

I guess I was always like that. You know, there's a certain type of guy, in his teens, his twenties, who says, "Screw it, man, I don't expect to live past thirty," and that's the way he lives his life? Well, I was that guy. I always figured something—some accident or whatever—would take me out, or maybe there were times I thought I'd kill myself. Never actually tried it but once, and I was already past thirty then, but I just felt something was going to get me before I had a chance to go gray.

Now I'm facing the possibility that I might get to experience all that—gray hair, arthritis, bifocals, all the joys of middle age.

And old age. I'm scared to death because I don't know what I'm going to do with that.

Oh ... you caught that, did you? I was kind of hoping to slip it in there without drawing too much attention to it.

No, you're right. Thanks for the flattery ... I don't know about "someone as smart as I am." But you're probably right that most people wouldn't casually slip in a reference to a suicide attempt and expect it to pass without notice. I'm sure I've got some kind of deep hidden motive for mentioning it.

Weren't you the one who said we were supposed to focus on the here and now? Do you really need to hear about my unsuccessful attempt to off myself eight years ago?

OK, I guess I did bring it up. And I'm sure there's a tie-in to the here and now. Fear of life, I guess. Maybe I've always suffered from that. Is there a name for that? Biophobia?

Of course being drunk a lot of the time shielded me from feeling it too much. Now it's hitting me hard because I've got nothing to fall back on. Does everyone have this? I look at other people and they seem to have it together, they seem to know how they're going to fill up the next few weeks and months and years. They don't seem terrified.

I'd like to think everyone is secretly just as screwed up as I am and they've figured out some amazing trick to cover it up. Then I could learn the trick and I'd be OK too.

So ... yeah. The one time I decided I couldn't face it was, like I said, about eight years ago. It was after I left Tammy and moved out here. I was working at the university running a computer lab in one of the departments. I'd been seeing a girl and it hadn't worked out, but I can't say I was crushed about that. I had a pretty safe, contained little life carved out for myself.

Then Tammy remarried and her and her new husband and the kids moved out to Vancouver Island. Suddenly my family was in shouting range again. She never made any attempt to contact me but after a couple of months I started to feel ripped off, like I should stand up for my rights as a father. Pathetic or what, eh? Not one minute's thought about what the kids might want or need—just wanting to make sure Tammy wasn't getting anything over on me. God, I amaze myself sometimes.

Anyway, there were phone calls back and forth to the lawyers. The kids were—what, about six and eight then. I used to go over to Victoria on Saturdays or Sundays, pick them up and do pathetic divorced-dad stuff with them—take them to McDonalds, out the museum, to the playground.

One weekend I asked Tammy if I could have the kids overnight. I'd promised them a trip to the zoo sometime and I thought it might work out if they came over on a Saturday evening, stayed the night at my place, and we did the zoo on Sunday.

God, it was exhausting. I'd forgotten what kids were like 24/7. Maybe I'd never really known. We survived the Saturday night—barely—and got ready for the zoo on Sunday. I was packing some pop for the kids in the cooler—my plan was to swing by McDonald's and pick up a something to take with us for lunch—when I suddenly decided to stick a couple of beer in the cooler for myself. Then—this is the good part—as an emergency measure, I filled up a thermos with vodka.

Yeah, I know. But despite everything, I was still living with the illusion that I could have a quick drink to pick me up or tide me over and that would be it. Why anyone who would take a thermos of vodka on a trip to the zoo with their kids could think this way, I don't know.

We made it to the zoo. It was hot, they were tired, we were all cranky. When we stopped for lunch they lit into the nuggets and fries while I had my beer, and we were all happy for the first time that day. I had a small internal struggle over the thermos, because I knew getting drunk while shepherding my kids through the zoo would be a bad way to demonstrate what a fantastic dad I was. But the afternoon was long and hot and the thermos was right there, and I'm sure you know where this story is going, haven't you?

After the lunch break, I was a lot mellower and the whining and fussing didn't bother me so much. I was so mellow, in fact, that it was awhile before I noticed Brett tugging at my sleeve, going, "Daddy, where's Sara?"

Needless to say she was nowhere in sight. And it took me longer than it should have to realize just how serious a problem this was ... six year old girl, lost in huge city zoo ... father has no idea where or when he last saw her. We were running around calling for her, and I remember that I was putting off going to security, because I knew they'd ask a bunch of questions—what she was wearing, what time I last saw her—and I didn't know the answers.

Yeah, eventually we went to security, and she was at the office, eating a popsicle they gave her when the nice security guard picked her up—happy ending, right? Except they saw I was drunk, and wouldn't release her to me. Ended up calling

Tammy to come get the kids. A happy day at the zoo, and my last overnight visit ever with my son and daughter.

When the ordeal finally ended there was nothing to do but go out and get drunk again, and it was while I was driving home that I was suddenly struck by how incredibly pointless and stupid my life was. I knew there was only one good solution: to quit drinking and get my shit together.

Then there was this other solution. I could make it stop. And the beauty of it was, nobody would be upset about me committing suicide, because it would look like an accident. It would *be* an accident. And without giving it much more thought than that, I drove over the edge of a cliff.

God, it's hard to tell this story now, to remember it, after what's happened to Jeff. I mean, I look back at myself eight years ago, deliberately driving my car over a bank because I was drunk and stupid, and then I look at someone like Jeff, a great guy, wonderful husband and father, best friend I ever had—remind me to tell you about the time he saved my life— and suddenly he's driving along and a semi goes out of control and bang, that's it. Stupid assholes throwing their lives away all over the place while good people, decent people, don't get a second chance.

Well, it wasn't much of a cliff. More of a slope. I walked away with a broken collarbone. Lost my license, of course—it wasn't my first DUI. At the end of the day I was back where I started, except with a broken collarbone, no car, no driver's license, and no further hope of seeing my kids. Oh, and my life. I got to keep that little bonus package.

I never directly tried to kill myself again. I figured I'd screw it up some way or another. Better just to rely on the usual method of blocking out the noise of life.

Yeah, that's what it's all about, isn't it? Real life is just so ... so intense. Sometimes I don't know how people can stand it. It just rushes at you all at once—so many emotions, so many choices, so many years rolling out ahead of you. It gets so I just want to turn down the volume. Drinking was the best way I knew of doing that. But now I can't do that anymore. I either have to find another way, or learn to live with the volume up on bust.

So here I am back to my real life, now, this week. And maybe this comes under the "making amends" category, I don't know, but I just had this stupid idea, walking home from the clinic, that I should call up Brett and Sara and ask if they'd like to come over for the weekend.

First I lined up tickets to the Canucks game, I figured that would be kind of a draw. Then I made the call. They were surprised, and a little suspicious, but later in the evening after they talked it over Tammy called back and said they'd both like to come.

I could tell she was worried. She warned me they aren't exactly at an easy age and that just because I'm sober I shouldn't think things were going to be easy.

Do I? Hell no. I'm figuring out that it makes everything a lot harder, in one way. But yeah. I really want to do this. It probably won't be easy, but I want to try it.

When I saw Liz yesterday, I asked her if she'd come with us to the game Saturday night and generally sort of—be around, for the weekend. It sort of made sense in the light of the conversation we'd just been having, the information she'd just given me.

No, I told you I'm not going to talk about that today. I need a little more time to chew that one over.

After I made those calls the other night, I went out to the convenience store to get some milk and bread and stuff. You know all that AA stuff about staying away from triggers? Well, I do pretty good with that. I mostly don't play or sing in bars, I avoid the liquor store. But there are things you can't avoid ... like when they rearrange things at the corner store and the fridge where you usually get your milk is blocked with cases of beer. I had my hand on the door and the fridge half-opened before I realized. And I stood there looking at this whole fridge full of cases of Molson's and—you know what I thought of?

Remember awhile back, early on when I started seeing you, I told you this story about hiding vodka in Coke cans when I was a teenager? Remember that? And about this one time when I was feeling guilty, and I looked at the Coke can thinking, *I don't need this* and realizing that yes, I did.

That's exactly the thought I had, looking at the beer cooler in the convenience store. I remembered that moment, and I said to myself, *I don't need this.*

That was—well, it was an amazing moment for me.

Want it? Hell, yes, sure I did. But there's a difference between want and need. I don't have to have everything I want, because there are other things I need. I need my kids. I need my friends. I need work and music. I need a functioning liver. I need God. I need ... I need to live. Life scares the shit out of me, sure, but it's a hell of a lot better than the alternatives.

ELEVEN

Jeff

I GREW UP EXPECTING the Last Judgement.

We always knew it was coming, right after the End Times. At the Last Judgement, God would open the books. Every act or thought you'd ever had would be laid bare and God would judge you worthy or unworthy.

There were different versions of the Last Judgement. You had the sheep-and-goats version—all that mattered was how kind you were and if you helped the poor. You had the saved-by-grace version, where nothing you did actually mattered. Jesus would step forward and say, "Jeff Evans claimed Me as his personal savior. I died for all his sins!" and you'd be in like Flynn. Then you had the version where you were judged on every idle word you spoke and every act you'd done. This was the version that my dad most of our teachers and pastors seemed to have in mind. Anything, from the beer you drank at a party to the dirty joke you repeated in the boys' washroom—anything was fair game for the Last Judgement.

Like a lot of things about dying, the Last Judgement is not what I expected.

The pain is now gone, cut off as if it has been unplugged. Unfortunately my body is gone too. I'm no longer present in the room where doctors still struggle to save my brain and heart and nerves. I'm no longer at this address.

I'm in a room, or maybe a courtyard—the walls are high but there's no ceiling. Very light, very open. And I'm alone. But I know what I have to do.

Dave told me once about a thing you have to do in AA which sounds horrible. You're supposed to go through and make a list, an actual written list, of all the harm you've done to anyone. Then you go ask forgiveness and try to make amends. Everything, from your whole life.

I think people who've been to AA should be exempt from the Last Judgement, just for having done that.

That's not what I have to do here. My sins—I've got plenty—don't seem to matter in this quiet place. Yet there's a question in the air, and finally I find the words to express it. I recognize it because I've been hearing it all my life.

Was I good enough?

I picture myself going around to every person I've known: my mother, my father, my brothers, my wife and kids, my friends. One simple question. Was I good enough?

Mom would say yes. But would she really mean it? She's always been good to me, but it's no secret in the family that Larry is her favourite—the baby. I was the one who moved home when she got sick, to be closer to her and Dad. But it's really Debbie who does stuff for them. She goes to Mom's appointments with her, cleans their house. She brings casseroles and homemade bread.

Mom would have been really happy if I'd become a pastor.

Was I good enough? Dad would say, *You can do better, b'y. Just give it your best effort. Was that your best effort?*

Was I good enough? My brothers would laugh. I'm sure they never ask that question about themselves. They know they're good enough.

My kids would say, "Daddy's the greatest." They're at that age. But I haven't really done that well. Brandon is a handful at school and Debbie does all the discipline. I lose my temper. I'm not a perfect dad. In five years Brandon will be a teenager.

I'll probably yell at him and tell him he's not good enough. If I were going to be there in five years, that is.

My wife. Debbie once told me she loved me because I was kind. But deep down, she must know she could have done better. I'm not as smart as she is. I'm not as good a person. I forget anniversaries, I work too many long hours and leave her alone with the kids. I could do better. I could have done better.

My friends. What would my friends say? I've tried to be a good friend. Only twice, I think, did I ever really have to go out on a limb to help a friend. I failed both times.

I got this call a few years back. When we were out in Vancouver. Dave and Liz both lived out there too. I saw Liz now and then but hardly ever saw Dave—we lost touch, I guess. Different lives. One night Liz called me. She said Dave had phoned her and sounded desperate, said he might be dying. My first thought was that he'd tried to kill himself. I drove over there as fast as I could. I'd never seen the dump where he lived and frankly I'd be quite happy if I never had seen it. The kind of place where rats nest in the mattresses. Hard to believe my best buddy had ended up there.

I got him to hospital and stayed with him for awhile. Just a side-effect of drinking too much. I knew he wanted to thank me for the rescue effort and leave it at that. But I had to go a step farther. Maybe God called or something, I don't know. I told Dave I'd help him get into rehab, even give him money. And I did. He went to rehab, and I put up the money. Dave said he'd pay me back but I wrote the money off the minute it was out of my pocket.

In the end it added up to nothing. He quit for a few months and soon he was back at it again. I call him sometimes these days and I can tell things are in a downward spiral. One of these days he really will kill himself. I couldn't stop my best friend from dying.

The other time I had a chance to be a good friend was just a few months ago. I had to go out to Central to look at a piece of land for a client. On the way home I stopped at a fast-food place in Grand Falls. I was barely sat down when Julie walked in.

I knew she lived in Grand Falls. We saw each other a couple of times a year, at Campmeeting or when her husband came into town for some church meetings. Julie and I never said much more than "Hi" to each other. But there's no doubt I always had a soft spot for her, my first girlfriend.

She still looked good. Older, of course, but in a soft and pretty way. She'd put on a few pounds but it looked good on her. Her smile was as warm as it used to be when she was thirteen, sitting on the dock at Southwest Pond wearing my Blue Jays cap. We took our trays and sat down together and had our first real conversation in years.

At first she was all bright and cheerful. But as we kept talking I knew something was wrong. I'm a guy, I'm not good with this kind of thing. Debbie or Katie or some other woman would have been all sympathetic and listening. I just said something stupid like, "You don't seem all that happy, Jules."

Like turning on a tap she started to cry, wiping her eyes with the cheap restaurant napkins and apologizing. "It's OK, it's OK," I said, doing this little patting thing on the back of her hand. "What is it, it's OK, you can tell me."

And she told me. I couldn't have been more surprised if she'd stood on the table and stripped. But all she did was roll up one sleeve and show me an ugly bruise, purple turning yellow, and tell me where it came from.

I never liked Julie's husband Roger. I thought he was the full of himself and with very little reason. I was suspicious of his big smile and firm handshake. Also, he used to be really possessive about Julie when we were out at CUC. Once he took a swing at me for hanging around with her. Still, I never would have imagined that he'd spent the last fifteen years beating the living crap out of her.

"If I got my hands on Roger I'd put him through a wall," I told her. "In fact I'd like to go over there now and do it. I'll run you by the house, you pack your bags. I'll punch Roger's lights out and drive you home to your mom's place."

Julie started laughing through her tears. "Jeff, I can't do that! I've got kids, and besides, you can't go punching out my husband. He's a pastor."

"I think you pronounce that *bastard*," I said. "Julie, seriously, you've got to leave him."

"How can I? We've got three kids together."

I hated the way she said that. So helpless. "It's the kids you need to be thinking of," I said.

I wanted to take her in my arms and kiss her. And I'm a guy who for all my faults has never once cheated on his wife. I mean sure, fantasy babes in movies and magazines, yeah—but in real life? Cheat on Debbie? Yet here was my first girlfriend, the sweetest girl I ever knew, crying because some hypocritical prick had been making her life miserable for fifteen years.

I didn't kiss her and I didn't go punch Roger. I stayed there with her for an hour, till she had to go get her kids from school. I swore if there was anything I could do, anyway I could help, she only had to ask.

"Just don't tell anyone," she begged. "And pray for me."

She didn't leave him. It was June when I met her. A few weeks later, I saw her and the kids with Roger at Campmeeting, looking like the perfect Christian family. It was like our whole conversation had been a dream. A nightmare. I never got a chance to pull her aside and ask how things were going. I just stood by and watched her walk away with the guy

I knew was beating on her, and I did nothing. Good enough? I don't think so.

So a jury of my peers has weighed in with their opinions. There's really only one person left to hear from: the Judge. God, have I been good enough?

I grew up in church, learned my memory verses, went to Sabbath School every week. Now I'm forty and I go to church, take my kids to Sabbath School, help them learn their memory verses. Except for a few rebellious years when I was a teenager, I've pretty much stayed on the straight and narrow. Last year, the nominating committee even asked me if I'd consider being an elder. They also asked Sam, Katie's husband, who's probably the best friend I have these days. Neither of us could believe it. Were we suddenly old enough, mature enough, to be elders?

But for me there was a whole other layer to it that I didn't mention to Sam, or to anyone. Me, good enough to be an elder? I always thought that was for the super-spiritual. Some days I forget to pray. I don't really read the Bible that much. I gave up working on Sabbath when the kids came along because I wanted to set a good example, but I always resented the way my business took a hit from that. God never seemed to pour out the blessings the way He was supposed to. When I think of how much better, kinder, more spiritual I could have been, there's no doubt. Good enough? Definitely not.

The empty room is silent. Nothing moves and no-one speaks. The light grows brighter. And brighter still till it hurts my eyes. I close them but I can feel the light, in me and through me and all around me. And suddenly I know it. I know the thing that's always eluded me.

It's not something you can put into words. I can't even come close, but my best stab at it is to say: *It's not about good enough. It was never about that at all. It's not about you. It's about Me.*

All those sermons about grace, the Bible studies on the book of Romans. They never scratched the surface on a lifetime of self-doubt. But now it's here and clear and the thought that I ever doubted it—doubted Him—makes me want to laugh. The desire to laugh leaps out of me and fills the air in this small, clear, joyful room.

Now that I've discovered this, it would be OK to die. But it would be better to live. To go back and live with the people I love and not spend all my time worrying whether I measure up. I don't care about how beat-up my body is. I'll live in a wheelchair if I have to. I just want to see everybody again and know that it's OK, that I don't have to try a little harder, that *good enough* is not the point.

The brilliant light all around is fading as if someone turned a dimmer switch, fading into a warm twilight, a safe and sleepy darkness where I could lie down and be at peace.

Oh, I want to live forty more years or one more day without worrying about *good enough*. I want to live. I want ... I need ... oh, God.

Oh, God!

Only the Good Die Young

2005

2000

Julie

I SHOULD BE AT GROUP *instead of home writing in my journal. I didn't go tonight. I skipped. First time. It's a twelve-week group and this was week eleven. Not a great time to pip off, as we used to say in school.*

I've gone to every meeting, I've done all the journal-writing exercises. I've done everything right since the day in August that I left home. Just like I was the model wife for so many years, now I'm the model abuse survivor.

I can't go to the group because I've made up my mind to go home for Christmas and I know what Michele and the girls in the group will say if I tell them. I can't tell them, I can't tell Katie, I can't tell Mom, even though I guess I'll tell them both at some point. Everybody who cares about me will be so disappointed.

I'm not going back to Roger, not permanently. I'm going home for Christmas so my kids can have both parents together for the holidays. We'll all be under our own roof again and I can sit down and talk with Roger about everything. I've learned a lot about myself in the last few months. I'm stronger now. Maybe we can work something out. Maybe he'll admit there's a problem and go get counselling.

Maybe pigs will fly.

I spent a lot of today wanting to cry, which worried me since I haven't felt like that in quite some time. I've been doing so well.

I remember the first morning I couldn't get out of bed. It was up in Ontario, a year or so before we moved home to Newfoundland. Kyle was in Grade Six, Mikayla was in Grade

413

Three, and Chelsea was still home with me. One Sunday evening I did all the usual routine—finished the housework, made the lunches and laying out school clothes, made a few phone calls. I went to bed and was asleep before Roger came in—he used to work late in his study most nights. Then in the morning, suddenly I couldn't get up.

I didn't feel any physical pain except that I was very, very tired. I thought maybe I was coming down with the flu but there was no cough, no runny nose, no fever. What I mainly felt was just this tremendous sense of heaviness, like weights were tied to my limbs. I felt such despair I thought it would be pointless to get out of bed.

I guess I'd been depressed for awhile and never really recognized it. But that morning the kids were jumping on me, Roger was out of the shower and saying, "Julie, are you crazy? It's seven-thirty. Come on, get out of bed!" And I just lay there. When he told me again to get up, I started to cry.

I got out of bed, finally. By lunchtime I was lying down on the couch and Chelsea was watching TV, which I never let her do in the daytime. Nothing was done, dishes weren't washed or anything. When Roger came home from his hospital visits expecting lunch, he flipped out.

Things got worse instead of better over the next few weeks. I tried praying, reading the Bible—all the things I'd always told people would help if they felt down or discouraged. I spent more and more time lying on the couch just crying. Roger was at his wits' end. One night he shook me as if he could shake sense into me.

I said I thought I should see a doctor and Roger asked what was wrong with me, did I have some physical symptom? He said he didn't want me to go to some doctor who would start shoving tranquilizers at me, that the only problem was I didn't have enough faith.

He was right about that, anyway. At that stage I had no faith whatsoever. Faith is the evidence of things not seen, the substance of things hoped for. I hoped for nothing at all. I couldn't even imagine hope.

Our family doctor was a good, kind man. When I broke into tears there in his office, he patted my hand and said it sounded like I might be depressed.

"But what could be causing it?" I asked him.

He shook his head and said they didn't always know. He said it could be some stress or problem in my life but sometimes it was just brain chemistry. He said even normal, well-adjusted people with happy lives could get depressed.

It really seemed like he didn't want to hear anything bad about my life. It was a small town and Roger was well-known and well-liked. He volunteered with a lot of community organizations on projects like the food bank, stuff like that. Part of me wanted to say, "Well, I'm under a bit of stress, because every time my husband gets angry he hits me or punches me or slaps me." But I knew I couldn't say anything like that.

But I had to have help. A depression that could be blamed on brain chemistry sounded perfect. Roger would have been angry about the meds, but I hid it from him. Soon I was able to get out of bed and get through a day without weeping all the time.

I've been on antidepressants for 5 years now. They do help. I understand a lot more about depression than I used to. We talked about it in the group one time and Michele said something that really stuck with me. She said that being depressed was like trying to put together a 1000-piece puzzle and having someone throw a tablecloth over the top of the puzzle and say, "OK now, put it together!" It's impossible. The puzzle pieces are the stresses and problems we face in our lives and the tablecloth is the chemical imbalance in the brain.

Getting on the right meds is like taking off the tablecloth. You still have a 1000-piece puzzle to put together ... but at least you can see what you're working with.

These last few weeks, I was starting to feel like maybe I had the outside of the puzzle done—that outer rim that you fit everything else inside, the part I always do first when the girls and I put a puzzle together. Last doctor's appointment before this one, I even talked with her about reducing my meds a little. It's so much easier to talk with this doctor because I've been honest with her. She knows I've left my husband and she knows why. She said maybe I would have less need for the meds now that my situation has changed and I'm feeling stronger.

That was a couple of weeks ago. Ever since first Kyle and then Roger talked to me about Christmas vacation, that strong feeling has been ebbing away. It's like I'm looking at the puzzle realizing that while I may have the outline done, most of the puzzle is still left to do and all the pieces look the same to me now. It's beyond me. I don't think I have what it takes anymore.

I need to talk to someone. One time a few years ago, about the same time I started taking the antidepressants, I was talking to Katie on the phone when I almost felt brave enough to tell her. But as soon as I admitted I was having a hard time, she said things were rough for her too—that was when she and Sam were trying for a baby, before they adopted Charlotte—and I ended up listening and sympathizing, keeping my own troubles locked inside like a good pastor's wife should. It was the same whenever I talked to my mom or sister in those days. We were talking about moving back to Newfoundland at that time and when I thought of seeing the people I was close to, all I could think was how could I keep them from getting too close?

Roger always reminded me we had to keep some distance from church members—that professional role. The goal for the ideal pastor's wife seemed to be: friendly with everyone, friends with no-one. Only later did I realize how much power that gave him.

So the silence went on, and maybe would have gone on forever if it hadn't been for a chance encounter with another old friend this past summer. If I hadn't met Jeff that day—if we hadn't talked—how differently might things have worked out?

If I were ever to go back to Roger, things would have to be different. So much has happened. I'm a different person now. If I went back, would I become that same frightened, depressed person again? And who will I become if I go on by myself?

Katie

LIZ IS WAITING FOR HER IN THE Arrivals area at Vancouver airport. "You're looking great," Katie says as they hug, wondering if there could be a more meaningless greeting for two old friends.

It's no lie. Liz does look fine: her dark hair now has a purplish-blue sheen and she's pierced her nose. It's a measure of her confidence that the nose stud looks in no way incongruous on woman of thirty-five.

In the parking garage Liz says, "Throw your bag in the back seat; there's a bunch of stuff in the trunk." Katie complies, thinking that unless Liz is keeping bodies in the trunk it can't be much more crowded than the backseat of her Honda Civic, which is completely covered, seat and floor, with discarded jackets and sweatshirts, books and magazines, empty take-out containers, loose tapes and CDs. The front passenger seat is no better: Liz says, "Just fling that stuff in the back. I love having a car; it's like having another apartment that moves around with you."

"I guess," Katie says. Dangling from the rearview mirror is a pair of baby shoes—Katie can't think whose they might be—and the laminated card from Shopper's Drug Mart that explains how to do a breast self-exam complete with diagrams. Catching Katie's glance, Liz says, "Those things are really made to hang in the shower, but I find it makes a better conversation piece in here." The CD player jumps to life, blasting Bif Naked, which Katie recognizes only from kids playing it at work.

"And the booties?"

"Oh, mine," Liz says. "Found them when we were packing up my mom's house. I'm mothering my inner child these days," she adds, in that tone of voice that walks the line between serious and deadpan. She uses the same voice on the phone to say that she's unlocking the centres of her feminine power through Goddess worship. After eight years of phone calls, Katie's been assuming it will be easier to read Liz when they're face to face, easier to judge when she's kidding and when she's serious. She sees now this might not be so easy.

"And your mom? How is she?"

"Not really any worse, except she wanders now and the nursing home staff have to keep bringing her back."

"That's awful. I mean, how old is she? Not seventy yet."

"No, sixty-nine."

"Same age as my mom."

"And your mom is, what, chairing half a dozen committees and writing a memoir?" Liz laughs. "She's the greatest, your mom. I never told her what an inspiration she was to me when I was a teenager. I mean, I never even realized there were other ways of being an adult woman until I met her."

Katie nods. "You should send her an email or something, tell her that. She'd appreciate it."

"I'll drop her a note. She's online?"

"Heck yes. She's got my dad designing a website for her."

Liz throws back her head and laughs. "More power to the both of them. They've lasted better than my folks, for all the clean living my parents did."

"It's so random. Who's going to make it and who's not. It must be hard for you, watching her like that."

Liz shrugs. "In some ways she's easier to take like this."

Liz turns onto a main road and the night city takes shape around them. "I was going to talk Dave into coming to the airport but I couldn't get hold of him," she says. "We're going to try to get together with Jeff and Debbie on the weekend, maybe go over to Victoria and see Butchart Gardens or something."

Katie has imagined an old gang reunion forming around her weekend conference in Vancouver. "Well I'll be in meetings all day tomorrow and Friday, but I'm free Sab— Saturday. It'd be great to get together with Jeff and Debbie can get up then. I can't wait to see the baby."

"Not so much a baby anymore," Liz says. "He's a holy terror, I'm sure the kid is ADHD, but he's gonna be a little heartbreaker. Big baby-blue eyes, blond hair—a little Jeff all over again."

Katie expects Liz's eighth-floor apartment to be a less mobile version of her car, but she's surprised. Yes, it's cluttered, but not so cluttered that Liz's decorating touches are overwhelmed. She has original art on the walls— "mostly by friends," she explains—bold, striking, abstract. Katie clears a space to sit on the futon and kicks off her shoes as she looks around at Liz's pictures, Liz's books, Liz's furniture. Nothing fussy, no knick-knacks—a lot of junk strewn around but if you strip all that away the room is strong, clear, unapologetic. Like Liz.

Katie's relieved to find there's no awkwardness; she and Liz talk as easily as if they were sixteen or twenty-one. Liz admits she's crabby—"by which I mean, of course, crabbier than usual,"—because she's just quit smoking. "Quite apart from the whole nicotine addiction thing, it suddenly struck me that the only reason I'm still doing it is because when I was thirteen my father thought it was the worst sin I could commit. It finally dawned on me that twenty years is a long time to spend sabotaging your body just to spite a dead man, you know?"

The next evening, after a full day of workshops and meetings, she meets Liz at an Indian restaurant for supper before returning to the apartment. "I finally got hold of Dave and asked him if he'd meet us here," Liz says, "but he said he was busy and maybe we'd get together later in the weekend. It's going to suck if you don't get to see him at all—did you call to tell him you were going to be in town?"

Katie shakes her head. "I haven't even had his number for, oh, two years. Since the last time he moved, I think. Totally lost touch. How's he doing?"

Liz shrugs, dipping a chunk of naan bread in chutney. "I don't see him that much either. Used to, but we've kind of drifted apart. I don't think he's—" she pauses, looks up at Katie as if measuring her. "I mean, you know he drinks a lot, right?"

"Well, yeah."

"Yeah. I don't think he's doing all that well, actually. We used to hang out a lot but—it's funny, I see Jeff and Debbie these days more than I see Dave. Even though their lives and mine are polar opposites."

"You mean the whole married-with-children thing."

"I mean the whole steady jobs, going to church, married-with-children thing," Liz says, taking a sip of her beer. "I'm not knocking it—I'm just saying it wouldn't work for me. No offense. I mean, I guess that's pretty much your life too, except for the children part."

"Not for lack of trying," Katie says, around the knot that suddenly tightens in her throat.

"Right. You guys still trying?" The word rolls casually off Liz's tongue. *Trying.*

"We're talking about adoption now. Maybe that's the way to go. We've been looking into these international adoptions...."

"God. Sorry. I mean, that must be incredibly stressful."

"Yeah it's that. And with the adoption thing—you know, there are so many questions. I know people say you love them just as if they're your own, but really—can you? And with a child from some orphanage in China or wherever—I mean, there's all these questions about taking them out of their own country, their own culture, all that."

"Right. Like language, history, everything—how do you raise them to honour their own heritage and still have them be fully a part of your own family, your own community."

"Exactly." Katie's takes a bite of curry that sets her mouth on fire; she takes a swig of water which doesn't help at all.

"Gene and Bob talked about it, actually."

"Adopting?"

"Yeah, one of those kids from like an orphanage in Eastern Europe or something. It's a whole hassle though, gay couples adopting. I think they're gonna stick with dogs."

Katie feels Liz watching her, trying to gauge her reaction to the idea of gay adoption. She's not sure herself how she feels about it, only that no matter what rhetoric she hears from conservatives in church, she can't imagine Gene and his partner being any worse than many of the straight parenting couples she sees at work. "That's too bad—I'm sure they'd be good dads," she says, although she's never met Bob. "Gene's a good guy."

"Yeah, he's still got a soft spot for you too. Is it weird now, thinking that you guys dated once? Like that your first love turned out to be gay?"

"First *boyfriend*," Katie corrects her.

"Right, yeah." Liz nods, and when she says a moment later, "Anyway, I hope Dave's gonna make it on Saturday, it'd be good to see him again," they both understand the connection without it being said. Katie's first love: that was never Gene.

Talking to Liz, she swings rapidly from feeling that they live on two separate planets, to feeling like Liz is the only person who really gets what she's saying. "What about you?" she asks Liz now.

"Me?"

"I mean, you just said you couldn't do the whole marriage-and-family bit. Have you been with anyone—seriously—since Flaming Bastard?" This is the official title of Liz's last long-term boyfriend, the married novelist who dumped her for a college student. "Do you ever regret not having kids?"

"Regret? Geez Katie, I'm not quite over the hill yet, you know—I don't think the eggs have passed their expiry date." Katie, whose own eggs apparently came already expired, nods apology. "I could still decide to have a baby—on my own, I'm a twentieth century woman."

"Twenty-first."

"Right. Or is that not till next year? Anyway, there's no-one I'd particularly like to have a child with. But sometimes…." Liz draws her fork through the basmati rice still on her plate as if creating one of those miniature sand gardens that is supposed to somehow soothe and calm you. "Yeah, I think about it. Maybe for selfish reasons, like it'd be cool to have a little mini-me to shape and mold. I imagine this little girl…." She shakes her head and goes back to raking her rice garden. "You're right, there hasn't been anyone since Flaming Bastard. No-one long term. But I went off the Pill. I always have condoms in my purse, but sometimes I think there'll be one night, one guy—maybe I'll just decide he's a good risk from a genetic point of view, you know? Sorry, I must sound like a notorious slut."

"No, you sound like a twenty-first century woman," Katie says. "Only you know what's right for you, Liz."

"You've gotten a lot more tolerant."

"Life does that to you. Or maybe it's working with an endless string of people with crappy lives in constant crisis. It gets harder to judge people."

"And yet there you are, every week, sitting in that same pew, hearing about how you're right and everyone else is wrong." It's the first time Liz has let bitterness tinge her voice.

The waiter interrupts to ask about dessert. Liz orders gulab jamun and chai tea; Katie asks for mango ice cream. After the interruption, it would be easy to ignore Liz's comment, but Katie decides not to.

"Sometimes it is like that," she admits. "And I don't like it. But there's so much there that's—part of me. My faith. My family. That whole sense of—community, I guess. Knowing there's this whole community of people who've known me since I was a kid, who have certain expectations. It's like, you know, the place where everybody knows your name."

Liz raises her glass. "Well then, what can I say but—cheers. Sounds like everything you love is everything I hated about it."

Dessert arrives. The mango ice cream is delicious enough to make Katie forget the earlier mouth-burning incident. The conversation drifts from Liz's new fascination with Wicca to her latest writing projects.

"What about you?" Liz says. "You still write?"

"Me? Oh—not really. I mean, not seriously. I haven't for years." It's funny. Katie can talk to Liz about her defective ovaries, their motley crew of old friends, Liz's gay brother and his partner, dead and dying parents, her faith in God—but there's still this one taboo. The small pile of short stories, labouriously written and edited, grows in a binder on the shelf at home. Every time she thinks about sending one out, she gets a call or an email telling her that Liz is up for another award, that Liz's latest poetry collection is coming out.

Jeff calls the next day to say he and Debbie are coming down with their son's flu and won't be able to meet up with Katie while she's there. Liz gets hold of Dave on Saturday night. He's got stuff on the go tonight, he says, but tomorrow afternoon he'll meet them for coffee before Katie goes to the airport.

"Sorry," Liz says to Katie. "Not much of a reunion."

"Never mind. *We've* had a good reunion."

They stop at the coffee shop on the way to the airport, Katie's bag packed and in the car. They've been sitting there for twenty minutes, drinking lattes, when Katie sees Dave enter. Rather, she sees a middle-aged man looking unkempt in jeans and a burgundy sweater stretched out of shape. He pauses inside the door, scanning the room like someone entering unfamiliar territory. When Liz catches his eye and waves him over, Katie is caught completely off-guard.

She expects people to change—was surprised, in fact, to see Liz had changed so little. When she last saw Dave he looked heavier, and she'd half-expected him to have gotten fat, but instead he's very thin—*gaunt*, is the word that comes to mind. His hair, now close-cropped, is graying. Until he smiles at her, she wouldn't have had any clue this is the Dave Mitchell she grew up in love with.

Then it's there—the smile, the eyes. She looks at his hands. Still the same, long slender fingers. "Sorry I'm late," he says. "Katie, you look—great."

"Thanks." She can't really say *you too*, even to be polite.

"Let me just go get a coffee," he says, still standing, searching his pockets for change.

"That's all right, I'm going up for a muffin. I'll get yours," Liz says. "Black, right?"

"Black, no sugar, none of your fancy cappucino shit for me. How's it going, Katie?" he says as he eases into a chair.

"Not bad. Been out here since Wednesday, going to a conference. I hoped we could all get together."

"Yeah. Sorry I didn't—I mean, I just had a lot on the go this week."

"What are you up to? Still computers?"

"Yeah, off and on." Dave shifts in his seat, glancing up at Liz who stands at the counter, then around the coffee shop. "Kind of between jobs right now." His fingers drum staccato on the tabletop.

"Doing any music?"

"Not really. Messing around on my own a little, but I haven't played in a band for—well, awhile. Haven't had my big break yet," he adds, the fleeting smile warming his face once more.

Liz is on her way back with coffee and a muffin. "I don't have your number anymore," Katie says. "I miss being in touch with you."

"Got a pen?" Dave pulls over a paper napkin and scribbles his number, writes his name under it. Katie writes hers above it and tears off the other part of the napkin to give to Dave. "Call once in awhile, OK?"

Dave nods, taking his coffee from Liz. His hand shakes a little, jingling the spoon in the cup. "I'll do that."

Twenty minutes later, the girls have to leave so Katie can catch her flight. Dave hugs her hard against his sweater, which reeks, mostly but not exclusively of cigarette smoke. "I'll try to do better with keeping in touch," he says. "You take care."

Liz hugs her, too, when they say goodbye at the airport. "It's been wonderful," she says. "And let me know what you decide to do, about the adoption and everything. I think you'd be a wonderful mother."

Katie grins. "I think you would be too," she says.

Two hours later, Katie is aloft, flying east on the red-eye, home to Sam and their house and her job and her life and decisions that need to be made. She sits under the soft glow of the reading light, staring out the window into a night she can't see. A guy at work has as his email signature line: "God is my co-pilot. But we crashed in the mountains and I had to eat him."

Tonight the seat beside her is empty. God rides beside her as they fly over the mountains. Like Sam, sometimes when they fly together, He doesn't say anything. But it's good to know he's there.

liz

I LIVE IN THE MOMENT. be here now my only mantra. cut loose from ties of past and present i soar free in this one and only moment. until the past reaches out with grappling hooks pulling pulling anchoring me to the ground.

first the nursing home. ms carter your mother she's had a fall. her hip it's her hip.

by the time i arrive she has been moved from emergency to a ward she is bright and agitated plucking at the covers.

-when will they let me out of here liz i need to be at home. your father likes to have supper on the table these nights when he works late.

-it's okay mom it's all taken care of. i cooked a casserole and left it for him.

i enjoy this fantasy role-play game in which i enter her fears and soothe them. i even imagine the casserole, fri-chik in mushroom soup always a favourite in the adventist home.

> *[fri-chik -- again the meat substitutes are probably not self-explanatory]*

i update gene with nightly phone calls. will she need more care we may need to make other arrangements. we murmur and commiserate about our problem child the way mom and dad once sat down at the kitchen table figuring out how to handle liz's bad crowd of friends or gene's latest suspension from school. we do this without the guilt blaming shaming recriminations. we neither love nor hate nor need each other as much as they did.

then katie comes for a conference. eight years and a continent of experience stretch between us. i prepare myself to have nothing in common with my do-gooder social-worker church-going girlhood friend.

she wants to get all the old gang together. i see only futility and disappointment in the venture but dutifully make the calls anyway. jeff is busy with work and family dave is busy with booze and despair but we will try we will try to get together they say for old times' sake.

she comes we sit up late nights talking and laughing the four days slip away like whispers not enough time. we embrace at the airport both near tears each wondering if we will ever see each other again.

and i beat my clipped wings and try to regain that soaring freedom but the hooks are in my flesh and i am yanked earthward again.

my phone vibrates after midnight. liz it's me oh my god i think i'm dying.

who the hell is this i think but do not say. what's the matter i say instead playing for time hoping for clues in the voice.

-my god my god i don't know what's wrong but i think i'm dying. help me please help.

the voice clicks like a key in a lock. dave what the hell is wrong. dave never calls me.

-just come over here please.

-i don't even know where you live.

he tells me and i shudder no way in hell am i going to the downtown east side alone at night. i'll be there i tell dave. i look up jeff's number.

no hesitation. i'm leaving now i'll pick you up.

we climb the stairs of what might be a crack house or god alone knows what the stairwell stinks of piss and booze. all the upstairs doors are closed no-one seems to be around but jeff finds dave in the bathroom at the end of the hall.

-jesus he says what a bloody mess. he says the name of jesus like my mother says it like a prayer.

i want to be a florence nightingale i want to help but all i can do is pass jeff wet paper towels and call an ambulance. jeff needs my help to get dave to his feet. his clothes are damp and reeking with vomit piss shit blood i do not want to touch him. already in my head composing an email to katie. if you wanted a real reunion of the old gang you should have stayed another couple of weeks.

no i can't tell katie this. she was so in love with dave i thought her heart would break. there's nothing left of that boy in this broken man who hangs between jeff and me as we stagger down the stairs like christ being taken down from the cross. jeff and i are nicodemus and joseph of arimithea too bad we haven't got the hundred pounds of sweet smelling spices we could certainly use some of that in this particular garden tomb.

[i like the scriptural allusion but do i really want to cast dave as a christ figure and if so what does this imply especially in light of recent developments? future generations of students writing their thesis on liz carter will want to know so i should figure it out before they do]

i am the mad voice in the head the detached commentator. jeff is all concern but underneath i feel his anger. dave peels away from us to retch on the sidewalk.

a similar night a thousand years ago in st. john's we all reeled home from a party at russ keating's house me and jeff in defiance of curfew dave much drunker than we were singing bohemian rhapsody at the top of his lungs. my first time being really drunk that night it was the boys who caught me as i hurled in the street and carried me home between them to face the wrath of dad.

three teenage kids learn everyday in church in school that drinking is a sin yield not to temptation touch not taste not. three kids laugh at the rules enjoy a few beers at a party. twenty years later two of them hold the other upright between them as he pukes up his own blood. a tribute to the enduring power of lifelong friendship sure but also to the total terrifying randomness of fate.

in the emergency waiting room i start to shake.

i am the coward who drives away from the wreck the levite who passes the man on the other side of the road. i soar above the pain and filth i am one of the lucky ones who will not spend tonight in emergency with a broken hip with a bleeding stomach with a dying child i am the lucky one. no blood no ties.

i sit at my desk with a piece of blank paper a pen gripped so hard my fingertips hurt. the smell of that stairwell the sight of a man who was once my friend sprawled on that floor the white white clean of the hospital waiting room all these things crowd my mind demanding words words words.

dress us in words make us palatable make us disturbing and beautiful maybe you'll win another prize a handful of ribbons twisted from the gut of someone else's pain.

[there's a lot of irony in reading this about dave and jeff now after all that's happened. maybe one more good reason this should never see the light of publication]

Dave

JUST TO SAVE YOU THE TROUBLE of asking, my week sucked.

I'm probably overstating my case a little. It didn't suck exactly. The weekend, with my kids? It wasn't exactly a Norman Rockwell painting, you know? When it was all over I phoned Liz to thank her for being around, and she pointed out that having teenagers isn't supposed to be a walk in the park.

I said, "Yeah, but having them for the *weekend*? Is that supposed to be this hard?"

Well, I let myself in for it. And when you consider the background, the kind of father I've been for sixteen years, actually it could have been a lot worse. The hockey game was OK, they both enjoyed that. Sunday morning they watched a video, although Sara bitched about me not having a DVD player. I tried to make them lunch and they wouldn't eat it and then they wanted to go out for pizza in the middle of the afternoon. They got into a fight about what to have on the pizza.

I guess it could have been worse.

How? Well, I guess either one of them could have turned to me and said, "Who do you think you are, you pathetic old bastard? Why are you suddenly trying to hang out with us and act all cool when you've had nothing to do with us for years?" They didn't say that.

I don't know what I expected from the weekend. Some kind of big reconciliation scene, them throwing themselves into my arms? I probably wouldn't have been able to handle that anyway. Sara remembered to say thanks for taking them to the game, before I put them on the ferry. And when I said, "Maybe we'll do it again sometime," neither one of them said, "Not in a million years."

Yeah, perhaps you're right. It wasn't really that bad, was it? And of course, what matters most is not what happened but how I handled it.

Well, I won't lie to you. When I left the ferry terminal the desire to stop into a bar was pretty damn strong and I figured I'd earned it if anyone had. But I'm learning that it doesn't matter so much what I feel like ... what matters is what I do. I went home and made a couple of phone calls — I called my sponsor, I called Liz. Then I picked up my guitar and messed around with this song I'm writing, and I—I tried to pray. I've been out of practice on that for the last few years.

There's this guy down east, Bruce Guthro, singer-songwriter type—ever hear of him? He's got this one song with a line in it I love: *I've hit the bottom and bounced back, to only rise up twice as strong, God only knows how I did that, God only knows indeed.* Great stuff, hey? If I'd spent one tenth the time with my guitar that I did with a bottle of vodka over the past twenty years, maybe I could've written something half as good as that.

No, can't ever see myself going to church again—well, in a regular way, I mean. I do still drop in on churches now and then. But don't expect to see me singing in the choir or jamming with the praise band anytime soon. Maybe AA is my church now. But God—well, I wouldn't be getting through this without Him. You could call that faith, or grace, or whatever.

So, yeah. I've hit bottom and maybe I'm bouncing back.

Hitting bottom? Yeah, that's a big thing in AA isn't it? I have no trouble telling you a story about me hitting bottom. But the idea that after you hit, there's no place to go but up—that never rang true for me. It was more like I fell a long ways, hit hard, and then found the bottom was a slope and I kept rolling downhill.

Oh yeah, you know I'd rather tell you a story than spend this time any other way. And it's not a bad story. Except—you know what I'm realizing? My stories—they're actually a little boring.

When I was a teenager in church we'd often get testimonies, sometimes from ministers and sometimes just from ordinary people, who'd lived a big-time "life of sin" before they got saved. Kinda like the stories people tell at AA meetings. There was always loads of detail about the sins they used to commit before—how drunk they'd get, how stoned, how much trouble with the law they were in, how many women they slept with. The "after" part, when they got saved, wrapped up pretty quick. So, probably like a lot of teenagers in church, I got the idea that sin was fun and interesting, and being saved was good for you but kind of dull.

But these afternoons I spend with you, going over and over these old stories—well, I'm starting to realize how dull and predictable it all is. Every story ends the same way—I get drunk and I screw up. When you're twenty and partying your ass off, you feel like you're really living, like you're going to have an exciting life to look back on. When you're forty and you've been living that way for years ... suddenly you look back and it wasn't all that exciting.

But still. I'll tell you this story, my hitting-bottom story. It is important, in a way.

After my car accident, the one that wasn't an accident, things changed. I lost my job. I stopped playing and singing. Tried to go onstage one night really, really drunk, and I sucked. So the next time I tried it stone-cold sober and that was worse—couldn't even find the chords. And I couldn't find the middle ground anymore, so I just gave up trying to perform at all.

I guess I stopped trying to—function. Ran out of money and went on social assistance for the first time in my life. Began my career of living in shitty bedsitting rooms. Lost touch with a lot of my old friends and what was left of my family.

These would be Dave Mitchell: The Dark Years. Oh, except all the others were dark too, weren't they? OK. Dave Mitchell: The Even Darker Years.

Probably the darkest, yeah. This isn't a lot of fun to talk about.

Anyway, one time about—what was this, about five years ago now? My whole memory of time these last few years is really screwed. I was living in a boardinghouse on the downtown east side. At that point I was passing out every night and puking my guts up every morning—a really glamorous and exciting lifestyle.

Then something unexpected happened. One night I started throwing up *before* I passed out, and only after I had vomited all over myself did I realize that I was throwing up blood. Like, a lot of blood. It scared me shitless. All I could think was that I had to get somebody to help me, and there was nobody, literally nobody I felt I could call on.

Apart from the other drunks and junkies that lived around me, I had two friends still in the city—Jeff and Liz. I hardly saw either of them anymore, and the last time I lost my phone I'd lost both their numbers. Jeff had a wife, a kid, a good job. There was no place for me in that life he was living. I lost track of Liz too for awhile, but then I saw her, not long before this whole puking-blood thing happened. Katie came out to Vancouver, and Liz kept calling, trying to get me to meet them for dinner or something. God, I so much did not want to do that. I finally agreed to meet them in a coffee shop for a few minutes and when I walked in there they were, these two beautiful women, so smart and successful and just—yeah, just beautiful. And there I was, this human waste product—I'm sorry but I'm trying to be realistic about how I felt about myself at the time, how I saw myself. I didn't feel fit to sit down at the table with them.

Yeah, I was sorry I'd met them. I wanted to disappear off the map. I wanted everyone to forget me. But because of that visit, I had Liz's number written down and I managed to get to the phone and call her. I think I said something stupid like that I thought I might be dying and could she come over.

I can't remember much after that. I kept throwing up and I was afraid I'd pass out and never wake up. When Liz showed up I remember thinking that I'd been embarrassed about seeing her in the coffee shop when I was upright and had had a chance to shave and shower. Why the hell had I invited her over when I was covered in puke and blood and God knows what?

Oh, yeah, I remember her reaction. The shock in her eyes. I also saw that she wasn't alone. At first I was mad because she'd dragged some stranger along, I figured for protection in my crime-ridden neighbourhood. But then I realized it was Jeff.

Jeff was great. Liz hung back like the whole scene freaked her out—I don't blame her—but Jeff came right over to where I was lying on the floor by the toilet, put his arms around me and kind of hauled me up to a sitting position. "Jesus, buddy, what have you been doing to yourself?" he said, but in a kind of gentle way, like to let me know that he didn't expect an answer. Liz got some paper towels from somewhere and Jeff cleaned me up a little and told Liz to phone an ambulance.

I tried to tell them I didn't want to go the hospital, because I knew that once I got into the hands of doctors they'd start treating me like an alcoholic—I didn't go see doctors very often but strangely I noticed they always treated me that way. Jeff told me to shut up, I was puking blood and I didn't get a vote.

He stayed with me in the ambulance. I think Liz must have gone home because I don't recall seeing her after we got there. I've never asked her much about what happened that night because obviously it's not one of those shared experiences that you like to look back on fondly and reminisce about. I was ashamed my friends had to see me like that, but if they hadn't been there—Jeff particularly—what would have happened to me?

Yeah, I guess we wouldn't be here right now, would we?

So that was the time Jeff saved my life. He stuck around the whole time, out in the waiting room, coming in and sitting with me whenever I wasn't having something disgusting done to me. When it was all over a doctor had a little chat with me, told me I'd suffered a gastric bleed and they were going to admit me and run some tests. She warned me that this was going to happen again if I didn't quit drinking, and that I could easily be dead within a matter of months or a year.

When Jeff came in I didn't know what to say. I was surprised he was still there, surprised he'd stuck around. What do you say when someone saves your life?

The obvious thing—I said thanks. And he told me I could thank him by making sure it didn't happen again. Only I knew it would, and I told him that.

Oh, I remember exactly what he said. Sorry, I just—anyway. Yeah. He sat there looking down at his hands, picking at a hangnail, and he said, "Fuck it man, you gotta stop this." Jeff wasn't real foul-mouthed the way I am so I knew he was really upset. He said, "Look, b'y, I been watching you do this for nearly twenty years now."

That made us both sound old. And I guess I was worn down, and scared, because I told him yeah, OK, I'd try. I'd check into rehab.

Well. I guess Jeff intended to save my life again. I wasn't exactly grateful to him while I was going through detox. It was a hell of a lot worse than it had been the other times. And I didn't really want to be there, and in all the counselling and groups and shit I mainly just said what I thought they wanted to hear. On top of that, Jeff fronted the money, the part I had to pay myself over and above what the government subsidized, and I'm sorry to say I never did pay him back.

How long? Two months after I got out. Then I convinced myself I could control my drinking, keep it under wraps and live a normal life. That lasted awhile and then ... yeah.

Well, you know the rest. Right back where I started. Out of work, living in shithouses. Last time I was in hospital was back in June when everything started to shut down and they pretty much told me it was a matter of months. And you know, at the time I was kind of OK with that. I didn't even make an effort to quit or cut back or anything—just figured I'd reached the end of the road and that was that.

Jeff? Oh, he moved back to Newfoundland not long after I got out of rehab. We lost touch again. I guess I was ashamed and he was disappointed. They few times he did call, we never talked about my drinking. Just tried to carry on with what was left of our friendship.

That was why the biggest shock of my life was August of this year. I was lying on the couch in my latest crappy bedsit on night, watching TV, working my way through a bottle, when the phone downstairs rang and somebody yelled it was for me. It was Katie—God knows how she got that number—calling to tell me that Jeff was in a car crash. She told me a semi went out of control and hit his car head-on and they weren't sure he was going to make it

I couldn't say anything ... she was there on the other end of the phone just going, "Dave? Are you there, Dave?" I—oh God. Sorry.

I remember walking back upstairs and sitting down on the couch. Pictures crowded through my vodka-soaked brain, right back to when Jeff and I were kids playing street hockey.

But mostly the picture of him sitting with me in the emergency room, cursing at me.

Yeah, sadness and grief and guilt ... mainly what I felt was, I loathed myself that night. He did this incredible thing for me, and there was only one way I could have thanked him for it. And that was the one thing I couldn't do.

TWELVE

Amazing Grace

2005

The Old Gang

KATIE'S CELL PHONE RINGS AT the playground. She's pushing Charlotte on the swing. Charlotte's round face shines more brilliantly than the sun over Kenny's Pond; sheer delight radiates from her. "Again, Mommy! Higher!"

"Just a second, honey," Katie says, digging into her pocket to grab the phone which is beeping "Ode to Joy." It's her mom.

"Katie, honey, have you heard?" Angela sounds breathless.

"I've been here at the playground all morning. What is it?"

"It's Jeff, Jeff Evans. He was in a car accident on the highway early this morning. I just got off the phone with his aunt."

"Is he OK?"

"He was alive when they brought him to the hospital but he's in a coma. They don't know if he's going to make it."

After her mother hangs up, Katie stares at the phone for a minute. She calls Sam's cell to tell him the news, then calls Julie out in Grand Falls.

"I just heard," Julie says. "Pastor Spracklin phoned Roger, asked us to get all the church members across the island praying for Jeff. I'm reeling—I can't take it in."

The phone keeps ringing, when Katie's not dialling out. Charlotte runs around the playground, making friends with another three-year-old, sliding down the twisty slide over and over yelling, "Mommy! Look at me!" News of Jeff's accident flames through Katie's circle of friends and church members, but nobody has any updates on his condition.

Finally Katie brings Charlotte to her parents' place. "I'm just going over to the hospital for awhile," she says. Adrenaline surges like an illicit drug through her veins as she drives across town. *Hello, my name is Katie Matthews-Patey and I'm a crisis junkie. I love to feed off other people's tragedies because it makes me feel useful and powerful. Is there anything I can do to help?*

In the Emergency waiting room she finds the pastor's wife and one of Jeff's many aunts. "We've just heard he's in surgery," Mrs. Spracklin tells Katie, "so we're heading up to Four North. Frank's already up there with the family."

Jeff's family crowds the small waiting room outside the OR. Debbie sits by Mrs. Evans, an arm around her mother-in-law's shoulder. Jeff's dad stares at a magazine on his lap with a fixed and unseeing gaze. The pastor talks quietly to Jeff's uncle.

Debbie looks up and sees Katie. "Hi," she says. Her face is blotched and swollen from crying. Katie kneels on the floor in front of her and takes her hand and Jeff's mom's hand. "I'm so sorry. We're all praying for Jeff."

Debbie nods, pressing her lips together.

"They almost lost him, before he went into surgery. His heart rate went right down," Pastor Spracklin puts in. "But they were able to stabilize him."

"How long has he been in surgery?"

"It's been—" Debbie glances at the clock. "Oh. An hour, for sure. His lung was punctured and there's a lot of broken bones, but it's the head injury they're really concerned about. They say even if he makes it—" Her voice breaks off in a ragged sob.

"Where are the boys? Do you want me to take them to my place? They can stay as long as you need them to."

"Oh—oh Katie, that'd be great ... yeah, I think that would be the best thing. Until my mom gets here anyway—the kids are at my neighbour's house, Shirley Hennessey, you know the one? You've met her, right?"

Only when she picks the boys up does Katie realize they know nothing. Brandon, a bright-eyed eight-year-old full of mischief, says, "Where's my mom and dad?" Jack, who is four, says, "I want Daddy!"

Katie picks Jack up and carries him to her car, buckling him into Charlotte's booster seat. Holding him brings back a visceral memory: Jack was born right about the time she and Sam were mired in paperwork over Charlotte's adoption. She remembers going to see Debbie in the hospital, holding baby Jack. Wanting to burst into tears because Debbie had what she, Katie, would never have—a child of her own, born from her own body.

She envied Jeff and Debbie for years. Now the world has snapped upside-down. She and Sam and Charlotte have everything; Jeff and Debbie and their boys dangle over the abyss.

Katie's house is full for supper; her parents bring Charlotte home and bring take-out pizza too. Sam gets home from work and takes Brandon out in the back yard to play soccer for nearly an hour in hopes of wearing him out. Midway through the evening, Jack and Charlotte fight over a stuffed toy and Jack sits down in the middle of the floor and howls. Katie gathers him in her lap and Charlotte, jealous, climbs up too. The phone rings several times. Debbie calls with news: Jeff has come through surgery but hasn't regained consciousness. Church members call looking for news. Jeff's dad calls to say that Jeff's brother Larry is arriving on the midnight flight from Toronto; could Sam go pick him up?

Sam and Brandon come back into the house, dirty and dissheveled. Brandon helps himself to a handful of nacho chips in a bowl on the table. "Is my mom still at the hospital?" he says. "What's wrong with my dad?"

Katie, who has already explained that Daddy was in a car accident and the doctors are trying to help him get better, says, "He was badly hurt in the accident."

"We should pray," says Brandon.

"You guys are having a sleepover with Charlotte tonight. Get your jammies on, and we'll pray for Daddy before bed."

Liz doesn't hear her cellphone at first. She's at a bar where her friends Andrea and Teresa are celebrating their anniversary and the band is loud. When she realizes it's ringing she excuses herself to the ladies' room. Even here the sax throbs through the walls. Two women at the mirror criticize their dates loudly while applying lipstick. Liz plugs one ear to hear the phone.

"Liz! It's Katie! Have you heard about Jeff!" It's terrible news, but because of the volume Katie's having to speak to be heard on the phone line it sounds like she's leading a cheer.

"He's what?" Liz says. "Sorry, this is a crappy line and it's really noisy here."

"He had a car accident! He's in a COMA!"

"Oh my God. Do they think he's going to pull through?"

"Don't know. The damage is pretty severe! They're waiting to see what happens overnight!"

What else could they do, Liz wonders. "I'll call you when I get home! Oh! Do you want me to phone Dave?!"

Pause. "No ... I'll do that. Do you have a number for him?"

Liz bellows Dave's latest number into the phone, leaves the bathroom and pushes her way back through the crush of bodies to the table. "You should turn your phone OFF," Andrea says. "What are you, some kind of high-powered executive who's got to close the deal before midnight? I hate cellphones."

"It was my best friend from back home," Liz says. "The first guy I ever slept with hit a semi with his car. He's in a coma and he might die tonight. But I guess if I'd left my cell home, she probably could have just left a message on my machine."

"I'll shut up now," says Andrea.

"Dave? Dave, are you still there?"

"Holy shit," Dave says, after a long silence. "No. That can't be right."

"I'll call you when we have any more news, OK?"

"Shit, this isn't happening."

Katie says goodbye and hangs up. The red numbers on her beside clock glow 1:34 a.m. Nine o'clock in Vancouver. She's worked her way west across the continent with phone calls. Beside her, Sam sleeps with Charlotte cuddled against his back. Charlotte was excited about having Brandon and Jack for a sleepover right up until she realized they would be sleeping in her room. Then she insisted on getting in Mommy and Daddy's bed.

There's no-one else to call and nothing left to do. No news from the hospital; no possibility of sleep. Katie checks on the sleeping boys in Charlotte's room, then goes into the study and turns on the computer. She posts prayer requests on a couple of her boards and then calls up a new WordPerfect file. If the adrenaline rush of wanting to be a hero and save the world is a drug, writing is her antidote. She's never shown a page to anyone.

Now, in the tangled yarn of emotions spun by Jeff's accident, she reaches in to find the one thread she can pull, the line that will lead her out. She could write about driving an eighteen-wheeler, having the tires snap and skid and feeling the huge machine spin out of control. She could write about a wide-eyed eight-year-old saying "We should pray," about what might happen to that innocent faith if prayers go unanswered. She could write the pain and emptiness she would feel if it were Sam in hospital, breathing by machine.

She writes about being fourteen. She doesn't write about Jeff, not directly. He is an unseen character in the story, the guy who dumped one of her best friends for the other. Katie writes about that triangle, about herself at the apex of another triangle, three girls growing up in a world of faith and doubt, hammering out who they would become. It's a story about very little, a moment caught and shimmering like a coin in the hand. She writes about her old gang, once tight as five closed fingers in a fist.

In the gray light before morning Jack pads into the study on bare feet. "I want my Daddy," he says. Katie pulls him onto her lap.

Julie rises before dawn and sits in the living room rocker with her Bible and devotional book in her lap. She's been praying for Jeff ever since she heard the news, but it's hard to find words. She doesn't want to pray *Thy will be done* because what if it's God's will for Jeff to die?

She's not prepared to accept that.

Jeff, she thinks, is the best and kindest man she's ever known. Yes, he dumped her in Grade Nine and was a bit of a jerk about it, but you can't resent people for stuff they did when they were fourteen. She remembers Jeff with his wife and kids, a gentle man who would never hurt them. She remembers Jeff the last time they talked, sitting across from each other in McDonald's.

What was it in Jeff that unlocked the door behind which she'd hidden all these years? Maybe, she thinks, Jeff was just in the right place at the right time. Maybe that day the camel's back finally broke and she would have spilled her guts to any sensitive person who sat down long enough listen. Or maybe it was the kindness in his eyes, the memory of their first tentative kisses twenty-five years ago. The curiosity about what her life would have been like if she and Jeff had stayed together.

It excited her a little, the way he was ready to go punch Roger's lights out, as he put it. No-one has ever stood up for her. For days after their meeting she played that image over in her mind, of Jeff driving her home and knocking Roger down with one well-aimed punch.

But that was just fantasy. Underneath the action-hero bravado was Jeff's assurance that leaving was the right thing, the only thing to do. One phrase from their conversation rings in her head: *You have to think about your children.* Jeff meant that if Roger hurt her, he might hurt the kids too. Any mother would protect her children from monster like that.

But Roger's not a monster, not with the kids. He's a strict and stern father, but a fair one. The kids love him. Kyle, before he left for Kingsway, had even begun to imitate him, talking to Julie with something of the same contempt he hears when Roger criticizes Julie.

Julie opens her Bible to Psalm 23, *The Lord is my shepherd, I shall not want.* The words and the images they call up are as comforting and familiar as a childhood blanket, even though she has never seen a shepherd in real life. On their living room wall, a few feet from her rocker, hangs a framed sketch of

Jesus, the Good Shepherd, a modern and smiling young Jesus with the lamb not draped around his shoulder as in most illustrations, but cradled in his arms in the exact same position in which Julie used to carry her children when they were babies.

She stares at the picture, the words drumming without meaning in her head. *I shall not want I shall not want.* Jeff's remembered voice now sounds like a command from beyond the grave: *You have to think about your children.*

Staring at the Jesus on the wall, she thinks that if anyone hurt Mikayla or Chelsea, she'd grab them in her arms like the Good Shepherd carries his lamb and she'd run a thousand miles to bring them to safety. Jesus, the Good Shepherd, loves her more than she could ever love her children. She's taught that in children's Sabbath School; she's assured other women of it in Bible study groups. Did she ever really believe it? If Jesus loved her that much, he would never let her stay where she could be hurt. He would gather her in his arms and run away with her, far away to a safe place.

Katie stands at the end of the driveway, looking up at Jeff and Debbie's house before opening the door of the minivan. Charlotte is again with her grandparents while Katie brings Jack and Brandon home. It's ten-thirty in the morning. Barely twenty-four hours since the accident.

She grabs the boys' hands as they climb out of the car. "There are a lot of people in your house, and your mommy will need you to be very quiet." It's a stupid time to be imposing rules on them, but she can't have them bursting into the house all energy and exuberance. She hadn't expected to bring them back so early, but Debbie wants them here.

One of Jeff's uncles opens the door. The boys spurt past him, looking for their parents. "Deb's in the bedroom," Jeff's uncle says. "She wants to tell them herself. Come on in, sit down."

"What time are Debbie's mom and dad getting in?" Katie says. "I can go get them at the airport."

There must be twenty people in the house but it's surprisingly quiet. Pastor Spracklin is in the living room with his Bible and a small spiral bound notebook. His wife stands with her arm around one of Jeff's cousins who is crying loudly. Katie wanders into the kitchen, trying to be useful.

Debbie comes downstairs to thank her. They hug and hold each other for a long time. "Did anyone tell you? He almost regained consciousness just before—before they lost him." Debbie says. "He looked like he was trying to open his eyes, to talk. I thought—I thought for sure he was coming out of it. And he actually said something."

"He did?" Katie knows most people don't get actual last words, not meaningful ones, anyway.

"I guess I was hoping he'd say my name or one of the boys' names. But he just said—oh, God, and then his heart rate went flat and they couldn't revive him. Oh, God. That was what he said. Like a prayer."

Katie lays her fingers on Debbie's wet cheek, a gesture of intimacy she could not have imagined yesterday. "I'm sure it was a prayer," she says.

"I think I'd like to come down for the funeral," Liz says.

"Sure. That would be—yeah. I'd like you to be here."

Liz looks at her calendar on the wall next to the phone. This weekend she has a workshop, a reading, and a party to attend. Cancel, cancel, cancel. She hasn't been back to St. John's since leaving there fifteen years ago.

"I haven't told Dave that he's dead yet. I wonder how he'll take it?"

"I'll call him. Don't worry about putting me up at your place, I'm going to get a hotel room. No, really, I insist." She tries to sound like she doesn't want to cause Katie any trouble, though it's really the thought of sleeping on a fold-out couch in a house with a three-year-old in it that puts her off.

In the dark room Liz lays down the phone and looks around at her surroundings as if she's in a stranger's house. Jeff is dead

She calls Dave and asks him to meet her at a bar near his place. He looks like hell, as he always does on the infrequent occasions when she sees him now. He stares into his glass when she tells him that Jeff never came out of the coma, that he died at nine o'clock this morning. "Can't get my head around it," Dave says. "I keep thinking I'm going to wake up."

"Me too. I'm going home for the funeral."

Dave's eyes lift to her, a tiny flicker of light that recalls another time. "Oh, God. That's good. That'd be ... nice."

"How long since you were home, Dave?"

"Ah—before Mom died, I guess. Must be ten years."

"You were his best friend, growing up. Come home with me, for the funeral." She lifts a finger to stop the obvious protest. "I'll buy the ticket. It's the least I can do."

"I got nobody left at home ... no-one to stay with."

"I'm staying in a hotel. You can stay with me ... I promise I won't take advantage of you."

The memory of a smile lights his face. "Not even if I beg and plead?"

Liz calculates quickly the cost of two standby tickets to St. John's. She's trying to write something now about home, about growing up there. She has a grant for the project, and a trip to Newfoundland could certainly be written off as a legitimate expense. Bringing along an old friend to attend the funeral of another old friend—it'll be a stretch, but she can cover it. Sometimes research is just the stuff that happens.

On the plane Friday morning, Dave concentrates mainly on not throwing up. The usual burning nausea coupled with nervousness and air turbulence makes it hard to focus on anything else. It seems like if you're travelling to the funeral of your best friend you should be able to think about something other than whether you're going to hurl.

He checks his watch. Soon the inflight service will start and he can get a drink. Thank God.

"What do you remember best? About him?" he asks Liz, looking at her smooth hands clasping a book in her lap, the nails burnished a deep burgundy to match her lipstick.

Liz is silent for a minute. "A lot of stuff. I remember a blue shirt he used to wear in Grade Ten, a polo shirt that he gave me and I used to wear it to bed. I remember him playing floor hockey in gym and how he'd go all out for it and be completely wiped after the game. I remember sex, obviously. I mean, it was our first time, both of us, so you don't forget."

Dave remembers a basement rec room. Jeff, a little stoned, explaining solemnly how he had to lose it with another girl first so he could do it right with Liz. Who were those two girls, what were their names? Dave decides not to share this memory.

"What about you, what do you remember?"

"Him playing air drums while I played air guitar to Ozzy Osbourne in my room when we were about twelve. Um ...

driving out to CUC in his old car listening to crap country music because that's all we could get on the radio. I remember the time we got in a fight and he knocked me down and I cut my hand open on a broken bottle." Pain like a knife in his stomach, his throat.

"Jeff did that?"

"Yeah, but he drove me to Emerg, so it kind of came out even."

They both fall silent. Dave sees with relief the stewardess coming with her cart.

Julie folds the girls' pants and shirts in the big suitcase. "I'm going to stay in town for a few days," she tells Roger. He's in the other room, can't see how much stuff she's packing. "It'll be a great chance to do some shopping for back to school clothes."

"Just remember we've got a budget for that. Don't get carried away buying them every little thing they ask for."

It's a break she never expected. Roger can't come in for the funeral on Sabbath; he's got to preach in the morning and host a long-planned benefit concert in the evening. It's appropriate, he decides, for Julie to go on her own, to represent the family, and to take the girls with her. He never liked Jeff, but he knows it would look bad if they all missed the funeral. Julie moves quickly, finding hairbands, dolls, favourite books to tuck in the pouches of the suitcase.

When Roger lifts the two suitcases into the car for her she sees his surprise and feels a stab of fear. "What have you got in here, bricks? Why are you taking all this for a couple of days in town?"

"I'm bringing some stuff in for Katie, books and toys the girls have outgrown, for Charlotte. I'll use the extra space to bring back the school clothes I buy."

Roger nods briefly. "Be careful on the highway," he says. The girls are already buckled into the back seats, squabbling about who owns the Barbie clothes. Julie waits by the drivers' side door. They are not in the habit of good-bye hugs or kisses. Still, she feels this moment ought to have more ceremony to mark it. She says nothing, though; nothing that would draw his attention. She is like a hunted animal moving slowly in camouflage across the forest floor, silently drawing the hunter away from her nest.

Out on the highway she turns on the radio. Josh Groban is singing "You Raise Me Up," and Julie joins in, her voice filling the car as miles of highway unroll beneath her wheels.

"Can you see Katie?" Liz asks Dave, who towers over her. She's lost in a sea of people and luggage, flowing down the escalator into a shiny and gleaming new airport terminal entirely unlike the one she remembers.

"No ... I don't recognize anyone ... oh, wait. There she is." Liz cranes her neck to see Katie, who stares up at the escalator. Katie's hair is longer and she clutches her daughter by the hand. Liz steps off the escalator, dragging her roll-along bag behind her, thumpity-thump as one of the four wheels has fallen off. She catches Katie's eye. Katie smiles, then looks past Liz to Dave. There's that little recoil that Liz realizes she'll see over and over again as people meet Dave on this trip. She feels suddenly protective toward him, this gray-haired man with lines deeply etched in his yellowing skin, this man who could easily pass for fifty or older. He steps forward, gives Katie an awkward hug.

Liz sweeps Charlotte up for a hug. "You don't know me, but I know you," she tells the black-haired, brown-skinned pixie. "I have all your baby pictures in a book in my house, did you know that?"

Charlotte wriggles. "Mommy, can I go play on the boat?" At Katie's nod she darts through the legs of the crowd towards a pirate-ship play area that dominates the Arrivals level. For a fleeting moment Liz things of the life Charlotte might have had, running as fleetly through dirt-packed streets in Guatemala begging for pennies, a child prostitute by age nine or ten. Liz hugs Katie, whose eyes are red. "You've been crying," Liz says. "I haven't. It hasn't hit me yet."

"You're sure you won't stay at my place?"

"No, the hotel's fine. We're at the Battery; I'm looking forward to the view."

Their room, when they get there, turns out to face the winding road up Signal Hill rather than the broad expanse of city and harbour for which the hotel is famous. "Oh well," Liz says. "It's tourist season, I should've known better."

She lies down on the bed, kicks off her shoes and falls asleep while Dave showers and shaves. He comes out looking almost respectable, though still old and sick. "Haven't you got anything better than that horrible sweater?" she asks.

"No. It's black, isn't that right for a funeral? You're being bossy."

"I'm paying your way, I've earned the right to be bossy."

Dave explores the minibar while Liz goes into the bathroom. "Please try to at least be conscious for the wake," she says.

"This is still part of you being bossy?"

Liz closes the bathroom door behind her.

Barrett's funeral home is crowded. Katie and Sam, who picked them up from the hotel, have to park out on the street because the parking lot is jammed. As they enter the building faces loom at Liz like flashcards in a menacing guessing game: do you know this elderly lady? That balding man? Is that Russ Keating, party animal and drug dealer, now insurance salesman? High school classmates, parents of friends, church members swarm around her. Katie performs introductions, treats Liz and Dave as her guests.

Everyone remembers Liz and envelops her in smiles and hugs, even the most uptight church people. Either they haven't heard about the erotic poems or they've granted her a funeral amnesty. Almost no-one recognizes Dave. Two women, both bottle-blond, one brittle thin and lavishly made up, the other plump and conservative. Liz draws a blank on the skinny one but says to the fat one, "Julie! My gosh! How long has it been?

"Too long, too long," Julie says. "Isn't it terrible it takes something like this to bring us all together? Liz, you remember Steph of course, from high school?"

Stephanie Hussey, school slut! *Why can't we all wear badges?* Liz wonders. *What would mine say?*

"They tell me you're a writer!" Stephanie bellows above the babble.

"That's right! And you?"

"I'm a Grade Five teacher. I live out in Clarenville, but as soon as I heard I said to Bob, that's my husband, Bob I said, Jeff Evans was the sweetest man who ever lived, and I am going to his funeral. And Bob said of course Steph, you go. What a tragedy, isn't it? Those poor little boys."

The whole scene is like a high-school reunion with a bizarre and grotesque centrepiece. People visit the coffin, stand solemnly in front of the framed photos of Jeff on the lid, run their fingers over the little brass plaque that reads: *Jeffrey Evans, 1965-2005.* They say, "Only forty years old. In the prime of his life. What a sin," and then turn to the people next to them to talk about babies and jobs, marriages and divorces.

Later, Liz sits with Katie and Julie on a couch in the lobby. They have both been crying; Liz still hasn't. "The pastor asked me I could sing at the funeral," Julie says, "but I don't think I could get through it."

Mrs. Kimball walks past, looking dazed. She focuses for a moment on the three women on the couch. "My, my, the three musketeers," she said. "How nice to see you all together here."

Liz looks at Katie and rolls her eyes.

"Debbie asked me to do a Scripture reading," Katie says.

"I've got you all beat. They asked me to be a pallbearer." Dave has come up quietly behind them and hangs over the back of the sofa looking down.

"Oh ... that's nice. They asked Sam too. And Jeff's brothers ... I don't know who else they'll get," Katie says. "Aren't there usually six?"

"I don't know, but I know they wear suits," Dave says.

"You haven't got one?"

"What do you think?"

"We'll find something," Katie promises. Liz eyes her friend: she can see Katie enjoys being Good In A Crisis. Well, she's in the right place this weekend.

The crowd thins till no-one's left at the funeral home but the family, Katie and Sam, Liz and Dave, and Julie. "We should get home," Katie says. "Sam's mom is babysitting." She drops Sam at their place first so he can relieve his mom, then starts up towards the Battery. "You'll come along for the ride, won't you

Julie? I can drop you off last if that's OK." Julie and her daughters are staying in her mother's tiny apartment.

"Oh yeah, that'd be fine," says Julie. There's something wrong with Julie today, something more than just attending the funeral of an old friend, Katie thinks. She's wound up, jittery. Katie thinks maybe after she drops Liz and Dave off, she and Julie can talk.

Liz invites them in. "I'm starving. I never had any supper, so I'm going to grab something at the coffee shop."

Katie, who wouldn't normally eat out on a Friday night, glances at Julie, who wouldn't either. Julie nods. "I didn't really get supper either," she says. "Maybe we could get a sandwich or something."

Katie isn't hungry, but likes the idea of the four of them sitting around a table together. But when they get in the lobby Dave says he's tired and he's going straight up to the room.

"Just remember it's my credit card," Liz calls as he heads for the elevator.

The three women sit at a round table; Julie and Liz both order sandwiches and Katie has a cup of tea. They are not, and have never been the Three Musketeers. Older people like Mrs. Kimball look at them and see a mirage, something that was never there. Katie remembers the tension from high school, balancing Julie's friendship with Liz's, needing both but knowing they were like the north poles of magnets, unable to come too close without repelling each other. Now, exhausted by grief, they are all relaxed and quiet in each other's company.

"Here we are, together again," says Julie, who has obviously been thinking along the same lines. "We haven't all done this since ... my wedding, was it?"

"Was that when we made that vow?" Liz says. "To get together every five years and celebrate our birthdays?"

"Well, it's that time of year again. We're not doing bad for forty, are we?" Katie says.

They all smile and nod, giving themselves points for survival. "I thought I'd feel older when I was forty," Liz says.

"I didn't think I'd feel this old," says Julie.

"Well, I feel old *now,* but that's mostly jet lag," Liz says as she finishes her sandwich. They say goodnight, make arrangements for the next day. In the van on the way back, Julie is quiet. Katie tries to find a space in the conversation to ask Julie how she's doing, but the moment never seems right.

Dave sits at the front of the church with the other pallbearers, across the aisle from the family. Sam's old suit hangs loose on him. It's half-past two and he hasn't had a drink since waking this morning. Dave swallows hard, stares at the coffin.

Jeff is inside there. A dead body, soon to be put in the ground. His friends' hands, his brothers' hands, will carry him over the rocky ground of Mount Pleasant Cemetery and lower him into a hole. Dave shakes his head. Nothing will make it seem real, except perhaps that final moment as dirt hits the lid of the box.

First there's church to get through. A hymn, a reading, a sermon. Pastor Kimball, Jeff's father-in-law, has the sermon. He talks about Jeff: a good man, a loving husband and father, a friend to all. *You don't know the half of it,* Dave thinks. Then he starts into his Bible text, a strange one for a funeral, not one of the usual ones about the resurrection and the life. He preaches about the paralyzed man at the pool of Bethesda, a man lying for thirty-eight years on his bedroll waiting to crawl to the healing waters before Jesus sets him free with a single word.

Dave can't follow the thread of the sermon. Thirty-eight years. Nearly as long as Jeff's whole life, as Dave's own. A long time to suffer. Pastor Kimball is saying Jesus doesn't always answer our prayers this way, doesn't always give a miraculous healing. "That's what we all wanted for Jeff in those hours after the accident, but it didn't happen." But Jesus comes to where we're lying and sees us in our pain, Pastor Kimball says.

Dave remembers the story like he remembers most Bible stories, like faraway voices or scenes through the wrong end of the binoculars. Jesus told the man to get up and walk. In defiance of all logic the guy picked up his bedroll and started walking away with it. Pastor Kimball is saying that Jesus is there for Debbie, for Brandon and Jack, for Jeff's parents, for all of them. They don't feel now like they'll ever walk again but they will, just like Jeff will on the resurrection morning.

Dave looks up at the coffin, the flowers spilling over the lid. Above it, the pulpit. He stood up there once, fifteen years old, talking about God's love. Thinking he knew something about sin and suffering and guilt.

The final hymn is *Amazing Grace*. The other pallbearers get to their feet. Dave follows them towards the coffin. A stab of the usual pain slices up through his gut, like a knife piercing his heart.

Amazing grace, how sweet the sound
That saved a wretch like me
I once was lost but now am found
Was blind, but now I see.

The final hymn. The pallbearers take their places on either side of the coffin. Owing to a structural flaw the main aisle of the church is not wide enough for them to walk beside the coffin as they should, so Jeff's brothers walk in front pulling while Dave, Sam, and two men Liz doesn't know walk behind, nudging it along.

Liz sings the hymn with a strong clear voice. This building again plunges her into a pool of memory, into a world where she is, in the eyes of most people here, lost, blind and wretched. Remembered words hammer in her brain, her King-James-soaked memory so useful for Liz the poet, so inconvenient for Liz the woman. *Thou thinkest thou art rich, and knowest not that thou art wretched, and poor, and blind, and naked.*

Wretched, and blind certainly, Liz thinks, remembering sitting here as a thirteen year old drowned in thirteen-year-old sorrow, wishing she could believe what the others believed. But not naked till she met Jeff, till they lay down together on the sagging mattress in Dave's sister's room and Jeff's touch brought her body to life. She recalls the pounding music from the cassette player and the pounding of her own blood in her veins, a kind of grace that set her free to make her own way in the world. She and Jeff were wretched, and poor, and naked together, and it was terrific.

For all those years this sanctuary with its high peaked roof felt like a cage; the broad wooden beams were bars that held her in. Then the roof lifted off and she took flight. Back here again, Liz feels no desire to be one of the people who huddle beneath that roof for weekly worship, yet she feels her kinship with them, a kind of tenderness for their frailties, their awkward well-meaning love. A cage can just as easily be a container, a safe place in which to be nurtured and grow. This building was never that for her, but for the first time she sees it with someone else's eyes. Katie's, maybe. Or Jeff's. Her life will never fit into this particular container, but she understands, at least, the value of a roof and walls. She no longer thinks of bars and shackles but of blood ties, ties of love and memory.

He saved a wretch like me, Liz thinks as the coffin begins its slow journey down the aisle. Her eyes have been dry too long, and tears begin suddenly.

The Lord has promised good to me
His word my hope secures
He will my shield and portion be
As long as life endures.

Debbie walks past the pew, her head down. *She shouldn't have brought the boys*, Julie thinks. She doesn't believe any good can come from dragging a four-year-old and an eight-year-old to their father's funeral. Her own kids are at home with her mother. On Monday, as far as they know, they're going home to Grand Falls, home to Daddy.

Julie sings as loudly as she can through her tears, through the seldom-sung verse about my shield and portion. The Lord has promised good to her. And he promised it to Jeff and Debbie, and to Liz, and Katie, and Dave. Some of them seem to be getting it and some clearly aren't. But Julie can't be mad at God. He promised to be her shield and portion, and you don't need a shield unless you're going into battle. No longer the gentle Shepherd but her shield and portion. Has she got the strength for this fight?

She feels she owes it to Jeff, to go through with this. He was so sure it was the right thing to do. And now his funeral has offered her the perfect opportunity to leave—without suspicion, a clean getaway. She has four hours of highway between herself and Roger, and enough time to breathe and think. A safe place to stay and friends who will support her, if she can only unlock the doors of silence and tell what's happened.

Katie will understand. She works with battered women, survivors of abuse, whatever you call them—she sees it everyday. Say what you will about Katie, she doesn't shock easily. And once Julie has let the barrier down, said the words, something magical will happen. The truth will be out, and she won't have to go back. If she can only tell one more person the truth.

The last of the mourners has filed past; they are singing the final verse of the song. Ten thousand years, bright shining as the sun. The next time Julie sees Jeff, it will be in that brilliant eternal light. And she will say, "Thank you, Jeff. Thank you, you saved my life."

Tears blur Katie's vision as she sings.

> *Through many dangers, toils and snares*
> *I have already come*
> *Tis grace hath brought me safe thus far*
> *And grace will lead me home.*

Safe thus far. Katie watches the boys—no, the men—push and pull Jeff's coffin up the aisle, almost parallel with her seat now. Sam lifts his eyes for a moment to hers.

She sits with Liz on one side and Julie on the other, all three of them singing about amazing grace. Katie wonders what the words mean to Liz, to Julie. What would they have meant to Jeff?

She thinks of Jeff's last moments. Did he cry out in fear, or curse, or ask for forgiveness? Does it matter?

They were close again in the years since he moved home, not so much Katie and Jeff as two people but all the four of them as couples. Jeff and Sam played hockey together on Saturday nights. Katie and Debbie taught together in the children's Sabbath School departments. She never spoke about faith with Jeff, never knew what he believed. Some days Katie's not even sure what she believes herself. She comes home from church after the sermon like her mother used to, with a long list of things she disagrees with. Sometimes she feels as much a cynic as Liz. Other times she has a faith as simple and sure as Julie's, a current that flows strong underneath the questions and doubts that ripple the surface. Safe thus far.

Jeff is safe now. Next stop for Jeff is ten thousand years bright shining as the sun. Does she really believe this? Did Jeff? Katie is safe thus far, and has accepted that this is all the certainty she's going to get in life.

In the front pews, the family stands to follow the coffin out. Katie can't look in Debbie's face. She remembers envying Debbie, once in another lifetime. One roll of the dice, one skid of a tire on pavement, changes everything. Safe—thus far.

Old words at the gravesite. "I am the resurrection and the life," Pastor Spracklin reads. Dave is the last to realize he's supposed to peel off the white gloves and lay them on the coffin. As it drops into the ground Debbie steps forward and throws a rose on top of it, then turns away and buries her face in her father's shoulder. Sobs tear across her body like waves of sickness.

Dave watches the coffin sink into the hole. He wonders when they'll get back to the hotel room. After this they'll all go back to the church for tea and cookies.

The wind has changed and the afternoon is cold for August, skies low with gray clouds. A drop of rain hits Dave in the face as he comes out from under the canopy. Liz moves beside him, takes his arm as she picks her way across the stony ground in high heels. Her fingers are warm on his arm. There's so much he wants to say, but he can't get words past the other fingers, the ones closing around his throat.

Back to the church. People flow around Jeff's family, around the old gang, offering hugs and kind words. Hardly anyone speaks to Dave, but one or two older ladies stop and lay a hand gently on his arm. He holds a styrofoam cup of coffee–real coffee, which he didn't expect to find in the church basement. In deference to the mixed crowd that shows up at a funeral, it seems some rules can be suspended. Not the particular ones he'd like to suspend, but you take what you can get.

The standing, the milling around, the chatting seems endless. A replay of the funeral home last night. Dave looks for a place to sit down and finally finds a chair against the wall, closes his eyes and tries to breathe.

Katie stops in front of him. "Everyone's coming back to my place after," she says. "I mean, not everyone. Liz, Julie. You too."

Dave shakes his head, rubs his face with both hands. "I'd like to come, Katie, thanks. But I can't—I need—"

Katie stands watching him for a moment and her shoulders drop, as if she's just conceded defeat in a very long battle. "You bring whatever you need," she says.

Of all the looks he's gotten this weekend, the pitying and the puzzled and the shocked looks, Dave hates this look worst of all, Katie's disappointed look. *I would be someone else for you if I could,* he tells her silently as she walks away.

Katie tucks Charlotte into bed, the accustomed army of dolls and stuffed toys lined up beside her. If even one is forgotten, bedtime cannot proceed. The rituals are intense and must be observed in minute detail, even during a crisis: *Morningtown Ride* must be sung, and *Hush little baby don't say a word.* The name "Charlotte" must be substituted for "baby" in the latter song.

She's settled at last. Sam and Katie both kiss her goodnight and stop in the doorway to look back before pulling her door exactly six inches from the fully shut position. Voices drift up from the dining room, a clatter of plates being cleared off the table. Liz's laughter rings a sharp note.

"Do you—would you mind if I did a few things down in the workshop, then turned in early?" Sam says.

Katie nods. He's a tactful man and knows what she needs tonight, whose company she wants. Knows, too, that when they've all gone he'll still be there. Katie squeezes his hand and he kisses her cheek.

She's a little worried about leaving Julie downstairs with Liz and Dave—will she be comfortable with them? Katie feels an odd need to protect Julie. But it's groundless: she hears laughter drifting up the stairs, and finds Liz, Julie and Dave deep into the reminiscing portion of the post-funeral program.

"Oh my goodness, do you remember that time at camp— the time you guys tipped the canoe over with me in it?" Julie says to Dave. "I was soaked, and *so* mad, and all Jeff cared about was that I'd gotten his stupid baseball cap wet."

"Remember the time we stole his backpack and threw it up on the porch roof of the school, Katie?" Liz says. "He had to climb all the way up to get it, and instead of getting mad he got even."

"Why, what'd he do?" Julie asks.

Dave says, "Remember we used to take yearbook pictures? Jeff told Liz and Katie he had the school camera in his backpack and it was broken and they'd have to pay five hundred dollars to replace it."

"I totally believed him," Katie added.

"Learned your lesson, didn't you?"

"Like you learned yours when we turned the fire extinguisher on you."

"Oh, I remember that," Julie says. "The white stuff got on Jeff's jeans and he was livid, just livid. He was always so particular about his clothes."

"God, yes. Remember the Miami Vice jacket?"

Words and laughter unravel into the night, creating a magical space in which they are briefly brought together, these four fingers closed around a bleeding stump. After an extended burst of laughter they all simultaneously let out a long sign and Julie says, "ANYway...."

"I couldn't stop looking at Debbie today," Liz says. "She's going to be a single mom. I don't know how anyone manages that."

"She'll manage," Katie says. "What choice does she have? She has two kids, a home, a job. She'll hurt like crazy, but she'll get out of bed in the morning and do what has to be done. When your choices narrow down so there's only one thing to do, you just do it."

"You really think so?" Julie says. The mood in the room has shifted, no laughter now.

"I know it," Katie says.

"I'm sorry Katie, but that is a huge pile of unadulterated crap," says Dave. "You're a social worker, for God's sake. You see people every day who know what they've got to do, but they don't do it. It's not that simple."

"I think it is," Katie says. "When it's life or death and you really know there's no other choice."

"There's always another choice. You can know the right thing to do but that don't mean shit if you don't do it."

"I think Dave's right," Julie says.

"Come off it, Katie," Dave says, leaning forward, more animated than she's yet seen him. "You know some of the people you work with are failures. I don't know what percentage, but you must know."

"No. I don't think of it like that. Call me naive, but I really hope for the best from everyone."

"OK, you're naive."

"I hope you're right," says Julie.

"She's not right and I'll tell you why. Katie, you're judging by people like you and people like Debbie, but strong people aren't normal. You're not thinking about everyday, average people like your clients, people like me. There's a hell of a lot of fucked-up people out there—excuse my language—who know what they've got to do, and maybe it is a matter of life and death, but they still can't do it."

"Why?" says Liz, the first time she's spoken in this newly serious conversation.

Silence. Dave shrugs; Katie shrugs.

"Scared," Julie says.

"Maybe that's it," says Dave. He takes a long breath, and they let a silence settle until he says, "Don't mind me, I get worked up over nothing. OK if I go outside for a smoke?"

Liz gets up to follow him. Katie sees Dave, as he goes through the kitchen, discreetly pick up the bottle he brought along and pluck two glasses from the drain rack. She looks over at Julie, who stares at the tabletop as if looking somewhere else entirely.

Out of the ocean of grief they're all sailing over, Dave's pain rises jagged as an iceberg, and Katie wishes she could help. But just like long ago in London, it's Liz who's outside on the step with him, lit briefly in the quick flare of a match. Katie Matthews-Patey, social worker and general superhero, fails again at helping a friend in need.

Julie draws on the tabletop with her fingertip. "Katie," she says. "Katie, I need to talk to you. There's something I've got to tell you."

It's a long walk from Katie's downtown house back up to the Battery, but neither Liz nor Dave wants Katie to drive them. She and Julie are curled up on the couch deep in some private discussion; Sam has gone to bed. Liz, giggly and lightheaded from her share of Dave's bottle of vodka, says goodnight. Walking up the steep slope of Signal Hill they are both puffing for breath. "Holy shit, I'm in such bad shape," Dave says.

"Me too," says Liz.

"Not in my league." He takes her hand. "Come on, I'll pull you up." It's easier, somehow, walking hand in hand. The wind off the water is so cold their breath is white. Hard to believe it's August.

In the hotel lobby, out of breath, they turn in different directions: Liz toward the elevator, Dave toward the bar. "Oh, come on," she says.

"No. Honestly, I'm just getting started," he tells her. "This has been a shitty, shitty day. I just buried my best friend."

"You're already drunk."

"Not nearly drunk enough."

Liz reaches up, touches his cheek with her hand. She's never been like Katie, driven by an urge to collect lost souls and save them. Nothing like that comes into play here. She looks into Dave's eyes and says, "Try something different. Come upstairs with me."

In the elevator she touches his face again. He catches her wrist, kisses her hand. "You know you're crazy."

"Like I said. Try something different."

"If you only knew how bad I want something different. If you only knew." His mouth finds hers as the elevator door pings open and she tastes the sharp alcoholic taste of the inside of his mouth.

They barely get through the door to the room, Liz fumbling with the cardkey as Dave leans over her, kissing the back of her neck, biting lightly till she moans. Her shirt is off before the door is closed, his long slim hands all over her skin.

In the blue light from a streetlamp outside she takes off the rest of her clothes for him. Liz has learned to like her own body, enjoys her round firm belly and ass, her powerful thighs: she strips with pleasure. Then she takes off Dave's clothes, drawing him down to the bed, their hands and mouths all over each other. He lies beneath her; her hands trace the concave well of his chest, the ribs that stand out clear and bare as the hull of an upturned and abandoned boat. In another light, another man, another night this ruin of his body might turn her off, might excite pity which would kill passion. Tonight it doesn't matter. She looks only at his eyes.

His long fingers that once played guitar now play her body, arouse it, draw her down into a place deeper than darkness. He moans with pleasure but his body is slower to respond. Finally, though, they find each other's rhythm. She is connected, rooted, tied with a tie deeper than blood to man whose ravaged face looks up at her from the bed as if from the bottom of a well.

Julie wakes to a quiet house, no children piling on top of her, no alarm clock. Sunday morning, and she's sleeping on the couch in Katie's living room. She lies there for a moment remembering, letting the pieces fall into place.

Jeff. She remembers Jeff, the funeral, the tears.

Her daughters. Asleep at her mother's apartment, safe from harm.

Roger. At home in Grand Falls, suspecting nothing. Last night she talked to Katie. Last night she told the truth.

Sam makes pancakes for breakfast; Katie drives to Julie's mom's place and picks up the girls, brings them back to her place for breakfast. "What will I tell the girls?" Julie asks Katie. "There's so much to decide. Finding a place to stay and — what am I going to do about money, a job?"

"All those things are Monday morning worries," Katie says. "We'll figure it out. For now, it's Sunday morning and we're having pancakes." Julie's daughters are playing with Charlotte, dressing her up in her princess dress and sparkle jewellery. Squares of sun spill from the window onto the big dining room table Sam made himself. Julie sits and sips orange juice. Is it wrong to be happy the day after a friend's funeral?

Liz wakes to find herself in the same bed as a naked man. Not an entirely unheard-of experience, but not one she expected to have on this trip. She leans up on her elbow and sees that it's

Dave. Last night comes back to her, not flooding back but dribbling back in unsteady bursts. What has she done?

Dave sleeps, his face looking more rested and peaceful than she's yet seen it. Last night was a drunken, grief-fuelled mistake, a one-time anomaly. He'll understand this. She traces a line down his jaw with her finger, brushes his lower lip. His eyelids flutter.

"Hello, sweetheart. My God, Liz," he says, two completely separate responses.

"Yeah. It's me."

"Oh shit. Did we—I mean were we—

"Yes, we did and we were. And I'm glad you have such happy memories of it."

He smiles. "No, I do remember, I just can't quite believe my luck." He takes her finger gently between two of his and bites it, and Liz feels another brief rush of desire. She leans closer, drawn despite herself. Takes her finger from between his teeth and traces his lips with it as she brings her own lips closer, closer. They almost touch. She thinks, *This can't be happening again.*

It's not. Dave sits up abruptly, says, "Oh, fuck," and goes into the bathroom. He leaves the water running in an unsuccessful attempt to cover the sound of his own retching. Liz lies on the bed and stares at the ceiling, thinking she really should get dressed.

So many instances of bad judgement it's hard to know where to start. Well, no, it's easy to know where to start. She can start with the calendar, and the unsullied box of condoms in her purse. It's a long shot. It may be the middle of her cycle, but she's forty years old, for heaven's sakes, not some rampantly fertile teenager. Anyway, she read somewhere that chronic alcoholics are usually infertile. Of course they're often impotent too, which was hardly a problem last night.

Dave comes out of the bathroom, a towel wrapped around his waist. His face and hair are damp, newly splashed with water. "Sorry. Guess that shattered the mood a little. Unfortunately that tends to be the way days start around here." He goes to the minibar. "Can I trespass on your credit card a little further?"

"Sure, take what you need. I'll be paying for awhile anyway."

He sits down beside her on the bed. "I'll pretend you're talking about your credit card, will I?"

"Dave, you don't have any idea whether—I mean, there's no chance you might have used a condom last night is there?"

He looks stricken. "Oh God, Liz, sorry. I didn't even have any on me—I really didn't plan it to be that kind of trip. Shit. But look, I think you're OK. I mean, it doesn't excuse me being a thoughtless bastard, but I do think I'm clean. I don't shoot up and I haven't been with anyone at all in a long time, so— you're probably safe."

That's a relief to hear—not that she won't get tested anyway—but not exactly what Liz was thinking. She realizes the other possibility hasn't even crossed his mind. He takes a long drink from an absurdly tiny bottle and frowns at the sun spilling through the window.

"I'm sorry," he says at last.

"Don't be. It happened. It's OK. Maybe it's kind of a post-funeral, grief recovery kind of thing."

"Yeah. Ask Katie, she probably gives seminars about it." He frowns again and rubs his face. "What Katie said last night—about knowing what you have to do and doing it. I wish it was that simple."

"Yeah."

"It's just—I never told you. I was in hospital a few months ago. Scary shit. I am seriously fucked-up beyond all repair."

Liz has the sense that Dave has said these same words to her before, though she can't remember when or where. She reaches across the blanket and takes his hand.

"I'm frightened, Liz. I watched—they put him in the ground. Under the ground." He sounds young and scared. His fingers tighten on hers. There ought to be words she can say. She is a poet: words are her tools and her toys. But she is empty, dry-mouthed. Nothing to offer but touch, the pressure of her fingers on his. Finally she thinks of words, just one handful of them.

"You've got my number, right?"

"I do. Thanks." He stands up, lays the empty bottle on the night stand. "What time is Katie coming to take us to the airport? We better pack."

They pack in silence, Liz's things in the three-wheeled roll-along; Dave's in his grey duffel bag. Together they go downstairs to wait for Katie.

Katie pulls the van out of the parking spot and hits her left-turn signal. Before she leaves the parking lot Liz says, "Do we have a few minutes? Can we drive up to Cabot Tower?"

Katie turns right instead of left, begins the slow winding climb up Signal Hill to the parking lot at the top. A few hours ago, in the dark of Saturday night, it would have been filled with carloads of teenagers making out. Now it's silent and empty; Katie's is the only car there. She slides into a parking space that overlooks the city. St. John's by early-morning light, spread out below them, looks cleaner and greener than it does when you're down in the middle of it.

Nobody says anything for a long time. Then Liz asks, "What was Jeff's thing?"

"What?"

"You know, the vow. Where we all added one word."

"Young, brave, outrageous ... what was it?"

"Outrageous ... that was me," Dave says.

They all search their fragmented memories; nobody can remember all five adjectives. Finally Katie says, "Positive. I think it was positive."

"Yeah, I think you're right."

"That sounds like Jeff," says Julie.

Katie remembers that her own word was "young." Forever young. Why did she want that? Why would anyone?

The radio is playing CBC's morning news, turned down so low no-one can really hear it. After more silence, Katie says, "We should get going. You're supposed to be there an hour before the flight, right?"

At the airport she and Julie say goodbye to Liz and Dave at the bottom of the escalator. Most of Katie's energy is already focused on Julie: she's thinking about finding a counsellor to refer her to, helping her look for an apartment. But she feels the sharp pain—a scab torn away—when she hugs Liz and Dave. This was their reunion.

Dave says into her hair, "You still pray for me, right?"

"Always. You know that."

"Don't stop, OK?"

Tears again. Katie fishes for a Kleenex in her pocket as she waves at Liz and Dave, gliding up on the escalator. Julie reaches over and hands her a clean one.

Epilogue

Same Old Lang Syne

December 2005

Dave

SO... THAT'S THE WHOLE STORY. I probably should have told you earlier about Liz and me hooking up after Jeff's funeral, but for a long time I thought it was just one of those things, you know? A one-night stand, no consequences. Obviously I was wrong.

Anyway, that's my little Christmas surprise. Quite the gift pack, isn't it?

So when do I see you again? Yeah, I can face the prospect of a couple weeks' break over Christmas. If there's one person in this building who deserves a holiday, it's you. If things get too intense I can always go to a few extra meetings.

Oh, I'm pretty sure they will. Get intense, that is. For the first time in years I have actual holiday plans. I can see why people find Christmas so stressful. I even had to go shopping, buy a few presents. How's that for re-entry into normal life? You give me a couple of years, I'll probably be sending out an annual Christmas letter.

Well, maybe not.

OK, so how am I feeling? Scared shitless. I'm sure that's a shock for you, eh? Dave Mitchell, biophobic. I can report progress on this front, though. I no longer have a vague, undifferentiated fear of existence. I'm now afraid of specific things that I can list, and I think that's an improvement.

You want the list? You got it. Dave's Christmas list.

First up, I guess, the obvious one: I'm scared about being a father again. When Liz finally broke the news—which was only about three weeks ago—I freaked out at her. What the hell was she doing, I wanted to know, sitting on a piece of information for nearly four months? What the hell was that about?

Cool as the cucumber she tells me she was waiting. Checking me out. Waiting to see if I could handle the information.

"Waiting to see if I was going to stay sober, you mean," I said.

Why'd that make me so mad? Because I felt like I was being interviewed for a job application or something. Like I was on probation. All this time I thought we were just hanging out, spending time together, and really she was test-driving me. She said that bringing a kid into the world was a big deal and she wasn't prepared to share that with me unless I was stable enough to cope with it. I said it was a bit late to start showing caution and good sense.

Then I remembered that thing they say about anger ... I think maybe you told me, or I might have heard it at AA or somewhere else. You know, that when you get mad, there's probably another emotion that came first only you didn't notice it? So I stopped to notice it, and of course it was fear.

I've already been a father. I've screwed up two kids ... not beyond all repair, I hope, but any good Brett and Sara manage to make out of their lives won't be thanks to me. I'm still trying with them, but I know it's really too little, too late. The idea of starting from scratch with another raw little human being just terrifies me.

So that's item number one: baby fear. Then there's woman fear, item two. Liz and me. My God, what a bizarre courtship.

Lifelong friends, a one-night stand when we were both drunk and depressed and crazy, and then four months of dating so chaste and careful we might as well have been Adventist teenagers again. I really thought all this time she was just being nice to me. We never touched, never kissed, not from the night after Jeff's funeral till the night she told me about the baby. And since then....

Yeah. Since then things have been on a whole other level. But there's still one more river to cross, if you know what I mean. And that's scary.

Well, obviously. On the most basic level, purely the mechanics of it. It's been awhile, and I've been in bad shape. Naturally there's a little—what would you say?—performance anxiety.

But that's only on the surface. Nothing that time won't heal. I've always figured that at some point I'd sleep with someone again. But all the other stuff ... intimacy, love, being in someone's life day to day, maybe even living together ... yeah. That's frightening. Something I've never done successfully, and now I have to do it on my own, no crutches, just me and the good old Higher Power.

I'm spending Christmas at her place. We'll see how that goes. After that ... who knows?

Items one and two are the big ones, but of course there's other stuff on this list too. My health. I'm trying to take care of myself but there's a lot of damage there and I'm still afraid of going to a doctor and ending up with bad news. I'm only just getting used to having a little energy, enjoying some exercise, a decent meal, a good night's sleep. Simple pleasures. I don't want to lose those.

And I'm afraid for my mind as much as for my body, if not more. I mean, given that one relapse back in the fall, I'm actually only at 90 days. I've been sober for longer than this before and ultimately failed. What if I fail again?

So that's the list, I think. All my biggest fears. It's not really as long a list as I thought it was going to be.

What am I going to do? I'm not going to run away. I've done enough of that.

I had a buddy one time who was into the stupidest stuff—bungee jumping, skydiving, rapelling off buildings, all that stuff. Spent all his money on these crazy extreme sports, which I thought was stupid. Although at the time I was spending all my money on booze, so who was I to say what was stupid? I tried to get him to explain it to me, what was the point of doing things that scared the shit out of you. He said unless I tried it I'd never know, and I said in that case I'd never know.

One day, though, just for a laugh, I came along and watched him bungee-jump. He offered to pay for me to try it but I said never in a million years. And I just stood there and watched this guy—sensible guy, good programmer, wife and kids—fling himself off a bridge into space. When he came back and we were heading out to his car I said, "I still don't get it."

Know what he told me? "What can I say, Dave?" he said. "It scares me every time. But the things that scare the shit out of you, those are the only things that make you feel alive."

Anyway. Thanks and Merry Christmas. I gotta go pick up a string of Christmas lights, if you can believe that. But I'll see you in the New Year. You hang in there, OK?

From: "liz carter" <yeahright.biteme@gmail.com.>
To: "undisclosed recipient"
Date: December 24, 2005
Subject: christmas letter

behold miracles and wonders, peace on earth goodwill et al. liz not only sends an annual christmas letter but sends it before christmas.

as you know standard christmas eve procedure in the lizworld involves intimate parties at chic restaurants with similarly single friends enjoying champagne and sushi thumbing our nose at holiday traditions.

christmas eve 2005 finds me placing gleaming pans of vegetarian lasagna in the kitchen to cool while significant other untangles long string of white lights in living room to accompaniment of potent curses. we have actual holiday decorations: a three-foot-tall artificial tree; a nativity scene in honour of somewhat christian dad2b; a yule log in honour of somewhat pagan mom2b, although log symbolic as apartment obviously has no fireplace.

they say christmas changes when you have children. apparently this applies to sixteen-week-fetuses as well. champagne flutes and sushi have been replaced by tangled tree lights and tumblers of eggnog — the nonalcoholic kind in cartons from the supermarket. dad2b has a 90-day chip on his keychain and mom2b is abstaining in the interests of baby2b's brain development.

my sudden commitment to family life may come as something of a shock to some of you. believe me when i say i share your surprise.

attached ultrasound photo is allegedly too early to determine sex but i know my daughter when i see her. one advantage of elderly pregnancy is close medical attention accompanied by frequent ultrasounds. one disadvantage is being called elderly when barely 40.

this year my new collection *storms over earth and sea* was nominated for the caa jack chalmers award and shortlisted for the dorothy livesay poetry prize, winning neither. my most outstanding accomplishment this year has been winning the fertility over forty award. significant other aka dad2b turns out to be surprisingly sane and balanced person despite extremely unpromising resume. good thing i bypassed application and interview process for prospective fathers.

to add to holiday madness my demented mother (using term literally not in a derogatory fashion) joins us for christmas dinner tomorrow. on boxing day dad2b's sullen teenagers from previous liason arrive for 2-day visit. supplies of dvds pizza coupons and earplugs already being stockpiled.

assuming all hurdles of elderly pregnancy are cleared without incident, sometime in may we expect to announce arrival of fiona morag branwen carter. or carter-mitchell. or mitchell-carter. she may also be named jane. or padraic if the y chromosomes carry the day. all possible permutations of name not yet negotiated. suggestions welcome.

peace on earth, goodwill to persons.

liz&dave

Julie

THINGS DON'T ALWAYS FEEL *the way they're supposed to, do they? Christmas is supposed to feel happy, full of goodwill and cheer. But everyone knows it doesn't always happen that way.*

Sitting alone on Christmas night in an empty apartment listening to Kenny Rogers singing "Carol of the Bells" should be depressing. You're not supposed to be alone on Christmas. But after the noise and chaos of today I have to say the quiet apartment is actually kind of soothing. More surprising—I kind of like being on my own.

We had Christmas dinner at Katie & Sam's today, along with her parents and my mom. My girls were in high spirits, wearing paper party hats & enjoying Charlotte's Lego set more than any of their own presents. Even Kyle, who has been a bit of a pain since he got home, relaxed enough to help the younger kids build a snowman. The first snow of the season fell last night—a postcard Christmas Eve—and although there wasn't really much on the ground Charlotte and Chelsea insisted they had to make a snowman.

At about five Roger & his dad arrived to pick up the kids. They're spending the second half of the holidays at Roger's parents' house with him. I didn't want them to spend a week alone with Roger, but at the same time I don't want them to lose touch with him & his family. When his mom called to discuss my suggestion I could hear the anger & resentment in her voice—how I'm making her poor boy suffer. It's certainly not an ideal situation but from what I've seen of divorced families people just have to work out the best arrangements they can.

Yes, I used the D-word. Divorce. First thing next week I'm going to call a lawyer and get things moving—at least a legal separation. Everyone needs to know this is not temporary.

Seems amazing, looking back through these pages—just a few weeks ago I was seriously thinking of going back to Roger for Christmas. In my heart I knew that if I went back for a week, it would be hard to leave again. He told me on the phone that he'd been praying. He'd had some serious talks with Pastor Kent, the conference president, and he knew things would be different this time.

I was reading my Bible one night after I talked to him & found myself in John 5 reading the story of the man at the pool of Bethesda. It was the one Pastor Kimball preached on at Jeff's funeral, so I had the funeral bulletin folded up and stuck in that page. Looking at the bulletin brought back that whole terrible weekend—the funeral, my decision not to go home. I remembered how sad & brave & frightened & free I felt then. I thought about the man by the pool, waiting all those years for an angel to stir up the waters, convinced every time that this time things would be different—this time he'd be the first one in the water & be healed. When Jesus came He offered the man something completely different—grace, I guess. A chance to break the cycle.

In the morning I phoned Pastor Kent and told him I wanted an appointment.

I've never talked to Pastor Spracklin, who I guess now is my own pastor, about this. He would be the appropriate person to go to for counselling if I wanted it from someone in the church. But I wanted to talk to the conference president because Roger's been talking to him. If anyone would have a sense of whether my marriage was worth saving, it would be him.

I went into his office that morning & he was all smiles, shaking my hand. I told him I was considering taking the children back to Grand Falls to spend Christmas with Roger and asked if he thought that was the right thing to do.

He folded his hands in front of him on the desk in a here-is-the-church, here-is-the-steeple grip. "Marriage isn't always easy, Julie. It takes a lot of hard work, but the marriage vows are not to be taken lightly."

I told him I understood about for better, for worse, and I'd been through a lot of worse.

He said that he and Roger had had a lot of what he called "fruitful discussions" and he knew Roger wasn't always easy to live with, that he had a bad temper, that I must feel like Roger didn't appreciate me enough. "Perhaps you've even fantasized about finding someone else, starting a new life with a man who's kinder and more patient," he said. He must have seen the shock on my face because he added, "It's not a sin to be tempted. But it is a sin to entertain those thoughts, to act upon them."

"I've never for one second considered being unfaithful to my husband," I said, feeling like I was choking.

I'm trying to remember it all, to write down what he and I actually said, just to have it on paper. I know he said that if I would give Roger another chance, maybe we could both meet with him, talk about how to make our marriage work.

I stood up, picked up my jacket folded on the chair beside me. Take up thy bed and walk. "Pastor Kent," I said, "is this what Roger has told you about our marriage? That I've been restless and feeling unappreciated, and that he's got a bit of a bad temper?"

"Yes, he's admitted all that to me," said Pastor Kent, still smiling but looking puzzled about why I was standing up.

"You're sure that's all he's told you? Nothing else."

"Nothing of substance, no."

"Thank you, Pastor."

He said he hoped I wasn't upset, that I could sit down and we could talk a little more.

I told him that wouldn't be necessary. I was shaking, but at the same time I felt so strong it amazed me, like I could kick a hole in the wall or run five miles if I needed to. "You haven't said anything to offend me, Pastor Kent, it's just that you're not in full possession of the facts in this situation." I was proud of that sentence. Not in full possession of the facts.

I drove home shaking, but more with anger than with fear. Stopped at Sobey's to get groceries—the place was a madhouse, just a few days before Christmas, but the shopping had to get done. In one of the aisles I passed Molly, from my group, and we said hi. Then on the way out I saw her with her groceries, getting ready to call a taxi. I offered her a ride home and, on the spur of the moment, asked her if she wanted to go to Tim Horton's for a coffee or something first.

We sat down together and I caught a reflection of us both in the window of Tim's. What an odd pair we made. I still look like a pastor's wife—sensible, conservative, middle-aged. Next to me is this teenage girl with her tattoos and nose ring, this girl whose boyfriend used to make her sleep with his friends for drug money. It was a little awkward at first—we talked about getting ready for Christmas and all, but our lives are so different I could tell we weren't really connecting & I started to think I was crazy for asking her to Tim's with me.

Then I told her I had been thinking of going home for Christmas and that I'd decided not to, and it was like a light switched on. Suddenly we were just there for each other, you know? We are so different, yet there's a part of me no-one can understand except someone who's been there. Half an hour later I dropped her off at her apartment on Graves Street and wished her Merry Christmas.

I walked back into my own apartment and for the first time it felt like home. If I hadn't talked to Pastor Kent, I might have believed Roger when he said he was getting help and planning to make changes. I could have been fooled. I could have been there right now, in the house in Grand Falls, surrounded by my own handmade curtains and quilted pillowcases, slipcovers for a life too shabby to put on display.

I sit alone in my tiny living room with the ugly wood panelling. Day after tomorrow I think I'll pick up some fabric and start making covers for these cushions. Or maybe I'll just buy some whole new cushions. A late Christmas present for myself. Why not?

Merry Christmas, Julie. And happy new year.

Katie

KATIE TYPES THE FINAL WORDS on the phantom white page trapped behind the glass screen. The words are pinned there now, solidifying into fictional reality. She's been writing all through the fall, spinning out the story she began the night before Jeff died. Now, on the second-last day of 2005, she's done. She types "THE END," and adds a title page with an epigraph—two lines from a favourite song—and her own name.

She looks at her name on the page, makes a tiny one-letter revision, saves the file. *Amazing Graceland*, it reads. *By Kate Matthews-Patey.* She has written a whole book.

Writing about the past makes her think of Liz. She remembers the thrill she felt in Grade Nine, finding a friend who liked to write, offering her own poems for Liz's appreciation. Why did she follow that up with twenty-five years of hiding, of refusing to compete, to see herself as a writer? It's time to come clean.

She was going to phone Liz to tell her about the book, but Liz called first. The queen of one-up-manship, Liz had news of her own which blew Katie's book project out of the water.

"You're *what?*" Katie said. "You *did?* When? Right after you left here that night? When did you tell him? What did he say?" Both her voice and Liz's were high-pitched and breathless. It was like conducting a celebrity interview after inhaling helium..

At the end of a half-hour phone call Katie remembered to say, "I've been writing something. I think I may be writing a novel. Sort of half-fiction and half-memoir. About, you know, us and growing up and growing older and all that. I guess when Jeff died, I started looking back. And now I've nearly got a manuscript."

"You have? Oh my gosh. That's great ... that's wonderful, Katie. It's funny because ... I've been writing about some of the same stuff. My new project—it started out as another collection of poems, but I think it might be fiction too."

Great, Katie thought. Liz, award-winning poet, is writing the same book Katie is. Complete with gritty realism, swear words and graphic sex, no doubt. Not hard to guess whose book will make the best-seller list.

"It was just an idea, something I was messing around with," Katie said apologetically.

"Don't say that! How much have you got written?"

"I don't know, about, um, 60,000 words? I'm not sure how many pages."

"That's not just messing around, that's real writing. Good for you. Look, do you want me to talk to my agent? She doesn't look at new writers without a recommendation, but I'd have no problem recommending you."

"You haven't read anything I've written except letters and emails since we were sixteen."

"And I can't tell from letters and emails what a good writer you are? Let me make the call. Come on, Katie."

"Maybe. It's not finished yet. We'll see. Anyway, enough about me and my book ... are you thinking about baby names and all that maternal stuff yet?"

Now, Katie flicks from WordPerfect to her email and hits "Reply" on Liz's Christmas letter. *Glad to hear you're mired in Dickensian Christmas domesticity,* she types. *God bless us every one. Give my love to Dave and baby2b. I vote for Jane. I finally finished my book manuscript. I'm going to fling it in a drawer for a couple of months and let it rest before I face revisions. I don't mind if you talk to your agent about it, if that's still OK. Merry Christmas, Good Yule, Happy New Year.*

As she hits "Send" she hears a whimpery cry from Charlotte's room. Charlotte's post-Christmas cold has had her awake sniffling and coughing the last couple of nights. Katie goes into her room and finds Charlotte sitting up in bed clutching her teddy.

"You OK, honey? Do you need the bathroom or a drink of water?"

"Of water."

Katie gets her water bottle and Charlotte takes a drink. "Ready to go back to sleep?"

"Rock me?"

Katie pulls Charlotte into her lap in the rocker and buries her face in Charlotte's silky black hair. *Hush little Charlotte, don't say a word, Mama's gonna buy you a mockingbird.*

Footsteps in the hall. Sam appears in the doorway. "Are you still up? We've got thirty-five people coming over tomorrow night—you should probably get some sleep."

"Sorry. I was coming to bed when Charlotte woke up. I'm just settling her down."

Sam stands leaning against the doorframe, smiling, humming along as Katie sings. "You OK? Do you need anything?" he says as he turns to go back to bed.

"No, I'm fine," Katie says. "I've got everything I need."

THE END

Made in the USA
Middletown, DE
23 August 2019